BLOOD *of* TEN KINGS

BLOOD *of* TEN KINGS

EDWARD LAZELLARI

TOR

A TOM DOHERTY ASSOCIATES BOOK

NEW YORK

BLOOD OF TEN KINGS

Copyright © 2018 by Edward Lazellari

A Tor Book
Published by Tom Doherty Associates
175 Fifth Avenue
New York, NY 10010

www.tor-forge.com

Tor® is a registered trademark of Macmillan Publishing Group, LLC.

The Library of Congress Cataloging-in-Publication Data
is available upon request.

ISBN 978-0-7653-2789-5 (hardcover)
ISBN 978-1-4299-4568-4 (ebook)

Our books may be purchased in bulk for promotional, educational, or business use. Please contact your local bookseller or the Macmillan Corporate and Premium Sales Department at 1-800-221-7945, extension 5442, or by email at MacmillanSpecialMarkets@macmillan.com.

First Edition: December 2018

Printed in the United States of America

0 9 8 7 6 5 4 3 2 1

For my daughter, Siena,
who has taught me things I never could have imagined
and to love more deeply than ever before.

No plan survives contact with the enemy.

—Moltke the Elder

WHAT HAS GONE ON BEFORE

Conquered by their greatest nemesis, the Kingdom of Aandor protects its royal bloodline by sending their infant prince and his protectors across the multiverse to Earth. Mysteriously separated from his guardians, Daniel Hauer is raised by abusive foster parents in the suburbs of Baltimore, with no knowledge of his true heritage. Thirteen years after the guardians arrive in our world, assassins from Farrenheil are suddenly hunting them, trying to find the prince. The chase culminates in a wizard battle that nearly destroys New York City. In the aftermath of these events, Daniel must decide if he wants to live a safe, ordinary life in our universe, or return to Aandor to fight for his birthright and save his kingdom from tyranny.

BLOOD *of* TEN KINGS

PROLOGUE

1

AANDOR

Chryslantha Godwynn floated through the castle's great hall on moleskin slippers, appearing plain as a pantry maid in a long teal shift and blue apron. Her dress was speckled with butter stains and bleached flour, emphasizing the rosy hue of her cheeks and lips. A smattering of flour graced the roots of her thick, wavy blond hair, where she had it pulled back into a horsetail and then wrapped under a blue kerchief. She looked to all the castle dwellers a common maid transporting a platter of freshly baked rolls.

The castle buzzed with the activity of a hive on a warm day. Lads darted through the corridors, moving all manner of things sturdy and fragile, threatening to collide spectacularly if not for last-second course corrections; maids giggled, beating the rugs and tapestries along the crenels and laying down fresh linens. The kitchens were permeated with scents of roasted mutton, boar, pheasant, grilled salmon, pies of all variety, and freshly baked loaves. Bright, fragrant flowers were stationed at every turn. Every nook of the old gray sentinel that was Aandor's seat of power was decked for celebration. Today, Archduke Athelstan and his wife, Sophia, would share their firstborn son with the kingdom—Aandor's first true prince in a hundred years.

Workers from every corner of the empire poured into the city on this bright spring day to contribute to the celebration: the rhythms of the carpenters' saws melded with the percussion of blacksmiths' hammers and the cymbalic tings of the gardeners' shears. Butchers sliced; cooks stirred; jesters, minstrels, and jugglers rehearsed; everyone with a trade came to serve the lords and common folk who gathered this day.

Outside a window, the Dukesguarde gleamed during formations in their finest white and gold dress armor under perfect blue skies. The bright red plumes on their polished helmets stood starkly against the sun's radiance, bestowing a certain grace to the troops' measured steps. Merchant kiosks dotted the fair grounds like a great herd. The lists overflowed with the names of great and minor knights awaiting their chance to joust. This was the greatest fair and tourney in a generation.

Ahead, Linnea Ashe arranged several lengths of garlands along the grand staircase.

"Has her ladyship traded down for the simpler life?" Linnea asked.

"Commoners have fewer rules and more fun, I think," Chryslantha answered. "Sophia is starving, and like any good lady-in-waiting, I volunteered to procure some victuals." Chryslantha drew back the towel and offered Linnea one of her steaming rolls.

Linnea took a bite and asked, "Does the archduchess have a shortage of maids, milady?"

"She is driving *all* the servants mad with minute tasks," Chryslantha replied. "The festivities weigh on her. Sophia will be judged and criticized by lords and emissaries. She has lost only half a stone since the birth—I fear she will give Alva apoplexy with the numerous alterations to her gown."

Linnea halted two young lads rushing past with several boxes of roses and inspected the flowers. "Take these to my sister decorating the archduchess's chamber," she ordered, but not before stealing one and offering it to Chrys. "For the Rose of Aandor."

"You've your father's touch for growing and your mother's skill at arrangement," Chryslantha said.

"That's very kind, milady. Pray that the archduke will appoint me royal gardener when Father retires."

"With Galen's consent, I cannot see why not. And speaking of your husband—where is he?"

"In hiding—scribbling an ode to the prince on behalf of the tanners' guild, which he is expected to recite after the feast. His unease matches Sophia's."

"How delightful to have landed a tanner-poet. I look forward to his recital, Linnea."

Chryslantha bid farewell, and ascended the grand stairs. She turned the corner of the upper landing when a gloved hand gently grabbed her from behind.

"Your pardon, but I must inspect items carried into the lady's chambers," said a deep, confident voice.

Chryslantha turned slowly to examine the tall guardsman. His helmet, with its high red plume, was angled downward to shield his eyes. His golden breastplate shone to mirrored perfection and the captain's insignia, three lightning bolts side by side, was etched into the upper left of the plate. His Murano steel sword hung at his side and on his back he bore his shield, decorated with the crest of the Kingdom of Aandor, a black phoenix rising against a red field, bordered by gold.

"Good sir, surely you would not keep the archduchess from her biscuits?" Chryslantha asked with mock distress.

"In truth, I care not for the duchess's biscuits, milady," he said earnestly. He moved in slowly to plant a soft kiss on her lips. Chryslantha pulled away.

"Brute!" she said. "My lady will hear of your . . . your uncivil interrogations of my person."

He pulled her against him. "I see. Well . . . if my life be forfeit then . . . let it not be from want of a biscuit."

Chryslantha put her hand up to fend off the next kiss. She could barely breathe as she failed to restrain her laughter. She laid her forehead against his breastplate.

The captain removed his helmet revealing periwinkle-blue eyes deep as a northern fjord, a nose long and straight as a prelate's sermon, full lips and a strong jaw, and a tussle of loosely curled dark blond hair with the faintest sheen of rust; a face Chryslantha had known her entire life.

"What?" Callum MacDonnell protested, with equal mirth. "I never claimed to be a poet."

"Some time spent with Galen Ashe would sharpen your wit and prod finer verse from your thick head," she said.

"Ahem . . . !" Tristan McLeod stood at the periphery of good manners several feet away. He was slightly shorter than Cal with gray eyes and brown hair, dressed similarly. He wore the smuggest of expressions on his sun-bronzed face. "Far be it for me to interrupt this brilliant mummer's farce—but we've been called to council."

"Tristan's contempt for romance is a sad, sad thing," Callum said to his betrothed.

"Fear not," Chryslantha responded. "Valeria has designs on

him, and like all MacDonnells, she's likely to catch her prey. With my help," she added with a smirk.

"*Him* as my in-law?" the two men said, pointing at each other.

"Fear not, my captain. I predict years of revelry ahead of me. Your beautiful sister will grow weary and marry instead one of those wealthy merchants of dubious repute that clog the archduke's court these days."

"Better to wed the fool," Cal said. Tristan was trying to get under Cal's skin, a talent the puckish lieutenant had gained an aptitude for over their long friendship. "Why have we been called to council?"

"Our messengers and carrier birds from the outer forts have not checked in."

"How many?" Callum asked.

"Enough. Celebrations started early throughout the kingdom," Tristan said. "Everyone's happy and a little drunk. I'll bet a gold sterling half the messengers are asleep on some pub floor and the other half are in the arms of farmers' daughters."

Cal sighed and donned his helmet. "Lord Alney wouldn't have called council over a few messages," he said.

"Concerned for your mother and sister?" Chryslantha guessed. Mina MacDonnell would not leave Meanmnach Castle until her younger son's fever broke. The matriarch of clan MacDonnell was currently en route to the city.

"My uncle awaits her at Crowe's Porte with his contingent from the Gate. She could be no safer than if Father escorted her. Still . . . what does Alney want of us?" he asked Tristan. "We're not standard army."

Tristan shrugged.

Cal kissed Chryslantha on her flour-dusted cheek. "I will see you tonight at the feast," he said, his mind already turning to missing messengers.

2

Activity in the archduchess's suite was no less frenetic. Valeria MacDonnell sat on the divan holding the archduchess's dress while Alva stitched along its side. The seamstress saw Chryslantha and made a face of frustration. Alva was a castle staple, having once been seamstress to the archduke's mother, and she'd grown close to Sophia. Such was Sophia's connection with everyone: a daughter, sister, or mother in all ways but blood.

Sophia sat in the center of the chamber in a coral-pink chemise as a handmaiden and Chrys's younger sister Niccole plied her with rouge, lip paint, and powder. Her lady's maid tended to her nails, and Zenoia unfurled rollers from Sophia's long golden-brown hair. The remnants of her Bradaanese olive tinge clung to her despite Aandor's cooler climate—less dark than the first summer she arrived, when the aristocracy spun rumors that a Verakhoonese pirate had leaped into her father's seat before his wedding night. Her green eyes were large and luminescent, rumored to enthrall even eunuchs.

"Shouldn't you be arranging flowers?" Chrys asked Zenoia.

"I've been levied, milady."

"As have I," said Niccole moodily. "Like some lowborn commoner."

Sophia rolled her eyes. "My chamber is fine. Linnea has the flowers in the halls well in hand?"

"She does," Chryslantha confirmed. She placed the platter before her lady and whipped off the towel.

"Gods bless you," Sophia said, grabbing the top roll and stuffing it in a quite unladylike manner into her mouth.

"One only!" ordered Alva from the divan. "Bread will tighten the fit!"

"Some wizard has duplicated my mother and inserted her here as my seamstress," Sophia said through a mouthful.

Chryslantha laughed openly. The others were unsure if it was appropriate; Niccole was not receptive to mirth at all. Chryslantha's and Sophia's fathers were old friends, and as young girls they had built lifelong bonds playing games like knight and tower maiden. The slightly older Sophia usually claimed the role of the knight. She had a strong mind, and having no brothers, was indulged by her father as he would a son. Now Chryslantha's friend was a mother—not to just any child, but the prince of the realm.

The prince slept soundly in his bassinet—bright red cheeks with tiny curled fingers and a tuft of sandy-brown hair. It was hard to believe that in this tiny being flowed the bloodline of ten kings of the once-mighty empire of Aandor.

"I love him best when he sleeps," the archduchess confessed. "He's been irritable the past few nights."

"Here in the north, a babe sleeps several rooms away with his wet nurse for the first twelve months," Chryslantha pointed out.

"A barbaric custom, as is the idea of letting some strange foreign woman feed my baby. That is not our way in Bradaan."

"So say you . . . is it the custom in Bradaan to appear at your husband's council meetings with your child suckling?" Chryslantha teased. "You should hear what the generals and ministers have to say about that."

Sophia's wicked smile said she knew what they thought.

"It smacks of peasantry," Niccole said a bit too boldly.

"Please . . . ," Sophia said. "I lived with commoners a few summers—a family tending my father's farm in the south. They dance and sing each night, and are happier than this lot with their airs."

"Spoken like a true duchess," said Chrys. "Still, you could be nicer, lest they regret their decision to invite you into the family."

"Docile ladies do not make history," Sophia pointed out. "I intend to leave a mark for my children's sake. Athelstan's family has no touch with the common folk. They personify awkwardness. I've never seen so many pasty, yellow-toothed, long-faced, freckled, redheaded scarecrows in one brood. In a stiff wind their ears alone could sail a caravel."

"Why should we care what the commoners think?" quipped Niccole.

Again Sophia rolled her eyes and speedily pulled the rest of the rollers out of her hair, shooing away those around her. "Anyway . . . appearing at the council meetings with Danel is just me jostling the swords they have shoved up their collective—"

"The dress is ready!" Alva declared forcefully.

This time the handmaidens laughed and caught a stern eye from the lady's maid.

"Wait, bring me Danel," Sophia ordered.

Chryslantha handed the archduchess her son. Sophia pulled her chemise down at the shoulder and put Danel to suck.

"I can barely fit the dress when I'm empty," Sophia said.

Valeria appeared with a damp handkerchief and dabbed at the flour on Chryslantha's cheek. "My brother's affections are pressed upon you," she said with a smile. She was tall, with the same eyes as Callum, straight waist-length sandy-blond hair with that same smidgen of rust, and a ruddier complexion.

The handmaids giggled. Girls throughout the Twelve Kingdoms dreamed of Callum. Chrys thought it best not to mention Alney's call. It could very well be as Tristan said . . . exuberant celebration.

"Cal's not bad-looking," Niccole said, "but you are worthy of a king. I hear it said the MacDonnells trade mostly in copper coin for they lack gold and silver."

Valeria shot the girl an icy look.

"Chrys has found a man of her own choosing," said Sophia. "Have you set the date?"

"My eighteenth name day—in the autumn."

Sophia gazed wistfully out their window. Chryslantha doubted her friend saw Aandor's marble towers, the gleam of its temples, the deep blue and terra-cotta ceramics of their guilds' roofs—or beyond these the sparkling froth of Emeline's Tears replenishing the lake beside the capital from the Sevren River's upper shelf. Chryslantha knew that her friend thought of Johan, her first betrothed. One of Farrenheil's finest writers and musicians, he'd scribed many a song to her before the hunting accident took his young life. The commoners called the distant falls Emeline's Tears because their beloved ancient empress was not fortunate in affairs of the heart. It could just as well be called Sophia's Tears. The archduchess smiled, aware that Chrys had concern for her.

"Such is how marriage should come about," the archduchess said. "Not bartered for and purchased like a saddle from a tanner's shop—though tanners' wares are often better fits for their intended than the unions fathers make for their daughters."

"You are archduchess of the greatest kingdom in the land, mother of the prince of the realm, possibly grandmother to the first new emperor," Chrys reminded her. A drum of sadness had overcome the archduchess. It was a sudden thing, not easily explained. Chrys herself noticed a change in the air. The breeze had turned cold. She sensed a pressure in her ears, like that of a coming storm. Gazing again at the grand capital—something was amiss—not in the towers and domes of the serene city, but beyond it . . . something intangible. Clouds formed on the eastern edge of the city, a shadow on the promise of a bright day. A chill ran through Chryslantha; she closed the window.

"I, too, will wed in the autumn," said Zenoia, arranging lilies.

"An epidemic of matrimony has befallen us," Sophia said, snapping free of her melancholy. "Pray, tell us, Zenoia, did you choose each other?"

"Aye, with Father's blessing. Zak's his name, beginning with a Z as does mine, and he is a potter by trade. And I, being a gardener's daughter, can find no shortage of pots in my life."

"Common sense from a commoner," quipped the duchess. "I shall petition you for a seat on the council, Zenoia."

"Oh no, milady. I am too practical to argue all day long." Everyone except Niccole laughed.

Chryslantha sponged off the rest of the flour and removed her shift. Her dress for the festivities was two-toned green velvet with patterns of diamonds made from the raised plush of the material; it was long to the floor, and clung to her in the right places. A thin decorative corset of dark green leather was sewn into the middle to accent her curves and support her bosom. The low-cut collar was fringed with decorative white and gold lace stitching and small white pearls. Her sleeves were long: tight against the skin above the elbow, but loose below. The cuff arched to a point over the back of the hand and ended in a generous smattering of white pearls. She pulled her hair from the ribbon and shook it vigorously. With a brush, she transformed it from a wild golden bramble to a well-coifed one. The others ogled in admiration.

"Five minutes," said Valeria, shaking her head in disbelief. "It took her all of five minutes, to look like that."

"By the gods, Chrys," said Sophia. "If I were a man . . ."

"You'd sit in your chambers all day polishing your sword, plotting to expand your influence, and lusting after maidens," Chryslantha cut in. The room erupted into giggles.

The nursemaid collected Danel after his feeding to change his clout and bring the child to his father, who lunched with the high prelate. Chryslantha and Valeria helped Sophia into her gown, stuffing her cleavage into their silos, tugging at the ruffles, and lacing up the back with tools that looked borrowed from the chief interrogator. Alva had done an excellent job of double stitching the seams.

"Well, you just wait," Sophia warned Chryslantha. "After all the poetry, the flowers, the oaths, and pleading of their undying love comes the wedding night. And it is not as the poets write. There's pain, there's blood . . ."

"I doubt my sister still has need of a wedding night," said Niccole absentmindedly.

The room turned silent.

Chryslantha flushed—she hid her face adjusting the curtains. It remained eerily quiet behind her.

"Everyone out," Sophia ordered. Chrys knew the command did not apply to her. "Not you," Sophia pointed at Niccole.

The door shut and Sophia exploded. "Stupid, careless words," she told Niccole. "Your sister has a far better reputation than you, girl."

"I-I . . . ," she stuttered.

"Do you have any idea what damage you can do to your sister's station . . . to her life?"

"I only . . ."

"Get out. Don't return until you find your wits."

Niccole fled from the room in tears.

"This is how rumors begin!" the archduchess said, turning to Chryslantha. Chrys could not look Sophia in the eye. Sophia studied her a moment and said only, "I see."

"See what?" Chryslantha responded cautiously.

"That explaining a wedding night to you *is* pointless. By the gods, Chrys . . . you're highborn! The property of your father until wed. What were you thinking?"

Chrys felt her ire rise. "I was thinking that he was lost to me, Sophia. Callum earns his keep and reputation by the sword; he is always in the midst of conflict. I have had that fear . . . that we may never be together, since I first realized I loved him. Cal was leaving for the Mourish rebellion—that evil, hateful war. My father has sent men to war. Half never return. The ones that do are but remnants of the men that left." Chrys sat next to the archduchess and looked deeply into those viridian eyes, daring her friend to challenge her convictions.

"I have loved Callum since . . . nine? Certainly before an appreciation for the fairer sex manifested in that darling head. I was thinking of *him*, Sophia, in the dark and deadly abyss of war— that place where soldiers prove their mettle to their lords and kings and fathers before first discovering it for themselves. I was thinking that my desire, my yearning, which I had contained so virtuously for so long, would be for naught. I thought that the man I loved might find solace from our union in his darkest hour."

The archduchess waved her off. "But if he'd been slain and left you with a swollen belly . . . your father would be brutal to the MacDonnells for shaming you."

"You are not hearing me, Sophia. In my mind, I'd already lost Callum . . . not a wholly irrational fear and even now at the height of Aandor's resurgence, with him safe in the castle under his father's command, that fear still vexes me. I do not regret my actions, Sophia. Your wedding night may not have been as the poets writ, but I have had mine—before war and fate could fiddle me of it—and the words to describe what we shared are beyond any scribe's facility."

"You are not wed!" the duchess said, exasperated.

"Only *you* know of this, Sophia."

"And your sister."

"Suspicious. But she's a known prattler of nonsense. My fate rests entirely on what *you* reveal."

"I shall say nothing. I pray you've sense enough to stay your desires until you wed?"

"It was but the once. Soon we'll be wed; none will be the wiser."

The sky had turned dark. A great thunderclap moved over the city. Horses whinnied in distress, shutters rattled as winds whipped through the alleys. Chryslantha thought she heard the faint echo of a scream among the clang and clatter. She cracked the window and the sound of swordplay entered with an ill-scented breeze—acrid and sharp . . . an unholy smell. Screams soon joined the chorus across the far length of the city—not just men, but the high-pitched shrieks of women and children. Lightning struck the fair grounds. Sophia and Chryslantha held each other by the window, confused.

A loud pummeling on the door startled them.

"Enter," said the archduchess.

It was Callum with two guardsmen and Sophia's frightened ladies. Palace soldiers ran through the corridors behind them. The frenzy in the old gray sentinel had changed in tone. Something was very wrong.

"Something's amiss in the city," Callum said. "My lady, is Prince Danel with you?"

"With Athelstan."

"Stay in your chambers, keep your servants close," Callum ordered. "I shall leave Erich and Gunter here."

"Cal . . . ?" Chryslantha started.

Callum smiled at her in that manner of suppressing concern that he did not yet realize she'd deciphered. "All will be well," he said. "I shall consult with my father and then guard the prince." Before heading out, he stopped, turned, and drank in the vision of his betrothed. "You look amazing," he said, conveying more with that single word than all the love poems in the Great Library. And he left.

The screams now cut through the windows—columns of black smoke began to rise above the city rooftops. "How is this happening?" cried Sophia. "Were they disguised as revelers?"

The ladies stayed huddled, distracting themselves with needlepoint, avoiding the temptation to look out the windows. Anarchy ensued. Men on the walls began to fire arrows at unseen assailants. Gunter shuttered the window and pulled the heavy drapes across to muffle the sounds. A loud shriek cut through the air. Chryslantha was surprised how clearly it came through drapes—surprised until it was clear the screams came from within the castle.

A rush of boots blew past the front door. The sounds of battle rolled up the grand staircase.

Erich barred the door to the suite. Gunter herded the ladies to the rearmost room. It had but one entrance, easily defendable. Erich joined him—his girth aptly filled the doorway, barring any from coming past. The castle walls could not muffle the pings and clangs of swordplay—the screams of the dying. Anguish permeated the stone—it rose from the courtyard.

Sophia was tense, but Chryslantha knew the archduchess thought not of herself. "Callum will not let harm come to the prince," she told her friend confidently.

Darkness shrouded the city and the shadows in the room grew blacker yet. One corner especially drew Chryslantha's attention . . . something was wrong. Neither light nor sound emanated from this area. The black spot was greedy, consuming the light of the room and growing, like shade rendered upon shade with no hard edges—the effect was unnatural, inexplicable. Chrys's ears popped from the pressure and the smell from this abyss burned the nose. Gunter approached this black hole. A spear thrust from that inky darkness pierced the guard. The women screamed and stumbled to the far side of the room, cowering behind Sophia and Chryslantha. A man emerged from that void holding the other end of the spear. As he came fully into the room, the tendrils of brimstone swirled around him. The man was swarthy with penetrating dark eyes lined with coal—exotic, with billowy pantaloons, boots that curled in the front, a low round helmet with caged face guard, and the curved forked sword of a desert warrior from the southeast.

"Sorcery!" one of the girls screamed.

Sophia pulled a dagger from the fallen soldier's belt and stood her ground to defend her ladies.

Another soldier emerged after the first warrior, this one bearing a crimson jupon with the gryphon of Farrenheil. Erich charged and gave good measure, but when a third assailant emerged, he was overpowered. Alva unbarred the door and led the way out as the ladies ran toward the front of the suite—all except Zenoia, who picked up Gunter's halberd and blocked the way to give the others time. "Run, my lady!" she shouted.

The swarthy invaders ran Zenoia through and pushed her aside.

"Oh gods!" Chryslantha screamed, in the thrall of terror.

Outside the suite, the corridor was mayhem. The Dukesguarde was matched in number. One of Sophia's handmaidens ran into a flanged mace, her face crushed instantly. Sophia tripped over the broken body of a servant boy. Chryslantha and Valeria, on either side of the archduchess, grabbed her arms and lifted her, crouching as they ran toward the archduke's chambers. Men of the Dukesguarde, seeing the ladies, positioned themselves between the archduchess and the assailants. Arrows sailed over them; halberds skittered by their feet. A hundred men clashed on the grand staircase as they ran.

"Valeria!" cried a concerned voice from above.

James MacDonnell fought his way down the staircase with the consistency of a man who had waged war all his life. His enemies fell before him like paper lanterns before a storm. This was where Callum's prowess in battle descended from. Red-faced and breathing hard, the elder warrior joined the women on the landing and immediately formed a vanguard with a stout guardsman to cut a path to the archduke's wing.

By the time they arrived, the rear guards and all of the handmaids, even Alva, were gone. A line of Dukesguarde barred the hallway.

"Open the line!" a corporal ordered.

"The shadows!" Valeria screamed, pointing at invaders materializing behind the defenders' line.

The once secure hallway exploded with battle.

James MacDonnell led the women into the archduke's chamber and barred the door behind him.

Except for the newcomers' heavy breathing, the room was otherwise quiet, untouched by chaos or the strange dark sorcery that had transported the enemy into the rest of the castle. A haggard high prelate, in his tall hat and pristine gold and white ceremonial robes, stood beside Archduke Athelstan. They were flanked by the valet and footman; three pikemen; Lord Alney, commander of the army; and Lady Mila Boules, a childhood friend of the archduke's.

"It would appear Farrenheil has made good on its threat of war," said Lord Alney.

"And the Verakhoonese have joined them," the archduke added. Athelstan bore the general traits of his family better than most, but with a strong, long nose that curved smoothly to a point like the edge of an executioner's ax. "Bastards. We need to contact our allies."

Sophia searched about the room—once, twice. "Where is our son?" she asked.

Chryslantha looked about as well. No nursemaid. No Danel.

"The high prelate has placed a blessing about the room, blocking access by sorcery," her husband said, avoiding the question.

Sophia walked right up to her husband. "Where is Danel?!" she demanded. The archduke looked anxious. Sophia had criticized him for being a political animal—more comfortable making deals than pressing his rights by steel. But this was war. The kingdom needed a leader, and the look on Athelstan's face said he was not up to the task. The archduke shook his head and pointed at MacDonnell.

"Magnus Proust claimed he could spirit the boy out of the city safely," said James MacDonnell. "I covered Callum's flank as he rushed ahead to retrieve the prince."

"They left before you arrived . . . before the corridors were fully choked with the enemy," said the high prelate.

The clang of swordplay ceased outside; it went very quiet. They wondered if their guardsmen were victorious . . . until the thunderous rap of a mailed fist on the door broke the silence. The pikemen took up positions between the entrance and the nobles. Lord MacDonnell and Lord Alney behind the guardsmen also readied their long swords.

"Pelitos, shine your light upon us—illuminate our path and keep us safe," the high prelate prayed.

The door burst open. The enemy soldiers wore black and crimson jupons over gray chain mail, with boots and gauntlets of black and crimson. Their commanders followed cautiously. One of them stepped up, standing just before the nervous pikemen, but he made no move to engage them. He was in his fifties, tall with a broad chest and shoulders, a shaved head that gleamed like the egg of a great bird, and an old scar that ran diagonally from his upper left forehead across the bridge of a once-broken nose, down his right cheek to his jawline. His eyes were a clear bluish-green, like the waters off some tropical port.

"I am Lord Blunt, vice marshal of Farrenheil, general of the southern legions," he said in a calm and clear voice to the arch-duke standing behind the pikemen. He had the slightest trace of an accent introducing a sharp staccato to his Aandoran. "Your castle and your city have been taken. Do you yield?"

Chryslantha had heard of Blunt. One of Farrenheil's greatest military minds, nicknamed the Desert Hawk for his unsanctioned subjugation of Verakhoon into a vassal state.

The archduke moved his pikeman aside to stand before Lord Blunt. "You've destroyed a hundred-year peace this day. This will escalate to bloodshed across the entire—"

"No," said Lord Blunt. "What remains of your armies is too far to help you—I have fifteen regiments entrenched just beyond these city walls. We've taken your kingdom whole in one afternoon. The war is over."

"Our allies . . ."

Lord Blunt closed his eyes like a man mining for patience—he shook his head slowly. "No one is coming, Lord Athelstan. Yield."

Athelstan looked lost. This was beyond his rudimentary understanding of warfare. Advanced notice of approaching armies and the enemy met on open fields. Under the conventional rules of war, you knew when you were going to lose, had time to prepare for surrender. He turned to the others in the room, struggling to come to terms with the situation. Everyone expected him to save them. He looked at Sophia and must have concluded there was more yet to lose because he found his spine and stood tall before the vice marshal. "If I yield, you will spare my people?"

"Your subjects will be spared to the extent that we have the power to do so," replied a striking, statuesque woman who emerged smoothly from behind Lord Blunt, like a cat on the hunt. Except for penetrating amethyst eyes, she looked blanched of color. Her floor-length white satin dress was decorated with white lace and white pearls, as befitted a wedding gown. It was not what anyone sensible wore to a war, and yet it was immaculate, despite the carnage beyond this chamber. Platinum-white hair fell to her waist, and around her throat was a white satin choker with a polished stone.

"My wife, Lara," said Lord Blunt.

Lara's voice was dulcet, yet deep and confident. She was a woman who did not need to raise her voice to be obeyed. "Those in the castle are safest, as these are my husband's most disciplined soldiers and would answer to him directly."

Blunt nodded in accord with this statement.

Athelstan hesitated a moment as any man contemplating the

end of his world might. Chrys knew no word for the look on his face; there were lines there she had never seen before. He pulled out his sword slowly, waiting for someone to charge in and say this was all some mistake. He contemplated the sword a moment . . . perhaps to strike down the general and his wife—Athelstan looked at his wife and the others in the room first before relinquishing the sword to Blunt. Aandor's guards put down their pikes, and the enemy surged into every chamber of the suite.

A tall, solid, blue-eyed officer, with a strong jaw, sharp cheeks, and tied-back white-blond hair, joined Blunt and the White Lady. "Where's the brat?" he asked.

Athelstan's face soured at seeing the new officer. "Set any maids afire recently, Dorn?" the archduke queried.

Dorn raised his arm to strike.

"Cease!" Blunt barked at him.

Lara touched Dorn's arm gently and brought it down with little effort. "There are still yet five kingdoms to negotiate with, nephew. We must convince them of our—goodwill—if we are to settle our conflicts."

"What do you want with my son?" asked Sophia, stepping forward.

"The whore speaks," said Dorn with contempt. "Where is he?"

"No one can get out of the city," explained the White Lady. "We would have the prince sooner than later."

"You gave an oath!" Sophia shouted at Lord Blunt. The archduchess turned to her husband. "He said they would not harm anyone if you yielded. Do something!"

"We promised we would not harm any *subjects*," said the White Lady. "The prince is not the archduke's subject. He is Athelstan's liege lord. Why would we have come all this way if not to cut off the usurper's head?"

"No!" Sophia launched herself at Blunt, banging her fists ineffectively on his breastplate. Dorn grabbed her wrists and shook her roughly. Five men held the archduke and his commanders at sword point when they threatened to interfere.

"Where is your brat?" Dorn spat at her. He threw her to the floor. Chryslantha and Valeria lifted Sophia, who wanted to attack him again; they pulled her to the divan.

Lara snapped her fingers, instructing her soldiers to grab the archduke's valet. Dorn slid his dagger between the valet's ribs and twisted.

The valet refused to cry out. He spat in Dorn's face. Dorn pulled the knife and made to slash the man's throat, but Lara stayed his hand.

"Temper, nephew."

She grabbed the valet's face roughly with her hand and peered into his eyes. He struggled and whimpered beneath her gaze. His eyes rolled back into his head and blood slowly seeped from them.

She continued until the valet stopped shaking. The man withered before them—his skin shriveled, aged years in seconds. Lara's hair transformed, turning a deep chestnut brown . . . she appeared younger, luminescent with a maiden's flush.

"Blasphemy!" cried the high prelate.

"Oh, shut up!" Lara snarled. "You're as useless as the wards you placed around this room." She turned to Blunt and said, "This man witnessed Proust and a knight leave here with the child."

Dorn snapped his fingers and pointed at the divan. Chrys thought Dorn had targeted her until they grabbed Valeria instead. Dorn played with the knife before her, balancing it on its point. He removed his finger, and the knife remained hovering in the air before Valeria's terrified gaze. This monster was a sorcerer as well—magic at the whim of a madman.

"I don't know where the prince went," said Valeria, trembling.

Chryslantha cursed silently for the stupidity of drawing attention to herself, but she stood anyway. In a loud and forceful tone she said, "Lord Dorn, we do not know where the prince is, I swear it by the gods. We arrived after Proust departed. Lord Blunt gave his word . . ."

Recognition sparked in Dorn. His leer sent shivers down Chryslantha's spine. "The Rose of Aandor is spoken of even in the halls of Farrenheil—and maybe a few brothels. Godwynn's eldest flower has steel in her stem," he said to Lara.

The mention of flowers brought up her last image of Zenoia. Chrys hoped that Linnea fared better than her sister. Fear worked to unravel Chryslantha's emotions. She wanted to cry, but for Valeria's sake bit her inner cheek and forced the grief from her mind. "Valeria does not have your answers."

Dorn examined Valeria closer. "You have a familiar look."

"She is my daughter," said James MacDonnell.

"Ah . . . then your brother is the master of the tourneys—the captain himself. No doubt with his prince as we speak."

An oily-looking Skilyte rushed into the chamber. "Milord, the prince and the magus are barricaded in the pantry. Proust has blocked access—magic or otherwise. Even Widow Taker cannot circumvent the wards."

"Leave Proust to me," said the White Lady.

"No," cried Sophia. Chryslantha gripped her, worried that her friend might rush the enemy again.

"Like all your lot, Proust is cunning," Blunt told his wife, implying a mistrust of magic and wizards—a sharp irony considering who shared his marriage bed.

"We have committed too much blood and treasure to allow this child to escape," Lara said. "Rudolf, send your dogs to the pantry . . . ," she said to Dorn. "Take her," she added, pointing at Valeria.

Chryslantha's heart sank as Valeria left their sight. Blunt departed, taking Commander MacDonnell and Lord Alney. Enemy guards remained; the duke's suite had become their cage.

Sophia sobbed inconsolably. She rested her head on Chryslantha's chest and Chrys held her tight, struggling not to choke on her own despair. Where the prince was, so, too, was Callum, and he would not let them take the boy while he still drew breath. He would never yield. Chryslantha needed to scream like a madwoman—to beat the walls bloody with her bare hands. Her fears had come true. She grieved for the future she would never have. Chrys wept silently, biting down her own pain for Sophia's sake—empathy for a mother whose infant child was about to be murdered.

CHAPTER 1

THE BOY IN THE BOX

Daniel Hauer balanced along the edge of the half-pipe ramp staring down the fourteen-foot vert. His truck kept catching the edge, and he'd tumbled to the flat in his last two roll-ins, cursing like an angry drunk and blaming everything from the brand of skateboard to the quality of the Masonite for the failure. Though he'd never fully embraced skate culture back in Glen Burnie, he knew he was at least better than this.

"Your Grace . . . our lesson," Allyn Grey said somberly. He stood behind the teen with placards denoting Aandor's various noble families and their banner men—a long hierarchy that stretched down to the humblest country squire. Daniel wanted to tell the reverend to bug off, but bit his tongue. Grey tapped his wristwatch, peering judgmentally at Daniel over glasses perched at the tip of his nose.

It was one of *those* days, Daniel thought—the one where the iPhone shuffled one wrong song after another, and you suspected Steve Jobs of putting impish AIs in those little fuckers just for shits and giggles; the kind where no number of four-leaf clovers, rabbits' feet, or Saint Christopher medallions could change the dice from coming up craps. Daniel tuned out the reverend, just as he tuned out his etiquette lessons, histories of Aandor, geopolitics of the Twelve Kingdoms, songs of Udiné, dances of Bradaan, sword fighting, hand to hand, battle tactics, and several other disciplines Callum MacDonnell had tried to cram into his beleaguered fourteen-year-old brain the past five months. He couldn't care less about who his great-great-grandfathers were. Luanne Gillie was what he cared about.

They'd been physically kept apart for "security reasons," their rapport limited to social media—but recently, their conversations had turned awkward. Last week, a day before her seventeenth birthday, she'd blocked him on Facebook. Colby said she'd moved to Buckhead—an Atlanta neighborhood she could never afford. Daniel suspected his "guardians." A generous bribe seemed to be Malcolm Robbe's style. What right had they to mess with his paltry social life? Reverend Grey cleared his throat and continued to tap his watch.

Spring's full vibrancy was in effect at Malcolm's vast Dutchess County compound, beckoning him to frolic after a cooped-up winter. On the helicopter field rose the standing stones of a henge, which Reverend Grey had just completed to draw magical energy from Rosencrantz's lay line at the meadow several miles away. This estate was home base for the retaking of Aandor. Rosencrantz and Lelani perpetually refined the return spell, keeping it at the ready, so *when* to execute really was up to the guardians. Callum and Mal continuously argued over timing. At the rate with which they bought soldiers of fortune and equipment, they might bankrupt the billionaire. This caused Daniel some guilt, as, unlike the others, he had mixed feelings about returning to the universe of his birth. He wanted to meet his real parents, of course . . . but Aandor had dominated his life lately to the point where it wasn't *his* life any longer. They offered him a kingdom—sort of. Daniel would only ever be prince regent. He had the blood of ten kings, but he fell two kings short of a quorum that would allow him to become the king of Aandor and emperor of a re-formed empire. That honor would go to his progeny depending on whom he married. To his handlers, Daniel was a chess piece—a sperm bank.

He was lured by money, magic, and a helicopter that day they found him in North Carolina . . . and fear of assassins hunting him for belonging to the wrong family. It'd been USDA prime cuts and Idaho potatoes ever since, but he realized he had accepted the guardians far too easily. Living with Luanne off the grid in normalcy appealed to him more each day.

Malcolm Robbe's generosity was a formidable leash; and yet Cal warned him of it, telling Daniel that dwarvs were miserly by nature and expected their favors repaid for the smallest of boons. Daniel didn't know how he could ever repay Malcolm, but he appreciated the skate park immensely, even though it riled Callum to no end (which Malcolm appeared to enjoy). But nothing that the billionaire could buy would abate his lonesomeness. Cal's family was the exception—Catherine treated him like a younger brother. But they could come and go from the compound at will while he was perpetually "under protection." They even balked at Adrian and Katie visiting. The isolation was depressing. Tilcook had offered him a professional escort as a distraction; Daniel was deeply offended, though he made no show of it because the mobster was being sincere. No one understood; when his face was plastered on the evening news and everyone under the sky hunted Daniel for the reward, Luanne stood by him. She had been Daniel's *only* loyal friend, even lying to her own uncle. Her rejection stung more than Daniel wanted to admit—more than Katie Millar's *just friends* speech.

Before the guardians, before Clyde's death, the future had

been an open slate. Daniel could have become an artist or writer, joined NASA, or married the girl of his dreams. Now his handlers laid out his future like a toddler's Sunday clothes. If not for the chance to meet his parents (and the skateboard park), Daniel might already have run off.

He pushed off, cleared the edge of the ramp, and surfed down, across, and up the other vert. Instead of catching air, he ground the coping, held it for a second, and reversed direction. He continued, navigating the half-pipe with rediscovered dexterity. When he came to a sweaty, exhilarated stop, life had become a smidgeon less claustrophobic.

"Got it out of your system?" the reverend asked.

"Need to work on my fakies," Daniel said.

From the reverend's expression, it was a sure bet he didn't know a fakie from a doughnut. "Do you give MacDonnell this much sass at sword practice?" Grey asked.

"Swordplay is actually fun, Rev."

"Says the boy who has never been to war."

"You'd never know it from my bruises."

"And Cal's only *pretending* to try to kill you."

Daniel wondered about that . . . Callum always seemed disappointed with him. He excelled at his studies, at fencing, horseback riding . . . but something was missing. Maybe Daniel was just Cal's job, and a friendship was asking for too much.

"Can I ask you something, Padre?"

"You *may* ask me anything, Your Grace."

"Why did Luanne quit me?"

If the reverend knew of some nefarious plot, he didn't tip his hand. He scratched his tight salt-and-pepper hair and gave the matter serious thought. "You'll find many writings on the fickleness of teenagers," Grey answered.

"But we were good . . ."

"You knew her but a few days. The excitement and attention around you perhaps was an aphrodisiac. Relationships need interaction, and you two are always apart. As your first love, she resides in a special place in your heart, but remember . . . you were not *her* first. Think of Luanne's perspective, and try not to judge her harshly."

"So Mal and Cal didn't do anything?"

A flurry of whistles and shouts across the compound cut off the reverend's response. At first, Daniel thought it was Cal's training drills for the mercs, but when MacDonnell emerged from the maple trees flanked by his top mercenary lieutenants, Francois Ladue and Graeme Van Rooyen, Daniel knew there was more going on. All three wore relieved expressions at seeing the prince safe.

"The schedule says you have a lesson," Cal said. His distaste for the skate park was written on his face. "Why aren't you in the mansion?"

"It's stuffy in there. I needed to catch some air."

"There are no skate parks in Aandor."

"There are in America!" Daniel sniped. "People invent things here—like SKATEBOARDS!"

"You have too many obligations to be wasting—"

"Gentlemen!" Reverend Grey cut in. "What's going on?"

Callum recalled his purpose and said, "Our wayward court jester, Balzac Cruz, and the frost giant, Hesz . . . they just showed up at our front door."

CHAPTER 2

CREEP

Seth sat against Rosencrantz's broad trunk under the isolating pall of his Beats headphones, disconnected from everyone who increasingly asked more of him than he thought he could give. He skimmed through notes on general magic that Lelani had prepared for him. A glint of the waning sun ran along the top edge of the small aluminum camping trailer parked just yards from the tree. The tree itself was the bull's-eye of a four-acre meadow protected by a forest and hills in Dutchess County, New York. The haunting melody of Radiohead's "Creep" harmonized with Seth's mood. The coming war dogged his mind. The guardians expected much of Seth, especially after his stellar performance against Lord Dorn in New York. And therein lay the problem.

Seth had been spectacular in Manhattan, harnessing elemental forces that had taken man thousands of years to master through science . . . but he had done it with Rosencrantz's guidance. The tree wizard sent Seth complex spells through a lay line, one of the many that crisscrossed the earth. But because Seth had never truly learned the spells, earned them through practice and perseverance, he did not retain them in his memory. In fact, all new spells Seth learned disappeared from his memory after he cast them, limiting his repertoire to a handful that he had memorized his first year at school, and even those with questionable control. Without Rosencrantz's symbiotic connection, Seth stumbled through wizardry.

Deciphering magic was like a stubborn safety cap on a medicine bottle—he could just feel the tabs and catches, hear the clicks, and still fail to open after twisting and turning. Seth wished the protection spell that had insulated him from magic most of his life had never come down. Then the guardians could expect nothing from him.

Lelani tutored him, if one could call condescension and castigation methods of teaching, and she chastised him relentlessly about using Rosencrantz as a crutch. She regarded his pledge to repair the damage he had done to people in his life a distraction. Seth did not disagree with her objective . . . he had to get his shit together, or else the next challenge from a wizard could be his last.

The song ran continuously on a loop; it was his anthem:

> *But I'm a creep,*
> *I'm a weirdo,*
> *What the hell am I doing here?*
> *I don't belong here . . .*

Seth had been twelve when his mother, Jessica, sent him away to study at Proust's Academy in Aandor City. She, along with his aunt Belle and older cousin Pipa, ran the Grog and Grubb two days east of Aandor City. Seth hadn't appreciated how hard his family had worked to create a good home. Jessica had been a vivacious tavern girl—smart and comely with a penchant for fun after long shifts. Nine months after some debonair "traveler" had visited the inn, Seth arrived in the world. She acquired the Grog from its former owner (with what money being a source of much speculation). The running theory was that Archduke Athelstan himself was Seth's father, and helped her out of guilt, or for confirming his virility with a spanking new bastard. But life had been idyllic at the inn: stabling horses, bussing tables, but especially the frolicking around the banks of the Sevren and countryside glades. His mischievous nature had been good-humored then, pranking friends with silent steps and a good supply of spry bullfrogs.

Seth had resented Jessica for exiling him, as he perceived it. He turned angry and challenged even his most patient teachers. But his mother had not exiled him—she recognized his rare talent for magic, and Jessica wanted more for Seth than their Podunk hamlet could ever provide; he was too young at the time to understand. Thinking of his daughter, Caitlin, how he wanted to see her thrive, Seth finally understood the sacrifices his mother made on his behalf, how hard it must have been to watch her son ride away. Nostalgia dogged him . . . that humdrum inn was constantly in his thoughts. There was, however, the war—and the matter of putting the prince back on his throne.

Daniel was a good kid who deserved his birthright. Aandor was a great place to live under the old status quo, prosperous, magical, and just as fiefdoms went—but propping up a king cost a lot, usually paid in blood by simple folk like Seth's family. Seth's place during war should be at the Grog and Grubb. At the very least, he should retrieve his family and bring them back here.

The multiverse had an ironic sense of humor to entrust a man of Seth's sins with the care of so many women. It seemed like a lifetime ago, but barely half a year had passed since he exploited girls for porn companies. The universe had a long memory, and apparently so did his daughter's mother, one of his models. He'd tried to heal his hurt by putting Caitlin and Darcy on a better path. But Darcy's initial gratitude gave way to resentment. Her rehab counselors and her parents did not trust his epiphany. They could not see the extent to which Seth would have gone to earn Darcy's forgiveness.

Darcy cut him out, agreeing to take his money for Caitlin's sake in exchange for the occasional email on their progress. Seth accepted her conditions, taking some solace in their success. Caitlin was doing gangbusters at her new charter school in Forest Hills, and Darcy was finally finishing college. As hard as it was for Seth to accept, these were good problems—the problems of the living. Tristan and Timian and Ben Reyes did not have such concerns anymore.

A tap on his shoulder startled him.

"Sorry," said Helen Reyes with a playful smile and a tray of fresh pastilles. "I called to you twice." Ben's widow was in her seventies and had assumed the role of caretaker of Rosencrantz's meadow. She had far more energy than when they'd first met, a benefit of Rosencrantz's healing arts.

The meadow's tranquility belied its history of carnage. Buried a few feet away was Ben himself along with the other men and women who'd taken care of Rosencrantz over the years. Seth had known Reyes for just a short time, but the old man had had a profound impact on his life. The sky changed to match Seth's gray mood; clouds rolled in, the wind began to whip.

"Oh my, where did this gale come from all of a sudden?" asked Helen.

It was more than sudden . . . it was damned unnatural. *Did I do this?* Seth wondered, having no true sense of his power's *subconscious* limits. The sky darkened further; a cold rain fell.

Thunder rumbled within the clouds. Seth recognized this storm . . . he had been in one like it fourteen years ago.

He escorted Helen back to the trailer, driving his wizard's staff into the muddy earth to brace them against the wind. They entered just as golf ball–sized hail began dinging the aluminum roof. Darkness enveloped the meadow, and Seth worried about Lelani out there in the woods.

Through rain-streaked windows, he searched for her, mistaking some piece of animated brush along the forest edge for human activity. It had gotten so dark, his reflection was opaque; hazel eyes like crescents balanced on their tips—the eyes of an older soul. Just when he'd written off all the outside movements to the undulations of boughs and branches, some new activity, a flicker at the far edge of the meadow, renewed his attention. The atmosphere outside was thick with water, refracting what little illumination the weather offered. He thought it might have been the local college kids who often camped to drink and smoke, until a crack of lightning lit the meadow. What he saw chilled him.

"Who are they?" Helen asked, peeking through the window beside him.

People emerged from a thin black gash as though the air were giving birth. The gash pulsed and wormed like a suspended black lightning bolt slowed to a millionth of its speed. Black threads emanated from the edges of the opening like frayed silk. Seth had never seen blackness like this—so deep and absolute, blackness that was brighter than light. The world around it appeared a low-resolution image by comparison.

"Helen, get back to Puerto Rico and lock the door behind you," Seth ordered. Without hesitation, she left through the back door portal of the trailer, and cut the junction to the meadow.

Seth communed with Rosencrantz and, with a gesture not unlike a Catholic priest's blessing, erected a protective umbrella of shimmering hyper-dense air above him. Seth walked out toward the travelers, who numbered almost a dozen, all wearing hooded cloaks and boots of leather or suede and sword belts. A tall lanky man in a dark gray robe and hood carried a torch. Half the party wore the gold dress cloaks of Aandor's Dukesguarde. *Rescue party?* was Seth's first thought.

The rip in space sealed itself behind the last traveler. The rain abated and the clouds started to dissipate. Seth was thirty yards away when he sensed Rosencrantz's discomfort, which caused him to exhale a soft, "Oh!" The men in black raised their crossbows toward Seth in unison.

"Wait!" Seth cried. He held his arms up in as peaceful a gesture as he could muster. "Friend! Friend of Aandor."

Rosencrantz's discomfort morphed into pain and alarm. Seth rolled his shield down in front of him just in time to fend off three quarrels. At his use of magic, the man in the gray robes quickly advanced before the others. He was gaunt with creased pale skin, black circles under bloodshot eyes, and a long sharp nose curved like a shark fin. Gray Cloak waved a rod composed of a human ulna bone attached to a skeletal fist gripping a polished black stone the size of a baseball. He pointed his spindly white finger at Seth and bellowed through gnarled stained teeth, "Tertan!" The gold cloaks turned in unison and marched toward Seth.

It was a clumsy march—a squad of palsied players. Seth couldn't make heads or tails of it until the rotting stench of death rolled in like a fog. Half of one soldier's face was gouged, another dragged a leg with a bone jutting out, and a third moved with a spear through the center of his chest plate and his left arm mangled. Their eyes were filmy, lifeless. These men were different from the Colby Dretch variety of undead. These were true dead men walking.

"Oh fuck me," Seth whispered.

He backed up, nearly tripping over his own staff. "Lelani!" he screamed. The woods ran deep . . . she might be miles away.

You're a wizard, too . . . get your shit together, he thought. Through his link with Rosencrantz, Seth hurled a bolt of lightning from his staff that blew wide holes through two soldiers. The effort drained him. They still moved forward.

Crossbowmen shot at him from the left, forcing Seth to drop his attack on the approaching dead to shield his flank. The soldiers had closed half the distance between them already. Seth wasn't sure if he should stay to defend the meadow or run to get help; Rosencrantz, being a tree, needed him to effect spells in real time.

A ball of blue-white fire shot out of the forest and set three undead aflame. The crossbowmen turned their attention to the attacker, as did Gray Cloak. That left five soldiers still advancing on Seth. He fired another lightning bolt and knocked the head clean off one of the soldiers. The body kept advancing toward him. "That works in the movies!" Seth complained. They were within ten yards. The rancid stench made him want to puke.

"That smell . . . ," Seth said to himself. "Decomposition!"

Remembering Rosencrantz's firefly spell when they fought the gnolls, Seth asked the tree if it could affect creatures a hundred times smaller. The spell entered Seth's mind through their link, and he executed it. Nothing happened; with the dead almost upon him, Seth began to panic. The soldiers slowed; their skin dissolved at an accelerated rate; thousands of larvae appeared, like an overflowing tub of popcorn, to consume the dead flesh. Soon, only the tattered bones remained, and as the meat that held them was consumed they collapsed into the heaps of larvae on the grass.

At the edge of the meadow, Lelani had taken down the three crossbowmen and held her own against Gray Cloak—until he pointed his rod at his dead crossbowmen and they rose in that same palsied way and lurched toward the centaur.

Seth was exhausted. He had enough left for only one more attack. A lightning strike up Gray Cloak's sorcerous butt—but his aim was off, and he only managed to singe the cloak. Lelani amplified those embers into a true flame, and skimmed some of it off the necromancer to ignite the dead bowmen. She was a big proponent of coopting magic that was already cast because it cost half the energy of a new spell.

Gray Cloak fled into the woods, patting out his robe. Lelani was about to give chase, when a flaming bowman lurched onto her.

Seth cast his personal spell for hard air, and swung his staff like a bat, knocking the other two crossbowmen to the other end of the meadow. Nearly spent, he still thwacked Lelani's assailant on the back mercilessly until a familiar silver dagger pierced the back of her assailant's head. The corpse went limp.

"I am so fucking glad to see you," Seth said.

"Are you hurt?"

"No, just exhausted. Too many spell—"

"Relying on Rosencrantz is lazy." She cut him off. "In fact, it's not wizardry. It's puppetry. I told you there would be other mages!"

"They kind of showed up out of the blue, Red. What was I supposed to do?"

"Of course! Do you expect the enemy to announce their attacks?! You are supposed to be expanding your own spell library.

It's been five months. At the very least, learn how to use another wizard's own attack against him for half the effort. What happens the next time Rosencrantz or I are unavailable?"

"I can tap into him from anywhere . . ."

A blue cloak rustled on the ground several feet away. The wizards prepared their spells and approached cautiously. A foot with a torn blue slipper stuck out at one end. The person under the cloak whimpered.

"Reveal yourself," Lelani ordered.

"Pl-please don't hurt me," said a soft high voice. The figure stood. She was tall, her dress ruined by mud. Tears fell from clear blue eyes, her long hair a tangled mess. "They forced me . . ."

The girl was oddly familiar. "Does she remind you of anyone?" Seth asked.

"Speak, girl. Who are you?" Lelani demanded.

"M-my name is . . . Valeria MacDonnell."

CHAPTER 3

HOOFPRINTS ON THE EMPIRE STATE

"There are hoofprints on the Empire State Building," Malcolm Robbe said, watching the storm beyond his library's windows retreat as quickly as it sprang—hail smoked on the lawn as spring reasserted its dominance on the land. Mal swirled his tumbler of Macallan 18 single malt and took a sip.

Callum MacDonnell understood Mal's dilemma: that despite best efforts, evidence was out there connecting Dorn's attack on New York City with the guardians. He sat stoically, resolute in his decision to lock up Balzac and Hesz.

"Just because the government pushes that wag-the-dog tripe about terrorists releasing hallucinogens in the water supply doesn't mean people are buying it," Mal continued. "People died. The Feds are pushing hard on this."

Cal ran his finger along the rough, planed edges of the antique maple-wood boardroom table. "Balzac Cruz is a traitor to the realm," he said.

Mal turned around, arms out to the room. "This is *not* the realm. I've spent a fortune covering up our trail. There comes a point when all that money and effort becomes the liability—a blinking red siren of attention. People will connect dots. Some will try to blackmail me, others will go to the Feds out of patriotic duty, and before you know it . . ."

"A spy acting against Aandor's first family—espionage, sedition, an agent of genocide, infanticide, regicide . . ."

Mal crossed the room, stepping over the centerpiece Afghan rug depicting the Assyrian king Tiglath-Pileser dominating the Mushku people, and said, "You should have heard what Cruz had to say . . . and then *let him go.*"

"Let him go?"

"I've had that jackass under surveillance for months, Cal. We're not the government here—we have to tread lightly."

"Let *him* go?" Cal repeated. "He has intelligence on the invasion, which we're not going to get over coffee and cake."

"I want to gut the guy as much as you do . . ."

"That son of a bitch tried to kill *my* wife."

Mal paused their debate. He poured a tumbler for Cal, put it on the table, and chose to sit on a rung of the rolling ladder against the inlaid bookshelves instead of a chair. "Building a mercenary army on American soil is risky," the industrialist said. "The government's paranoid enough—the FBI will eventually figure out we were involved with New York. Then this whole endeavor will screw the pooch. Jesus, Cal—if we don't get back, Farrenheil's going to slaughter my people once they lock down the kingdom. Thousands of us just escaped from there in the past generation to find sanctuary under Athelstan. No other kingdom would take us in. Aandor is the only stability in our universe. You keep advocating for more time before returning to Aandor, but time's an illusion in both universes—we *never* had it. Our clock's been ticking down here since those monsters crawled out of the sewers. Now we kidnap a tenured university professor? We're already in the broiler."

"He came of his own accord."

"Semantics!" Mal shouted. "We locked him in the basement! Is there something else here that I don't know about?"

Cal debated whether this was the time to bring up his concerns. He downed the scotch; its heat slinked to his belly. "Daniel isn't ready," Cal finally admitted.

"For what?"

"To fight. To rule."

"You've lost me. Are we talking about the same kid?"

"He doesn't think or act like a prince. He pines for that girl."

"Xbox, pizza, and pretty blondes . . . surprise! He's a red-blooded American teenager, Cal."

"He's compromised."

"Daniel goes through my library like vampires at a blood bank! He's learning *your* shit in spades, too. His swordsmanship is sublime. He'll challenge even you when fully grown. But you gotta give him a longer leash, or he's going to snap."

Cal knew he'd been pushing the boy hard. He couldn't see any alternative. "He's been raised by peasants." Cal cringed as the words left his mouth; they sounded snobbish even to a lord of the realm. "He has the wrong mind-set," Cal continued. "Daniel lacks the little snippets of wisdom we attain from our fathers—the things they teach us at odd moments when they aren't trying to teach us anything at all. What we become as men—as leaders—is shaped by those unscripted moments. It's more about character than intelligence, as much about confidence as wisdom. Daniel's deficits in these things have created emotional vulnerability—he's too eager to please, to be accepted . . . to be loved. Look at this thing with the North Carolina girl. It's more a crutch than a choice." Hypocrisy weighed on his argument. Cal had married a commoner himself . . . over the most desired woman in his kingdom. He knew what Daniel needed to do for the kingdom's sake, and yet, knowing his family, Cal would still not give up Catherine for all the land or gold in the world.

"That the kid emerged as clean-cut as he is with those worthless foster parents says plenty about his character," Malcolm said. "He got different lessons from his father—how to take a punch to the gut and stand up again."

"Mal, a royal has to exude a sense of entitlement—to convey that it's natural for others to serve him . . . that he expects it. Princes aren't just born . . . they're molded. People have to want to die for him."

"You want him to be an asshole."

"No. I'm grateful he's compassionate. Cat and Bree love him. But Daniel is royalty—when Grey teaches table etiquette, he's uncomfortable keeping others standing until he's ready. That awkwardness can set the men around him ill at ease . . . men who are looking for a strong leader. It will chip away at their respect. All the letdowns in his life—his pill-popping mother, the childhood crush who dumped him, his abusive stepdad—these are the bricks of his insecurities, the very opposite of the experiences needed to build a prince. A confident man never spends time wondering how to make everybody love him. Deposed monarchs are always surprised . . . shocked, as though it were not possible to not love them."

"You're making the opposite case. No one wants to work for a jerk."

"When you lay off a thousand workers, people with mortgages and children in college, you still pull the trigger. That's the burden of leadership. He'll have to send men to their deaths."

Mal pointed to Cal with his empty glass. "A lot of good rulers don't fit the divine-right mold you're thinking of."

"The boy is only now receiving the kind of instruction—and love—a young leader needs. Yes, *love*," Cal emphasized. "I do love him. I want him to enjoy a long, happy life. All I need is a few years to balance out the damage done."

"We'll have time in Aandor, Cal. We tuck him away with his grandfather in Bradaan. Daniel isn't fighting this war. We're his generals, his advisers. We're building this army. He's a figure-head. He just needs to sign the orders and make the babies."

At the mention of babies Cal let out a deep sigh and rubbed the bridge of his nose. Catherine's ultrasound was today, and he'd for-gotten to call. His cell was still on mute from maneuvers—there were two voice mail messages from Seth, which he ignored, and a text from his wife that read: Everything fine. Blue paint, Bucko :-)

The problems of two universes suddenly took second place to simple joy—serene warmth radiated through the niches of his be-ing. Mal must have guessed the message because he gave his friend a dopey grin.

"I'm going to have a son," Cal said.

"Congratulations." They clinked glasses and toasted to baby boy MacDonnell's health.

Mal let the silence linger, but what he had said about their timetable still troubled Cal. "If we don't have years . . . ," Cal said like someone accepting a harsh verdict. "I ask one thing of you—stave off the wolves for five more months. I love Aandor, but I'd rather Catherine give birth in a hospital natal unit here, and the babe find its strength."

"I'll do my best," Mal said.

A commotion in the foyer commanded their attention. They hurried to find Seth and Lelani with a disheveled young lady. The strangely familiar woman looked lost, scared. When she locked eyes on Cal, she sprinted toward him.

"Cal!" she cried.

In the space of a heartbeat, Callum realized he held his sister.

"Dude, answer your phone," Seth scolded.

CHAPTER 4

SVENGALI OF WESTCHESTER

Daniel entered Balzac Cruz's basement cell flanked by Francois Ladue, a white-haired ex–French commando in his fifties who was Callum's top new Dukesguarde, and Reverend Grey. Ladue was against Daniel meeting the prisoner, but the mercs had been instructed to follow the prince's wishes—an exercise to build his authority.

Cruz sat on the bed with a copy of Plato's *Republic*. He looked much the same as last time they'd met: glasses; tweed jacket, leather elbow patches; brown slacks; and sensible leather loafers. He still raised Daniel's hackles.

The cell was sparse—cinder block walls, throw rug, chair, a small television at the foot of the bed. Cruz favored a single desk lamp to the overhead light, throwing the corners in deep, claustrophobic shadow. Hesz by comparison was in a much sturdier cell with a steel vault door. The guardians had planned for this necessity, though Daniel was certain Cal never anticipated the pair would simply waltz in of their own accord.

Cruz rose and bowed. "My philosopher king," he said without a hint of sarcasm—though there was mockery in the words; Daniel would never be king.

"Please sit," Daniel said.

That people one day would not sit or eat without his leave baffled Daniel. Cal said making folks stand longer demonstrated his power over them. Daniel didn't understand the difference; however, he regretted not making Cruz stand longer. The man was key in the invasion of Aandor . . . the reason Daniel grew up without his true parents. He should hate this man, but Daniel's connection with the people Cruz hurt was abstract. He couldn't match the others' vitriol. Only Cruz's attempt to kill Cat registered anything. The MacDonnells were the only normal family Daniel ever had, even if Cal was a hard-ass.

"Have you read this?" asked Cruz of his book. "Would you categorize Aandor as a timocracy, oligarchy, or tyranny?"

Daniel had read *Republic*—along with Machiavelli's *The Prince,* Rousseau's *Social Contract,* and other similar texts. There was no point learning to rule a kingdom he didn't technically possess, though. Sun Tzu's *The Art of War* was more germane to his predicament.

Cruz was dangerous—so devious, no one even knew he was the enemy until it was too late. The jester-turned-professor steered the conversation subtly with an innocent enough question about a book. He was gauging Daniel. Every word out of the jester's mouth was a subliminal attack. Daniel came to a startling self-realization—the teen had always subconsciously assumed he was the smartest person in any room he occupied. It was a completely arrogant notion, and probably not true in a lot of cases. Cruz's russet eyes bore into a person like a mental drill—his gaze, bordered by wizened creases under thick salt-and-pepper brows, declared that he knew all you knew and more. Attempting to discern Balzac's motivations was like matching wits with Socrates . . . or stumbling about a dark room with a hungry panther. Daniel hoped years of thwarting bullies like the Grundy brothers had hardened his poker face.

"Your Grace, why have you sought out this man?" asked Reverend Grey.

"That is obvious," Cruz explained. "His Grace has been fed a steady diet of the party line since you captured him. He has mental indigestion."

"Captured" was a tactical word to seed dissent. Daniel was with the guardians because he wanted to reunite with his parents, because the law was after him for Clyde's death; and who knew how many agents of Farrenheil were still out there?

"The same fare day in and day out is not healthy," Cruz continued. "Good advice is scarce, and a gifted mind such as His Grace's seeks alternative points of view."

Gifted mind. Flatterer. The jester may not be wrong, though. Options were the key to a long and happy life. The state of Maryland might put him in a warm prison, with three squares a day and medical coverage for only seven years, with good behavior. Compare that with Aandor, where tens of thousands of enemy soldiers were vying to lop off his head for the glory of their lord. *Would Mal and Cal even allow me to stay here if I didn't want be their prince?*

Cruz was trying to divide and conquer. To halt further drilling into his brain, Daniel asked, "Why did you do it?"

"I thought we could improve upon the status quo," he said solemnly.

"Anarchy, chaos are not improvements," said Reverend Grey. "People were happy."

"Peasants and serfs work long, hard days for their lords and lack the energy or education to advocate for their own interests,"

Cruz said in his most professorial tone. "And the gentry, in frenzied concupiscence to ascend the social hierarchy, are blind to the realities that bind them. They, too, have been fed a steady diet of hope. The odds of the lower gentry attaining a title, of marrying a child into the upper classes, are astronomically against them. There are only so many resources in Aandor. Show me a lord happy to parcel out his own land for a newly minted earl, and I shall show you vegan frost giants and altruistic dwarvs."

"That is a cynical view," Grey said. "I knew many commoners. The kingdom flourished. You speak of the overly ambitious—like yourself."

"The rich protect their own," Balzac continued, unperturbed. "Scholars, however, recognize the patterns that maintain our status quo. Oh, yes . . . I was a scholar in Aandor once. We tried to form a republic in Teulada, free from your extended family's squabbling, but both Aandor and Farrenheil undermined us. What chance had we thinkers when even mortal adversaries were willing to collaborate against change?"

Daniel pictured the empire map in his head; Teulada was a small kingdom in the south wedged between Udiné and Karakos. It was inconsequential to Aandor.

"You've fallen far for a *scholar* . . . or are you not also master of the Phoenix Nest, where you rent flesh to the debauched, ply patrons with spirits, and separate them from their earnings?" Grey said. "How many fathers leave your den shamed for gambling away their children's lunch and making mockery of their marriage vows? You are in league with an oligarchy of the merchants indifferent to your iniquity and vested only in their own interests."

"We don't have Las Vegas; people need to have fun. Daniel's father himself is my silent partner in the Nest . . . our trade is endorsed by ducal warrant."

"What hardened your heart that you turned your back on true scholarship, Balzac—what drove you to overturn the happiness and stability of the world?"

Balzac fell back into his memories like he'd bitten a rank lemon.

"Tell me, Balzac . . . before the spell returned our memories, were you happy here? Did you find peace, absent of the ambition that haunts you? I could soothe your pain . . ."

"Do not touch me," Balzac growled. "I am not here seeking redemption. I came to ask the prince what *he* wants."

"What he wants is to go home and meet his parents," Grey insisted.

"Ha!" spat Balzac. "You are an even bigger fool than your god. You give the boy a list of ancestors to memorize and tell him to wait patiently for a throne that will be served up to him like gruel at the commissary. There is not one among you that does not believe he may be better off here drawing his pictures, wooing his buxom Southern belle.

"Tell me, *Reverend*"—the honorific dripped acerbically—"on your list of Daniel's ancestors, *who* is *the* king?"

Reverend Grey looked unamused. "Daniel, this is a waste of our—"

"They were all kings except for the last few generations," the teen answered.

Balzac smiled like a fisherman jerking a hook. "Once, long, long ago, there was a village . . . ," Balzac lectured, "and the men of a rival group—possibly a neighboring village or a group of brigands living in the hills—came into the village and took their crops and probably their women. And this continued to happen until, one day, someone grew tired of being a victim. And this *someone* inspired the men to rally around him, to pick up a club or a pitchfork, and he led them against the raiders—or neighboring village—and if they lost, no one ever heard from them again. But if they won . . . if they won, they put this man on a pedestal and said, 'Lead us!' They gave him an honorific; let him sleep in the biggest hut and claim the most beautiful daughter in the village. This man has legitimate authority. There were no ballots, no records, nothing formal to record the event beyond a hearty cheer, but he earned the power bestowed on him by the villagers. This story has played out on every continent, on every world in the multiverse.

"Our villager who led his kinsmen to victory . . . he has a son, and people, being creatures of habit, do not think it a bad idea when dad and son conspire to maintain rule within the family. The son has done nothing other than come out of the womb that everybody believes their king inseminated. The son resembles his father and may be an intelligent amiable fellow whose company many enjoy. This may go on for generations. Rule is institutionalized, and handlers come in to maintain the power base and it becomes a prosperous business. Then king number nine comes out cruel or stupid, and believes his right to lead is divine by virtue of his connection to the first man who actually earned his authority. What follows are wars fought for personal grievances, ideological cullings—paranoia springs up because the king is acutely aware that everyone else believes he's not fit to rule and that he could never have forged a kingdom on his own had he been born a blacksmith or thatcher's son. The decadence, the neglect of your subjects' needs—royal properties badly managed lead to famines, plagues, and wars with neighbors over the most trivial offenses. It happens cyclically. So I ask again, who was the king of Aandor?"

"The first one . . . Atheling the Calm," Daniel said.

"Very good."

"Preposterous," Grey said. "Aandor has had many magnificent rulers. Alfred saved the kingdom during the White Hag Wars and expanded it twofold—was he any less a king?"

"To hear the tales, his mad brother Egwyn had as much to do with the kingdom's fortunes," said Balzac. "And for nearly destroying it. He lost his life and their wealthiest city, Meadsweir, to the spirits and ghouls of the Blue Forest. Wouldn't a republic be better? A nation, guaranteed the right to replace a bad ruler from a pool of its brightest citizens?" Balzac's eyes glazed over idealistically. "I used to think my ideals a pipe dream—some crazy dementia out of place in a corrupt world ruled by force. But then I awoke here, and I see this nation that reinvents itself like a phoenix. The notion that men need not be pawns traveled to me across time and space."

"We've had bad presidents, too," Daniel said. "Sometimes the electorate gets it wrong."

"What is it that you want, Balzac?" asked the reverend. His arms were folded, hand tapping elbow.

"Give up the throne," Cruz said to Daniel. "You would be happier here than an exiled prince over there. You cannot imagine the resources that went into the invasion—the wealth, man power, and sorcery. Lives were sacrificed before one soldier's foot touched Aandor's soil. Returning is a fool's errand. Trust me."

"So egalitarian," Grey said. "So self-sacrificing, jeopardizing your life to come here for the sake of the prince's happiness. I ask again, what do you want?"

Balzac thought about it for a moment, petitioning the ceiling for answers before admitting, "Farrenheil emptied itself of soldiers for this invasion . . . they have but one army remaining at their capital, Höllentor. Those fools actually think they've won something. The invasion was at best a stall. It will bring down both Aandor and Farrenheil, and hopefully, without a king to unify the remnants of the old empire, its debauched inheritors will fall with it. Daniel's return would only perpetuate hope with misguided inspiration. I want to see the fruits of my labors flourish; I deserve it. I want to go home."

"You're mad," said Reverend Grey. "They will throw you in the lowest dungeon and leave you to rot. You would have been better off at your university."

The explanation nagged at Daniel. Cruz always knew something Daniel didn't. He played the world like a chessboard—stacking the odds, planting seeds, and setting adversaries against one another. Reverend Grey had asked the wrong question. "Why now?" Daniel queried.

Cruz smiled, checked his watch, and went back to reading his book.

CHAPTER 5

TWISTED SISTER

1

Catherine MacDonnell's nerves danced like droplets on a hot skillet. She deemed herself silly to be in such a state, considering everything she'd been through in the past six months: otherworldly assassins, being kidnapped and tortured by an insane homicidal sorcerer, the lingering guilt of having executed a person (though Dorn had it coming). Icing on that cake was the revelation that her husband's former-current fiancée in Aandor looked like Charlize Theron. So why would meeting Cal's sister, an eighteen-year-old ingénue from a medieval universe, scare Cat into a cold sweat?

Maybe she was upset that more agents of Farrenheil had come over, and that meant her family was still in danger. *How many had come through in the past months?* To always be looking over her shoulder was no way to live—never sure if the creep on the corner was just selling a dime bag or casing her family.

Traffic on the northbound Taconic was light. Bree played a game on Cat's smartphone, oblivious to her mother's butterflies. The MacDonnells had debated whether letting Bree play with tech was a good idea. They might soon be living in an alternate reality devoid of electric outlets; but by that same logic, Cat would also have to cut off indoor plumbing. Cal swore there were other attributes to make up for the loss. Aandor was idyllic to him. *At least we'll be together,* she thought.

Six months earlier, Catherine had believed she would be working toward her MBA. Instead of financial models and market analysis, she was reading about barter economies, agriculture, and horticulture . . . skills that would be practical in a medieval world. Catherine was certain no amount of reading would prepare her for the culture shock. *There's a lot more manure everywhere,* Cal had joked, regarding a world where horses were the primary mode of locomotion. But all the food was organic, there was no air pollution, life was slower, and people loved deeply. Folks interacted with each other instead of their smartphones—after dinner they gathered around a fireplace and told stories, played games and instruments. How much of what Cal remembered of Aandor was left, though? The baby kicked; Cat rubbed her belly to soothe the little guy. The thought of bearing children without medical doctors, NICUs, sterile instruments, and, most important, epidurals, scared her more than a hundred Lord Dorns. Fortunately, Cal was of like mind on this issue.

She pulled up to the porte cochere. Some Hudson Valley steel magnate had built the mansion at the turn of the century; its double-oak main doors with their massive brass lion-head knockers were wide enough to drive a Ferrari through. Cat pulled down the sun visor and checked her makeup. *This isn't hard,* she told herself.

She collected Bree and headed in. This house symbolized everything that complicated her life. It sheltered the prince of Aandor, served as a camp to train her husband's army, and was the launching point from which Cat's family would leave this universe and everything they knew. She was still only ninety-eight percent sure that she was going anyway. What would she tell her family? As she approached the drawing room, her stomach rumbled.

The usual suspects were conversing in groups, noshing on appetizers. Mal put out a nice spread. The room had been arranged with clusters of comfy chairs, two massive couches, and love seats in the center around a large maple-wood coffee table. A warm palette of terra-cottas and tans complemented cream walls, clean white trimmings, deep rust drapery, and other maple-wood furnishings. The far wall had three evenly spaced glass-paneled doors that led to a patio, and above them, half shell–shaped transom windows that currently framed the twilit sky. Lelani, Seth, and Malcolm conversed with Daniel by the far left patio doors.

Daniel had filled in nicely under Cal's workout regimen. He'd grown an inch since they'd recovered him. His hair had grown into that moppy boy-band coif the tweens swooned over—and not just them . . . Bree had taken to Daniel like an older sibling. Daniel maintained a sense of humor in the middle of all this insanity, but Cat worried about the strain they'd placed on him. He was just a kid, not a savior. The average fourteen-year-old who paid no rent, bought no food, and played hours of free video games already complained that the world overwhelmed them—Daniel actually had a world riding on his shoulders. Still, Cat would be happy if her son turned out like the prince. He was a genuinely good kid. She wanted him to meet his true parents and didn't mind playing his guardian in the interim.

She still couldn't bring herself to call him "Your Grace," for which he'd confessed his gratitude. But Cal had high expectations and pushed the kid to his limits. They were all impressed with his intellectual and physical progress but no one, except for

Cat, monitored his emotional state. She advocated for the boy consistently. What did it matter if Daniel mastered all things Aandor if they just ended up breaking him?

The Debonair Don, Dominic Tagliatore, aka Tilcook of Aandor, chatted by the patio door with his wife Gina and Tony Two Scoops. They, too, would be going back to Aandor, along with their families and as many mafia cronies as they could take. This gathering must be important—Cal and Mal avoided Tilcook as much as possible because of surveillance by law enforcement. Lelani must have cast a veil to get them here.

Just inside the room's threshold, Reverend Grey conversed with the undead detective, Colby Dretch. Colby was working through his legal troubles. Mal had secretly arranged for a better lawyer to defend him and delay the state's prosecution. Grey and Lelani had not yet settled on the process to restore Colby's heart, but he was looking better since he started applying makeup to his normally pale skin. Cat spotted Cal in the inside corner of the room opposite the patio doors sitting alone with his thoughts and a glass of something deep amber in a tumbler. No sign of Valeria.

"How's Tory?" she asked Colby.

Colby beamed. "Doing great, thanks to the padre," he said, though in Brooklynese it sounded like *tanks ta da pahdrey*. "He's struggling on crutches—but walking, damn it. And he's got thirty-thirty vision in one eye. Baby steps."

Cat was so pleased to hear this she forgot her nerves. She took the detective's cold fishy hand and gave it an affectionate squeeze. "I'll visit him soon," she said.

Cal stood and kissed his wife and daughter.

"Where's your sister?" Cat queried.

"Upstairs asleep. I gave her the broad strokes of what had

happened to me since leaving Aandor. She was exhausted, so we gave her a bed. All of this has frazzled her." A hush in the room turned Cat's attention.

Cal's sister hovered at the entrance, taking in the newness of everything. She was as tall and lovely as a model, though a healthier size eight instead of a waif. She had the same blue eyes and radiant blondish hair as her brother. She wore a cerulean-blue summer dress with prints of small white flowers and white tennis shoes. There was no mistaking her for anything other than Cal's sister, though Valeria's features were softer. Valeria spotted her brother. Cat's gut tightened, and she wondered if her sister-in-law shared her nerves. After all, when Valeria awoke this morning, her brother was still a twenty-one-year-old bachelor.

Valeria walked through and hugged Cal for what seemed an eternity. Or was it the other way around . . . did Cal cling to her? Bree scrunched her face to indicate she was impatient to meet her new aunt. The girl had had the audacity to ask if this new addition to the family would increase her Christmas presents.

Cal introduced them in their native tongue. Valeria curtsied and said something that almost sounded like English, but wasn't, and with what appeared to be a hint of a Scottish brogue. Cal had said there were similarities between their two realities.

Valeria looked quite solemn, almost unhappy in her curtsy. Catherine was not aware curtsies needed to be so ice-queen serious and looked to Cal, unsure of whether she was required to dip as well. A subtle shake said "no," and then the lessons kicked in. *Of course not, she's younger, I'm married, and I'm the future matriarch of our family when their mother passes.*

Valeria straightened, and Cat opened her arms wide and said, "Welcome to our side of the universe." Valeria accepted the hug hesitantly; Cat wondered if their height difference was the reason for the awkward embrace.

Bree mimicked her aunt's curtsy, which put a large smile on Valeria's face. She scooped up her niece and kissed her repeatedly. *So not an ice queen,* Cat thought.

Lelani came over with a silver tray bearing a wide stone bowl, a copy of Webster's English dictionary, mortar and pestle, an olive-colored fluid in a lead jar, and a box of matches. She ripped out several pages of the dictionary and tore them into strips, which she placed into the bowl. She added a few sheets of parchment with strange writings and used the pestle to grind some buds that were in the mortar to a fine powder and sprinkled them into the bowl. The wizard set everything aflame with the fluid and a match. As the contents of the stone bowl burned, they produced a pleasantly scented white smoke that reminded Cat of almonds. Within the white smoke wafted thin black wisps, but not continuous; like tiny long sentences on microfiche. Lelani instructed Valeria to breathe in the smoke. Valeria stood over the bowl while Lelani chanted in Aandoran. Cat was worried Valeria would begin to choke, but she exhibited no discomfort. Then Lelani motioned for Cat and Bree to come over as well and breathe the smoke. Apparently, all the others had done this already.

Once the fire had died out, Valeria took a step back and said to Lelani, "Is that all?" in English, with that hint of Scottish inflection. And Cat now understood the greeting Valeria had given her moments before. The others applauded and went back to their own conversations.

"Wish that worked for me," Daniel shouted from the far corner of the room. His immunity to magic meant he had to hit the books.

Lelani scooped up the items from the spell and left.

"Honey, you and Valeria acquaint yourselves," Cal said, as though the language barrier was their sole cause of awkwardness. Catherine shot her husband a look that would have killed a bull elephant as he walked away to gather the others. Valeria gave her brother the very same look.

"So you understand me now?" Cat asked her.

Valeria thought about the question before saying, "Your words, yes." Valeria's response was layered. "I disapprove of witchcraft . . . but as it goes, this was a boon," Valeria finished.

Cal's sister would not smile, not even nervously. A cloud of deep sadness . . . or hostility permeated the girl. Had her kidnappers mistreated her?

"I'll just be honest," Cat said, pulling her sister-in-law aside and facing the corner away from earshot. "This is weird, and now that we can speak to each other, I don't want to say the wrong thing."

"Yes," Valeria said flatly.

Cat smiled harder to hide her frustration. This was not the reaction she had anticipated. Putting a bullet in Lord Dorn was easier. "Is there something wrong?" Cat asked her point-blank.

Valeria gave her a steely gaze. She straightened her back, shoulders high, and said in the most somber tone, "Chryslantha Godwynn is my dearest friend."

Ah. There it was . . . the other woman, smacking Cat in the brain like an Acme mallet. From Valeria's perspective, a few hours ago her "dearest friend" was going to be her sister-in-law, the mother of her nieces and nephews, the bridge between the Mac-Donnells' middle standing in the nobility to the upper echelons. No one in Aandor was going to be happy about this, except maybe the family that ended up getting Chryslantha.

"Did Callum explain what happened?"

"Aye," said Valeria, though her tone indicated it didn't offer much comfort. "I'm aware of Tristan's fate here as well. We were not betrothed, but I cared for him and always hoped . . ." Her thoughts trailed off from their point. "Callum says he, too, had a wife—family."

"I never met them. Mal has helped them financially."

"Knowing my own heart at this news, I cannot imagine what she who has loved my brother most of her life will do upon learning of his marriage to you. And of your child."

This was worse to Cal's family than if he'd died honorably in battle—to see him live on with another woman bearing his children, while Chryslantha's family was humiliated, would ruin the MacDonnells' reputation for generations. Cat thought often about what she would do if their roles had been reversed, and could never find a satisfactory answer. Cat had Bree and her unborn son, a part of Cal that would forever be intertwined with her own essence—something to comfort her if things ever reached their worst. What did Chryslantha have? She was as yet unaware that her hopes had been dashed—her marriage, a faded dream. Her heart broke for Chryslantha Godwynn, as though Cal's betrothed were also dear to her.

Bree tugged at her aunt's dress, annoyed at having been forgotten. Valeria knelt and cupped the girl's chin. "You're the wee image of your auntie Meghan."

Bree giggled. "You talk funny."

"Valeria, I just wanted to—"

Valeria stood and with a raised hand indicted that Cat stop. She ran her hand through her hair, pulling it back and away from her face, and dug deeply for her next words.

"I'm grateful," Valeria started. "My brother did not spend years of his life alone; he met someone worthy of him. I'm grateful for my new sister's willingness to embrace me with openness and warmth." Valeria paused for a moment, searching. "Do not let my sadness for my friend . . ." Valeria's eyes glistened and pleaded. "I pray thee, Catherine, give me time . . . time to accept this new world I find myself in."

Valeria spoke of her vanquished nation as much as this new universe. Her family and friends killed or kept hostage, Tristan dead, her brother a stranger—her best friend about to have her dreams crushed. Valeria bore it bravely and asked only for patience. She was infinitely more mature than Cat remembered being at seventeen. If all of Cal's family had this much grit, Cat would need a month in boot camp to catch up.

2

Valeria MacDonnell spoke in calm and somber tones. "Lord Blunt was confident they would find the prince—that even if you'd escaped the castle, you could not have made it past the tens of thousands of enemy soldiers in and around the city and the countryside. They scoured every alley, every drainage canal. As the day dragged on, their concern over your escape grew.

"They possessed intimate knowledge of our court . . . that the prince would be with Callum, groomed to command the Dukesguarde under Danel's reign. And still . . ." Valeria paused. Her face tightened recalling things she'd rather forget. Emotions overwhelmed her. "They knew the prince would be with Callum . . . and still . . ." Her voice cracked.

Cat did not share the guardians' emotional connection to Aandor, but having met Dorn, she knew how evil the enemy was and dreaded Valeria's next words. Callum put an arm around his sister and Bree brought her aunt a Kleenex. The group waited silently for Valeria to catch her breath.

"It was the White Lady," Valeria continued. "Lord Blunt had ordered all newborns in the city brought to the castle . . . the babes of merchants, peasants, and noblemen alike were rounded up. They knew that Danel had the mark of Aandor's sigil—that the prince would not be far from Callum . . . they knew . . . but the White Lady believed Proust might have veiled the mark with sorcery. It was she who . . . put the newborns to death."

A gasp rippled through the room. Cat worried for Daniel the most. He was sensitive and would feel responsible.

"One every hour, sucking their life force before their very parents, until they surrendered the prince," Valeria continued. "A dozen had been killed before I left."

"Farrenheil had gambled heavily with this war," Reverend Grey said. "To not succeed in their goal has made them desperate."

"To his credit, Lord Blunt asked his wife to stop and she capitulated. Archduchess Sophia's anguish was indescribable. She bore the pain of each death. She was so strong before, and this broke her."

Valeria struggled to keep her composure and wiped away a tear. Ladue and Van Rooyen, even Tilcook's stoic veneer wilted in the face of this tale.

This is the world Callum wants to bring us to?

Malcolm broke the silence first. "One babe an hour . . . and you counted twelve?" he asked. "How long was it since the invasion began until you yourself came to this reality?"

"One day," Valeria said.

Malcolm and Cal's expressions soured. They looked at Lelani, who was tapping furiously on an iPad.

"You left Aandor about two hours after we did," Malcolm said. "But you came through thirteen years later. How can the better part of a day have gone by for Valeria?"

Lelani looked up from the pad to find all eyes on her. She put the pad down and licked her lips.

"The time differential between our realities does not appear to be constant," the centaur said.

"No duh," said Tony Two Scoops. Gina smacked his ear.

Lelani put her hands together and thought carefully before saying, "The trip across dimensions does not occur in a straight line. There's a Coriolis effect . . . a curved trajectory due to the rotation of the multiverse." Blank faces told more than words ever could. Lelani blew a stray hair out of her face and tried again at a slower pace.

"Do you recall the records in Tilcook's jukebox? Imagine a point at the center of the disk and another at the edge along the radius. If the record is not spinning, the line between the points is straight. However, if the record spins along its axis, and one were to try and roll a tiny ball from the center to the edge along that radius, the ball would in fact take a curved path in the direction opposite the rotation and end up several degrees away from the intended point. The same effect occurs when traveling from the pole of your world to the equator along the same longitude. Unless you corrected for the rotation, you would in fact end up several degrees west of your intended position."

The group nodded mechanically.

"Rosencrantz and I have had a little difficulty plotting our return. If the Coriolis trajectory has changed this could account for the change in the time differential. We've sent through some light energy bursts to confirm the path, but we seem to be overshooting the mark. The curve is shorter and more extreme than when we arrived here. I've consulted a few theoretical physicists on a university message board," Lelani said. "We can correct the trajectory."

"What do they know about us?" Cal queried.

"Only that I am considering matriculating to Caltech."

"How did you end up here?" Catherine asked Valeria.

"Blunt believed Callum had bested Dorn. Proust's acolyte confessed under torture that the grand magus had sent a wizard with the guardians. No one knew that the guardians had left our world entirely. Lara was certain they had to be within a given radius of the city based on what power Proust had at hand to cast the portal spell; apparently it takes a lot of magic to move people as they did. Blunt sent a second party across the portal to scout the situation and report, but they, too, were not heard from again. I was sent with the third party—as leverage against Callum.

"Leading us was an acolyte of the White Lady named Chasaubaan. He had brought to life, if one calls it that, the corpses of our fallen guardsmen. We entered the mirror frame in the pantry— blacker than the darkest winter night. A force within threatened to tear me apart, bones and all, as we traveled—it pained the ears and pressed against our eyes—I thought I would splinter like a beehive fallen from a high branch. Shortly after, we emerged in the meadow."

"Lord Blunt's second scouting party would have arrived in the past few weeks," Lelani confirmed. "They are likely lost in our world with no money or knowledge of the language. It would be a long time before they were in any position to track us."

"Another bunch of psychos out there?" said Daniel. "Great. Can't I just renounce my title and have them leave me alone?"

The guardians flinched at his comment. Daniel blew out a long, regretful breath. "So what now?"

"We stick to the plan," Callum said.

Mal, who looked ready to hit something or someone, was about to argue again, but Callum appealed to his better nature.

"We all know how soldiers in our reality behave during war," Cal said to the group. He turned to Catherine. "They'll have burned crops and silos. Food will be scarce this year. Families left destitute. Women assaulted." Cal turned back to the group. "What's changed? That we have Valeria's confirmation that it's exactly as we knew it would be?"

"That is not all," Mal stressed. "We believed we had the luxury of time . . . years spent here were only hours there. That's not the case anymore. Every day we lollygag, thousands more die over there."

"We don't know that for sure," Lelani interjected. Cat was grateful for Lelani's loyalty. It had been their best leverage against Malcolm's hasty desires.

"The prince is not returning to Aandor until he is prepared," Cal said. He scanned the room for a challenge, but knew it would only come from one person.

"You're the boss," Malcolm said reluctantly. "But my dime's funding this resistance, so I want some consolation."

"What would you have of me, Mal?"

"Simple . . . let's talk to the clown."

CHAPTER 6

JESTER MINUTE

1

"Love what you've done with the place," said Balzac Cruz, at the foot of the library's posh board table. "Very Lex Luthor."

Opposite Cruz, Daniel occupied the most ornate chair in the room. The mercs were stationed along the periphery, and behind Daniel, Callum and Lelani cut imposing figures. Malcolm sat to Daniel's right and Allyn Grey to his left, leaving Balzac isolated at the foot. "And your lovely chair, Your Grace—is it hand-carved oak?"

Daniel suddenly felt self-conscious of his fancy chair. When Cal's hand gently gripped his shoulder, he thought it was to reassure . . . until he pulled Daniel up to correct his slump. A scold lurked beneath Cal's neutral mask as well. Balzac saw it. The guardians went to great lengths to make Daniel feel important, but that chair was damned big, and Cal's expectations were equally oppressive. The lives of his few friends were in Daniel's hands. What if bad decisions turned his small cadre of companions against him? How would Cat ever forgive him if he caused Cal's death?

A year earlier, twenty-sided dice initiated the only violence in

Daniel's life. Now he hacked at sides of raw beef with a sword, which was harder than one would think. *Get used to piercing real flesh,* Cal insisted. At first, Daniel could barely penetrate the meat. It was disgustingly bloody, and each thrust haunted him. Three weeks of MacDonnell barking about angles and momentum, he finally cut through. Cal had cheated, though. The first few cows had been frozen through to toughen his strikes. Cutting flesh reminded him of Clyde. The guilt still nagged him. Daniel wondered if he could ever kill again. *Would it be easier to keep my hands clean by ordering someone else to kill for me?*

"I suppose you want to know why I did it?" Balzac said serenely.

Malcolm snorted. "Couldn't care less," he said. "Neither will the mob when you hang."

"Logistics are only part of the story," Balzac said.

"Let's start with them anyway," Callum insisted.

Balzac graced them with an oily grin. "A map would help."

Malcolm and Allyn pulled apart two large leaves of the grand table split in the middle and turned them over back onto the table. Carved into the underside was a topographically rendered map of Aandor—not just Daniel's kingdom but the entire empire—an oval continent slightly smaller than mainland Europe with a freshwater sea called the Spoke at its center.

West of the Spoke, terminating at the Endless Ocean, lay the Kingdom of Aandor. Below Aandor, its staunchest ally, Udiné, stretched southward to the Sapphire Sea. To the east of Udiné sat a contiguous mass of smaller kingdoms under the Spoke: Bradaan, the kingdom ruled by Daniel's maternal grandfather, and the neutral kingdoms of Jura, Teulada, and Karakos. To the north, separating the borders of Aandor and Farrenheil, was neutral territory—an unclaimed stretch consisting of swamps and mountains stretching from the top of the Spoke to the northern kingdom of Nurvenheim.

To the east, Farrenheil stretched to the Black Ocean. Below it and on the Spoke's eastern shore resided Moran, a publically neutral kingdom that voted with Farrenheil and represented one of the two kingly bloodlines missing from Daniel's lineage. In the southeast portion of the continent resided Verakhoon, with the Sapphire Sea to its south, Karakos to its west, and the Black Ocean to its east. Tucked just under a corner of Verakhoon was the tiny Kingdom of Nakuru, more its neighbor's vassal these days and representing the other bloodline Daniel's heir would need to be emperor. The final kingdom, Hodonin, was a peninsula to the east of Farrenheil. The only remaining entities were small city-states beyond the southeastern mountain range that constituted the border of Verakhoon. These were petty fiefdoms at the cusp of a treacherous desert, deemed unworthy of assimilation.

Balzac steepled his hands and rested his chin on the thumbs. He looked each of them over with measured patience. "Forty thousand enemy soldiers are bivouacked on Deorwine Plain outside the north and eastern walls of Aandor City. Thousands from this force were sent into the surrounding countryside to quell towns and villages. A few thousand elite soldiers are in the city proper and in the castle—more than enough to dispatch the Dukesguarde and the city watch."

"Not possible," Callum said sternly. "You could not have marched that many troops that far without our notice."

"I guess I'm free to leave, then?" Balzac said with a pleased expression. He stood, causing Ladue's men to move toward him; Balzac sat back down, hands appealing for peace.

"I jest," he said. "Lord Blunt is the commander of the invasion force. He has never lost a war. His wife Lara is the illegitimate half-sister of Dorn's mother—also known to many as the White Lady—though there is nothing 'white' about her. She has an aptitude for sorcery that can match any wizard on their council. Ironically, Lord Blunt despises magic—doesn't trust it—but being supremely practical, he accepts that only fools rush into battle without a wizard.

"The plan was to draw away from Aandor City as many banner men and friendly forces that might aid the archduke. A few days before the main invasion, Verakhoon landed ten thousand cutthroat mercenaries and pirates from the free states east of Gull Harbor in the south, by sea. Their purpose is not to win, but to pull Lord Dormer's forces away from the capital and cause Udiné to bolster its coastal garrisons with troops from its northern forts." Cruz looked at Daniel. "Udiné is like Canada—friendly border."

"Farrenheil doesn't have the coin to launch this big an invasion," Malcolm said.

"You think *this* is big . . . I've yet to finish my tale. As for coin, I loaned Farrenheil the gold to finance these grand distractions. Not shabby for a peddler of spirits, flesh, and games. The opiates trade was also lucrative—I shipped it in with tea and spices."

Cal's knuckles cracked loudly behind Daniel's chair as he tightened his fist into a singularity and stifled the desire to pound Balzac. "Go on," Daniel told Cruz, praying his captain could hold it together.

"In the west, we lured Lord Heady's forces to the tip of White Hag's Peninsula with more fleets of raiders—Athelstan's western army went with them, at least twenty days' march from the capital. Lord Gillen of Wolfram in the east has been bought— he will not honor any banner call. Most other lords were in the capital for the celebration and with the city lost, they will sue for peace to save their own necks."

Missing from the table map were the duchies and earldoms within the Kingdom of Aandor. These were his father's banner men: dukes, earls, margraves, and other titled nobility who were obliged to defend the archduke's claim if called upon. At one time, these had been small kingdoms unto themselves until Daniel's ancestors conquered them. Daniel's father would be king of Aandor, if not for the continental accords between the Twelve Kingdoms that abolished the title until such time that a proper emperor born of all twelve bloodlines came into being. Daniel's ancestors had been shrewd; they cut their lands in a way that stretched to all the corners of the kingdom and isolated the other duchies. Athelstan commanded the only full-time militias—each only ten days' hard ride from the capital.

"Athelstan has as many soldiers as all his banner men combined," Malcolm said, mirroring Daniel's thoughts.

"Athelstan's southern army is gone," Cruz said.

The guardians looked at each other, disbelieving. Malcolm dismissed the statement as bravado. Balzac made no effort to convince them otherwise.

"What do you mean gone?" Callum inquired.

"As in, it no longer exists." Balzac observed each guardian's reaction as the news sunk in.

"That's the largest standing army on the continent," Malcolm said. Aandor's southern army was one-third of Athelstan's entire military—strategically garrisoned to help Jura and Bradaan should they be attacked from the east.

"Was . . . ," Cruz continued. "Lara found some old magic. I never saw it . . . couldn't tell you if it was a scroll or a whalebone, but it could move armies in a blink."

"She toys with the very fabric of existence," Grey said. He looked to Callum. "The gods did not intend for men to rip holes in their creation. This is old magic . . . lost arts beyond Lara's ability to harness safely. Like nuclear plants running at breakneck capacity."

"Jesus," Mal said. "What's the point of winning the kingdom if you lose the world?"

"Wizards!" spat Reverend Grey.

"Lord Blunt heartily agrees," Cruz consoled. "Nevertheless, the White Lady transported an overwhelming ninety thousand soldiers to your southern fortress. Sheer numbers would win the day. Forty thousand troops would then march north toward the capital, razing and pillaging, to join their comrades at the capital. Ten thousand would march east and pin Lord Dance's forces at Eel's Tooth. What's left of Udiné's northern army will dig in defensively rather than attacking our entrenched troops along Aandor's border. It's all an illusion, you see . . . the two sides were comparably matched, but Aandor's strengths were maneuvered into disadvantaged positions, distracted by tactical skirmishes of no value. The effect is that Aandor and its allies feel surrounded and overwhelmed."

Callum leaned into the table and braced himself on thick arms. "Red King's Gate?" he asked in his deep baritone.

Daniel sensed a personal stake in that fort. He searched the map for Red King's Gate. It was in the northeast on the border of the unclaimed lands—a neutral zone that separated Aandor from Farrenheil. The region was mountainous with a river and the only marked road that led directly to Farrenheil from Aandor.

Balzac tapped his fingers together. "That fort's proximity to the Wizards' Archives presented a challenge. The archives and the

Gate are really a twin-fort defense—each committed to help the other," Balzac continued. "But the White Lady needed something from the archive, perhaps the very magic that would power the invasion plan. Lord Blunt incorporated the problem into the solution."

"The archives was the staging point?" Cal said. "Impossible. The wizards—"

"Were neutralized." Balzac sat back in his chair, digging for dirt under a fingernail. "You're all very dense. Farrenheil emptied its entire treasury, emptied all the eastern kingdoms of anyone with even a modicum of magical talent, and used them for this attack. I can only imagine what a battle of so many wizards would be like: so many physical laws bent—even ignorant of science as I was at the time, I feared it would undo us all. Farrenheil obviously persevered, plundered the archives, and commenced the war. From there they moved their armies across the kingdom. But there were limits to that magic, and so several battalions were dispatched by traditional transport—over the mountains—to subjugate Red King's Gate. And they will raze all in their path from the east until they, too, reach the capital."

"The Gate will not fall," Callum said.

Cruz shrugged his shoulders and raised his hands in that *what do I know* way. "I was told it would not be a problem."

"And what was in it for you?" Malcolm asked coldly.

"Lord Heady's lands in the west. From White Hag, I planned to quietly foment my revolution while the entire continent fell to anarchy. Eventually, Udiné and Bradaan will find their balls and attack Farrenheil's forces in Aandor's south. Moran will attack Bradaan while most of its army is fighting for Aandor. With the eastern kingdoms virtually emptied of their military, Hodonin will march west to reclaim disputed territories from

Farrenheil. Eventually, Farrenheil will have no choice but to retract some of its force from Aandor and send them back east, weakening their hold in the newly conquered lands.

"Neither Aandor nor Farrenheil ever had the capability to dominate the other. The advantage of magically transporting armies was a delusion. Magic is no substitute for diplomacy and good politics—a dominant weapon is no guarantee of success. The Soviet Union once had twenty thousand nuclear missiles in its arsenal. Where is it today? It can barely hold Ukraine. The United States isn't any better—it can't stop a diminished Russia from taking Crimea or stop fanatical Muslims from wreaking havoc in the Middle East. Power is an illusion, and those who play the game of distraction well are victors."

"Bastard," Malcolm said. "You've destroyed a beautiful kingdom . . . a fair land with rulers who were just and learned."

The jester locked eyes on Daniel. "Your handlers promote an idealized version of your kingdom, my prince. Your father called the centaurs 'partners' and convinced them to patrol the Blue Forest for Aandor, pretending to do them a boon by letting them coexist peacefully. Athelstan simply didn't want to put up the coin to secure the forest himself. The deep woods weren't really his to give to anyone . . . too many other species living there—some far older than man. But he made its safekeeping the centaurs' burden and it doesn't cost him a single gold phoenix. Diplomacy." Balzac laughed—an annoying chortle that made everyone bristle. Through an oily grin, Balzac asked, "Did they tell you about your father's mistress—"

"We're done!" Cal interrupted, slapping the table hard.

"Perhaps another day . . . ," Balzac said.

"Lock him up!" Cal ordered.

"I came under a flag of truce," Balzac insisted. "Imprisoning me is a criminal act."

"You tried to kill my wife!" Callum said.

"Then let me have my day in court!" Cruz said defiantly. "Arrest me!"

That's not what he wants, Daniel thought. *He knows they would never do that. Can't the others see . . . ? He is still engaged in that game of distraction. That's why he is here spouting off.*

"I'll not let you or the frost giant out of my sight again," Callum promised.

"I came to broker a truce in good faith. However, I made assurances for my safety," Balzac warned. "People know I am here. What's more, a detailed report of the guardians' activities exists—including names and photos, even of the father killer Daniel Hauer in the Waldorf a few months ago. My report connects the dots regarding the deaths at the dairy farm in North Carolina and the golem attack in New York City." Cruz checked his watch. "My attorneys will be delivering them to several government agencies in moments. The paramilitary operation on this compound alone would unsettle authorities . . . third-world mercenaries operating just a hop and a skip from the elite in Westchester. West Point's just over the Hudson. Malcolm's money can't buy its way out of everything; we live in a paranoid world. The authorities will crush your little resistance before it ever flies."

Callum crossed the length of the table in a heartbeat and grabbed the jester by his collar. He yanked him out of the chair like a rag doll. "What makes you think you won't rot in a cold cell in whatever world we end up in?" Cal said. He shoved Balzac toward Ladue. "Lock him up."

"War favors the schemers," Balzac preached. "It prefers the lucky and the rich. I'm all three! I've rolled my dice, but whatever my outcome, Aandor's insurgency dies here."

2

Cal filled the others in the next day while Malcolm evaluated Balzac's threat on the phone with his partner Scott. In another corner, Seth tried to coopt Lelani's practice fireballs. He yelped often and had singe marks all over.

"Balzac will surely hang should he return," said Valeria.

"Balzac has been playing both sides," said Reverend Grey. "We consider fools inconsequential, no one of importance guards their tongue around them. He's made a fortune trading on inside information—blackmail, usury . . ." Cal wondered how many of his men had lost their pay at one of Balzac's gambling dens. Balzac himself was the biggest gambler of them all.

Malcolm approached the group somberly.

"A friend in the Justice Department confirmed Balzac's package arrived today. You can bet there's a package at the NYPD, FBI, CIA, and every other acronym that's looking for us."

The group fell silent.

"How long?" Callum asked.

"The packages have to be vetted to omit crackpots. It'll move up the chain fast as it gains credibility. A week, if we're lucky. They'll figure out we only arrived in this country fourteen years ago from places unknown. That's been no end of frustration for me as I've applied for security clearances over the years. My engineering talents helped them look the other way. But with so many of us, it will appear conspiratorial. We'll be hauled off as persons of interest. This is going to be rough."

"That's it then?" Daniel asked. "Game over?"

That Daniel almost sounded relieved broke Cal's heart. They had put a lot of pressure on the kid, robbing him of his childhood. Had Daniel lost interest in his birthright? What would become of Aandor without him?

"Game not over," Malcolm said. "We have a contingency. A compound in the Canadian Rockies near Calgary registered under dummy corporations—no one around for miles. I have accounts in the Caymans that will keep us liquid as well as gold bullion I've been hoarding for the trip home. We're going to buy Balzac's pirates out from under him."

"I'm not moving to Calgary," Cat said.

"Cat . . ."

"No, Cal! You may not have a past here, but I was born in New Jersey. I'm spending what little time I have left in this universe with my family . . . I haven't even told my mother that I'm going. And what of Bree's school and friends? Do what you have to, move your operation to Canada, but I am staying in the Bronx until we leave for Aandor."

"She has Mother's spirit," Valeria said approvingly.

Graeme Van Rooyen, an olive-skinned fireplug of a South African, stepped forward. "Sirs—Francois and I have fifty good men. If we leave for Aandor now, with our weapons, we can take back your castle—probably the whole city. Put a dozen M2 fifty-caliber heavy machineguns on the city walls, and we'll take out half the enemy while the other half stampedes back home in a panic."

"Combustion science and electronics do not play well around

magic," Lelani said. "Aandor is saturated with such energies. Your weapons won't be as reliable as you are used to."

"With all due respect, mademoiselle, we maintain our weapons religiously," countered Francois Ladue. "Against men in archaic armor who have never confronted automatic weapons, we will not need much time."

"Don't sell our warriors short for being less advanced," Cal said. "Farrenheil has fast knights on winged horses who'd pick your machine gunners off those walls."

Cal didn't fault the mercs for their exuberance. When you were used to surface-to-air missiles, it was hard to take men with swords seriously. He counted himself lucky to have found Van Rooyen and Ladue; they belonged to a bygone age—one where the paper pushers served men of action. Their elite warrior skills were out of place in a civilized world where lawyers and politicians vied for influence through money and elections, trading in securities and broken promises. Malcolm and Cal offered them a world they never dreamed still existed . . . and they were chomping at the bit to get there.

"We appreciate your enthusiasm, Graeme. Our goal was to return with a thousand men, but now we'll need ten times that number." Cal stole a glance at his wife, pregnant and more beautiful to him than ever. "There are also other reasons that we can't leave yet," he finished.

"I don't want to live on the run," said Cat, bringing the conversation back around.

"They're not going to make it easy for you just because you were born in New Jersey," Mal said. "You'll be questioned, watched continuously."

"Helen Reyes's house in Puerto Rico is a nexus," Lelani offered. "There are doors that lead to rooms around the world. I'm certain Rosencrantz can alter one to go to Mal's base. While authorities are looking for Cal at airports and train stations, you can pop into Calgary for a day—or even have family time on the beach in Puerto Rico. The authorities do not believe in magic, and no one will be the wiser."

Lelani was trying to put a positive spin on this, but Cal only heard that his pregnant wife and daughter would no longer be part of his daily life. And how could he be there for his son's birth without the authorities poised to grab him? The price for every foot forward was paid with two steps back.

"Do me one favor," he said to Catherine.

A cautious look surfaced, careful not to agree quickly but also cognizant of Cal's heartbreak. No one expected today to be the day family life ended as they knew it.

"I'm going to be busy with the bugout the next few days—but this party of soldiers that supposedly came through in the past few weeks has me worried—as does the necromancer. I'll be tackling logistics, loading trucks, copters—concern for your safety and Bree's will distract me. Would you consider spending a few days in Puerto Rico with Helen Reyes? Take Daniel and Valeria, too—and Seth for protection. I'll have Lelani and Ladue escort you to the trailer. Will you do this for me? Lay low for a few days while I sort out this mess?"

In a deadpan that would have made Aubrey Plaza proud, Cat said, "You want me to lounge on a Caribbean beach, white sand sifting through my toes, sipping virgin piña coladas, a thousand miles away from evil wizards and henchmen that are trying to kill me? Really? You're asking me to do *that*?"

He hugged her, relishing her petite form under his strong arms, and Cat broke character to squeeze back. She fit just right. She always had since the first time they embraced, as though some sculptor had crafted her just for him. He committed her scent to memory. In a muffled voice aimed at his chest she added, "You do know that was a yes?" He bent down to kiss her. She reached up to meet him on tippy-toes, like bobbing for a hanging fruit.

"Ooo-wee, they're in luuuv," Brianna sang—something new she did anytime people kissed on TV. Even Aunt Valeria cracked a smile.

CHAPTER 7

BUGOUT

1

At sunup, Daniel took one last run at the skateboard park. Mal promised to build a new ramp at the Canadian Rockies compound, but Daniel didn't think he'd need it since the snowboarding there was epically awesome.

In the driveway, large trucks promised to move the guardians to a new land. Malcolm's men were already packing crates into nondescript eighteen-wheelers, which would soon blend among the millions of others traversing the continent. Daniel showered, slipped into his jeans and a black T-shirt, and his favorite pair of Converse, and headed to the dining room.

The mood was both apprehensive and excited. The morning sun projected through a transom window and settled on Valeria at the buffet. It illuminated her cotton floral print summer dress with a glow, a film halo that accented her beauty. The dress clung to her flatteringly, its pleated hem falling to her knees just short of her graceful calves. Daniel was suddenly alarmed. He had completely forgotten Luanne. *Am I that fickle?* He'd decided to slip away after Puerto Rico and drop in on Luanne in Atlanta.

Reverend Grey was in the midst of a conversation with Brianna about the various colorful pins on her jacket. Daniel had started Bree off with a *Dora the Explorer* pin; both their collections just mushroomed from there. At the buffet, Valeria laughed at the wit of Francois Ladue. Daniel felt a tinge of jealousy, which was stupid. *Stupid hormones.*

Valeria considered herself Daniel's subject. The notion troubled him. She would gladly go for a walk if he but asked. *She'd probably do a lot of things,* he realized—and just like that he was very cognizant of the nature of power. A yearning stirred in Daniel, something dark and dangerous. It was not magic but very much human. "Power corrupts, and absolute power corrupts absolutely," he muttered to himself.

"What's that, Your Grace?" Reverend Grey asked, drawing a line from the boy's gaze to the young lady.

"Something from a dusty old textbook, Padre."

Daniel focused on the heap of bacon in front of him. That it actually distracted him testified to bacon's soothing prowess in all things—that is, until Valeria chose the seat across from him. She smiled and curtsied before sitting.

Clean thoughts, chum, Daniel chanted internally.

Valeria, too, was impressed with Bree's collection of flair, lamenting a shortage of jewelry for her own adornment. Thinking nothing of it, Daniel reached into his pocket and pulled out his Green Lantern power battery pin: green, black, white, and gold in the image of a lantern. He held it out and offered it to her. Valeria turned serious.

She rose from her chair and knelt before him, her head solemnly down. "I am deeply honored, Your Grace," she said, as though accepting the Congressional Medal of Honor. The act drew eyes around the room, and Daniel was flush with the heat of embarrassment.

Reverend Grey's face was stern and critical—he had managed to produce the tone of an eye roll without actually rolling eyes. "Well . . . pin it on her," the reverend said. "Unless you plan to keep her on her knees."

Daniel did so and she rose, stroking the metal pin and showing it off to Bree as the two girls excused themselves to finish packing.

"I didn't realize it would be a big deal," Daniel whispered to the reverend. Grey stared at the boy with a stiff, mildly amused expression reserved for someone who stepped in dog crap on a street he knew ten dogs lived on. After all their lessons, Daniel *should* know better.

"You planning to turn Cal's sister into your consort?" Grey asked.

"A what?"

"Friend with benefits."

"Absolutely not!" Daniel insisted.

"Good. Don't give her things . . .'cause you can't marry her, either."

The idea of returning to Aandor without Grey scared Daniel. He hadn't learned nearly enough. "You coming to Puerto Rico?" he asked the reverend.

"Driving back to North Carolina after my coffee. Should make it home by nine. I've already missed one Sunday service, as Michelle likes to remind me. Rosemarie says hello."

"Bring her up next time. I'd love someone my own age to hang with. Seth doesn't count."

Allyn Grey laughed. "Well, we'll see . . ."

"No really. Unless . . . I mean if you think I'm a bad influence . . ." Daniel's thought trailed off into the ether.

Allyn looked at him sternly. Daniel knew that gaze of

preacherly discourse well. "Daniel, you are a most noble young man. Every problem in your life, every bad thing you've had to do is because of our failures as your guardians. And you lay sole claim to all your positive achievements. We're lucky you did not fall into crime or gangs. You are nothing short of a miracle, young man."

"Then why . . . ?"

"It's my wife, Daniel. Michelle's not had an easy time with this Aandor business. Last time Rosemarie came up, Michelle nearly broke with anxiety. She won't come up herself—feels she needs to remain uninfluenced in order to pull me back from the abyss. I love that woman, but her zealotry is not an easy thing for me to contend with. None of this is your doing," he emphasized.

Daniel felt responsible, nevertheless. If he had died, everyone's lives would be easier. Well, maybe not Cal's . . . he'd go back to Aandor to fight regardless. Daniel excused himself.

He walked the grounds and came upon the new henge. Daniel could not feel a stitch of the power Grey insisted was coursing through the construct. Magic didn't affect him the way it did others. On the meadow next to the henge, and far more interesting to Daniel, were Malcolm's surplus CH-47F Chinook helicopters. Most surplus copters were stripped of their weaponry, but because of Malcolm's ties to the Pentagon, these came fully loaded with two 7.62 mm M240/FN MAG machineguns on side pintle mounts, and an aft 25 mm auto cannon. They were loaded with weapons and ammunition. The guardians' most sensitive assets would fly out with Malcolm and Cal, including their two prisoners.

"Are you packed, Your Grace?" asked Callum from behind.

Daniel cringed. Why couldn't Cal call him Dan or Danny in

private like his wife did? "Boxes are in my room," he said. Cal monitored the workers' activities around them as the two walked toward the copters. "Just need to box my gun," Daniel added.

"No, put the pistol in your backpack."

"For Puerto Rico?"

"Keep it at *all* times. Make it a habit. Also a med kit, phone, backup charger, your vest . . ."

"Kevlar sucks."

"It's state-of-the-art light armor. Better than what I wore for work. Look, we'll always have people around you, but I'd feel better knowing you're armed. You remember how we practiced?"

"Yeah. I'm not killing anyone, though."

After a contemplative second, Cal forced a smile. "I'd rather you make that choice from a position of strength. Practice your sword forms in PR—you're getting good and I don't want you backsliding. We'll spar next week."

"I prefer sparring with Seth. *He* doesn't leave me black and blue."

"He doesn't elevate you either. Welts mean you try harder not to get hit. It means no pierced spleen."

"Yeah, yeah."

"Do you know how *many* medieval combatants expire? That little sword scratch on your shoulder may not seem so bad at first, but it was made by a blade that had been through a man's intestines two minutes earlier. The last victim's crap is all over the sword and now it's festering in your open wound; antibiotics didn't exist, so sepsis sets in . . ."

"Enough! Ewwww . . . !"

Cal chuckled warmly. "Get your pack and meet Ladue by the van. I want you all in Puerto Rico by noon."

2

They parked on a dirt patch near the hidden trail, strapped on backpacks and canteens, and began their trek to Rosencrantz's meadow. Lelani took point with her bow. Next were two of Ladue's soldiers; Cat, followed by Bree with a *Dora the Explorer* backpack; Valeria; and Daniel. Ladue, Seth, and two more mercenaries brought up the rear. Everyone was dressed for a spring nature hike except Seth, who had taken to wearing a dark gray duster of late. He insisted the large pockets carried a "crap-load of stuff." Ladue and his soldiers for hire lived the cliché in black baseball caps and sunglasses.

Lelani regularly patrolled the hills surrounding the meadow, and other than local college kids who periodically camped in the woods, it had been quiet these past months. These had become her woods while she lived in this reality and she would not suffer a gnoll or a Skilyte anywhere near the tree wizard. Still, Daniel would be glad when they shut that trailer door behind them; he looked forward to a swim on the beach before setting out for Atlanta.

Valeria and Bree giggled while randomly looking back at Daniel.

"What's so funny?" Daniel asked. The question launched another round of tittering. If he read through the entire Library of Congress collection, Daniel would still never understand girls.

"*Vive la différence,*" Ladue said.

"So do you think we'll actually find ten thousand men who want to move to a medieval alternate reality to fight?" Seth asked Ladue.

"Do they exist? *Oui.* Many feel out of place in the modern

world, *mon ami*. Men like Van Rooyen and me are reduced to working for despots and amoral corporations. It is not that we are against peace—but we prefer straightforward goals in a less complex world. However, recruiting ten thousand mercenaries without tipping off the authorities . . . perhaps two thousand, maybe, over time. But ten . . . ?" Ladue shook his head as if to say that was a tall order.

Time was key. They'd thought they had plenty of it—until Valeria arrived.

Everyone stopped to let Cat catch her breath before the final hill. Seth, a lifelong smoker, looked grateful for Cat's pregnancy. Daniel took a sip from his canteen and approached Lelani, who had barely broken a sweat.

"Ever talk to your scientists about that time differential between the universes?" Daniel asked.

"One in particular offered the most logical theory. We applied it to our formulation and it appears to have fixed the problem."

"Is scientist guy smitten?" Seth quipped. "You're quite smittenable . . . from the navel up."

"It is a *she* . . . and yes, I suspect she is smitten with me. She has invited me to California for coffee."

"Now we're talkin' . . . ," Seth said, rubbing his hands together.

"Cut it out!" Daniel said. Seth always made him feel like the adult.

"Multidimensional oscillation is altering the Coriolis effect," she began. The others crooked an ear toward the conversation. "Imagine the multiverse as an onion, each layer, or brane, a universe unto itself. The core is pure energy and dimensions farthest away are dry of this energy. Each universe is separated by an inert, lifeless layer that has its own mass and volume; it would seem that these interbrane regions expand and contract—like an accordion—varying distances between universes."

"Huh?" Seth grunted.

Lelani let out a frustrated breath. "The multiverse is sometimes the size of a grape, and other times the size of a basketball. Multiuniversal oscillation means universes don't rotate at a constant rate relative to one another . . . they speed up and slow down, thus affecting how time moves in relation to one another. This influences the Coriolis trajectory and keeps the time differential fluid instead of constant. It makes sense, really . . . nothing in creation is static. Moon orbits earth, Earth orbits sun, sun orbits galaxy, galaxy orbits universe, universe orbits multiverse . . . and so on."

"Can't we just fly faster to make up the difference?" Seth asked.

"We're already traveling between dimensions at near infinite speeds as it is," she said. "But the time differential has shortened since I've been here, and our two universes are near synchronicity. That will change again soon enough."

"My brain hurts," Seth said.

"Your brain hurts watching *The Bachelor*," Daniel said.

"True. But this stuff . . . why did Proust expect me to ever become a wizard?"

"I simplified it as much as I could," Lelani said apologetically.

"The bottom of my heart thanks you."

"Monsieurs MacDonnell and Robb do not have the time they once thought to rescue their nation," Ladue said. "*Très difficile pour les hommes de bonne conscience.* I suspect we shall return to Aandor before the year is out."

"I wouldn't take that bet," Cat whispered to Daniel.

3

Bree and Valeria prodded Lelani for wizards' tidbits as they hiked. Seth wondered if the normally stoic centaur simply missed the company of young women.

"So you see," Lelani concluded, "where power has to do with the ability to tap into, channel, or store magical energy, magical proficiency dictates what level of matter you can affect, with lesser wizards able to manipulate only at the molecular level, and the most powerful at the subatomic levels influencing even photonic light and magnetic force—"

Lelani switched gears so quickly Seth barely registered her draw before she shot the arrow into the woods. A cry rang out at the same time a hail of gunfire took down their lead guard. Ladue had Daniel kissing dirt in a blink, shielding him with his own body from a deadly barrage. Cat also had the girls flat on the ground while Ladue's second man and rear mercenaries returned fire. They gave good measure, emptying clips on full auto before someone took them out from the other side of the path.

"We have to get to that trailer!" shouted Ladue.

Seth put a hard air bubble around himself, Ladue, and Daniel—Lelani did the same for the girls, and they sprinted for the meadow as their assailants fired. Lelani's shield deflected bullets solidly like steel while Seth's more pliable enchantment protected like super taffy. The occasional stray came through, but reduced to a mere sting.

Once through the tree line, Seth absorbed the rush of power from Rosencrantz's lay line and timed a split-second switch from defense to offense, casting the most powerful hard air spell he could behind himself. A hurricane-like gale blew the trees back hard, stripping branches and leaves and creating a swirl of debris so thick, it was almost a solid wall. Fatigue set into Seth for the effort, but the attacks from behind them ceased.

More assailants poured into the field from the woods to their left and right. It would be a footrace to the trailer, which was just beyond Rosencrantz at the north end. Fortunately, these new attackers were unarmed. Lelani shot off several arrows in a row, hitting her mark each time, but the people heedlessly advanced.

"The necromancer!" Lelani warned. She put away her bow to free her hands for casting.

Seth gripped his staff tightly, ready to back her up however he could. He tapped it into the grass and connected with Rosencrantz. Immediately he located Chasaubaan behind the trailer—too close to the portal and Helen's home for his taste. The necromancer's presence in the meadow was painful to the tree wizard. The undead appeared as bland gray voids in Seth's colorful magical radar. There were dozens more in the forest that the others couldn't yet see, plodding toward the meadow.

"We're severely outnumbered," Seth declared. "Death wizard's hiding behind the trailer calling in more corpses."

Ladue targeted their heads as anyone who'd ever watched a zombie movie knew to do. A few went down—but most did not, debunking that myth for posterity. Daniel and Valeria shielded Bree, protecting the girl from witnessing their attack on these innocent stiffs. Lelani fired phosphorous balls, setting the closest undead aflame. They continued forward as moving pyres, deadlier than before. Seth drew up another hard wind to knock the flaming dead back to the tree line and almost passed out from the effort. The dead emerging from the woods ran into their flaming brethren, broadening the wall of fire, which resumed its march toward the guardians.

Cat drew her pistol and helped Ladue take out every other undead with proficient accuracy. He lobbed some grenades at the fiery herd and tore them to pieces. The flaming parts were still flexing, hands now crawling.

Lelani launched a phosphorous ball in a high arc over the trailer. It exploded on the other side and flushed Chasaubaan out. He stumbled into view, patting out flames on his robe. She fired a second ball directly at the necromancer—he deflected it into Rosencrantz with his bone wand, singeing trunk and leaves. Seth winced with pain from their connection. Lelani hesitated before attacking again. Chasaubaan then did something that would haunt Seth to the end of his days: he began patting the grass beneath him, like a man searching for a lost jewel. Chasaubaan had discovered something far more valuable to him, and with a sinister sneer, he jammed the pointy end of his bone wand into the dirt.

Searing pain shot through Seth's head. The necromancer's wand poisoned all living things, but a life-oriented wizard such as Rosencrantz was exceptionally sensitive. Seth raised his staff to cut off their connection so he could function again.

"Oh no," Lelani said. She turned to Seth with horror and regret.

"What'd he do?" Seth asked. Grass and dirt began to tilt upward . . . and Seth remembered—Rosencrantz's old caretakers were buried in the meadow . . . all of them . . . *including Ben*!

Seth witnessed the former caretakers rise in various states of decomposition, some little more than bones with a tatter of skin hanging off. The more recent ones were—gummier—still hosts to nature's minute beasties. Ben's rising corpse, freshest of them all, still looked like the man Seth called friend except for those gauzy murderous eyes. Seth was grateful Helen didn't witness this desecration . . . it filled him with revulsion.

He left the newly risen dead to Lelani—he just couldn't strike at Ben. While she engaged them with a multitude of spells, Seth charged the necromancer with a feral cry. He'd almost closed the twenty feet between them when the necromancer pointed his wand, instilling the most awful sensation—his heart stopped, his lungs stopped. His flesh smelled of rot and the spark of life he knew as himself diminished to a precious flicker. Seth wished he still had the magical defense shield that had protected him most of his life.

Lelani threw a brain hex at Chasaubaan, forcing him to repel it and drop his attack on Seth. She followed with fireballs, phosphorous, and even a dagger at the man, but he was too quick, deflecting each attack with his death wand. While Seth recovered, Lelani volleyed with the death wizard, casting and deflecting with the power and speed of a centaur Serena Williams. Seth targeted the necro-wand and tried the only transmutation spell he could pull off; those purple blossoms had gotten him out of a few tight jams. The recoil almost broke Seth's brain. That death wand wanted nothing to do with flowers or any other living thing.

Hurled lightning would have come in handy right now, but Rosencrantz was in too much agony to help Seth. Seth cursed, trying to think of something . . . anything that would take this death wizard down. Most of what he remembered was rudimentary; he couldn't even get the shield right . . .

Shield? That was it . . .

Seth cast a hard air bubble around the necromancer. A few of Lelani's kinetic attacks bounced off.

"What are you doing?!" she yelled.

Seth concentrated, shrinking the perimeter of his bubble, tightening it more and more until it became the size of a fishbowl around the man's head. Chasaubaan threw a spell at Seth, which Lelani deflected. With her on defense, Seth could focus entirely on this off-the-cuff attack. Even a necromancer needed to breathe, and Chasaubaan, realizing he was running out of air, fired spells at Seth wildly, each one deflected by Lelani. Ladue and Cat joined them, firing at the death wizard at cross angles. The necromancer jerked and spasmed as the bullets hit. And then Lelani pulled out the big gun . . . the faerie silver dagger, which, when in contact with any magic user's blood, neutralized them. She hurled it with expert finesse into Chasaubaan's thigh.

Chasaubaan let out a cry, more emotional than physical pain. His end was imminent; he made a desperate, hobbled dash for the tree wizard. Seth maintained his vacuum bubble, shrinking it ever more. The guardians fired everything they could at the necromancer, rendering him little more than a living corpse by the time he reached the tree.

With his last iota of life he lurched desperately at the tree, and jabbed his wand into Rosencrantz's trunk.

Every tree, every bush and flower, every single blade of grass in the forest screamed. The power of Rosencrantz's anguish almost ejected Seth's eyes from his skull.

Cat and Lelani also writhed on the ground, praying, like Seth, for someone to end the siren that melted their minds. Ladue withstood the scream better than the others. Daniel was suddenly beside Seth, mouthing, "What's wrong?!" over and over. The boy couldn't hear the death cry; but neither could he do anything to help short of a merciful hammer to the brainpan.

Seth could not disconnect from the tree wizard—the bond was fixed, and so he sensed Rosencrantz drawing power from the lay line. So much power—all the magical energy on this side of the world—definitely more than what was natural. It rushed beneath Seth, around him, penetrated him like water through a turbine, quickening into the dying tree wizard. Rosencrantz was casting—the spell was of a magnitude Seth had never experienced . . . greater than harnessing lightning. *Was the dying tree trying to save itself?* A light, simultaneously bright and dark, the way something intensely cold can also burn, seared their eyes with a wicked flash—and then the world dropped out from under them like a carnival ride broken at its apex. And that was when the universe went completely mad.

CHAPTER 8

BREATHE

Cat found herself in mud—disoriented, and facing a puddle of her own vomit just inches from her face. She heaved again, emptying the last vestiges of her breakfast. The last thing she remembered was that sound—white noise amplified a thousand times, scrambling her senses. The ringing in her ears was worse than the hours after a rock concert.

Cat rose slowly on shaky knees. The added weight of her pregnancy unbalanced her—she stumbled lopsided into a tree and grabbed it to brace herself. An ethereal haze smelled like a country barbecue. Even through the gauzy air she knew the forest had changed—the trees were larger, older than the ones around Rosencrantz's meadow, with thick unruly roots that sprawled and gripped the earth like arthritic knuckles; the lush greenery permeated the air with a thick floral sweat—nature's version of a locker room after a well-fought match. Thickets and thorny brambles ran from tree to giant tree, a scrappy, bristled maze except for one well-traveled dirt path that cut through the ancient forest like a scar. Beyond the road's edge, scant sunlight broke the dense, miserly canopy. Even during day's apex this was a dark place. And Cat was alone.

"Bree!" she called out.

Nothing.

The stench of roasting meat threatened to make her retch again; but Cat could not afford to be sick with a deadly necromancer in their midst. She searched her immediate surroundings, behind each tree along the sides of the road. Her backpack lay on top of a bush, a good sign that anything that was close to her in the meadow was likely still in her proximity. She had lost the Glock she was using, but had packed a spare in the bag and verified that the clip was loaded. She pulled out her camping belt, which held a fully charged Taser, a hunting knife, and an extra clip for the gun.

The dirt road had deep ruts etched into it. Cat wondered if they were near an Amish town or maybe a dude ranch. She spotted one of Bree's pink sneakers several feet away in one of the muddy ruts.

"BREE!!!" Cat shouted. *Necromancers be damned.*

A white sock poked out under a bush. Cat was ecstatic to find the rest of her daughter attached to the foot. Except for a few cuts and scrapes, the girl was alive and whole. She patted Bree's cheeks and forehead with a wet wipe. The girl's eyes fluttered.

Cat heard men approaching from around a bend in the road. Behind Bree's bush was a small enclosure where the soil was too hard for growth; it was also out of view of the road and the forest behind it. Cat pushed through and dragged Bree in with her. She laid the girl against a tree and started putting her daughter's shoe back on in case they needed to run. Bree cracked an eye. Cat made the *hush* signal.

The men spoke in a language Cat didn't understand. About thirty feet away, one of them cried out. Cat gripped the Glock tightly—she gently fingered the little safety nub on the trigger. The men were laughing—sounds of shrubs being ruffled. A woman screamed and cried out "No!" The protesting woman sounded very much like Valeria MacDonnell.

Cat cursed silently. She took off her backpack and placed it next to Bree.

"Do not come out of this hidey place," she whispered. "Stay down and out of sight. Find Lelani if I . . ." Bree waited for the rest of the sentence, probably as much as Cat did. "If I don't come back soon."

Brianna grabbed her mother's wrist and shook her head *no*. Cat took her daughter's hand and kissed it. "Your aunt's in trouble. No one else is around to help." Cat snuck out the back of the enclosure and circled around to emerge on the road from a different spot. She peeked out from behind a tree.

The men were greasy, slovenly—all armed with swords. Two men wore steel breastplates, one had a ring-mail shirt, and the other two wore leather vests with metal studs, all in some variation of red and black. Despite the uniforms, they projected undisciplined anarchy. Cal had said that most feudal soldiers were amateurs, pulled from their fields by liege lords, with no real knowledge of war and little training. One of the leather-studded soldiers had a bow and arrow and stood watch as the other four men pinned Valeria to the ground. She struggled and screamed as they rolled her dress up over her waist. The biggest of them knelt between her legs with an evil leer, struggling to unknot his leather belt. *Valeria's virtue still intact for want of a zipper*, Cat thought. With a deep breath, she stepped onto the road and casually walked toward the soldiers.

"Hey, asshats! Come play with a grown woman!" she said, certain that her tone would convey the meaning well enough. The men looked around nervously for an ambush. She was only thirty feet away when the archer decided to train an arrow on her. She aimed the Glock at the archer. None of the men seemed concerned about that small piece of gray metal in her hand. They all beamed snarky smiles, believing the size of their debauchery had doubled. Cal had taught her to aim for the chest, the biggest target on any body, but the urge to wipe that smug smile off the archer's face got the best of Cat—she put a 9 mm slug in the center of the archer's unibrow; his left temple exploded with bones and brains. Three soldiers charged her. She put two shots through the lead guy's steel plate, and then she blew the ring-mailed man's brains out all over a bush. As she fired on the fourth man the pistol jammed.

"Fuck!"

She ducked to avoid the arc of his sword. The momentum of his wild swing exposed his side. Before he could bring the sword back, Cat jammed her Taser into his ribs. The man convulsed and fell hard. The Taser sparked and sputtered; she ditched it into the mud where it died. The big guy still hovering over Valeria drew a spiked mace from his belt. He was the best armored, and Cat was out of weapons. They didn't really teach her how to take on savages with chest plates in self-defense class, and in truth, six months into her pregnancy, she wasn't feeling as spry as her usual self. She pulled her hunting knife out and started to backpedal, wondering why this asshole was too stupid to be afraid of a person who had just killed four of his friends in under a minute. He charged her, revving his mace like he was about to pitch softball.

Cat dreaded the thought of that mace impacting any part of her. *Mace! Of course!* She pulled a canister of Mace from the back of her belt. The soldier was ten feet away when she doused him with a long stream. He went to his knees hard, rubbing his burning eyes with one hand and swinging his weapon wildly with the other. Cat wasn't sure how she'd get close enough to use the knife. Behind him, Valeria crept forward with the archer's dagger. Cat shouted at the warrior to draw his swings toward her. Valeria plunged the knife into his exposed neck, putting all her weight into it. He grabbed her, but she held on to the knife, twisting and grinding it in the wound. Cat rushed in to help, holding his sword arm at the elbow to prevent him from crowning Valeria. They were rag dolls to him. He wasn't dying fast enough, and Cat quickly determined why; the knife's pressure prevented the wound from bleeding out. She grabbed the handle and yanked up. Blood gushed like a geyser. In a panic, the soldier let go of Valeria to cover the wound, but it was a vain effort . . . he wound down under the weight of his armor as his life's blood streamed into the ruts—a red river flowing east and west—until finally he lay still.

Cat shook like she'd just taken an ice-cold bath. She had blood on her jacket and face. *Sacks of juice,* she thought. *That's all we are.* The art of ending life was perforation. It was that easy. This was the second time she'd had to kill—six men now, counting Dorn; their blood on her hands—a damned growing spot on her palm that all the Ajax and Brillo on earth couldn't remove. Tears welled as much for the release of tense nerves as for her lost innocence—until Cat realized Valeria was shaking worse than her. Cat swallowed her self-pity and embraced her new sister, as though their combined shivers might cancel each other out and restore equilibrium to their lives.

She led Valeria to the enclosure where Bree awaited them with grateful hugs. They rested there hidden for God knew how long, until a white rainbow made of sparkling mist came over the hedge and terminated in their enclosure. A minute later the bushes started to rustle.

Cat tensed and gripped her knife. She almost stabbed Lelani in the eye as the centaur poked her head through the shrub.

"Jesus H. Obama Christ! You scared the hell out of us," Cat said.

Lelani sported a few cuts and welts, as though she'd been in a fight herself. "The men on the road?" she inquired of Cat.

"That was me."

Cat witnessed a new level of respect write itself onto Lelani's face. She didn't know whether it was a compliment or an insult. In truth, Cat didn't know her own limits.

"We have to pull the bodies into this hiding place," Lelani said.

"I'm not sharing my hidey place with corpses that tried to rape us," Cat said.

"We must go," Lelani insisted. "The prince and Seth are missing. The countryside is teeming with enemy patrols searching for treasure and pleasure."

"Jesus, Mary, and Joseph!" Cat exclaimed. "I've fucking had it with these assassins! Can't we stop them from coming into our world?"

Lelani gave her friend a quizzical look. She took a deep breath and said, "Catherine, these men did not come into your world. We're in the Blue Forest. This is Aandor."

CHAPTER 9

A PRINCE AMONG MEN

1

Daniel awoke in a dark wood. The queasiness, aching joints, and vertigo were bad, worse than the morning after he and Adrian snuck off with Mr. Lutz's pint of Jägermeister—which he and Adrian had surmised must be the German word for NyQuil.

Daniel tried to stand up, but his head weighed fifty pounds and pressed him back on his ass—the world was two sets of swaying phantom images attempting to converge into a single picture. He closed his eyes and put his head between his knees for a moment. Then, slowly, he lifted his head and looked around.

The brush was dense and riddled with thorns and thistles that threatened to scratch out an eye and scar you like a rabid coon. A smoky haze softening the edges of the world reminded Daniel of old Hollywood movies that used nylons over the lenses to soften actresses past their prime. The forest smelled of bacon.

The last thing he remembered in the meadow was trying to help Seth and then a searing light. Then just infinite blackness— he and his friends were specks of dust flying through an immeasurable vacuum. Daniel couldn't gauge their velocity, but millions of lines of light, what he could only imagine were entire universes, riffled past like the edges of disks in a cosmic jukebox. In the deep reptilian recesses of his mind, he knew that if they'd collided with so much as a stray proton, they would be obliterated. And then they fell toward one disk . . . and then they were pulled toward the darkest pool in that light, like a still lake as seen from the air. It drew them like a beacon in the storm. Lelani did something—though how she could move or think in that state was beyond comprehension—she changed their course. The wizard found a stream away from the dark spot and diverted them all—but it was rough . . . literally fighting momentum and thrust from midair.

And then he woke up here . . . alone.

His heart was beating rapidly; cold shivers ran down his back despite the warmth. *I can't be here,* he thought, realizing tens of thousands of men beyond these trees wanted to kill him. Daniel balled his fists tight, his fingernails dug into his palms. *Don't panic,* he thought over and over, trying to stave off exactly that.

Something bounced off his head and onto a bush. It was a granola bar. Twenty feet above, his backpack dangled from a branch. With the wooziness fading, Daniel shimmied up the tree and crawled out on the branch to retrieve it. Someone below was making a racket, running toward his spot.

Daniel cautiously climbed up to the next large branch to put more foliage between him and the ground. A young boy of about nine or ten broke through some brush. He was breathing heavily, dressed in drab browns with leather sandals. Behind him came heavier footfalls with the clanking of metal. The lad ran ahead a few more steps before backtracking over his own footprints and diving into a hollow log behind a shrub, disturbing a family of porcupines that had scurried out irritably.

Two men in red and black uniforms were on the boy's trail.

They followed the false footprints, and beyond, no doubt thinking to recover their quarry's trail. The boy exited his log, pulling painful-looking spines from his arms and face as he started back until they heard more men coming from that direction.

"Pssst!" Daniel signaled. The boy squinted to find Daniel in the tree. Daniel waved for him to climb. The boy scurried up, reaching the branch just below him. He was a wiry kid and tried to make himself even thinner on that branch. They faced each other, Daniel looking down and the boy looking up wide-eyed and scared.

Three new men approached with a girl and boy on rope leashes, both slightly younger than Daniel's new friend. They shoved and tugged at the children mercilessly. The girl was scratched up and crying—her rope chafed at her neck. The lad who Daniel assumed was her brother tried to help, but his handler yanked on his rope and then smacked him on the head with a studded glove. The kid wavered on rubbery legs and collapsed, but immediately sprang back up and steadied himself. The men who'd run by moments before rejoined their friends beneath the tree, having realized they'd been tricked. They conferred with each other in Farrenspiel, which Daniel did not speak. He'd exclusively been studying Aandoran—which was close enough to Middle English for him to be grateful for that Chaucer elective in junior high—but had yet to start any of the empire's other languages. The tone of the men's conversations was not lost on anyone though. One of them began shouting angrily into the woods; this time, Daniel understood them even through a heavy accent.

"You are fast rabbit, but come now or we will hurt little ones!" To illustrate their point, the man handling the girl took her face in his studded leather glove and squeezed. She cried out.

The boy on the branch closed his tear-streamed eyes trying to pray this situation away. Daniel wished he had retrieved his pistol from the pack.

The boy on the leash tackled the soldier manhandling his sister, slamming into his hip with his whole body. His handler yanked harshly on the rope, harder perhaps than intended because the boy's neck bent with a sickly snap, and the lad went limp.

The young boy's leg jittered. Daniel heard the child struggle to draw breath, like a wet and raspy wheeze. The other soldiers chastised the man who had broken the child's neck, but the tone lacked human concern—it was anger at having lost chattel. The girl wailed over her fallen brother. On the branch below, the older boy's face turned wet and twisted with helplessness and rage.

Don't do anything stupid, thought Daniel, a little too late.

The boy rolled off his branch. He landed badly, but that didn't stop him from battering the nearest soldier ineffectively. The soldier laughed and bound the boy with his brother's leash. The younger boy still jittered on the ground, seizing up as he suffocated slowly. The soldiers dragged the two siblings away as they pleaded not to leave their dying brother.

Daniel climbed down and approached the dying boy. His wheezing grew fainter. He was very aware of his dwindling life, his fear painted in the whitish blue of his face. He gaped at Daniel with bulging eyes that said he'd intended to do much more living than his scant few years. That strained glare seared itself into the prince's memory; it was the most disturbing thing Daniel had ever witnessed. The boy's raspy grunts pleaded to put him out of his misery.

Daniel knelt next to him, unsure if he should touch the kid— his mind a jumble of thoughts. Lelani or Reverend Grey would know what to do, but neither was here. Daniel retrieved his pistol from the pack and aimed it at the boy's temple—and stayed like that, hand and gun quivering for far too long. *What if they hear it?* he thought, justifying his delay. Daniel's eyes welled with the realization that he was unable to follow through . . . he couldn't end this child's suffering. Time relieved him of this burden; Daniel didn't even hear the boy's final breath to mark his passing from the world.

Daniel was not cognizant of how long he sat beside the body. He was overwhelmed—by this child's death, by the fact that he was in Aandor, the very last place he should be without protection. When he emerged from his daze, the sun was past its apex. He pulled the cell phone from his pack. No signal whatsoever. He was truly on his own, in a strange universe.

Daniel donned his protective vest, clipped his hunting knife to his belt, and holstered his gun. Malcolm had given him the Rock Island M15 for his fourteenth birthday in February; there wasn't a piece of antiquated armor that could stop a .45-caliber slug. He looped the nylon holster onto his belt.

The child looked so innocent . . . at peace. Daniel had a hard time tearing his eyes away. He'd watched his stepfather drown in his own blood. But cruel Clyde had earned that death. This boy . . . this could have been Bree MacDonnell or his stepsister Penny. He touched the boy's face—a fading remnant of warmth remained, just enough to confirm the lad was once a living being. These children were his subjects.

I hid like a coward, he admitted, disgusted with himself. Daniel's hand rested on the pistol. Cal spent hours teaching him how to properly handle the weapon. Those animals rounding kids up like chattel wouldn't have had a chance against him. If Daniel had acted, that kid would still be breathing . . . running to safety with his siblings.

Fuck!

Daniel sobbed as though he'd lost his own brother. Why was he filled with shame? He didn't know these people. The guardians had just started forging his chains of obligation without asking if he wanted to be the prince of anything. All he had ever prayed for was a dad who wouldn't beat the tar out of him and a mom who wasn't addicted to drugs. *How the hell did I end up becoming the savior of a million people?*

He couldn't explain what propelled him to pursue those soldiers—rage at his own impotence, shame for being too weak to end the boy's suffering, fear because a gunshot might have brought attention to him. Daniel wouldn't look at his own reflection right now. But if he rescued those kids it might set things right, and then he could search for Cat and the others.

The trail was easy enough to follow—he heard their bellowing fifty yards out. The forest ahead thinned. The soldiers and kids were in the backyard of some homestead—a log-built structure with a thatched roof. A makeshift chicken coop was against the house and beside it a bloody tree stump for chopping the poultry. A few feet from the coop a large wagon wheel rested against a shed. A three-wheeled buckboard leaned toward its missing limb. Twenty feet to Daniel's left, near the edge of the tree line, was an outhouse that was unfortunately upwind of his position; the lingering odor of smoked barbecue took the edge off the shit smell. From his vantage, several columns of black smoke rose over the forest into the sky in the distance. A dirt road ran in front of the log house—Daniel suspected they were on the outskirts of a town that wasn't faring very well.

The kids were tied up, listless. Two new soldiers came around the corner of the cabin dragging a muddied, beaten woman and a bloodied man who was an older version of the boy Daniel met in the forest. The children cried out, "Mama! Papa!" The soldiers handed off the pair to the backyard crew.

"Where's Aldrich? Where's Aldrich?" the mother asked repeatedly, counting only two kids where there should have been three. She became hysterical as the realization of what happened to her younger son set in. One soldier began slapping her. Her husband, also anguished over his son's death, stupidly rushed the man and punched his jaw. Daniel was frozen with fear behind a bush. There were too many soldiers, and they were all psychotic. The invaders pounced on the father, stabbing him in the back and neck until he went limp. The family wailed as soldiers threw his bloody body into the chicken coop. Then they separated the hysterical mom from her kids. She slapped the man who stabbed her husband and tried to claw his eyes out. She took out a good chunk of his cheek. He punched her nose, and she fell hard on her knees. They bent her over the chopping block facedown, bound her wrists with rope, and staked the rope into the ground.

Daniel's heart caught in his throat. Were they going to behead her? He unholstered his weapon and clicked off the safety. His hand was shaking . . . he forgot to breathe. He had no plan. Should he walk into the yard and order them to release the hostages? Would they even recognize the gun as a weapon? What would Cal do?

Another soldier rushed out of the cabin cheering that he'd found the family's money stash. Most went to claim their cut, but not the main instigator that the mother had attacked. He dropped his britches and urinated on her hands, then wiggled his manhood before her face. His cohorts joked that she would bite it off. The instigator grabbed the daughter and dragged her before the woman. He placed his dagger point on the little girl's throat, and with a huge grin, again shook his prick before the woman.

Daniel was about to shoot him, when gunshots in the distance froze everyone in place. Birds rushed from the trees as the echo reverberated through the forest. It had to be the guardians, but the echo made it impossible to pinpoint where it came from. After a minute, the soldiers resumed their thievery, leaving strange noises for others to investigate.

A fat soldier abruptly exited the outhouse. He turned to his right and spotted Daniel crouching in the brush. The soldier got over his shock first and drew his long sword. Daniel blew a doughnut-sized hole through the center of his chest. The others turned toward the gunfire and pulled their weapons. Daniel just began shooting in the order closest to him; proximity had become the plan. While this happened, the young girl slipped out of her captor's grip, and got away. True to the soldiers' predictions, the mother lunged forward as far as she could and did indeed bite down on the instigator's cock. The soldier squealed like a slaughtered pig, screaming bloody murder as he battered her head with his fists. When he freed himself of her, he fell hard on his ass, bleeding profusely from a raw stump. *Go Mom!* Daniel thought.

One soldier grabbed the son as his shield. Daniel aimed carefully, let out his breath, and squeezed the trigger, evacuating the soldier's right eye and everything behind it. Only a single soldier remained standing—he drew his sword clumsily.

Daniel fired—click, click, click—the fucking thing jammed. Up close, the man was older and more portly than any soldier had a right be; he approached Daniel, wary of the gun. Daniel looked around and grabbed the outhouse guy's long sword. It was cruder than the weapons he'd trained with . . . the balance was off, it was slightly bent, and riddled with nicks and dings. But it was sharp. Daniel's stance was instinctual, drilled into him over months. This was it, the bullshit test to see if he was a big poser.

The young boy suddenly slammed into the soldier from behind throwing the man off balance. He swiped back with his sword, just missing the lad by inches, tripped over his own feet. He fell toward Daniel, landing before the prince on his back. Daniel almost felt bad for the man, with his network of spider veins across his pasty white neck. The old soldier swung up at Daniel and nearly took his ear off. Daniel easily deflected the next blow from his vantage. Daniel couldn't tell if it was because the man was stunned from the fall, or if he was truly a pitifully bad swordsman, but windows of opportunity kept presenting themselves. The prince was annoyed . . . didn't this asshat realize he was being merciful? With the soldier's next backhanded slash, Daniel stepped forward and put his full weight on the man's sword arm and slid the tip of his sword into the soldier's throat. The soldier gurgled and died.

The instigator, meanwhile, composed himself enough to retrieve his short sword and was about to stab the still bound mother. Daniel ran forward thinking this was it—*this* would be his dreaded first real sword fight, but the solider, in the throes of a myopic rage at the woman who'd performed his penectomy, ignored the prince entirely and managed one jab at her shoulder before Daniel lunged his long sword into the man's lungs. The soldier staggered back, stunned. He fell on his knees then collapsed backward.

Daniel cut the mother's bindings. She slipped off the chopping block, rubbing her wrists. Her mouth was bloody. She crawled to her sodomizer on hands and knees, locking eyes with him as he coughed up blood, and shoved his own cock into his mouth while pummeling the man and wailing loudly. Her children rushed in to pull her off him.

A squad of six new enemy soldiers rounded the house and faced them. Daniel couldn't fight them all. The men advanced on them. *This is it*, Daniel realized. *I finally make it back to the land of my birth, to die without ever meeting my parents.*

A strong gust whipped the soldiers off their feet and slammed them into the cabin, smashing the wall. They landed in the dirt with an inglorious thud.

"You gotta be more stealthy, kid," Seth said from the edge of the tree line. He held his wizard's staff at its end like a stickball bat. "Going all gangsta in these woods is going to get you stabbed."

2

Daniel had never been happier to see anyone in his life. He had a million questions for Seth, but the wizard waved them off and signaled a silent retreat into the forest.

"Shouldn't we go in the direction of the other gunshots?" Daniel asked.

"No. More soldiers that way. Lelani can find us with a spell—if she's still alive. If not, it doesn't matter."

"Don't say that." Daniel started to follow but stopped. The family appeared exhausted—brutalized, huddled tightly in the dirt at the end of their world. The woman stared into nothingness, lost in the memory of the life she'd woken up to this morning.

"Come with us," Daniel told them.

The mom didn't budge, but her son was happy to have a plan and began to pull her up. His sister helped him.

"There's a thousand enemy soldiers ten miles in every direction," Seth objected. "We can't take on refugees."

The son ran into the house for items they'd need, and emerged with two sacks. Daniel rummaged through the defeated soldiers' belongings for the best sword and scabbard among them. Then they all slipped into the woods.

The boy steered them along the barest of paths through brambles and bushes and ancient trees. Ten minutes in, the woods to their left thinned, and they had a clear elevated view of Yarmouth. Four thousand souls called this town home. The main street was a grubby muddy line that served as both road and drainage ditch. The dwellings were built mostly of thick wood timbers, plaster, and thatch. A few larger buildings had the look of stone, probably government offices or the homes of the affluent. Enemy soldiers stood out in their red uniforms like an angry infection among the browns and grays of the feudal town. A section of the outer wall was aflame, threatening to ignite the structures built against it. Woolly black columns of smoke rose from deep within the small city, writing the account of this siege on the sky.

Beside the western gate, someone had stacked wood and dead bodies. The soldiers lit them up. Daniel watched the flames grow higher. His heart caught in his throat when the enemy began hoisting up on a winch a well-dressed portly man nailed to a wooden frame. They dropped him in the center of the pyre. He writhed and struggled, but even if he freed himself, there was nowhere to go. The man's shrieks carried through the forest and sent a cold shiver through the group. Below, the soldiers fed the flame with more wood and wagonloads of the dead. The scent of roasting meat grew thicker, and Daniel wanted to retch, now knowing the source of that smell. *How many of these pyres have they lit?* A tugging at his sleeve pulled him away from the flames. The boy made gestures to leave now. And Daniel agreed, having seen enough. They crawled cautiously behind shrubs as they passed this area to avoid being spotted.

Twenty minutes on a thin, barely trodden path brought them to a rocky outcrop that looked like the top of an underground mountain jutting from the earth. High trees and bushes surrounded it. A small stream burbled in front of an overhang shaped like a rocky lean-to that could shelter them from sun and rain, and more importantly, would dissipate the campfire smoke as it hit the roof and fanned out into the sky. A hammock hung between two trees, and the remnants of a campfire lay beneath the overhang.

"Me and my mates fish here," the boy said. "There's a stocked pool behind the rock and berry bushes all around."

The woman started a fire in the stone pit and set up a kettle. The girl foraged for greens and herbs while her brother went to catch some fish. Daniel sat on a low flat rock beside the pit and tried to come to terms with the cruelty he'd witnessed; all to annex this piece of real estate for Farrenheil.

"What shall we call you, milord?" asked the mom. A mother in her late twenties calling Daniel "milord" felt as natural as a prostate exam. Her soft voice was a harsh contrast to its hard tone; if feudalism did one thing well, it was to ingrain subservience when in the presence of one's betters—even, apparently, when experiencing your own personal catastrophe. Steam from the kettle brought a growl to Daniel's belly. He didn't recall getting hungry.

"Daniel. Danel, actually," he said after remembering his birth name here. "But my friends call me Daniel or Danny."

"Like our new prince," remarked the little girl.

Fiona introduced herself and her son Jack, named for his

grandfather, and Sally, a little clone of her mom. Her dead son was Aldrich, Sally's twin, named for his father, a wagon maker. Fiona washed herself in the stream, wading in up to her knees and immersing her head like a baptismal aspirant seeking to let the cool rush carry away her sins with the dirt and mud. With the grime and mud removed, Fiona appeared younger than Daniel realized . . . little more than college age. She had fair skin and golden hair that accentuated her blue-green eyes.

"So, this is Aandor?" Daniel asked.

"Oh, this is definitely Aandor," Seth confirmed. "I was exhausted in the meadow fight after just a few spells, but I woke up here charged with energy. Magic is everywhere. I would have struggled to create that hard wind force at their house if this was New York—here, it was easy breezy. Pun intended."

"Great. So you can lightning blast these Farrenheil fuckers all the way to the capital."

"It's not about having *enough* power. Lightning is complex mojo. Haven't been able to replicate the advanced stuff on my own. I know a few spells reasonably well . . . the hard air for example. I can make a halfway decent shield . . . not very effective against spells or machineguns though without Rosencrantz. The tree was my crutch; now it's probably dead."

"Dead?! You sure?"

"Didn't you hear it scream?"

"No . . . But I heard all of you. Speaking of the others . . ."

"Gunshots woke me," Seth said. "I was heading in what I thought was the direction they came from when I heard your fire. You only got off five of an eight-round clip. What happened?"

"Pistol jammed."

"Combustion sciences don't play well here. The gun's probably cursed now. You should throw it away."

"That's stupid. Why would magic care about combustion?"

"Hey, I didn't write the laws of physics for this universe. One story says ancient wizards placed a spell over this world to neuter science as a competitive power. Remember, wizards are scientists, too. They know how to make gunpowder and stuff. Another is that magical energy is sentient—intelligent electrons or something. Combustion works on superheated air and explosions, so maybe it disrupts the energy—hurts them? Who knows? All we know is that engines, electricity, and guns don't work for long in Aandor. It's meat cleavers all around. I'm keeping my pistol a virgin until I'm desperate. And you should throw your gun away. Seriously."

Jack returned with three fair-sized fish, which they cooked with some parsley that grew along the edge of the outcrop. The meal barely satisfied. The thought of high-fructose corn syrup and corn-fed anything didn't seem so bad about now.

"Fiona, is Yarmouth the only town in the area?" Daniel inquired.

"Aye, the only town. There's a village between here and the capital ten leagues west. The village of Iibswitch is ten leagues north near the Sevren, and there's a proper river town—Crowe's Porte—half day's ride east along the Blue Road. They have a bridge to the north."

"Iibswitch," Seth said. "That's near where my mother runs an inn."

"Wrong direction," Daniel said. "Our best bet is to head away from the capital."

"The enemy's all over the countryside," Seth said.

"Yeah, but they were magically air-dropped on Deorwine Plain outside of the capital and fanned eastward from there."

Daniel grabbed a stick and sketched the kingdom in the sand. Fiona and the kids watched in fascination as he wrote the names of major landmarks as best as he could remember.

"You can write?" Jack noted. "You really are a lord, then."

"You couldn't possibly guess . . . ," Seth responded.

"The enemy's south and west of us," Daniel continued, ignoring the budding adoration society. "The farther east we run, the less saturated the countryside will be with enemy squads."

"But Farrenheil is pushing west from Red King's Gate," Seth said.

"No. Farrenheil hasn't taken that fort *yet*. Time differential, remember—the Gate's probably still unaware of the invasion."

Daniel looked at the map again and circled a swatch of forest southeast of Yarmouth. "I guess we can trek deeper into the woods here; stay away from the road entirely."

"Them's centaur lands, milord," Sally said, pointing to the area.

"Centaurs patrol the Blue Road for my fath . . . umm, the archduke? Friends, right?"

"'Friends' is not the word I'd use, milord," Fiona said. "Aye, they mind the forest about the road, but 'tis for their own interest s'much as ours. None of that lot takes kindly to men who stray from the path. We're not welcome in their villages. There's much sorry history between them beasts and men."

They probably don't think too highly of being called beasts, Daniel thought.

"It's a moot point anyway," Seth said. "We should find the others. Cat will have kittens when she realizes she's in Aandor."

Daniel chuckled. Seth took a moment to warm up to his own subconscious wit.

Voices came out of the forest, many footsteps heading their way along the path. Daniel pulled his sword and Seth readied his staff. A boy slightly older than Jack came around a tree carrying a young girl in his arms.

Behind the teen were four more, a young girl and boy, a young pikeman, and a woman of comparable age. They carried only their fatigue covered with soot and ash.

"Hail Jack, Aldrich's son," said the teen. "May we warm ourselves by your fire?"

"Aye, Fulbert, you may," Jack said, without consulting anyone.

"There are more behind us," said the pikeman.

"They're going to lead Farrenheil right to us if this keeps up," Seth said. "We're barely two miles from town."

"What are they supposed to do?" Daniel said. "Stay there and die?"

"The lads come to this glade to escape chores and pestering sisters," Jack said.

"Hey!" cried Sally.

"It is not on any map, nor easily found."

Oswin, a pikeman for the lord magistrate, had been off guard duty when the attack happened. He saw the magistrate cut down by archers and returned home to his wife and then escaped through a drainage tunnel. The two children with him belonged to a fellow guardsman who had died defending the magistrate.

As the sun fell toward the horizon, eight more townsfolk appeared led by another young boy. Soon, four hearths blazed in their little camp. People settled in as much as they could in a dark wood. *My people,* mused Daniel.

"Aye . . . I'd sooner take my chances with the centaurs," the pikeman said as they discussed Daniel's plan. "These men of

Farrenheil are vicious with lust and plunder. They assault as though seeking revenge for some heinous wrong. They are enslaving everyone. I'd sooner die by a centaur's spear. We'll follow you, milord."

Follow me? Daniel thought. Oswin was about eighteen, and Daniel hoped that, as the only local man in uniform, the pikeman would take charge and organize everybody. Seth chuckled at the look on Daniel's face.

"What? I'm in charge just 'cause I can fucking read?" Daniel said in English.

"You have straight white teeth, shiny hair, and your clothes have a high thread count," Seth said. "You ooze smarts—everyone's begging for someone smarter than them to take charge and save them."

"I'm fourteen."

"Great. Next February, you can legally marry, join the army, and own property."

Daniel countered Seth's smirk with a smoldering glare.

"Look, kid . . ." *Kid* was Seth's signal that he was about to impart serious wisdom. Seth was so seldom serious, Daniel felt obliged to listen when he got this way. "You're from a higher station than these folks, and they sense this. More importantly, you're a survivor, and they sense that, too. Until now, you survived for yourself . . . your street smarts and book smarts were your umbrella. To save these people, you have to let them under that umbrella. Same skills you always used to get by, only bigger scale. That's leadership."

Every once in a blue moon, Seth revealed intelligence beyond what he was credited with. What he left out was how much harder it would be to factor everyone else's safety into Daniel's decisions. Like playing five chess games at the same time.

"We can't stay here," Daniel said finally. "Eventually the patrols will find this place. Tomorrow we move deeper into the forest—all of us. Hopefully Lelani will find us before we run into her people."

CHAPTER 10

THE GILDED CAGE

1

The archduke's chambers, lavish as they were, had become a stifling prison after two days. Their captors had brought to the suite anyone they believed to be part of Aandor's nobility, and they now numbered seventeen—many were extended family, a few, like Earl Francis Gibbons, the court's chief solicitor, were part of Athelstan's privy council. *Does the earl appreciate having his family here with him?* Chryslantha wondered. Niccole Godwynn was not among their group, much to Chrys's dismay. Every time the door opened, Chryslantha held her breath, hoping her sister would cross its threshold.

Archduke Athelstan divided his consoling duties between his wife and his childhood friend Mila Boules, neither of whom could stand to be in the other's presence. Sophia was inconsolable and uncharacteristically quiet—her usual bravado silenced by the death of those innocent babes and the threat to her son. That Lady Boules had to remind the archduke to tend to his wife from time to time did not help Chrys's opinion of Athelstan. Chryslantha comforted her friend as much as possible, reminding the archduchess that Farrenheil so hated the new prince, they would shout it from all the towers if he were dead. This gave Chryslantha hope for Callum's life as well.

Colonel Falkyre entered the room. He had been assigned liaison between the two ruling families in Dorn's absence, amid rumors of the latter having disappeared chasing the prince's party. The gods had built Falkyre of interlocking blocks—square head and jaw, square shoulders—stiff, yet fit for a man of his years and as gray and hard as iron. He was humorless without being somber. His eyes were a penetrating grayish-blue and conveyed curtly that they were intimate with death. This was a man Lord Blunt trusted to impose order. Falkyre's eyes settled on Chrys.

With a quick bow he said, "My lady. I have a proposal, one that would see you out of this chamber. Will you join me?"

His tone was polite enough, but Chrys's stomach knotted nevertheless; she wasn't in any position to decline.

They walked down the grand hallway shadowed by a fat sergeant who reminded Chrys of a human mated with an ogre. The palace staff, those who survived, had been put back to work under the Farrenheisi's watchful eyes, mopping up blood and removing the dead. Guards in red and black lined all the hallways and the staircase. All the garlands and bunting were removed as though the prince's naming day never existed.

"Many have died," Colonel Falkyre said matter-of-factly. "Among them, members of the nobility and officers of the military. We would have them all identified before disposing of the bodies."

"But why me?"

"The palace staff speaks well of you. You apparently took the time to remember everyone's name. I can count on one hand the number of nobles I know who can do this. I would not even need all the fingers."

She followed him down the stairs and into Athelstan's great hall. The interior rose to the top of the castle—bolstered by marbled stone columns, caryatids of the goddesses, an elaborate overmantel carved of wood depicting cherubs and nymphs adorning Athelstan's ancestors, two balconies, and large sheets of lead glass high above, both stained and clear, that focused the sun on the coat of arms and many works of heraldry and sculpture around the room. Here she was to have danced with her betrothed on the polished teal and gold-veined marble floor.

The stench of running bowels poorly masked under the incense struck her first—then the lines of linen-covered bodies on the floor from entrance to dais. Black flies zigzagged over the sheets. Everyone working in the room had a kerchief over their nose and mouth. Chrys hesitated. She'd never seen so many dead.

"Disregard the first line on the right," Falkyre said. "Those were our men. The next six rows are your people. We brought them here from the surrounding grounds and the other levels to make listing easier. I would have you walk down these columns and note persons of substance."

"None in this room are persons of substance," Chrys answered solemnly.

Falkyre nodded, appreciating her dark wit.

"Nevertheless . . . ," he continued, "I would be thankful for your help. This task of liaison is more political than I am used to. For your help, I would see you rewarded with your own chamber for a time, a change of clothes . . . a bath."

"May Archduchess Sophia join me?"

Falkyre looked perplexed. "Would she not prefer to remain with her husband?" Chrys let the question stand. "Very well, if she wishes," he said, wanting to move things along. Falkyre called over his aide-de-camp holding a tablet and quill and left them alone; the fat sergeant remained and strolled the aisles casually as one would a garden. He was, it would seem, her personal guard. Something about that man's demeanor disturbed her.

The aide handed Chryslantha a kerchief that had been soaked in rosewater. She tied it over her nose and walked to the first column. They pulled back the sheets. Chrys fought her dread of finding Niccole among them. *Better to know for sure,* she convinced herself, and let out a long breath. They reached the end of the first column and she counted sixty bodies. Six columns of sixty—three hundred and sixty departed innocents.

Chrys spotted Zenoia in the second row; she would never be a Potter now. Farrenheil would not consider the gardener's daughter a person of note, but she gave them the name nevertheless along with eighteen others from that row. The list would be thorough . . . it was her countrymen's petition of retribution.

The fat sergeant, who was called Kalbfleish, hovered in a corner, leering at the young boys lighting incense. Chrys shuddered to think what the castle would be like if not for Blunt's decree of protection. Athelstan at least did that much for them. A soldier entered the hall and approached the sergeant with a list, which he read. She could barely hear Kalbfleish saying, "That's not enough." In an irritable grumble, he told the soldier to "sell them all."

"Are we taking a break?" the young aide asked her.

"No . . . let's get this done," Chryslantha said, wanting to be rid of this room.

In column three Chryslantha noted sixteen persons; in column four, ten; column five, twelve; and column six, twenty-seven. Column six was the hardest—Alva and a few ladies-in-waiting lay there. The aide was impressed with how many of the castle staff Chryslantha knew by name. Niccole was not among them, though, nor was Callum or Tristan. A tension that had been quietly building released, and Chrys began to cry.

"Milady?" asked the aide.

"Please ask the colonel if he would grant me one more request," Chrys asked. "My sister Niccole . . . if he would inquire as to her whereabouts, I would be most grateful."

2

Sergeant Kalbfleish escorted Chrys to Sophia's apartment—the last place she had known happiness. It had been thoroughly cleaned—the violence erased. Servants filled the archduchess's large copper tub with hot water. The sergeant and another guard, each at opposite ends of the room, about-faced, and stared unmoving at the walls directly ahead of them. *I will not be left alone*, Chryslantha realized. She was too drained to care anymore, and disrobed and submerged into the splendidly hot water. She tried to relax, but guilt nagged her because the other nobles were still trapped in Athelstan's suite while she enjoyed this moment of civility. The heat of the water eventually convinced her to accept the boon for what it was, and she turned her mind to Callum and the prince.

Proust had a plan, they said. The mage was brilliant, but plans were never foolproof. What if they escaped the castle only to fall into one of the many squads in the city? What would she sacrifice to have him still live? Chrys prayed to the Gray Lady that the prince and his guardians were far, far away, safe from the ravages of this war. Helene was not the patron goddess of Aandor, but Pelitos had failed epically in his duties, and could perhaps use help from an older, more seasoned goddess. She prayed for her betrothed . . . promising anything, *any sacrifice* the goddess asked of her to keep him safe.

Blunt insisted the war was over, but how many conquerors throughout history had called their conflict *the war to end all wars*? Men had the unfortunate tenacity to consistently prove themselves wrong. Callum was brilliant at war—men rallied to him. He could cobble an army—cause great trouble for Farrenheil.

Her betrothed's touch came to mind—his kisses—never more passionate than that eve before he marched to the Mourish queen's rebellion . . . when he realized Chrys had no intention of staying her own passions. In that heated bath, it was easy to imagine Callum, pressed atop her, his breath on her neck. She was both the happiest and most frightened of her life that night. Chryslantha didn't remember nodding off . . . she became aware that someone had joined her in the bath when a foot brushed her leg.

Across from her sat the White Lady. The guards were gone—they were alone.

"A pleasant dream?" Lara asked.

Chrys quickly crossed her arms to cover her chest.

"Invasion is dirty work," Lara noted with dark humor. With an ample sponge and scented oil, Lara caressed her own shoulders. Her skin was smooth as a mountain slope after first snowfall—nary a blemish, mole, or freckle to interrupt its serene whiteness; in dress she appeared buxom because of her corset and slender frame, but naked before Chrys, the White Lady was sized more modestly—her nipples dark pink carnations in contrast to her flesh.

Chrys grasped the edge of the tub and made to stand . . .

"Stay," Lara commanded, and placed the ball of her foot on

the soft tuft just above Chryslantha's sex—she gently pressed her back into the water. "Relax. I would talk. We are both ladies of breeding and power."

"It is you who has the power," Chrys reminded her.

"I must confess . . . I expected to be disappointed on meeting you—the Rose of Aandor—another vapid beauty with a wealthy father. I find instead that no poet or minstrel has yet done you justice. They write solely of your obvious virtues . . . like an auctioneer spelling out the qualities of a horse for gold purses: hair of spun gold, lips of rubies . . . teeth as straight as . . . well, I don't know—something very straight. Physical beauty is but the surface facet of a complex gem. One needs to look deeper to discern its true purity . . . its true worth. You are smarter than most, kinder than a well-fed prelate, and are not afraid to dirty your hands . . . I doubt a scullery maid exists anywhere with your work ethic. No, your true beauty, Chryslantha Godwynn, resides within and radiates outward like the sun's shine."

None had ever spoken of Chryslantha as lovingly. But Chrys could not bring herself to thank the monster, for monster was what Lara truly was despite her own inhumanly beautiful appearance—never more so than after she stole the life from Athelstan's valet to commandeer his memories, and left him a withering husk. Though Lara's hair still retained its chestnut hue, traces of white platinum resurged. She caught Chrys staring.

"My grandmother was a succubus," Lara said. "Do you know of such creatures?" Chrys nodded. Her nanny Rae had shared her vast repository of fantastic tales.

Lara slid deeper into the tub, sliding her legs forward along her bath mate's thighs. She gently massaged Chrys's hips with the balls and arches of her feet. Lara's soles were soft as silk and hot to the touch; heat swirled into Chrys like cream into tea, and settled into niches Chryslantha didn't know existed. Chrys's nipples grew erect and the bud of her womanhood engorged and pulsed with pleasure. Lara's irises turned a deep amethyst. Chrys discovered that Lara was cycling their life energies, taking from her and giving back. It created an intoxicating sensation. Lara's sleepy gaze and slanted smile conveyed her own pleasure.

Chrys was drunk and excited simultaneously. The urge to reciprocate with affection grew; she daringly stretched her long slender leg and found Lara's soft sheath with her toe. Chrys's foot played around Lara's softness, but her hands gripped hard the edge of the tub, fighting the urge to lurch ahead and kiss the White Lady. "Why . . . ?" Chrys mumbled in a dreamlike haze.

"With our life forces linked, I can tell if you lie to me. There are things I would know," Lara said.

"What things . . . ?" Lara had barely moved, yet phantom lovers caressed Chryslantha with strong hands and dexterous tongues. Chrys shut her eyes. Her toe gently brushed Lara's flower. It was hotter than the water—completely receptive, inviting.

Lara made a soft accepting sound. "Isn't this better than how I interrogated the valet? I can do that, you know . . . siphon the knowledge in your head. But it would destroy you, and I have other plans."

"Wha . . . what would you have of me?" Chryslantha asked.

Lara gazed at her for a long moment, long enough for Chrys to catch a glimpse of a conflict beneath the White Lady's rapturous veneer. "No one we have sent after your gallant young Captain MacDonnell has returned to Aandor," Lara continued. "They enter a portal in the pantry and end up . . . well, who knows? Believe me, we are scouring the city and the countryside. I've cast spells. It's as though they have vanished from all existence."

He has probably killed them all, you witch, Chrys thought, struggling against her basest instincts. Lara's body implored to be embraced . . . her lips, to be kissed.

"Where are they, Lady Chryslantha? I know what power is required to move things great distances through the ether of creation. It was I who dropped two armies in the middle of your kingdom. The cost was more than a kingdom of dwarvs could mine in their lifetime."

"Mmm . . . don't know . . ." Chrys floated in a haze.

"Please, Chrys . . . where has Callum taken my—my nephew?"

"You . . . you want to kill him."

"Kill my nephew?"

"Callum . . ."

Lara relaxed her thighs, she took Chrys's hand, inviting her to come across the bath. She rested Chrys's head on her breast, and embraced her the way a mother comforted a child, stroking her long hair. "No, my dear. You may have your betrothed . . . marry and live a happy life. Have many children with the captain."

"Th . . . the prince."

"Will be reunited with his mother, of course—and together will live out their lives peacefully in exile . . . a secluded temple in one of the free cities perhaps? If he has a daughter, we can marry her to our line, solidify our claim."

"Li . . . l . . . liarrrr . . ."

"You wound me, my dear . . ."

"Liar!" Chrys said, forcefully pushing herself off Lara and to the other end of the tub again. She grappled with her passions, wresting control, and expelling the lust from her core. "Liar," she repeated. "But it does not matter . . . I know not where the prince or my betrothed have gone. Leave me be!"

Lara stopped her power. It was as though she'd withdrawn the sun and air itself. Even the heat of the water could not abate the cold in Chryslantha's soul. Everything was less bright, made of shadow; Chrys felt isolated, abandoned. The witch's power was like the tears of the poppy used by healers for those in unbearable pain . . . withdrawal came with a cost.

"I believe you," Lara said. "Not just because I could taste your mind. It is not the habit of men to confide in women, regardless of how able they are. We have to fight harder, be stronger just to settle for the meager scraps they throw us." They stared at each other from across the tub for a moment.

Chryslantha curled up at her end of the tub. She'd enjoyed what had transpired—wanted to reignite it; she wished Callum were there for her to pounce on and ravish; she would make him forget their eve before the Mourish rebellion with feral abandon. She was mortified by her feelings.

Lara could read this; she threw her a wicked smile. She exited the bath and put on a robe.

"Know this, Chryslantha Godwynn—few have the will to resist the allure of a succubus—even from a quartus like me. None who were successful, however, still retained their maidenhood. Virgins are feebly vulnerable to the seduction." Lara's smirk changed from mirthful to victorious. "So was it the good captain, or have you cuckolded him even before your vows?"

Chrys pulled her knees in tighter. She would never leave this bath.

Lara crouched down at the edge of the tub, her face just a foot away from Chrys's. Her breath was sweet like spring blossoms.

"My my . . . your virtue is an illusion worthy of the greatest wizards. Perhaps we sent the wrong woman across the void? We'd hoped to leverage MacDonnell's sister against him—but that group, too, despite boasting a powerful sorcerer, has not been heard from. Before we send you or anyone else through the portal, though, I would know where it leads. For this I would have you speak with Magnus Proust."

"Have you not asked him yourself?" Chryslantha said.

"Of course. Care to guess how that went?"

"Why would the magus tell *me* anything?"

Lara's eyes restrained a frightening rage, the very fire from which her reputation was forged. "I do not care what you must do, *Rose of Aandor*. You are a capable woman and an important noble in this kingdom. Bribe him, appeal to him as a maiden searching for her beloved, drug him, torture him—fuck him if that's your fancy—but I want to know where the prince is. I want to know what is Lord Dorn's fate. If you fail me in this, I will add persons from the archduke's chambers to the rows of sheets in the great hall—starting with that cow Sophia."

Chryslantha saw the witch with renewed eyes. She was a creature of pure lust—for sex, for power, for wealth. How did the archduke of Farrenheil hope to restrain her? Her appetites ran deep—so, too, were the lengths she would go to satiate them.

Lara leaned in and kissed Chrys tenderly on the lips. She sent a small pulse of her power through and Chryslantha kissed back, tasting her, needing more. Then Lara withdrew. "Good hunting," she said, and left Chrys to her yearnings.

CHAPTER 11

LAY OF THE LAND

"We can't be in Aandor!"

Cat's hands were shaking, a paralytic cold marched down her spine, and the muscles in her neck tightened like racquet strings. "We—we haven't sold the house . . . I haven't told my mother. My sister . . . myfriendsandneighborsandandandIhaventhadthe-babyyetor . . . I . . ." Cat turned crimson, exhausting the fuel for new words. She grabbed her throat frantically and began to turn purple. "I cah . . . I cah . . . breeh . . ." Lelani placed a hand on Cat's chest and chanted until breath flowed again.

Cat composed herself and came to terms with the here and now; she was in another universe—like some character from a C. S. Lewis story. This wilderness was harsh, lonely, isolating—beyond these trees and shrubs, there were no power plants making electricity, no airplanes, no Internet . . . no rock music or copies of Dr. Seuss's *Green Eggs and Ham*. A muddy, rutted highway was the only civilization here, and even it subsisted under threat from the tsunami of ancient trees that threatened to swallow it.

"Cal and I were supposed to come over *together*."

Lelani watched the woods nervously. "The spell to return us to Aandor is long and complex," she whispered. "Rosencrantz had been sorting it out over many months, keeping it at the ready. But death and life magicks are antithetical forces. When the necromancer plunged his dagger, it drove the tree mad."

"I heard it," Cat said. "That poor tree."

Lelani noted Cat's confirmation. "In its death throes, Rosencrantz cast the return spell—whether for our benefit or in a fit of madness does not matter—the results are the same."

"But have we left Cal in Catherine's world?" Valeria asked.

"I do not know, my lady. We are lucky to have arrived where we are. As we approached this universe, we were drawn to the pantry gateway in the castle. That would have been disastrous for us. Changing our trajectory midcourse was most difficult. Thank the gods we survived."

What would become of her family now? Cat wondered. Lelani took Cat's hand. "The kingdom is infested with enemy troops, my lady. And the prince is missing."

Shit. Lelani wouldn't waste a second finding a way home while Daniel was unaccounted for.

The centaur pulled out a small vial with hairs in it. "These belong to Daniel. With them I can cast a tracer spell. The problem is it would be visible to everyone, including the enemy. If it becomes our last resort, I would use it at dawn when most are asleep and the morning's brightness obfuscates the trail."

Gunfire echoed through the forest from the east.

"That's them!" Cat said.

"Aye," confirmed Valeria. "But to remain on the road invites trouble."

"We will travel through the woods parallel to it," Lelani said. "Slow, but safer."

Lelani hacked through shrubs and brambles with a machete. Life claimed every inch of ground here, scratching, biting as you trespassed. The extra weight of Cat's pregnancy was also taking its toll. She wondered what it would be like twelve weeks from now . . . *if she was still alive.* They needed to set up camp before the sun set. As Cat finished this thought, they came upon a modest homestead.

Dead soldiers littered the rear yard. The crude construction of the house, the thatched roof and muddy road helped drive home the reality that Cat was in a world of leather and wood—stone and iron. Despite its lack of polish, touches like curtains and flower boxes on the sill told of a cherished home. A family much like hers had lived here.

"Mayhap Aandor's knights did this work," Valeria suggested. "A patrol we might seek refuge with?"

Lelani sniffed the air and clopped over to one of the corpses. She pointed at a bullet hole and to a shell casing nearby. "A spell had been cast here as well," she said. "See the wall of the house, how it buckles as though these men were heaved against it in one powerful thrust. Seth's hard wind."

Lelani clopped over to the tree line. "They left this way, using the forest for cover," she said, pointing to Daniel's sneaker prints in the dirt. "We can follow . . ."

"We need to make camp," said Cat, eyeing the sun. Her lower back demanded relief. "Maybe this cottage . . ."

"Farrenheil will come looking for these men," Lelani said

"Indeed they will," said a brightly dressed stranger as he rounded the corner of the house. If not for his statement they would not have known he was there, so quietly did he move.

The women quickly jumped beside Lelani, who positioned her hands for a quick spell, but the man made no hostile gesture. He stood there demurely, fiddling with one of his many jeweled rings.

He was short with curly black hair and a thick broom mustache that reminded Cat of Freddie Mercury. His tunic was an iridescent blue with shiny patterns stitched in gold and bronze thread. He wore just a dagger on his belt—his brown suede slippers curled up at their tips. Both ears were adorned with earrings stacked from his lobes to the top. He looked around the courtyard calculating the carnage and then smiled at Lelani.

"Friend or foe?" asked Lelani.

"A stupid question," answered the man. "I know not your allegiances, therefore I cannot say one way or the other. And if I did know, why would I tell true to a foe? You're one of the hopelessly honorable, hmmm?" He waved at the dead around them. "Your work?"

"No," said Cat. She'd killed enough today—no need to take credit for these.

"I don't believe you," said the flashy man. He twisted a ring on his pinkie and pain cut through Cat's skull, worse than any migraine. A voice in her brain compelled her to her knees. Bree and Valeria were in the same state.

Only Lelani stood immune. "Wizard!" she cried out, and hurled a blinding white phosphorous ball at the little man. He touched a ring on his index finger and the ball bounced off an invisible wall to fizzle in the dirt.

Lelani prepared another spell but suddenly cried out in pain before she could cast it. She reared and Bree fell off her back landing hard. The centaur slapped her neck and came away with a small silver dart. Soldiers in red and black poured out of the trees around the house; their movements were quiet as a grave—not a crunch of a boot or clank of a metal, until their wizard touched one of his earrings, and the sound of their movements materialized.

Lelani cast her spell. Nothing happened. She tried again to

no effect. "Faerie silver," she whispered in horror, looking at the dart.

Lelani produced a spear—from where it came Cat couldn't say—but the centaur charged her assailant. Lassos flew around the centaur's limbs—and soldiers pulled her down from every direction. A rope hoop at the end of a long stick collared Lelani's neck. Valeria and Cat were also surrounded. The flashy man shut off the PA system blaring in Cat's head.

Unlike the rabble they'd met on the forest road, these soldiers wore crimson tunics that were truly uniform and shimmered like silk; they were loose and billowy in the sleeves with new studded black leather mail and accessories. Two lightning bolts were inscribed side by side on their collars. These soldiers were not the usual army fodder. A strapping young officer rode in on an impressive black destrier to examine the takedown. He could have been an Aryan recruitment icon.

"Are we safe, Ahbahdaan?" the officer asked.

The wizard in blue approached Lelani and stripped the protection charms that hung around her neck. He was most impressed with the dream catcher made of strands from Lelani's red tail hairs. "Yes," replied the wizard.

Cal had drilled Cat on certain rules of his culture until she could recite them in her sleep; not because he hoped she'd ever have to use them, but from an overabundance of caution. Cat stood and addressed the man on horseback directly. "The Lady Catherine MacDonnell of the House MacDonnell yields to the noble captain from Farrenheil!"

"Lady MacDonnell?" he mused and studied her with a calculating eye.

Cat thought of Lord Dorn in the Chrysler Building and his attempt to yield to the guardians—how she put a bullet in him anyway. Would this knight do the same? The promise of her ransom was their only hope. "I am wife to a lord of Aandor, a captain of Lord Athelstan's, and this is his sister. My signet is in that satchel."

They retrieved the sterling silver ring from her bag. Cal had had his family's seal—a red kite hawk in profile under a blazing sun— custom made for her in the diamond districta, a basic piece of jewelry for any lord's wife. The ring was too big for practical use. Behind the hawk image was inlaid black onyx, in the sun's center was a two-carat round diamond, and the hawk's eye a tiny ruby. Circling the seal outside the stamp edge were even smaller rubies only slightly larger than grains of sand. The workmanship was exquisite, far better than anyone in Aandor could ever have done. Cal's version was plain silver, without the jewels, for pressing wax seals.

"I pray thee, my lord, protect us under the accords of war."

The officer brought his horse closer. He took the ring and examined Cat and Valeria the way one inspected livestock sold by a disreputable merchant. Bree clutched Cat's leg tightly as the knight judged them.

The flashy man in blue approached his superior. He pointed at Lelani and said, "Just her."

The knight looked like he smelled money. In a strong Farrenheisi accent, he said, "I am not a lord; just a poor lieutenant in the archduke's service. You may call me Sir Arnulf." He put the ring in a pouch. "The accords of war are not what they once were. But my grandfather taught them to me, so I will honor his memory and take you as my wards until I can verify your identities."

The knight gave instructions to his men in Farrenspiel. The tone sounded right. Lelani lay unmoving on the ground; she stopped struggling once Cat formally surrendered.

They were marched onto the road in the direction of the town. The knight secured a wagon for the ladies but not Lelani, who with hands bound was tied to a post at the rear of the wagon, collared like a mule. Two of the elite soldiers rode on either side of her. Cat wished she could do more for her friend, but there was no cart that could carry a centaur anyway.

"Tell me, my lady—the MacDonnell lands . . . are they near?" asked the knight.

Valeria saved Cat some embarrassment by saying, "North of the Sevren River, good sir—toward the eastern mountains."

Arnulf knitted his brows. "I see. It's just . . . well, I thought your family might be the local nobility." He kicked his horse lightly and pulled ahead toward the head of the column.

"Why?" asked Cat.

Over his shoulder Arnulf added, "You are not the only MacDonnell in our custody." He rode ahead, leaving them to wonder.

CHAPTER 12

HORSE SENSE

1

Refugees trickled in through the night, hobbled, injured, and exhausted, grateful for a place to rest their bones and consume some meager soup. By the time Seth and Daniel were ready to set out the next day, their number had swelled to thirty-two. Seth was not happy with Daniel's insistence to bring them all.

Of the rabble, six were soldiers of note like Oswin who could fend for themselves, though one was too injured to join their trek into the deep forest. A few local farmers safely navigated their families around the enemy patrols—men with broad backs and thick arms, but little to no skill with a sword or halberd. Women, children, and the elderly made up the majority of the group. The ones remaining behind would not see their next sunrise; their injuries were too severe and Farrenheil would find this camp soon enough anyway.

Daniel was sick over abandoning the injured and infirmed, but carts would not go where they were headed. Seth pestered his friend to get as far from the town as possible; if Farrenheil caught the prince the game was over.

Despite Daniel's inexperience (and the buzz of his strange dress), the group readily accepted him as their "lord" and put their fate in his hands. Seth looked from Daniel to Jack and back again. Just four years separated the boys. Daniel carried that extra muscle MacDonnell put on him with a tall, straight back that could shoulder burdens. He held his head high and looked men in the eye when he spoke. *When did our wiry little prince become a man?* Seth wondered. Maybe leadership was genetic. Seth was older, taller, and equally as literate, but it was the prince who received the goodwill and benefit of the doubt.

Seth hoped that Daniel knew what he was taking on with this rabble of hungry mouths and quick tempers. Why would anyone punish himself with the responsibility? The kid had been a snail's tit away from running off in New York—suffocated by the guardians' grand allusions. Seth would have helped him, even though Lelani would have kicked his magical ass to Timbuktu. Lelani was loyal to the prince so long as he returned to Aandor, which was in her people's best interests. Everyone had skin in this game and had pinned their hopes and strategies on Daniel.

They traveled east three miles and made camp by a secluded lake at noon. Seth sat by the water and broke into his dwindling stash of Slim Jims and granola. He studied the woods and couldn't shake the notion that he was being watched; or more accurately, talked about. He sensed . . . *A buzz? A murmur?* Whatever the word, it was something. Maybe it was magic itself. Aandor was rife with the stuff, and now that his lifelong magic defense was porous, the energy filled him like a teen's first can of Jolt soda. *Bathing in magical radiation all day . . . probably why the local life expectancy is forty. We're all getting cancer.* Seth was primed to cast a spell in this environment—two pounds of pressure on a three-pound trigger—but his lack of experience and limited spell book made him a poor shot. No wonder his mother sent him off to Aandor—as much to protect those around him as himself.

Twenty-five miles north, near the village of Iibswitch, Seth's mother ran an inn. The invasion must have reached Iibswitch by now. Seth worried for his family and hoped they were smart enough to cross the Sevren and head for the mountains. Any army coming west from Red King's Gate would march through Iibswitch. The yearning to check on his family only grew.

Fulbert bolted out of the forest as though the devil himself was chasing him. Between short, quick gasps he conveyed something to Oswin and the guardsmen that soured their faces.

Seth reached Daniel at the same time as Oswin.

"Enemy soldiers," the pikeman said. "Guarding prisoners over the next hill."

A scouting party made their way over the hill quietly and spied the scene. A makeshift camp around another lake—four centaurs were captive in a makeshift corral, bound by ropes and chains. Imprisoned with them were four soldiers of Aandor, and a few other men.

"They have taken the Blue Forest patrol," whispered Oswin. "Both men and centaurs."

"'Tis disconcerting to look upon beasts with men's faces," whispered one of the farmers.

"Aye-yuh," said another farmer. "Mix with that lot, soon enough yer daughters will bear ye kin with hoofs 'stead of foots."

"There's gratitude," Seth noted in English.

"They keep to the woods around the Blue Road," Oswin finished. "Our patrol rides the highway and liaises with the centaurs to report. Farrenheil penetrated the forest to ambush the beast-men's patrol."

"Great! So the woods aren't as safe as we thought," Seth griped.

"Two men to a tent?" Daniel asked.

"Standard bivouac," Oswin confirmed.

"I count twenty tents and forty horses. Where are the other fifteen men?"

"I know," whispered Jack.

All the men, including Seth, were surprised to see Jack, who had snuck his way into their midst.

"I told you to stay by the lake," Daniel said, doing a great imitation of someone's father.

"Aye, ya did, milord," Jack said smiling. "But then ye wouldn't know where the other half of these soldiers have gone."

2

They quietly climbed back down their hill. The clinking of pots and chatter of children at their camp made Seth wince. The noise probably couldn't make it over the hill, but there was no reason to dance so close to the hornet's nest.

"Get back to camp and tell everyone to quiet down," Daniel told Fulbert. "Pack everything and head a few yards into the trees out of view. Wait for us." Daniel turned to Jack. "Is there any way you can just point to where the other soldiers have gone?"

Jack shook his head impishly. The boy was determined to skip ages eleven through fourteen and move right to manhood.

They were lucky Jack had turned out to be so stubborn. The route was anything but easy—a dense old part of the forest likely untrodden by men. The party scratched their heads wondering how the lad had even thought to take this path, and how he was able to find his way back. Oswin remarked that the boy must be half wood nymph—Seth couldn't tell if it was a joke.

They came to a creek lined with a congress of birch, ash, and maple trees with branches that arched over the water to form a natural vaulted roof. A few rocks cleared the surface enough for a thin path over the water, which Jack now hopped across heedlessly, finding solid purchase and ducking lower branches across the course. Daniel went next. Seth was in the middle of the group; four rocks across he thought he would slip and grabbed a branch to steady himself—his mind suddenly went on an acid trip. Seth fell backward into the creek. The water was only two feet deep, but he still went under—the cold current tugged him downstream, limp and weighted down by his gear. Strong large hands from the big bearded farmer that reminded Seth of Mr. Garvey from *Little House on the Prairie* grabbed him under the armpits and hoisted him out. They carried him to the far bank where he coughed out his lungs under Daniel's concerned gaze.

Seth's head cleared and he sat up. He reached around for his staff but couldn't find it.

"Pole's flowed down yonder," said Mr. Garvey.

His staff was twenty yards downstream and moving fast.

"I'll whittle ye another . . . ," the farmer began.

Seth stood dripping. His "pole" was more than just a stick. It was a magical appendage, whittled from the branch of a sentient tree wizard; he shared a symbiotic relationship with the staff—his till for navigating the currents of magic. Seth would no more accept its loss than he could his arm. He closed his eyes and felt for the lines of connection between the staff and himself. He caught the link, like the strings that connected master to puppet. The stick jerked and stood up on the water. The staff flew across the top of the creek toward Seth's outreached hand. He knew it was going to smart like a motherfucker even before it slapped into his palm with a loud *THWACK!* But damned if it didn't look cool as all hell.

"Sorcery!" cried many, making signs to ward off evil. Jack looked at Seth with sheer awe.

"I'm partial to *this* pole," Seth told the big farmer.

Seth identified the branch he'd grabbed on the water and followed it back to its trunk. It was an ash tree, ancient by the look of it. The buzz was strong around it.

"It's like Rosencrantz," he said to Daniel. "The spell Rosencrantz cast on me to be able to communicate with it in real time is still active. When I touched this tree we connected and were both overwhelmed. I think I can establish a safe rapport now that I'm prepared."

The farmers had convened a safe distance from Seth. The wizard didn't blame them—this was hippy-dippy stuff to practical people. The soldiers were less bothered and had probably met hedge wizards in their duties. Seth knelt by the tree and placed his hands on its ancient gnarled roots. He was prepared for the rush this time.

Fraxinus was a thousand years old and it protected this piece of the forest. There were many sentient trees in the Blue, and they communicated through their own pheromone version of the cloud. The forest knew that something was wrong. Acres of farms had been burned, and even a few sentient floras had lost their lives. The enemy killed the horse men that had always showed great reverence for the woods. Seth explained who he was, where he came from, and how he was able to communicate. Fraxinus had never heard of Rosencrantz, nor was the tree a wizard itself; that ability was as rare for flora as it was for men, although Seth suspected the tree did use magic but was unaware that it did so. Seth was certain magic was at the root of any sentient flora.

He asked Fraxinus for help against their common enemy. The ash shared an image of the area from its point of view; Seth was suddenly aware of every brook, creek, and stream, where the deer walked, the dark areas that led below the earth to other worlds murky and dangerous, gnolls' dens, an ogre's cave—and he knew where the other half of Farrenheil's troop was, and more importantly what they were up to. Seth thanked the tree for its aid. Fraxinus wished him sun and water and blessed seedlings.

The buzzing stopped once Seth withdrew. It had been the flora all along, not magic. Maybe they wouldn't die of cancer by forty after all. "We don't have much time," he told his crew.

3

From high cover they spied a deer path through the woods. To their left, a wooden bridge of centaur design traversed a deep ravine. About twelve feet down was a fast stream. The missing Farrenheil soldiers lay in wait around the bridge, behind trees and bushes, and a section of hill overlooking the ravine from the other end. They had the usual weapons: swords, mace, morning stars, spears—but they also had hoops on the ends of long sticks that reminded Seth of something animal control would use back in New York. The soldiers were so silent, that had Seth not forewarned the group of their positions, they would have stumbled blindly into the trap themselves.

"These are Farrenheil's special forces," Daniel whispered.

"What makes you say that?

"You wouldn't hunt centaurs with draftees. That rabble we fought at Jack's homestead cobbled their gear and uniforms from anywhere they could—rusty, bent swords. These guys have new weapons and matching uniforms, and the reds are downplayed, browned out for hiding in a forest."

"Milord speaks true," Oswin said. "Their camp banner bore the sig rune—two black lightning bolts on a yellow field."

A hundred yards up the path, heading into the ambush, was another centaur patrol: five bearing spears and one in the vanguard with an impressive golden bow.

"We're not letting them take down the centaurs," Daniel said.

All the men, even Seth, stared at Daniel like he'd lost his mind.

"We are but nine men . . . ," said Merick, a lanky but solid guardsman.

"Ten," added Jack.

"Three are farmers who have never used a sword . . . and no offense, milord, but ye and yer wizard don't have the look of hard battle."

"Gillette face cream for men . . . ," Seth quipped. "Nips worry lines in the bud."

"They're beasts," said Jarin, the huge farmer who had saved Seth at the creek. "Risk our necks for the likes of them?"

"They're definitely going to want to bed *your* daughters after we save them," Seth added.

Jarin nodded, missing the sarcasm, and added, "Milord, we have a good plan. Move deeper into the woods away from the patrols, hide our kin, wait until Archduke Athelstan arrives to repel these bastards." A round of "ayes" from the others made public their consensus.

Daniel took a deep breath to control his frustration. These farmers weren't bad men; they were afraid and didn't see the big picture. "The archduke partnered with them," Daniel said. "They have honored the Blue Forest Accord. The kingdom thrives from the commerce of a safe forest road."

"Aye, but—" Jarin started.

"They're our allies!" Daniel pressed. They'd gotten his ire up. He took a deep, calming breath. "The entire kingdom's been taken; Farrenheil used ancient sorcery to cheat. Aandor City has forty thousand problems of its own bivouacked on Deorwine Plain—between us and the capital. There's no help coming. We can run, but eventually we'll have to fight—or there will be nowhere left to run to."

The men looked somberly at their feet, ashamed that they still preferred to hide.

"What about you?" Seth said to Daniel. "Is your life worth risking in a fight?"

Daniel could only think of Jack's brother lying dead in that clearing as the consequence of doing nothing.

"You're too important," Seth added, seeing him struggle with the decision.

"Who are ye, milord, if I might ask," queried Oswin, "to travel with your own wizard and such?"

Daniel was stuck. They certainly had the right to know who they were following.

"He is a close relation of Archduke Athelstan and Archduchess Sophia," Seth cut in. "It would be best in the event of our capture that few know his lordship's true identity." The men murmured and grunted affirmatively, as though confirming what they already suspected. The archduke and duchess's portraits hung in every town and many inns and pubs. Daniel's resemblance to his mother came into focus.

"We have the element of surprise," Daniel said. "We have a

wizard. And we'll have six soon-to-be-pissed-off centaurs fighting with us. The plan is to ambush the ambushers."

4

The hill was steep, but manageable. The trees thinned out about halfway down before disappearing entirely, but Seth had cast an almost competent veil over the group, and helped them get to the tree line. The final thirty feet was high grass that ran down to small boulders and rocky outcrops along the path that the ambushers hid behind. Seth spotted only twelve of the combatants; seven were on the far side of the footbridge. They intended to trap the centaurs on the bridge. Farrenheil would lose its advantage without the trap if the centaurs fought half as well as Lelani. Too many "ifs" for Seth—but he recognized the cool killer's eye of imagination in Daniel's plan. Daniel was creative, able to see what could be—he unraveled the action in his mind clear as if it had happened. The plan hinged on the centaurs joining the fight—but if they bolted into the forest, Daniel's squad still had the cover of the trees against assailants charging uphill.

Daniel used his Zippo to light Merick's arrows dipped in oil, inviting whispers of his own magical ability—an irony considering as a royal he was insulated from using or being affected by most magic. Merick let an arrow fly, hitting a soldier nearest to the centaurs. The man screamed, as one would when pierced with a flaming arrow, and sprung up to pat out flames that had caught on his tunic. The centaurs were alerted to their presence. The ambushers attacked prematurely, their shrill war cries ineffective against the wary centaurs. The soldiers on Daniel's side of the road charged up the hill toward them. The men at the other end of the footbridge hastily charged across to help their brothers. It would be bad if they made it over the bridge.

Seth used the high grass to get within a few yards of the bridge. The edge of the ravine, a sharp, rocky drop, lay a few feet to his left. Daniel's prediction was on the mark; Seth now had seven soldiers in a line over a tightly controlled space. He cast his hard air spell and swatted them off the bridge with a hurricane gust so powerful, the bridge groaned and threatened to come off its mooring. The men cracked bones on the rocks as they fell in. Some struggled to stay up as the fast current pulled their armored forms down.

Seth was breathing hard and cursed his decade-long smoking habit. He was physically spent and hard-pressed to cast again. He couldn't understand it—weren't they in the land of magical milk and honey?

An enemy archer climbing the hill spotted Seth and turned his arrow on him. Seth made the priest's blessing to produce his shield, and the arrow glanced off and lodged into a bridge post. The archer's expression turned forlorn as he notched his second arrow, now aware that he confronted a wizard. Seth fought the urge to pass out and used his last scrap of concentration to convert the soldier's bow into a collapsing bouquet of purple blossoms. That put Seth on his hands and knees, steeling himself to stay awake and trying to find enough energy to fend off the man with his staff. An arrow perforated the soldier's chest, saving him. Merick gave Seth a hearty salute from atop the hill.

Daniel's team had taken down the remaining soldiers who had charged the hill with no casualties to themselves—the centaurs had made short work of their attackers as well. In this tiny corner of this world, at least, Farrenheil had been vanquished.

It occurred to Seth that he'd taken out half this enemy squad by himself. And he was not even a good wizard by any stretch of the imagination. Daniel and his merry men came down the hill to join him. The prince had the biggest grin.

"You were amazing!" his friend exclaimed.

Daniel's admiration was disarming. His praise had a quality drawn from some well of communal acceptance. Daniel's power stemmed from his unabashed sincerity—his acceptance, flaws and all, of those who he considered friends. He was bigger than life. By contrast, Seth was mired in the experience that anyone who liked him once would not continue to do so for long. He was used to being tolerated.

"Uh . . . yeah, thanks," was all Seth could respond. He'd feel better if three hills over, the rest of this enemy platoon wasn't building a makeshift prison. Daniel wasn't going to let that go, either.

The centaurs approached them cautiously. Daniel's men were nervous, even though they had just earned a basketful of good-will. The leader was over six foot four from head to hoof, with red hair and an ornate golden bow. Where Lelani's equestrian half was svelte like a racehorse, this centaur was thicker, hairier around the hooves, and built more like a workhorse.

"Clydesdales," Seth whispered.

The prince was the only one who didn't show discomfort in their presence—in fact, he radiated confidence, as though he had every right to be standing on that spot deep in their forest. He approached the lead centaur a little too easily for Seth's comfort. The horse people were not all as progressive as Lelani. They were skittish around humans, unpredictable, and sometimes ornery. And they outweighed men by hundreds of pounds.

Three of the others were like their leader: hairy upper bodies, swarthy, unibrows, and slightly crooked teeth. Two were more polished like Lelani. The centaurs surrounded Daniel's squad, spears at the ready. While the men shifted nervously, tightening their grips on their weapons, Daniel showed no fear; he maintained his smile and calm.

"You are deep in our lands," accused the lead centaur, with a heavy accent that reminded Seth of his Slovakian dry cleaner in the East Village.

"Lucky for you," Daniel responded.

That earned a crack in big red's gruff demeanor and the centaur squad put up their spears.

"Our patrol did not return home," Big Red said.

"Aandor has been invaded," Daniel replied. "Farrenheil has no love of centaurs."

This appeared to confirm what the centaurs suspected.

"We need to palaver," Daniel said.

"Palaver?"

"Talk. I know where your missing people are."

CHAPTER 13

MUM DEAREST

1

A dozen black smoke columns were the pillars of a billowy canopy over the town of Yarmouth. The town was dusted with a gray ash—high piles of razed bodies were stacked against the gate's entry towers like sacks of sand in a flood, and where Yarmouth lacked a natural moat, rivers of blood mixed with mud to create a wet red ring below the walls. The din of looting and mayhem echoed within—feral cries ricocheted through the streets in rhythmic succession like big cats in heat. Nothing could have prepared Catherine MacDonnell for the reality of medieval warfare. Her gut knotted at the idea of riding into that bedlam.

The enemy regiment, however, had set up camp outside the town. Sir Arnulf marched them around that red soppy mud to a dry patch down the hill, away from the madness. There were about sixty moth-eaten old tents that Cat had expected to be more regimented—but this camp was chaotic, like a montage of different armies slapped together by virtue of having black or red in a banner or uniform. Valeria had said many of the lowborn would don their grandfathers' uniforms when their liege lords called them to war. The peasants and common folk were loyal to liege lords who in turn were loyal to themselves first and then their own higher lords. Everyone waited for the opportunity to absorb their neighbor's fief. It was a paranoid command structure.

Arnulf's squad wasn't rabble; their corner of the camp was pitched in rows with larger tents, latrines, and a corral. His platoon was called the Entzerrei—wizard hunters who kept battles fair for their numerically superior forces by weeding out the enemy magic users. When squads from the vicinity of that homestead failed to report back to camp, Arnulf and his men were dispatched to investigate. They believed Lelani was responsible for that backyard slaughter.

They halted before the largest tent in the row, an ambitious circular piece of canvas.

"You will remain in my tent under guard," Arnulf said. "There's bread, cheese, and wine; you'll remain unmolested, provided you abide by the rules of surrender."

Lelani remained tied to the wagon; the flashy little wizard they called Ahbahdaan led the cart away with her in tow.

"No!" cried Brianna.

"Where are you taking her?" Catherine asked, loathe to lose the only person she knew in this crazy universe.

"The wizard must be interrogated," Arnulf said. "There are rumors of a magic-wielding centaur studying at Proust's Academy. Is this her?" he asked. Cat shrugged her shoulders. "My superiors will be interested in her, either way."

"You can't take her!" Bree insisted.

"Best to calm your whelp and enter your lodgings. We are at war, after all."

Cat steered Bree into the tent and half hoped to find Callum—the *other* MacDonnell—within. It was empty. The canvas was a mint green like hospital colors with a sturdy cot in the corner, a plain wooden desk and two chairs, a large chest, a washbasin, and a pitcher filled with clean water, all resting atop worn, faded woven rugs. Two oil lamps hung on the center pole. Arnulf might not be a "lord" but he was certainly no pauper, either. Cat piled thick pillows together for Bree to lie on, then plopped herself on the cot, grateful to have something soft beneath her. She massaged her back and wanted nothing more than to lay her head down and sleep.

"Valeria, what do I need to know right now about being a hostage?"

"Patience. The men will do what it is men do in these matters. Arnulf will consult his superiors. They must validate your claim."

"How? There's no record of our marriage in this universe. No witnesses."

"Perhaps Callum is his prisoner," Valeria said.

Nothing would make Cat happier than to see her husband right now—but that would mean he was subject to torture and execution. Cal was their biggest threat after the prince. He could rally men behind him and make a lot of trouble.

A knock came at the entrance. Two guards entered with a tall soldier dressed in Aandor's blue, white, and gold. He was about fifty, but still fit with a full head of white hair and a beard to match. Valeria refused to exhale until she accepted this was not a mirage. She rushed the man and threw her arms around him.

"Child, I had heard you were in the castle attending the archduchess. How came you to be in these woods?" the man asked.

"A strange tale indeed, Uncle Roland." Valeria glanced at the guards. Roland picked up on this and asked them for privacy, confirming that she was in fact his niece.

"They said Callum's *wife* had been captured?"

"Aye," confirmed Valeria. "This is she. Catherine, this is my father's younger brother Roland MacDonnell, commander of Red King's Gate."

Cat curtsied as Cal had taught them. Roland was at a loss. They poured him wine as he took a seat. Cat encouraged Valeria to speak since it was she, and only she, who could give Cat's claim any validity. He listened to the story of Cal's mission—Magnus Proust's escape plan upon the invasion, the alternate reality—Cat interjected to clarify those things Valeria couldn't know. The general listened with the skepticism of a career soldier. Cat pulled out her iPhone and showed him photographs of her family. After Roland's initial shock, sure that this *sorcery* was a magic mirror out of a child's fable, he settled into the history of Cat's life with his nephew. She played "In My Life" by the Beatles as he scrolled through the pictures. If this didn't prove that she was not business as usual, Cat didn't know what else would.

"'Tis all true, Uncle," Valeria emphasized. "I have been to this other world and seen my brother there but three days ago, an older man than we remembered." Roland settled on the last picture Cat had taken for a long time—Cal and Valeria posing at Malcolm's mansion the morning they left for Rosencrantz's pasture.

Cat tried to imagine how a Pentagon general would react to a story like this. Roland thought about it, and thought about it, running fingers through his beard as he studied Cat's eyes.

"What of Chryslantha?" Roland asked his niece.

Cat bit her tongue. *Really? Of all the questions you could ask about iPhones and alternative universes, she comes to mind?*

"Chryslantha remains a prisoner in Aandor," Valeria said.

"Callum's heart weighs heavy with the breaking of his betrothal. It vexes him."

Vexes him?

"But Catherine has been his wife of seven years. This child, Brianna, is Callum's daughter and Catherine bears his unborn son."

Uncle Roland studied Bree with compassionate blue eyes fair as a summer sky. He pulled something from his pocket and handed it to Cat. "Your ring, Lady MacDonnell," he said. "For ill or good in these strange times, welcome to the family."

Cat let out a breath she didn't know she'd been holding. If Roland repudiated her, Arnulf would have thrown them to the wolves—probably literally around here.

"Uncle, how did you come to be *here*?" asked Valeria.

"Taken on the road to Aandor. Our honor guard was outnumbered; my men, except for my sergeant and lieutenant, were killed. I would have continued to fight, but had your mother and sister to think of."

"Mother?" Valeria asked in a near panic.

"I was her escort. Much good it did." He saw the concern on Valeria's face. "They are fine. We are being kept in the regiment commander's tent. Lord Onyx."

"Fuck," Catherine said. An unhappy mood descended upon her, severe enough to concern Valeria, who took Bree into her embrace. "Fuck, fuck—fuck!"

Roland disapproved of her profanity, likely because women in his circles simply didn't speak like longshoremen. "I assure you, Catherine, we are treated well as our rank and privilege afford us," he said, trying to calm her. "Lord Onyx is my second cousin by marriage."

Cat just shook her head and began to groan. "No. You don't

understand . . . I've been assaulted today and nearly beaten. I killed four men. My husband is on the other side of the universe, my only friend here has been carted away in chains . . . I'm six months pregnant in a medieval forest where I'll be lucky to find a barber to deliver my baby with rusted knives and no epidural. I look like shit. And just when I've gotten a handle on it . . . all that the universe has thrown at me . . . just when I've made my peace with God's sick sense of humor . . . I find out . . ." She looked up them, flustered and bleary eyed. "I find out I'm going to meet my fucking mother-in-law!"

2

Valeria and Roland jointly agreed they should break the news of Callum's marriage before Mina met Catherine. Cat was quite herself again, taking deep breaths to regain her composure while Valeria explained her mother's strong will and cold resolve for planning her family's ascension in society. Forewarning Mina would be the safest approach for all parties. That such drama should even exist in the midst of a full-fledged war was a little surreal to Cat.

Mina had dreamed of Callum's marriage to Chryslantha since they first played together as children. Chrys, as Valeria called her, was rich and beautiful, and if Cat were to believe the hype, kind, generous, and intelligent as well. Cat despised this woman's bond to her husband with a passion. She'd fairly fought off her competitors—not that she ever needed to worry about Cal's fidelity, but that didn't stop women from trying . . . flaunting their assets (some not so God-given) like forbidden fruit on blue light special. It never got under Cat's skin before because Cal was so decent. But Chryslantha was different from every other woman—she shared every bit of Cal's undying devotion that Cat once thought reserved solely for her in all the world. Here, Cat was the usurper—the late arrival that pilfered some poor bride's groom. Chryslantha's father was incredibly powerful, second only to the archduke himself. Could he make Cat and Bree "disappear" for the sake of his daughter if he wanted to? Only two things protected Cat right now: Callum's love for her and the unfortunate fact that Lord Godwynn was probably a prisoner himself, or possibly dead. Cat was grateful for that advantage right now. *When did you get so petty?*

Cat had fantasized about meeting Cal's mother since before she'd ever heard of Aandor—in her imaginings, Mama Mac-Donnell was eternally grateful for Cat taking care of her lost baby boy. Cat was always confident she could win that woman over with grandchildren, charm, and casseroles. In Cat's wildest dreams, she would never have imagined this. The fact that she could even cook at all worked against her with Callum's crowd. Highborn women in this land existed to breed men. And when they had daughters, they chalked it up to the necessity to breed the next generation of powerful men. Even when not at war, it was a flawed system, the only perfection being Callum Mac-Donnell and Chryslantha Godwynn.

Everyone in Aandor, especially Mina MacDonnell, was of the opinion that Callum and Chryslantha were soul mates, destined for a harmonious life. Then there was Chryslantha Godwynn's dowry—five thousand acres adjoining the MacDonnell lands—which would have elevated Callum's standing in the nobility as well as his family's income. Catherine Hill's dowry of a 1991 Nissan Sentra, a diabetic cat, and massive student loan debt was considerably less impressive.

"I'm bored," Bree complained. Cat was bored as well. Several hours had passed. She couldn't risk them catching Bree playing with her iPad, which she'd convinced the enemy was a mirror. The last thing they needed was to get branded magic users and thrown in Arnulf's stockade.

"Bored is good," Cat told her. "Bored means nothing bad is happening to us right now." Then she looked to her sister-in-law. "What do you think is going on?" she asked Valeria.

Val bit her lower lip. "Mother may have broken things."

Cat thought it a joke until Val frowned.

Sir Arnulf knocked and let himself in. Rested and relieved, Cat was able to better appreciate Arnulf's handsomeness . . . a Brothers Grimm prince with hazel bedroom eyes, a thin line of a mouth that accented his strong chin, and just as commanding a presence as her husband. He'd proven to be honorable, despite his choice of allegiances. "Roland's request to have you join him has been granted," he said. "We're to escort you to Lord Onyx's tent. You would do well to remember that your uncle has accepted responsibility for you, and that your actions reflect on him."

"Why did you look at me when you said it?" Cat asked.

Arnulf gave her a wolfish smile. "There is something to you, Lady MacDonnell . . . at first I thought it my affinity for gray eyes, but there is some other quality that sets you apart from the doe-eyed hens I am accustomed to. Perhaps it's the way you carry yourself in the most fearful situations—even heavy with child. You consider yourself the equal of men?"

"Absolutely," Cat said before she could censor herself.

Amused, Arnulf nodded. "I see that you truly believe this. How fortunate a man is Callum MacDonnell to cull such lovely women with sharp minds and masculine spines. And what a fool he is to play them so poorly. I did not realize at first whose wife you claimed to be, but it became clear soon enough—the jousting champion of the Twelve Kingdoms, captain of Athelstan's Dukesguarde himself. I thought for sure Lord Roland would reveal your deception, but he has confirmed your marriage, which, I will confess, had shocked me. So I wonder, my lady, what manner of woman can turn the head of Callum MacDonnell from the Rose of Aandor herself—a woman I had the pleasure to once see at court and found lacking in any flaw."

Cat was fed up with Chryslantha's *perfection*. You'd think the woman never used a toilet. "Actually, Cal said she snores. Horribly . . . like a pregnant pig." Cat hated women who turned on the sisterhood and regretted her remark. "I don't care to discuss my husband's old girlfriends," she said, in a most aristocratic manner. "Are we leaving?"

As they walked through camp, they passed a corral whose only occupant was a broken centaur languishing in filthy mud. It broke Catherine's heart. They had gagged Lelani, manacled her hands and legs to thick posts. They'd shorn her beautiful red hair and horsetail. Around her neck, a leather collar with inward silver spikes sent rivulets of blood down her shoulders and bare breasts. She was dappled with dark welts; her left eye was swollen shut, her demeanor forlorn. Three grizzled soldiers sat on the fence posts with crossbows.

"You bastards," Cat said.

One turned to Cat and held up a cudgel about the size of a long eggplant.

"Milady . . . do you think this cosh is the size of a centaur's cock?" he asked. The other men sniggered.

Another showed his baton, the size of a baker's pin. "He's daft, milady. I'm sure this is a proper centaur's cock."

"However shall we know for sure?" the first man added. They laughed at their low wit.

Arnulf took Cat's arm to nudge her along—she shook him off defiantly and stared him down. "My husband would never treat a prisoner like this."

"The Butcher of Gagarnoth?" Arnulf let out a short laugh. "If the stories are even half true, the Mourish queen would not agree with you. Her end at your husband's hands is legend."

Cat's heart sank at the thought of Cal behaving like these monsters. Cal might have had to kill people in his duties, but he would never have abided their torture and humiliation. He would never have enjoyed it.

"The centaur is under the purview of the Entzerrei. Ahbah-daan decides her fate. Shall we . . . ?" He motioned ahead.

If Cat thought Arnulf's tent was luxurious, then Lord Onyx's had to be the Versailles of all tents. The rugs were bright; the furniture equal to anything you'd find on an English antiquing trip; the back of the tent was segmented to create additional rooms on either side of a center aisle. Multiple lamps illuminated the interior. They were led to the first of the sectioned-off rooms where Roland awaited them by the entrance with a girl of about ten years who looked like the very image of Brianna, or what Bree would eventually become. For her part, Bree hid behind her mother, suffering an annoying bout of sudden shyness. Meghan lit up at the sight of her sister.

Roland gave Cat a sympathetic gaze that broadcast the unease they were about to encounter and ushered them through the flap. Meghan and Valeria embraced, both crying. The space was comparable to a modern living room; three cots lined the outer wall while in the center, wearing a decorative shiny teal dress, sat a regally beautiful woman on a green velvet ottoman. She refused to look at the new arrivals, choosing instead to ponder something of interest on the tent's bare wall. This woman was unmistakably Callum's mother; because she had Cal at the tender age of seventeen and due to the time differential between their universes, she was just a few years older than Catherine. Nevertheless, her blond hair was transitioning to white and she bore a few more crow's-feet than a woman of the same rank and years in New York would have.

"Are you well, Valeria?" Mina asked, moving her head slightly to note her daughter.

"I am, Mother." Valeria relayed her discomfort over Mina's cold detachment to Catherine with a subtle glance. Cat, however, had braced herself for just such a reception. "Mother, this is Callum's wife of seven years, Catherine Hill."

Mina turned her stoic eyes toward Catherine with mechanical slowness and took her daughter-in-law in from head to toe. Cat felt like a prize heifer going up for auction. It gave Mina's blue eyes—Callum's blue eyes—an icy, remote countenance. It pissed Catherine off to no end . . . yet she would hold her tongue and behave for her husband's sake.

After an eternity, Mina deigned to speak. "You're not very tall."

And there you had it . . . the first disapproval of the mother-in-law.

Cat noted the poetic justice—her own father criticized Cal when she announced their engagement: *He has no people . . . ,* Matt Hill had barked regarding Cal's lack of relations—no family to help out in their lives. Her father could not have been more wrong.

If there was one lesson Cat learned from her father's treatment of Cal, it was that there was such a thing as being too good. Cal took everything her parents threw at him with good humor—always excusing their actions as parental concern for their child. Cal was chivalrous as a knight, even before he recalled he actually was one. There were times when she'd get so mad at him for not fighting back, for being a punching bag. She loved her mom and dad, but they had a few snarky remarks coming to them. Now it was Cat's turn to tread the fine line—but she was not the emotionally patient person her husband was. Still, she knew enough to keep the legendary mouth under wraps until they had some plan of action to get out from this situation.

"I ate my vegetables and drank my milk, but this was all the height I could muster," Cat offered.

Valeria, Meghan, and Uncle Roland smiled stealthily. Mina continued to measure Catherine impassively as though she had not heard her. "Chryslantha Godwynn is very rich, very smart, very powerful, and always gets what she wants," Mina said in a tone that conveyed quite transparently that Chryslantha Godwynn would eat Cat alive.

"This is Callum's daughter, Brianna," Valeria said, pulling the reluctant girl out from behind her mother in an attempt to change the trajectory of this conversation.

When Cal's memories returned to him, he marveled at how much Brianna reminded him of his youngest sister, Meghan. The resemblance was in fact uncanny because Bree garnered the first unreserved reaction from Mina. She drew a sharp breath and held it a moment.

"Say hello to your grandmother, sweetie," Cat said through clenched jaw.

"How can this be?" Mina whispered. She touched Brianna's cheek gently; surprised to find the girl was not an apparition but a solid living being with her family's resemblance. "How can this be so?"

"I've explained," Roland said. "Twice, in fact." He reached out to Catherine. "Your tablet, niece."

Cat handed him the iPad instead, where she had edited the images so that as they scrolled, it would give a chronological account of her life with Cal: her wedding photo, Bree's birthday parties, the day they dug the car out from a snowstorm and snuck in a snowball fight and a family of snowmen; Bree's first lost tooth, her first day at kindergarten. Cat even had video of Bree's last birthday party. Cat hit the play button for them. The sound of her son's voice in the moving image shocked the uninitiated. Mina touched the screen over her slightly older son and jiggled the image. She put her hand to her mouth and tears ran down her cheek. She saw in the device not just her son, but also another world she could never have imagined—and a beloved son living a life he could not have planned for. She came across a photo of Cal in his dress blues from Erin Ramos's funeral.

"What uniform is this?"

"A policeman's—a knight of our world protecting and serving the people." Mina took pride in this.

"And this?" Mina asked, having come across an ultrasound image.

"That is our son," Cat said, rubbing her swollen belly.

"How is this possible? That Callum would take a witch bride from a world of sorcery . . . !"

As words that ended with "itch" went, Cat could live with that one.

"Lady MacDonnell . . . Callum was popular with the ladies of my world. But it was me he courted . . . me he moved heaven and earth to woo—and I fell in love with him, very hard." Mina looked up, and Cat locked eyes with her mother-in-law. "I know I am not Chryslantha Godwynn. Fate has dealt her an unimaginable injustice. Both of us have suffered from this. But Callum is my sun and stars, my husband of seven years, the father of my children." Cat rubbed her belly to emphasize this. "This is his son. I will not willingly give him up or stand aside. I will not be relegated to a mistress or any other such nonsense. I do not even know if I will ever see him again because he did not transition to Aandor with us—but I will fight for my family against *anyone* that would tear us apart," Cat said in a hard-edged yet dulcet tone.

Valeria and Meghan held their breaths. People in Aandor knew better than to threaten Mina MacDonnell, but Roland nodded his subtle approval. Mina's expression was unreadable—those cold calculating blue eyes bored into her, searching for the secrets in Cat's head. Cat stared back unflinching, digging back for her own information. She'd always won at the staring game as a kid—it was one of the things that unsettled friends and foe when dealing with her.

Mina turned first, using her granddaughter for an excuse, and stroked Brianna's soft hair.

"If I were to salvage any one bit of good news from this catastrophe, it is that at the very least my son chose a woman with some steel in her," Mina said. Cat was willing to chalk that up as a victory. However, Mina was not yet done. "How that will interpret what needs to be done to correct the dishonor yet remains to be seen."

"There's no dishonor," Cat insisted. "Cal did not know about his betrothal."

"You have a commoner's simplicity, Catherine Hill. Lord Godwynn will not care for the details. His daughter has been humiliated, and my family will suffer for the indignity. We cannot even begin to calculate the cost."

"Cost? Lady, you don't even have a kingdom right now. You're in the same prison I'm in. Godwynn's up the creek, too! There's no guarantee that Farrenheil will continue to honor your rules of chivalry. Farrenheil will be extracting the prizes it wants from Aandor—and you're too in denial to really comprehend what that means. Do you know how many times Valeria and I were assaulted today? So you can take your *costs* and—"

Valeria grabbed Cat's arm and shook her head pleadingly for Cat to stop. Cat took several short breaths, counting to ten in her head.

Mina smiled victoriously. "Much strength and fire—unfortunately fixed to a temper ill suited for court." Mina pulled Bree in front of her and cupped the young girl's face with her hands. She looked to Meghan and then again to Brianna. "Leave us," she said. "I wish to speak with my . . . my granddaughter."

The others, except for Catherine and Roland exited. Cat did not want Bree out of her sight. Roland approached her. "No harm will come to your child, Catherine. My brother's wife is known for many things—her love of children is foremost among them. On this I give you my word."

Cat let Roland escort her out. The meeting had not been as lovey-dovey as she'd hoped. She was crazy to think that woman would ever embrace her. Mina MacDonnell was a schemer on a giant scale, moving her children up the ladder of power and influence with delusions of having a grandchild or great-grandchild sit on a throne one day. She'd give Livia of ancient Rome a run for her money. Cat thought she could trust Roland and Valeria, but she was certain she could never trust Mina. That woman would stick her in a ditch the first chance she got. She was enamored with Bree though. Maybe the girl was their ticket to softening her grandmother. *Or maybe when Mina puts me down in that ditch, she'll just take Bree for herself.*

CHAPTER 14

THIS OLD MAN . . .

Magnus Proust resided in one of the cells reserved for political prisoners—nobles whose offenses were less dire than treason. He was chained to a chair bolted to the center of the room, however, and could not utilize the fireplace, feather bed, or desk with parchment and quill. Magnus wore only a bloody loincloth—they had castrated him because a hag who'd read Lara's future once said his descendant would be her undoing—a senselessly cruel act since wizards of the council vowed abstinence and never married. His fingers were broken, teeth were missing, and his right eye was swollen shut and crusted with pus. Trickles of blood dripped from under the leather collar around his neck. Below the chair was an overflowing bedpan that reeked of stale blood, urine, and feces. Chryslantha would have to spoon-feed him the soup she'd brought. The bearskin rug under his feet at least kept the granite's chill off the old man's bones, but the barred window was too small to let in much sunlight. The wizard nevertheless looked pleased to see Chryslantha Godwynn—or maybe it was the hot soup.

Proust was an enigma—ancient, almost sixty, with a balding pate that he often covered with a skullcap. Chrys had known him for most of her life—amiable, often jovial; he enjoyed playing tricks on children to their delight. Yet, as children became adults and became cognizant of his great power and its burdens, they politely shied away from the magus as did all men from things that made them feel small and inadequate. All except his students, who were proud to study under a sitting member of the Wizards' Council—the very council that protected the Twelve Kingdoms from ambitiously deranged sorcerers and had been frustratingly quiet through this invasion. Did even they fear the White Lady?

"How fares your father?" Proust asked, his voice hoarse and low, but his one good hazel eye bright and alert.

"I am told he still lives, but have not seen him or my mother. It is for my sister I fear—there has been no sign of her." She pulled up a chair and sat so as not to make him crane his neck. She fed him two spoonfuls of soup. "Master Proust, I've been sent to question you regarding Callum and the prince."

"Would you truly have me divulge where I've sent them?"

"I would not. But the White Lady is . . . insistent. Athelstan has yielded. Lara believes she's won this conflict fairly and that our continuance to resist is bad form. She has threatened to kill the nobles, starting with Sophia. I've agreed to this inquiry to bide time until . . ." *Until what? Litigate a truce?* Her authority and privilege had been stripped; this was the new world order.

Proust swallowed a mouthful of soup and finished her thoughts. "Until we are rescued?" he said.

It sounded foolish when said aloud.

"You will keep your promise to the White Lady and curry her favor. I shall speak true to you, as you should to her. Lara can sniff out a lie like a . . ."

"No, Magnus!" she said, horrified. *Surely he knew enough to lie.* "I cannot put Callum and the prince in jeopardy."

"I have known you since you were three, Chryslantha . . . you would risk yourself to save as many as you could—but believe me when I tell you this—the truth will not help Farrenheil and it will extend your life and that of Sophia. Callum and the prince are not in the city—or even in the kingdom. They are not on this world."

"Have they beaten you senseless, Magnus?"

He chuckled. "Listen, and open your mind, child. Our universe is but one of many realms in the gods' creation. A celestial rind separates each realm. In each reality exists a world connected to its counterparts in the other realms. I visited one such world—a beautiful place, with knights and maidens much like ours . . . I helped a young king attain his throne and defend it against his half-sister, a sorceress cut from the same rotted bolt of fabric as the White Lady." Proust looked lost in his nostalgia. "She broke my heart."

"I do not recall you being away for any length of time, Magnus."

"From Aandor, no. How old would you say I am?"

"Two and fifty . . ."

"Flatterer. I have seen sixty-three winters, but I was born in Gull Harbor forty-one years ago."

"That is not possible. They've addled your mind."

"The not possible is the currency of wizards. It's what we trade and barter to elevate our renown and finance our learning. But I assure you I am not mad. Time between this realm and the other is not constant. Imagine two men cast off in parallel rivers at dawn, one slow, the other a raging rapid. By noon, the man in the faster river has traveled farther in the same length of time. So it is between these realms. When I returned to Aandor after a few years, only a few days had passed here. Magical energy is sparse on that earth, so of course they develop other philosophies to compensate. They had made many wondrous advances in engineering and the sciences the second time I visited that realm. Since then, I wondered what new marvels they might have . . ."

He looked off and turned melancholy, shaken.

"Magnus?" Chryslantha prodded with a spoonful of soup.

Tears fell from his one good eye. "I was blind," he confessed. "Excited for my return . . . addicted to my wanderlust . . . my desire to again visit this other realm. I was negligent of my chief responsibility . . . to protect this family and this kingdom. The signs of this invasion were evident. But I was not paying attention. Resources spent preparing for my return, anticipating changes in their language and science, would have been better served spying on Farrenheil, conferring with my peers. I failed those that placed their trust in me—and one that was dear to me . . ."

"Magnus, men have waged war since the dawn of time. You cannot control the hearts of men."

"I tried to make amends for my shortcomings. I used the spell prepared for my journey—for I had planned to leave soon after the naming day ceremony—and instead sent the prince and his guardians. I gave the guardians spells to acclimate them quickly to that foreign land and gold, which has value even there. I covered their escape and delayed pursuit. Dorn and his party would have arrived years after the guardians. That arrogant leech had no clue what he was walking into . . . no money, no language on a world where magic was virtually nonexistent."

Proust began to laugh. Chrys was worried . . . the strain of imprisonment could crack anyone. He read her concern.

"I still have my wits," he said. "I was relishing the greatest of ironies. Any great portal requires tremendous magical energy, more than is readily available. I use a druid's circle in the Blue Forest—it collects magic like a reservoir and takes years to replenish. But Lara's spell to transport whole armies within this realm required even more power; she created a singularity to bend space. The gods do not take kindly to those who chip away at the foundations of their creation. Wizards died and relics were destroyed for sure, and I dread to think what else she'd sacrifice to harness such power. But there was much of it. For those such as clerics and druids who can see the flow of power, Aandor City would have appeared brighter than the sun on the day of the invasion. Spells shed magic, and the bigger the spell, the more the excess. As the enemy moved men into our city, I siphoned this excess magic to *my* portal." Magnus grinned wickedly—a harrowing sight in his current state. "Lara herself supplied the magic for the prince's escape!"

In this cold and desolate cell, Chryslantha found the unimaginable. Hope. Callum lived!

"How will they return?"

"With the help of an old friend. I sent an acolyte—a very capable young lady—to contact this wizard and lead the guardians to him."

Chrys looked kindly upon the old man. He smiled back—a grisly visage of pummel marks and broken teeth, stubborn white stubble on a face wizened by numerous creases for the effort. *Only forty,* Chrys thought. "Magnus, if years pass quickly over there . . ."

"The prince may be close to twenty when he returns—a man of legal status instantly capable of reigning. That should give so-called *neutral* kingdoms a kick in the arse," he said. "Should they renege on their obligation to the accords, contracts signed in blood with the blessing of the prelates and witnessed by the Wizards' Council, the council will step in to set their affairs straight."

"And Callum . . . ?"

Proust turned sullen. "I am sorry, child . . . truly. If your betrothed yet lives, he will be almost as old as I."

Her heart turned heavy. Again her fear of losing Cal manifested . . . the fates conspired against their union. Her emotions dipped and peaked as though fixed to a bandalore. How much longer would the gods toy with her?

"I could not risk simply moving them to some other part of the kingdom," Proust explained sympathetically. "The White Lady is cunning and powerful. With just Daniel's blanket, she would have found the boy anywhere on the continent. Please forgive me, Lady Godwynn."

Chrys took but a moment to recall whom her betrothed was— Callum MacDonnell was as honorable as a summer day is long. He would count the days, dream of her until their reunion. It would be less time by far for Chryslantha, so how could she not receive him in whatever condition the fates returned him to her? Almost twenty years separated Mina from Cal's father, James, and their devotion was truer than most. "I would have him back at any age," she whispered to herself.

"Aye," Proust agreed. "Love conquers all."

"You saved the prince. You saved my beloved from a certain death. For this I am grateful."

An explosion shook the city. The cell rattled slightly, bits of mortar and dust rained around them. Chryslantha propped a stool under the window and lifted herself to it. "By the gods!"

"What is it, child?" asked Proust.

"Fire and smoke in the Aavanteen. Soldiers running in alarm."

She cheered in her heart for the insurgents; she hoped soldiers of Farrenheil lay dead. She hated them more than ever. Those who resisted Farrenheil struck for her as well. She would see the Farrenheisi all dead for what they had done to Aandor—for what they had done to her life.

CHAPTER 15

IF A TREE FALLS IN A FOREST . . .

Allyn Grey headed south on the Taconic belting out Aretha's "Respect" to the stereo and trying to decide whether the Tappan Zee would be faster than the GW at this time of day. Then, it was everywhere—the howl—for what else would one call the excruciating interruption that battered his senses like hammers on porcelain? He quickly put the car onto the shoulder until he could reduce that wail to a whisper.

Something familiar resonated in that connection—some hint of wizardry. It was inhuman . . . a plea for help, the sound of earth itself dying. Allyn turned around at the next exit and headed back to Malcolm's mansion.

The trucks were gone—so were the helicopters . . . and people. Did anyone else hear it, or only the blessed chosen sensitive to the gods' energy? The reverberations of the scream led back through the henge, which functioned like an amplifier. He followed the cry back to its origin along the lay stream—back to Rosencrantz.

The group's vans sat locked and empty at the foot of the trail into the woods. Allyn took a flashlight and began the hike. His shoes were not the best for it, but he hadn't time to change . . .

the cry was fading. Three-quarters of the way there, the bodies came into view. Some looked fresh, soldiers brought down with bullets—others not so fresh—rancid corpses raised from their rest. *Necromancer's work.*

At the final ridge, the trees leaned toward the road, many torn up at their roots. The meadow was dying—it had been hit by blight. Fetid bodies littered the once pristine field. Some of the undead remained animated, but he didn't fear them, for the undead could not harm clerics of a god of light in daylight; they wandered around him with no purpose. As he approached the wizard tree, ozone lingered in the air. He remembered that smell like it was yesterday . . . the scent of a portal to another universe.

Chasaubaan's body lay slumped against Rosencrantz, his hand still clutching the bone wand that had pierced the trunk. *That would do it,* Allyn thought. Allyn knew touching the wand would mean his instant death as well. Perhaps if he pulled on the necromancer's arm? Except, Allyn didn't want to touch the necromancer's corpse any more than he wanted to handle the wand. *Necromancer's corpse?* There lay an ironic quandary if Allyn had ever heard of one. *There ought to be a special word for it,* he mused to distract from the fear of what had happened to his friends . . . and the prince.

In the trailer, the portal to Puerto Rico had been cut. Allyn didn't have Helen Reyes's number, but could find it back at the mansion. He found a large open-ended wrench and a trash can liner. The necro-wand tapered from the fist and ball to the pointy end that stuck in the tree. Allyn slipped the wrench around the thin section closest to the trunk and slid the tool up until the wand's girth filled the socket. Then he jimmied it out of the tree, but the wand remained in the necromancer's death grip.

Lelani's dagger stuck out of Chasaubaan's leg. *They certainly threw the kitchen sink at this bastard.* He pulled out the dagger and used it to cut the wrist, putting the wand and hand into the trash bag.

Dark sap oozed out of Rosencrantz. Its foul odor choked the senses. Allyn was not sure how to heal a tree. He placed his hands on Rosencrantz, wishing he'd studied more of the druidic disciplines at seminary. Allyn cast the only blessing he knew on the tree. He sensed Rosencrantz pulling magic from the lay line as he did this, casting a spell, and this gave Allyn hope that the tree might heal itself with his aid. This went on for a time until it abruptly stopped. All of Rosencrantz's life energy dissipated— the spark of sentience gone. Its leaves turned brown, red, and white, and began to fall.

Allyn sat back on a root in disbelief, struggling with sorrow for the loss of one of God's most unique and magnificent creations. He thought he'd been helping the tree. He cried until long shadows reached toward him, and the cleric realized he needed to get out of that meadow before sunset. As he stood, a golden acorn dropped on his shoulder and landed on his shoe. There were no other nuts beside that one. It had a shine about it. He picked it up. It throbbed warmly with life and energy—the gods' energy. The acorn dispelled Allyn's grief. He stood in awe of it for a moment before leaving. The sun had set by the time Allyn returned to the mansion; he went to his room to nap before heading home.

Consciousness crept back like a sneaking teenager at dawn. He'd slept longer than intended. The amber-reddish glow of the sun on his lids said it was morning—the rustling said he was not alone. He cracked one eye open slowly and found the dark muzzle of an assault rifle staring back. The men were covered head to toe in paramilitary assault gear, much like Ladue's men; the key difference being that on the gunmen's vests, in yellow vinyl, were the letters "FBI."

CHAPTER 16

THE PRINCE OF AANDOR

1

They'd feasted on roast pheasant and small potatoes sautéed with peppers and dried tomato, poached fish, something rolled that they pronounced "al-oh-wed" that tasted like veal, and string beans and asparagus doused in a delicious apple cider vinegar. Whatever Cat MacDonnell expected of medieval fare, this meal surpassed it. She was certain the peasants never ate this well—something about the meal troubled her, though—she couldn't shake the feeling that this was like the meal they served on death row the night before an execution. The comfort with which Mina accepted their gilded cage troubled Cat.

Mina believed this war was like the previous skirmishes in her experience—she hadn't seen Aandor City under occupation, was not cognizant of the enemy's dominance in her nation, scouring the forest, rooting out farmers, peasants, and wizards. While she was safe in this canvas castle, she could not envision the breadth of the invasion, which left no room for Aandor's nobility to surrender or capitulate. *Farrenheil needs land—forests, farms, mines, and castles with which to reward its own lords and knights for their great risks,* Cal had told Cat. Castle Meanmnach, the Mac-Donnell ancestral home in the north, might not yet be in enemy hands, but eventually Mina would come to a rude awakening. Her husband, James, was simply too close to Archduke Athelstan. If Mina were lucky, she might be allowed to live out her life in some backwoods cabin, and that only because she had no blood rights to the MacDonnell lands except through her children. But did a soldier of Roland's rank and experience know better? That was the million-dollar question.

Mina was enamored with Bree and sat her to her immediate right. Cat was placed at the other end. Mina no longer doubted the truth of their story—if the iPad photos weren't enough, Cal's features were stamped strongly on Bree's face. Cat remained wary of her mother-in-law and recognized some element of scheming behind the matriarch's eyes—some way of saving face at court and repairing Cal's betrothal with the most desired maiden in the kingdom.

"What?! Is this true?" Mina decried in response to something Bree said. Mina turned her attention to Cat and said, "Brianna does not yet have her own pony?" Cat gave her mother-in-law a weak smile, a shrug, and decided to try the wine after all.

"My bairns had their first pony at the age of five," Mina declared.

Mom is chapping my ass, Cat thought, but continued to smile. "I'll talk to Cal," Cat promised. "If I see him again."

Mina dazzled Bree with all the presents awaiting her at Castle Meanmnach once they returned. The fallacy that they would ever see that castle was too much for Cat to bear. She turned to Roland and bluntly asked, "Do we have a plan? Other than bloating ourselves with food and floating down the river like pontoons?"

"Not one that would see my brother's family away safely," Roland said. "There is too much chaos out there right now."

"Then you don't disagree that leaving here's a priority?" Cat said hopefully. "We have to find the pri—"

Roland grabbed her wrist and squeezed hard enough to make Cat wonder if her bones would snap. He looked around the tent subtly before settling a steely gaze on her that said, *Not here.* Roland had not been fooled by the rules of honor and chivalry.

"We have to do many things," he whispered. Roland released her arm. "The timing is not right."

"We don't have time," she whispered back.

"For myself, I do not care," Roland said. "I am an old soldier and prepared to die. But Mina and the girls . . . I cannot jeopardize their safety."

Two guards entered the tent followed by Sir Arnulf and then a short, portly, colorful blond man of about forty decked in loose robes of green and yellow velvet with gold embroidery and gold silk slippers. His rosy cheeks brought to mind cherry tomatoes; periwinkle eyes, wispy golden eyebrows, and a magnificent mustache that curled up and around on the ends completed the doll-like visage. Each stout finger sported a jeweled ring and glittered as he waved his hands about as he spoke.

"Cousins!" the round man exclaimed. He looked remarkably happy to see them. "I hope that your feast was satisfying."

"The pheasant was dry," Mina critiqued.

"Ah, yes . . . well . . . apologies. That will not be a problem in the future. I have wonderful news," he said stressing "wonderful" and making it twice as long as it ought to be. "A fresh company marches east from Aandor City to relieve us in Yarmouth."

"This is good news," Mina confirmed. "Shall they expect us in Aandor, then?"

Onyx looked as though he'd bitten a bitter olive. "Ahhh . . . well—you see my dear—my troops have been ordered north . . . to Castle Meanmnach. You are going home."

Mina looked disconcerted. "Will you now bring this war to the north?"

"Cousin, cousin . . . there is *no* war," Lord Onyx stressed. "The conflict is settled and the sooner everyone accepts this, the better it will be for all."

"You would do well to remember that Roland has an army to the east," Mina said.

"Yes, and its general and officers are my honored guests here in camp. And soon enough, that won't matter because it's all part of the plan, you see. The eastern army will cease to be soon enough. So please, cousins, help me . . . I truly wish an end to violence."

"Yes," said Roland with a mild touch of the sardonic. "We would all like to see an end to that. What would you have of us, Onyx?"

"I am to establish a command post at Castle Meanmnach. Your husband has approved this, of course, Mina."

"Of course he has," she said drily.

"You will encourage the people to a peaceful transition. If they do not resist, your tenants will hardly notice us. My soldiers will hunt and fish your lands with nary a bother to your folk. All the great lords of this land are agreeing to such compromises. Why even Lord Godwynn has agreed to a full battalion stationed on his property by next week . . . his gratitude for looking after his daughters at Aandor Castle during this terrible mess."

Mina stared at the rotund little man with a look Cat would

dub *cockroach on the dinner table*. The truth finally nestled into the matriarch's bones. Cat wished she could enjoy Mina's epiphany more, but she was sad for the woman. To her credit, Mina smiled and nodded, submitting to the thinly veiled charade. Cat hoped this latest news would prod Roland to action—survival had become day-to-day.

"One more thing," Onyx said, snapping his many-ringed fingers as though just remembering, "to ensure the peace. Valeria and I are to wed."

"What?!" they all said in unison.

"By the gods, man, you're already married to my wife's cousin," Roland pointed out.

"A union that has failed to produce an heir," Onyx countered with a pout. "Grand Duke Vaulknar has annulled my marriage. Poor Lucretia. But I think life with the Sweet Sisters will suit her better. Let us hope that my marriage with Valeria will be more fruitful."

Valeria looked to be near panic and Cat could not blame her. "I . . . I cannot," Valeria said. The girl clutched her chest, trying to draw breath. She found the pin Daniel had put on her. "This . . . this token. The prince bestowed it on me," she said in desperation. "I am under the prince's protection. I cannot marry without his leave," she said, grasping, trying to clutch at some legal loophole in a world without laws—forgetting that no one knew Daniel was of age.

"Are you the consort of an infant?" Onyx asked amused. "And they call me wicked."

"When?" Mina asked curtly, suppressing intense rage at the rotund little man. Someone other than her had arranged a marriage for her eldest daughter, which on any normal day was offense enough to invoke her wrath, but it was doubly distasteful now.

Onyx spun his hands as though to stir the answers from the air before him. "Well . . ."

Four soldiers entered with two prelates in tow, dressed in ceremonial garb.

It was a squeeze play. Valeria's marriage brought hereditary legitimacy to Onyx's claim to Meanmnach, especially if she got pregnant with a boy . . . Cat doubted James MacDonnell, Mina, Meghan, or Laurence would make it through the month alive. Valeria was shaking. Mina put her arm around the girl, the first show of tenderness Cat had seen since meeting the matriarch.

The prelate from Yarmouth—a prisoner—refused to officiate the marriage. He was rewarded with his own left hand. They dragged him whimpering from the tent clutching his bleeding stump.

"In Verakhoon, they don't consider it a proper wedding unless some blood is spilled," said Lord Onyx, with a giggle for his wit. "I'd hoped to involve some local clergy for posterity's sake but oh well . . ."

The second prelate was Onyx's personal man. A garland was placed on Valeria's head and she was dragged next to Onyx.

"Mother . . . ," she pleaded.

"Fear not," said Mina. "You may yet be a maiden by week's end."

Onyx grew redder than usual. "I don't like it when people say such things of me!" he complained. "If that bitch speaks again, give her the back of your gauntlet," he said to Arnulf.

"So much for chivalry," Cat said in a mock whisper.

"Can we get on?!" Onyx snapped at his prelate.

It was a very short ceremony performed at swordpoint. The

bride cried through all of it; it broke Cat's heart almost as much as Valeria's. Cat held Bree tightly before her, praying that Cal's daughter would go unnoticed in the plots and schemes of these barbarians.

"My bride and I shall be in our wedding chamber," Onyx declared, pulling Valeria to the back of his tent. "As tradition dictates, you're all welcome to watch as I claim her maidenhoo—"

Someone outside the tent raised an alarm. Several horns followed.

"Pray tell, what now?" said Onyx.

A soldier ran in, panicked. "We're under attack, milord!"

"Attack? Impossible. By whom?"

"We don't kn—" An arrow pierced the speaker's throat from behind.

"Go! Fight!" Onyx ordered Arnulf and other soldiers in the tent; only his two personal guards remained.

Roland subtly herded the women behind him. Cat suspected this was the moment they'd been waiting for. The enemy soldiers had ignored her Mace can, not recognizing it for a weapon, and she readied it. Cat nudged Bree into Valeria's arms just as Roland very calmly picked up a small iron kettle and brained the guard closest to him. The other guard rushed in, and Cat doused him. As he went down crying in pain, Roland brained him, too. Onyx and the prelate tried to run past Cat toward the exit; she tripped the rotund lordling. As Onyx tried to resume his escape, Roland put one of the guardsmen's swords to his throat.

"Guards!" Onyx cried out, but the din of battle outside the tent was fierce—no one heard.

"Cry out again, *cousin.*"

"Let's not be hasty, MacDonnell. I have four hundred men. Exactly where do you intend to go?"

"Can we trade him for horses?" Cat asked.

Roland shook his head. They had the upper hand at the moment but were short one very good long-term plan.

Cat grabbed the other guard's sword and poked her head outside of the tent. No guards, no sign of the prelate, and bedlam everywhere. The attackers looked like peasants and farmers. Onyx's soldiers were too busy trying to stay alive to pay attention to the tent. "Good a time as any," Cat said. "Do we kill him?"

Roland and Mina looked uncomfortable with the suggestion. "He's a nobleman . . . ," Roland said, as though that explained it.

Onyx began to threaten with all the slow tortures he would heap upon their family. Roland struck the glass-jawed aristocrat unconscious with a solid right hook.

"Now can we kill him?" Cat repeated.

A flask of burning oil struck the wall of the tent, and it caught flame.

"Everyone out now!" Roland commanded, leaving Onyx to his fate.

Val carried Bree, and Mina held both her daughters; Cat found a large horse blanket to cover them, like a moving tent. The Mac-Donnells exited with Cat and Roland in the front. They snaked their way through the skirmishes trying to look as unassuming as possible. Along the way, they came across Roland's lieutenant, Manus Bryce, armed and battling.

"Manus, to us!" Roland cried. "We make for the forest!"

Cat let the two soldiers handle the bulk of any resistance ahead of them. "Wait! We have to get Lelani," Cat said.

"There's no time!" Roland objected.

But as they passed the pen that held the centaur, Cat climbed over the rail.

Lelani failed to recognize her at first. Her eyes were swollen; she was black and blue all over and bleeding from that damnable collar. Her back legs were manacled to an iron spike in the ground. Cat hugged her friend, choking back tears for what they'd done to this beautiful woman.

"Catherine, we must go," Roland pleaded.

"Not without Lelani," said Bree.

Cat sliced the ropes that bound the centaur's hands. "Can you whammy that lock on the manacle?"

Lelani shook her head.

Cat found a mallet in the corner. She swung at the spike several times, loosening the dirt, and then began to dig with her fingers. Lieutenant Bryce helped her and they pulled the spike out. They placed the tip of the spike on the chain between Lelani's legs and Bryce struck the head over and over until it snapped. They could worry about the manacle bracelets later.

They resumed their creep through the fighting. Cat saw a male centaur battling in the mix. Lelani saw him, too, and was just as perplexed. Near the camp's edge, they pressed themselves against a large outcrop of granite jutting from the earth. Fifty yards at the bottom of the hill were the trees. Together they dashed for the tree line . . . they were halfway there when Sir Arnulf's company cut them off. A singed and bruised Lord Onyx was with them.

"Kill them all," Onyx ordered. "Except for my wife."

So much for nobility, Cat thought. She pulled Bree out of Val's hold and turned her back to the archers. The archers drew their bows. Cat said her first prayer in thirteen years. She heard the twang of their bows . . . and . . .

Nothing.

Cat looked up to see the arrows stuck in space, as though the air had become taffy.

Standing above them on that granite protrusion, like Moses parting the Red Sea, was Seth. "I really need to work on making that shield harder," he said.

Ahbahdaan's wizard squad rushed forward.

"Seth, run!" cried Lelani, but too late. They'd pegged him with several darts.

"Fucking ow!" Seth cried, plucking them and throwing them down.

"Take him!" ordered Ahbahdaan.

Seth cast a hard wind and batted the wizard hunters away twenty feet. They were shocked at his ability, but quickly recovered and fired another salvo at him, which Seth dodged. Seth sprang up and cast again . . . all the bows and dart guns transformed into purple blossoms and fell apart in their wielders' hands.

"Swords!" ordered Arnulf and they marched toward the MacDonnells. Out of the forest behind Onyx's men came a terrifying war cry. Twenty large, armed, and very pissed-off centaurs charged out of the trees and took Arnulf's squad down from the rear.

"May I borrow this?" Lelani asked of Cat's sword.

Lelani charged Ahbahdaan. He twisted a ring and her sword deflected off a shield. She struck again and again to no avail. He touched an earring and she went down into the mud as though a great weight pressed on her. The wizard hunter drew a dagger and hovered above her. Cat couldn't reach them in time to do anything; she looked in horror as Ahbahdaan readied to plunge the knife. Lelani jabbed the hunter in the foot with a small object that cut through his shield. It was one of those faerie silver darts. She rose and jabbed him in the neck with it. Ahbahdaan screamed and lost his concentration. He put his hands up to fend off Lelani's next attack, and she sliced his fingers off, rings and all, with one swipe of the sword. Then she sliced upward and hacked off his ear, then the other. They jangled like chimes as they tumbled through the air. The hunter fell to the ground crying. He begged for mercy. Lelani reared up and crushed his head with three hundred pounds of hoof.

Arnulf's troop was the last squad standing. With a hundred enemy combatants closing in on them, Arnulf yielded, and they threw down their weapons.

"Fight!" ordered Lord Onyx. "I am the lord of Castle Meanmnach! I must get to my castle! Fiiiiight! You miserable cowards!"

The field turned quiet, except for Lord Onyx and the wind. Citizens of Yarmouth silently spilled out of the town to witness the carnage on their slope—to confirm that the enemy army had been vanquished.

A knight on a huge chestnut-colored warhorse rode slowly down the slope toward the MacDonnells, leading a retinue of men and centaurs. Next to him was a man who looked a lot like François Ladue. As the knight drew closer, Cat realized the knight was not a man but a boy. A black phoenix rising against a red field bordered by gold was painted crudely on his Kevlar body armor. He wore bronze shin guards over his jeans and a bronze barbute on his head. His sword was bloody and the remnants of someone's brain decorated his sneakers.

"Daniel?"

"Robin Hood," Daniel said from atop the warhorse and smiled. He saw Valeria crying tears of joy and asked, "Are you okay?"

"I am now, Your Grace," she said, touching the pin he'd given her as though it had protected her.

"You are addressing my wife," said Lord Onyx. "This . . . this *victory* is a farce. There are forty thousand soldiers of Farrenheil on the plain of Deorwine outside the capital."

"Who's this guy?" asked Seth.

"I am the rightful lord of Meanmnach Castle and all the lands that once belonged to the MacDonnells. Valeria MacDonnell is my lawful wife . . ."

"Oh shut up," said Mina.

"And this . . . this farce of a win means nothing. Six hundred men ride east to relieve us here. You will be routed within a day."

Sir Arnulf looked like he wanted to plant a mace into Onyx's skull for revealing their troop position.

"I'm gone barely two days and you get hitched," Daniel said to Valeria. She smiled weakly.

"You're gone two days and you show up with your own army?" Cat shot back.

"This is the prince, then?" Roland asked his niece.

"Aye," confirmed Valeria.

Ladue jumped off his horse and ran to Lelani, the anguish at her appearance evident on his face. He removed his jacket and covered her. She embraced him, put her arms around his strong shoulders. He caressed her and kissed her tenderly.

"Cat?" Daniel inquired about the scene.

"Well that's news to me," Cat said. "But the white-haired guy is Cal's uncle—big-time general. The lady is Cal's mother—real piece of work. Pissed-off guy is Lord Onyx of Farrenheil who sacked Yarmouth and just married Valeria at swordpoint to claim her family's lands."

"I saw a telenovela just like this once," Seth interjected.

Daniel rode up to the portly blond lord. "Onyx, you and Valeria are not wed by order of . . . well, me."

"I do not recognize your authority, pretender! The true prince is but a babe still in swaddling and secreted by radicals somewhere in this land. As for my marriage, an ordained prelate performed it, and what the gods have blessed only they may tear asunder."

Daniel dismounted and approached Onyx.

"Your Grace, Onyx has not yielded," warned Roland. Daniel acknowledged this with a nod.

2

The bodies of friend and foe littered the battlefield. Daniel finally understood the toll of war: *Even when you win, you lose.* Daniel could see Grohk's corpse, one of the original centaurs they'd saved from the ambush—an amiable fellow with a talent for whittling. Next to him lay Collin, one of the farmers that originally was against anything having to do with the centaurs—they'd fought back to back. Only this morning, Collin and Grohk had exchanged humorous comparisons of child rearing between their races. They'd planned to introduce their sons once the conflict had settled. And now they were dead.

Daniel looked up at the town, the columns of smoke still streaming up from earlier fires. He thought about all those innocents on the pyre—that sickly smell of barbecue, which permeated the forest. He thought of Fiona's dead son. How many more people suffered like that across the kingdom? And then he looked at the little man before him demanding his rights as the victor of a war like it was all some neat little game with rules. It was a sneak attack, a cheat . . . a sucker punch—just because Daniel was born.

This little shit thought his rank and position protected him . . . that he had some value for barter. Onyx might be right. Who knew what allies they could trade him for? Daniel wanted to be merciful. Each person he killed he hoped would be the last for the rest of his life. But he had read all the books—from Machiavelli to Sun Tzu—and everything he'd learned pointed to the reality that somewhere between ruthless and soft was a balance that made an effective leader.

He looked around at the thousands of eyes on him. One pair, green like moss under moonlight, struck him hardest—a centaur, swollen, black, blue, burned, and bleeding—her once long red hair shorn, her tail hacked, her beauty transformed into a metaphor for this conflict.

"Your Grace," Lelani acknowledged with a painful bow.

Daniel seethed. "Lord Onyx . . . I agree with you," he said. "Do you?"

"Valeria is a virtuous woman. A divorce would be disreputable to a maiden of her station." Daniel faced the little lord. "What is it priests say in marriage vows . . . about parting?"

Daniel drew back his sword as Cal taught him all those hours hacking at beef. It seemed to dawn on Lord Onyx at the very last instant that maybe this young man didn't give a pig's fart whether he recognized him as the prince or not. Onyx began to say the words "I yield," but only got as far as "ye—" before the sword sliced through his voice box and sent his head tumbling onto the blood-drenched earth. Valeria sighed in relief—as did her mother.

The victors began to chant—men, women, and centaurs stomped and rumbled in a deep baritone that shook the hill.

"DANEL! DANEL! DANEL! ALL HAIL THE PRINCE OF AANDOR!"

CHAPTER 17

ROLE PLAYING

"We can't stay here," Daniel told Sadon Althalus, one of the surviving aldermen of Yarmouth. By "we" Daniel meant townsfolk as well as his men. They met in the late lord magistrate's dining room. Roland MacDonnell and his two remaining officers sat to Daniel's right; Cat, Seth, the MacDonnells, Lelani, and Klaugh—the leader of the centaurs Daniel saved in the woods—stood on the fringes; Ladue stood behind Daniel as serious as a heart attack; and on the prince's left sat the leaders of Yarmouth.

"Your Grace . . . ," Sadon began hesitantly—not everyone was sold on Daniel's pedigree, despite his birthmark. But it would appear ungrateful to argue with the town's savior. "Where are we to go?"

"North . . . or east with us. Just not west."

"But we must defend the town."

"We cannot hold the town," Roland MacDonnell interjected a second time. Daniel had found an able ally in the general, thanks to Cat and Valeria. With that, Roland's support was absolute, including accepting Ladue as Daniel's captain and bodyguard. Roland had Cal's best qualities plus years of experience, which translated into a deep, calm confidence. Sadon, however, was draining everyone's patience. "Yarmouth's water source is outside the city, and the walls will not withstand a siege."

"Red King's Gate is the safest place for folk," added Sergeant Urry. Roland's chief soldier was a large man, strong but amiable, with a thick black head of hair and a beard that would be more at home on a pirate ship than a battlefield.

"Such a trek," Sadon fretted.

Sadon's concerns about the old and infirm, the women and children, were valid. Some of them might die on a long journey. Daniel felt guilty forcing a march on the townspeople, removing them from their homes. He'd barely solved the logistics of making it to microeconomics from gym class; now he was transporting a whole town to the edge of the kingdom. He needed to pull a rabbit out of a hat.

Considering magic, Daniel naturally turned to Lelani. Food, first aid, and a hot shower improved her considerably—less torture victim, more Marine camp grunt. She had been elbowing Klaugh in the ribs for the past ten minutes; he kept swatting her arm. The two redheads reminded Daniel of bickering siblings.

"We can shelter those who cannot journey north," Klaugh offered, reluctantly.

Daniel and Roland simultaneously realized this was the solution. The aldermen gave each other grave, perplexed stares.

"Are you to trust our people to these . . . these . . ."

"Don't say it," Daniel warned with a stiff finger. "The centaur village is just a few miles into the Blue. They can defend it better than Yarmouth. We took out Farrenheil's camp in the forest and they're not yet ready for a full affront. There are ogres, trolls, gnolls, and other things that still scare the crap out of them."

"I'm well aware of what lies in the forests, young man . . .

errr . . . Your Grace," added Sadon. "Will *we* not be prey to the very same monsters?"

"If you remain with our escort, all will be safe," Klaugh assured them.

Roland brusquely dismissed the town leaders, who fretted on their way out over how to tell their folk they were either going to live in the woods with centaurs or joining the army. Daniel made the right decision—and shoved it down their throats. They resented him for it.

"You got what you wanted," Daniel told Jarin and his farmers. "Into the woods with your families."

"Nay, Your Grace. The wives'll be taking the wee ones and going with the horse folk . . . the men will be joining you east." Jarin smiled in that way that said, *We're following you no matter what.* The other farmers agreed.

So Jarin and his neighbors now trust Klaugh enough to let him guard their families. Will wonders never cease?

"We'll be targets," Cat said.

"We're already targets," Seth noted.

"What I mean is, is it really such a good idea for the prince of Aandor to be riding through the forest playing soldier?"

"His Grace is not *playing* at anything," Roland said, perplexed by Cat's concern. "He has a hundred men pledged to him."

"His Grace has saved us the trouble of levying soldiers," noted Sergeant Urry. "Townsmen are volunteering five at a time."

"He's a child," Cat said.

The officers looked at each other, collectively baffled.

"The prince is but months from legal age, milady," said Lieutenant Bryce.

"It's a hundred miles of open road to that fort," Cat said.

"What's wrong with *us* hiding? Can't we can go with the centaurs?"

"It would dishearten the men if I ran," Daniel said. "And we've already dropped hints that I'm the prince of Aandor, returned as a man thanks to Proust's magicks."

"You're not a man."

Cat wasn't wrong. But people didn't fight for leaders who hid in the midst of trouble. "Farrenheil will come after me wherever I am. The townsfolk are safer without me among them. There's no strategic value right now in breaching the Blue Forest for women, children, and the infirm."

"Then hide somewhere else!" Cat shot back.

"Hiding's not a long-term solution . . . build a citadel, someone invents the cannon . . . hide in the desert, someone invents drones. Farrenheil would eventually find me wherever I holed up."

"The prince should be protected by his army," Roland said. "He has but one that we can reach safely, at Red King's Gate."

"And they're going to be attacked soon," Cat said.

"We have to warn them," Daniel said.

"There's no safer place for the prince than the Gate," Sergeant Urry insisted.

"Am I the only one who sees the lunacy in this?" Cat scolded the room. "They outnumber us. The only wars Danny's won were played with trading cards!" She grabbed her cup of wine and haughtily walked away from them.

The magistrate's servants piled the table with cheeses, bread, salted beef, fruit, more wine, and mead. They curtsied to Daniel and left. Daniel was amused by the notion that no one would stop him from pouring a flagon of mead—except maybe Catherine.

She was the older sister he never had, with a talent for morphing into his mom when she chose. Daniel appreciated the affection, even when delivered by her temper.

"Mina and the girls will go with the centaurs," Roland said.

Mina MacDonnell chuckled. "No."

"Mina . . ."

"We're heading north to Meanmnach . . . with Catherine and Brianna. You will do what you must, but I must go to Laurence. He is lord of the castle while his father and brother are away and will need my help rallying our vassals and banner men. Oh don't give me that look, Roland . . . His Grace has informed us that the enemy is south of the Sevren—once we've crossed the river, we should be safely ahead of their van."

Roland threw up his hands in frustration.

Cat stood silently in the corner rubbing her belly, nursing a cup of wine, and staring out of a small lead window that warped the street beyond it. Daniel approached the way one might a tiger and asked, "You okay?"

"Mmmmm," she murmured noncommittally. Daniel could have used Callum there to interpret that. She sipped her wine like medicine, looking tired and older than her scant thirty years.

"Should you be drinking?" he asked.

"It's medicinal," she shot back. "Doc said a glass a month was okay."

"You did well, Cat. Even with the belly."

"I'm channeling the sheriff from *Fargo*," she said.

"Darn tootin'," Daniel responded.

She turned dour again. "I don't know how to get home. I don't know where to go in this world." She laughed, with a touch of the maniacal. "God, that's a line out of a sci-fi movie; but here we are. You, Seth, and Lelani are my only friends; I don't want to separate . . . I don't want anyone to die."

"Cat, I thought I'd be in Puerto Rico right now, sneaking rum drinks and checking out beach girls," Daniel admitted. "I don't understand how I got *here*, but my instincts have kept me alive—all my life, in fact."

"And they tell you to lead this war from the front?"

"People who lead from behind all have the same stupid expression on their face when the jackass they put up front has them charging toward a cliff."

"You're assuming Balzac told the truth. They could have double the men he said and this whole effort really is hopeless."

"They could have half the men he said, and we'll have missed an opportunity to end this."

She took another sip, conceding the futility of their argument. "But why tell everyone who you really are? If things go south, you could have quietly made a life here. As anything."

"Fair point." He looked out the window as though the answer was on the street. "I was going to live a lie . . . after I killed Clyde. Convinced myself Costa Rica and a new name was my best option for a normal life. But it never sat well with me. Live or die, I'd rather do it as myself. These folks could have thought I was crazy claiming to be the prince of Aandor when rational thought says I'm an infant at this moment. They believed me."

"They're starved for a savior," Cat explained. "Even an impossible one."

"I don't know about savior," Daniel said. "But I do know what's right . . . like going back to take out that prison camp after we saved the centaurs. Turned out they had Ladue in there. He staged an escape just as we were figuring out a plan of attack—blew up the command center and their officers with grenades. We rolled in to help and shut them down. I won't lie—I was scared. But we got intelligence on all the enemy's piddly companies out there disrupting the local hamlets, to keep them from unifying. We added the prisoners from the camp to our ranks and started shutting those patrols down and taking on more men to fight. I learned how good a swordsman I am . . . how great a teacher Cal really is. This region's clean for ten miles.

"People commit themselves to a person they see is in their best interest. And for what it's worth, I believe what Balzac told us. He wanted something from us, and the truth was the only way he would have gotten it at that moment. That was the only strategy he could play."

"It's all a game," Cat said.

"Yeah. Look, maybe I've only ever played RPGs up to now. But strategy is strategy. I learned a lot playing against great players, and it still taught me how to allocate resources effectively, when to dig in, and when to risk striking out. A superior force doesn't guarantee a win. If it did, we'd all be speaking with British accents."

"Daniel . . ."

"I know this isn't a game, Cat. My decisions could put real people in coffins. But they want to fight. They *have* to fight; because this *isn't* a game—it's their lives. Numbers can't measure heart or determination. You can't quantify the lengths a man will go to save his family. This is not a hopeless cause."

Cat took another sip of wine. If she was aware that Daniel sought her approval, she wasn't letting on. "You're smart and you have a good heart, Danny. I want to believe you are right. But I have Bree. Back home, I know how to tie up the venetian blind cords and buckle her car seat and teach her about stranger danger. What can I teach her about here . . . I'm utterly lost."

"The MacDonnells will look after you until we can find Cal . . ."

"Ha!" she blurted. "Mina is willful and stubborn about the things she wants; and she never wanted me."

Daniel chuckled.

"Not funny," Cat stressed.

"No, of course not. I didn't mean . . . it's just . . . Mina reminds me a lot of . . . well, you."

Cat's smoldering glare made Daniel's point for him, except the irony, for lack of a mirror, was lost on her.

"I'm just saying, you're both tough—and stubborn, digging in to stand your ground even when it would be smarter to bend."

"She's an eight-hundred-pound gorilla in this kingdom . . . and I'm '*short.*' Her words, not mine."

Daniel spotted Mina fussing with Valeria's summer dress at the other end of the room, and looking quite cross with her daughter.

"Excuse me!" Daniel shouted above the din. He snapped his fingers and the room went silent. Daniel made a point of facing Mina and always coming back to her as he scanned the room with his eyes. The sudden attention unnerved the matriarch.

"Catherine is Callum MacDonnell's wife of seven years, a union I fully recognize. This is a matter of settled law as far as I'm concerned, and Catherine is due all the courtesies that befit her rank. She is like a sister to me. Those who treat her well in my absence will curry my favor. Those who do not . . ." Daniel let them fill in the rest with their imaginations—he had after all just beheaded a lord.

They all nodded graciously, even Mina with the most dumbfounded expression.

Cat opened and closed her mouth, searching for something to say.

"In a feudal monarchy, I'm the eight-*thousand*-pound gorilla," Daniel pointed out. "Now I'm going to catch some Zs before we ride out."

CHAPTER 18

BRIDGE OF SORROWS

The company had set out before dawn with more than two hundred men, leaving in Yarmouth the prisoners that neither Daniel nor the centaurs were equipped to restrain. It was frustrating—to have won the town only to realize they must abandon it.

Cat was relieved that Daniel left Arnulf alive, though he would surely inform his superiors of the insurgency. Except for his men's treatment of Lelani, Arnulf had acted honorably. The knight could just as easily have thrown them on a pyre or into a brothel after he captured them. They were safe now, in the company of family, and headed away from the mayhem.

Daniel had a knack for how this society worked. He'd earned Roland's respect in a short period—in fact, Daniel's talent for earning the loyalty of those around him was on steroids. They had all been psychologically defeated, disconsolate. No one expected a hero to arise . . . certainly not out of the forest leading farmers and centaurs. Those that would have fled instead bound themselves to him, put their lives in his hands. It saved them because scattered, the roving bands of the enemy would have picked them off easily. Together, they were a force to be feared. Daniel, whom Cat thought of as the little brother she never had, seemed older, bigger than life now.

Despite being six months pregnant, Cat chose a horse over riding in the coach with Mina. They found her a docile mare, and from this vantage Cat could see the wonders of Aandor the way she'd hoped when her plans included coming over with Cal. The air in Aandor, never touched by industrialization, was so pristine and oxygen rich it energized her like a teenager—she was high from simply breathing.

The company exited the forest canopy two miles south and uphill of Crowe's Porte. The vista looking down at this river town was like one of those grand oil paintings at the Met. The Sevren flowed west through a valley that cut the line of a mountain range to the east like a bike tire over a long earthworm. The plain on either side of the Sevren accommodated a patchwork of farms along the river. Farms carpeted all the empty space outside of town up to the forest and rolling east to the mountain range's base. The colors—greens, yellows, reds, and purples of nature—radiated Technicolor vibrancy, the noon sky was a Renaissance blue, and the majestic river, a line of glimmer glass that stretched a quarter mile wide to Crowe's Porte's sister town on the other bank. Spanning the river was a beautiful bridge of white marble abutments laid across in a series of barrel vaults topped with a smooth wood plank roadway. The bridge could have been designed by Michelangelo and transported directly from sixteenth-century Florence. The farmers, smiths, and tradesmen of Yarmouth talked of the bridge as one of the kingdom's great wonders—and surprisingly to Cat, most had never seen it though Yarmouth was barely thirty miles away. Once over the bridge, the company would part; Mina, Cat, and the girls would ride north to Meanmnach Castle while Daniel, Lelani, Seth, and the officers headed east to Red King's Gate.

Roland sent the company across the river to Hull's Porte, right away. It was the smaller of the two towns, and provided more open space for the men to bivouac in; they could rest and resupply there before the final push east.

"The general and I are going to update the town leaders before crossing over," Daniel told Cat.

"I'll stay with you and Lelani, if you don't mind," Cat said. "Just let me get Bree." She rode back to the middle of the column to the former lord magistrate's coach where Mina rode with the girls.

"It is undignified for a lady to ride in breeches" were Mina's last words to Cat for refusing to change into a dress or ride sidesaddle. Cal had said something similar when he started giving her riding lessons, but Cat held firm to learning how to ride like a "normal" person. Cat could run, kick, jump, and ride much better in pants and didn't intend now to let her mother-in-law saddle her with burdensome medieval lady garb designed to render women nothing more than objects of a man's attention. Valeria, however, had given up her lovely summer dress that made her look like "a brothel tart" for something conservatively long and brown.

Inside the coach, Bree and her aunt Meghan were curled asleep against each other on a bench.

"What news?" asked Mina.

"They are sending the company through to Hull's Porte while we parley with the leaders here. I came for Bree."

"Let her sleep," Mina implored.

"I'm not comfortable having a river between us . . ."

"Yes, yes, you want her close . . . I understand, Catherine. There's a tailor near the magistrate's home that I have business with. We will be but up the street. I will not ride over that bridge without you."

The image of Bree sleeping peacefully tugged at Cat's heart. Whatever else Mina might be, she *was* protective of family, in which she now included Brianna. Still . . .

"You'll stay with her, Val?"

"Of course," Valeria confirmed.

The town was very much what she'd expected: tightly built wooden homes, many with wood-tiled or thatched roofs, but for those who could afford stone or brick dwellings, their roofs were tiled with a dark blue clay that was uniform throughout the city, giving this river port a tranquil quality despite the bustle. Naming day bunting and decorations were still up. The home they sought was on a hill with many storefronts along a stone street. This was where the affluent dwelled.

From the magistrate's terrace, Cat and Lelani watched Lieutenant Bryce march the company across the bridge double file toward Hull's Porte. The lord magistrate himself had gone to Aandor for the naming day festivities. His son, the town's portreeve, was the most senior official available. "No nepotism there," Daniel said sarcastically in English. They found one other alderman who had also passed on traveling to the capital because of his gout. Sergeant Urry and Seth picked at fresh grapes in a bowl while Francois Ladue watched the horses, and the street, below.

"We'd suspected something was wrong," said the portreeve. "Until you appeared, no travelers have come from the west for three days. We sent out a treasury guardsman yesterday to investigate the smoke in Yarmouth and he never returned. We put a call out to reserves . . . mostly retired soldiers and guardsmen . . . and sent messengers to the archduke's banner men. There are a few east and north of town who would not have gotten caught up in the invasion yet. Earl Grafton comes to mind—he's older, but has led men in war—but then, there's no way to know which lords went to the capital and which are still available to lead. Men must have leaders."

"In desperate times, leaders emerge," Roland noted and looked at the prince. "How many fighting men do you expect?"

"A few have trickled in already—a hundred on the morrow."

"Too slow," Sergeant Urry said. "One hundred thirty thousand soldiers wreak havoc in the center of our kingdom while we build our force piecemeal on the fringes."

"I thought we were heading for an army," Seth noted.

"'Tis but ten thousand at the Gate," Roland said. "If we reach them in time."

Lelani continued to gaze at a specific spot on the river. She hadn't moved since they arrived.

"Worried about your magic?" Cat queried.

Lelani shook her head. "The magic will return once my body expunges the last of the silver. Something's amiss with the river . . . and I cannot tell what." This drew Seth and Sergeant Urry to the railing.

The river from this close did not appear as calm as when she first saw it. Spring thaw was in full effect—it ran fast with ropy currents and waves that lapped against its banks. But nothing looked out of place.

Seth shifted uncomfortably beside them from foot to foot as he gazed over the Sevren. Cat noted his discomfort. "Does something prevent you from making water?" Lelani asked Seth.

"What are you, my mother?" Seth responded.

Lelani waited for an answer.

"All the horseback riding's probably chafing something," Seth said defensively. "I've felt worse after Buffalo wings."

"Perhaps it's some trick of the sunlight," said Sergeant Urry, still scrutinizing the river for that thing that wasn't there. The sun glinted off the whitecaps like a scattered flock of gulls.

"West of the bridge . . . a disturbance in the current," Lelani said.

"What safety remains lies north and east of here," Roland told the portreeve. "If Crowe's Porte should be overrun, fall back to the northern bank and barricade the bridge. I will leave behind a hundred men . . ." Roland stopped and bit his lip. He turned to Daniel. "With your permission, Your Grace."

"Works for me," Daniel said, biting into a juicy apple.

"To arms! To arms!" came a loud cry from the watchtower gate. The watchmen rang their bells and trumpeted frantically.

At the edge of the forest, where they had just themselves come from, was a contingent of Farrenheisi knights and foot soldiers charging down the long path, emerging from the canopy like a long angry snake.

"We miscalculated," Daniel said. "With nobody left in Yarmouth to police, the relief company had no reason to guard it!"

"They'll be at the wall in ten minutes," said the portreeve.

"Close the gates and marshal your defenders," Roland commanded. "The prince must get across that bridge."

The streets were chaotic; Cat spotted the girls' carriage outside the tailor shop. She led her horse over by the reins as swiftly as her condition allowed to rally her family.

"Where's our driver?" asked Valeria.

The massive charge of two hundred horses shook the ground. "Never mind him," said Mina. She climbed into the driver's seat as Cat piled the girls into the coach.

"I'll be right behind you," Cat said.

Mina whipped the reins and took off for the bridge.

As Cat attempted to mount her horse, she discovered to her dismay that Murphy's Law traversed universes. With one foot in the stirrup, horse and rider made a comical circular dance as she tried to climb onto the skittish beast. The enemy's thunderous charge and the town's anxiety proved too much for the gentle mare, which decided to suddenly bolt. Cat let the reins slide from her fingers rather than be dragged along the street. She couldn't see her people anywhere, and now she was minus one sweet, but very stupid, horse. She forced herself to delay panic and followed the crowd toward the bridge. She could find the others in Hull's Porte if she could get over the river. Thousands fled, the bridge became a crush of humanity. It was at best wide enough to allow two coaches side by side, and soon panic broke out among the fleeing.

Cat was wedged between two large and sweaty men who were most definitely fishmongers; their stench alone could repel the enemy. Their collective body mass threatened to crush Cat. She covered her belly protectively for all the good that would do and yelled to be noticed. Someone tripped her and she tumbled. It was dark down there on the planking, the sky blotted by a herd in flight; desperate legs battered. She couldn't get up . . . she thought she was finished, until daylight suddenly broke the throngs—a man was forcibly hurled aside, then another; Lelani's face appeared—never more beautiful than at that moment—framed by a patch of blue sky. Lelani stood over Cat, her equestrian mass clearing enough space for Cat to regain her breath—and peoples' prejudices helped as the crowd now pushed to get clear of the centaur.

Daniel rode behind Francois Ladue on a gray courser and Seth was on his own packhorse.

"I thought you guys left me," Cat said.

"You think any of us want to tell Cal that we lost you and his baby?" Seth remarked.

The thud of a battering ram echoed from the front gate, kicking up the crowd's frenzy. The bridge was bedlam.

"We need to get to the other side!" Daniel shouted. Everyone in Crowe's Porte had the exact same thought.

"Lelani?" Ladue asked, hoping her abilities had returned.

The centaur shook her head; the silver was not yet out of her. She lowered herself to allow Cat on her back—something centaurs despised as it reinforced human prejudices of them.

"Wait! Where is Bree?!" cried Catherine.

"Other end of the bridge," Daniel said.

Cat spotted Mina's coach pressing on slowly toward the far bank. The crowd was thinner on that end, a boon for the quick thinkers who made for the other town right away; the bottleneck was around Cat and the prince. Lieutenant Bryce had the company amassed at the other side ready to defend the north bank.

"Seth, it's up to you," Cat said.

"I'm not turning these people into blossoms or blasting them into the river," Seth protested.

"Use hard air to push the ones around us back just a bit," Lelani instructed.

"I've got two speeds—dice and monsters. I don't know how to do in between."

"Yes you do," Lelani argued. "When you do it powerfully, you approach it like a baseball batter going for a home run . . . approach it instead with less follow-through, a staccato pulse; think of the spell like a bunt instead of a hit. Envision the end result."

Seth cast it—with more gusto than he intended. A few people

were blown over the balustrade into the river, a few bones snapped, and many behind him were pressed back like sardines. Nevertheless, they had room to maneuver. Ladue kicked his horse, weaving and jumping over the recovering crowd and Seth followed close behind. Lelani leaped onto the stone balustrade and charged for the other bank, swatting aside the occasional human copycat with her spear. The balustrade was only two feet wide and disappeared from view under Lelani's bulk. The best rider on horseback could never duplicate this run, and Cat suspected neither could many centaurs. Cat leaned forward into her friend and held on for dear life, eyes shut to the deep, fast river on her right that threatened to engulf them with a single misstep.

Mid-bridge the people density lessened and Lelani vaulted back onto the planking. Cat thought they were in the clear, until screams alerted them to the new threat. Arrows shot past them from on high and lodged into the planking. They looked up to find knights on black winged horses with crossbows. Cal had warned at length about Farrenheil's deadly winged cavalry.

"*Mon Dieu!*" cried Ladue.

"They don't know us from Adam," Daniel said. "It's Lelani they're homing in on . . . and anyone with her."

Five knights hovered over the guardians while others corralled the crowds behind them, pushing them back off the bridge. Seth raised a large shield around the group just in time to block a volley of bolts, but one got through and lodged into his horse's neck. The poor creature went down, pinning Seth's foot under its weight. His shield faltered—but it was ample delay for Ladue to have pulled out a bulky black weapon from his duffel bag; on full automatic the M4A1 tore through the targeted knight—armor, horse, and all—with hellish vengeance. Shells rained on the bridge while Ladue cried out, "*Mourrez et allez en enfer, sales bâtards!*" The knight and his mount plunged into the river while his cohorts tried to regain control of their startled animals—but not before Ladue loaded a fresh cartridge, and pureed a second knight. The remaining cavalry scattered in long, far swoops above the river before regrouping a hundred yards away to parley.

"Your weapon will not last," Lelani said.

"She make love long time, *ma cherie.*"

"It has nothing to do with the weapon."

"*Oui,* I remember—magic will curse her. However, if the explosion happen *là-haut,* why will the magic punish *ma belle fille?*"

Ladue stuffed a very fat green bullet with a gold tip into a tube under the weapon's muzzle and aimed cautiously for the hovering knights. With a pneumatic pop, he fired at the center knight. The explosion tore into all three knights and they spiraled into the river.

Eight hundred feet to the other bank, and the bridge ahead was all clear; Cat thought it too good to be true, and was rewarded for her skepticism when something big hit the bridge. The thing that surfaced out of the river looked like a whale made of sewn bladders and hemp rope netting. Its stink was wretched— men began to pour out of it and climb the side of the bridge with hook and rope. Their skintight black suits were slick, seal-like, and even their hair and skin had an oily sheen to them. The men brandished knives, bolo nets, spears, and tridents and climbed so quickly, soon three dozen stood between the guardians and their end point.

"Skilytes," cried Lelani.

Ladue handed Daniel the M4; he jumped off their horse, stuck a detonator into a belt of C-4 bricks, and hurled it with the grace of an Olympic discus thrower at the new arrivals. The explosion blew the planking to splinters; a gapping hole too wide to jump trapped the surviving Skilytes on the other side of the gap, but at the same time, severed the guardians' link to the north bank.

Another of those bladder whales surfaced, then a third. Hook lines flew up to the railing—Lelani severed the ropes with her spear tip as Ladue remounted his horse.

Ladue charged his courser back toward Crowe's Porte, their only viable option. Daniel fired his bodyguard's *belle fille* at the winged knights who corralled what remained of the crowds with a large chain between them. He got one, and the other three fled. A fourth bladder whale tapped the bridge closer to the town, threatening to cut off the guardians from a retreat. Daniel loaded a grenade and blew a hole in the submarine. It deflated around its crew, trapping them in the water.

Cat tapped Lelani and pointed to the road that led out of the Blue Forest. The attacking host was no longer on the hill slope, which meant they'd broken the gate and were likely heading for the bridge.

"Halp!" cried Seth, whose foot was still pinned.

Lelani grabbed him under the armpits and pulled him out. As Seth tried to balance himself, his hand and Lelani's came into contact—something strange happened to all three of them. Magic coursed through Lelani like a conduit and into Cat. Seth whipped his hand away, and all three of them asked, "What was that?"

Lelani tried to cast a spell, but nothing happened.

"Figure it out later," Cat insisted. "We need to get off this bridge." Seth ran beside them as they followed the prince.

Daniel and Ladue came to an abrupt stop at the foot. The earthbound knights of Farrenheil had arrived and blocked their

exit. They allowed the townsfolk to disperse. Lelani and her col-
laborators were their priority.

"Take my hand!" she commanded Seth.

He grasped her right hand and Cat felt that charge again.
With her left hand, Lelani made motions to form one of her hot
phosphorous balls. She blew on it and the whitish-blue ball transformed into red and yellow flame. She blew on it again and it
grew and bubbled with convection like a miniature sun. The heat
was intense.

"Seth, the man in the green robe to the right of the knights is
their mage. Take him out before he counters my attack!" Lelani
commanded.

Lelani hurled the ball of flame. It shot down the length of the
bridge like a comet past Daniel toward the knights. Seth whipped
up a potent hard wind and focused the spell at the magic user in
green, who ducked for cover just as a hurricane gale force tore up
the wall behind him. The fireball exploded ferociously, blowing
horses and knights into the air and even devastating parts of the
town's bridge gate.

Seth passed out from his effort. Lelani grabbed the young wizard and tossed him over her shoulder. Cat could feel the strain
on the centaur's legs and hoped Lelani would hold up a bit longer. The four guardians and their prince rode past the tattered
blockade, heading due east along the riverbank. An enemy contingent pursued, gaining on the guardians' weighted mounts.

Ahead, someone rode toward them like the devil in a wagon
of flaming hay and logs. Cat thought they were cut off, until they
recognized Sergeant Urry. His own horse charged beside the
wagon. The guardians hugged the edge of the path to let him
pass. The sergeant leaped from the driver's bench to his horse
moments before the wagon skidded, teetered over, and sent an

inferno of logs and terrified horses flying into the pursuing host. The horrible flaming mess, its mass of pinned and broken horses, covered the entire path, blocking pursuit.

Urry caught up with the group and took Seth from Lelani. They heard shouts from the town above to their right. They were about to make a run for it when Lelani yelled, "Wait!" She motioned for everyone to get close and took Seth's hand again. Then she cast another one-handed spell. "Shhh . . . ," she told her cohorts. Knights of Farrenheil rumbled down the short hill to the river road . . . they charged past the guardians as though they were not there.

"A veil," Lelani whispered to Cat.

And with that, the mercenary, the prince, the sergeant, the photographer, the centaur, and the expectant mother from New York quietly followed the river out of Crowe's Porte.

CHAPTER 19

A QUEEN'S GAMBIT

With his family and the prince safely away in Puerto Rico, Callum focused on the final stages of the group's bugout. The trucks had already left—only the helicopters remained to transport their most sensitive items and their prisoners.

Graeme Van Rooyen and his mercenaries escorted Balzac and Hesz to the landing field. Their manacles—wrist-to-wrist, ankle-to-ankle, with a long chain running between their hands and feet—rattled with their short, constrained steps. Hesz tripped and fell on the graveled path twice. Mercenaries lined the entire route to their copter. Malcolm, Cal, Tilcook, and Tony Two Scoops observed the progress from beside the henge.

"Overkill?" asked Tilcook as he puffed on a half-finished Cohiba. His purple shirt shimmered with iridescence, his rings and gold chains flared under the bright sun. "These guys ain't wizards."

"Never bet your life against Balzac," Cal said.

Balzac had been a step ahead ever since they regained their memories; the man seemed to know the impossible. Despite the professor's modest resources, he had compromised Malcolm's financial empire and political connections. The division at the FBI devoted to Tilcook had just been folded into the New York attack investigation thanks to Balzac. That was the last bit of bad news they were able to get out of Malcolm's *former* sources. The billionaire was now too hot even for "friends." The jester's intelligence on the scope of the invasion also demoralized them. That man had a talent for screwing with your psyche.

Van Rooyen approached. "The professor would have some words with you before he boards the helicopter. He was adamant."

"He'd have nothing left to say if you'd a let Dominic and me do the interrogation," Tony Two Scoops said.

Cal motioned Balzac over. Hesz remained behind, rubbing his knees and blowing on his scuffed-up palms.

"I wish to confess," Balzac said amiably. He was in a pleasant mood, which put Cal immediately on his guard.

"We already know you're a seditious bastard," Tilcook said.

"Yes. But still, I have not been entirely truthful with you. I have actively been plotting against the prince and his guardians these past five months."

"Bullshit," said Malcolm.

Balzac confirmed this with a nod. "You watched my bank accounts, my travels, my email, my cell phone—even though such actions are highly illegal. Had you discovered impropriety, you would have checked me into your luxurious basement much earlier, no doubt. Nevertheless I've been a busy subversive."

"Why you squealing now?" asked Tilcook.

"Timing."

"Timing?" Two Scoops repeated.

"It's key to all the best-laid plans."

Malcolm rolled his eyes. "Get to the point, Ball Sack."

"Ah, yes—very funny," the jester said, contemplating Mal the way an anaconda contemplated rodents. "I'm a tenured professor. Good standing, in line to chair the literature department one day. Interesting thing about college students—they have liberal concepts of currency. Every school has its stragglers, its grade-grubbers, and what wouldn't they do for an easy A to bolster their grade-point averages? I created a work-study program—something green and eco-centric—available online to the lads and lasses of the colleges of this region. I was partial to students from Bard . . . very resourceful, but my best intel ended up coming from art majors at SUNY Purchase. I won't trouble you with the syllabus details; suffice to say, it required them to camp in the local woods, where they could earn credit drinking, smoking weed, and screwing to their hearts' content—so long as they kept me abreast of who was going in and coming out—through burner phones, of course."

A pit materialized in Cal's gut.

"So you knew our ins and outs?" Tilcook asked.

"Oh, I had already surmised what you guardians were planning. Soldiers are predictable—it's always more men, bigger weapons. I simply needed updates. What truly interested me were parties from Farrenheil who would have languished on this world lost and confused, like the squad that came through four months ago . . . and the one that came through last week, which was a scouting party for a bigger group with a wizard of Dorn's caliber that would have arrived a few days ago. My students guided them to me; I set them on a new agenda to claim this wizard when he arrived and acclimate him to the situation. Knowledge is power, after all."

A vein of dread harried Cal. He wanted to rush Balzac into a copter, take off—instead, he eyed his commandos suspiciously—uniformly dressed strangers really. *Too many men hired too quickly.* A glance from Mal said the dwarv shared his paranoia.

"Why spill now?" Tilcook asked. "You ain't goin' nowherez."

"Good question!" commended Balzac. "Why indeed have I chosen *this* very moment, as you are about to whisk me away to your Rocky Mountain stronghold?"

How did he know they were going to the Rockies?

Balzac hesitated for dramatic effect. "Do you recall what I said about plans . . . about what they rely on to succeed?"

"Timing?" said Tony Two Scoops, as though vying for credit.

He was toying with them. They were blind to something they should have been on top of. "We need to get moving," Cal said.

"Timing!" Balzac emphasized, pointing at Tony. "Pieces on a game board must be in place before the endgame. Sometimes it's a row of complicated maneuvers, and other times, the simplicity of a delaying tactic—an action intended for no other purpose than to allow pieces to sync up . . ."

Frost giants breathe cold! Callum remembered.

A rocket fired from the cover of the woods. It took out Cal's soldiers closest to the helicopters. Machine guns followed. Hell broke loose as the mercenaries returned fire. Tilcook, Tony, and Mal hit the deck. Callum tackled Balzac to the ground, though he was inclined to leave the traitor standing in the maelstrom. Suddenly, Hesz snapped his chains, the links rendered brittle by his frost breath.

A mercenary guarding Hesz began firing on his own squad. *Fucking mole,* Cal confirmed. The turncoat took out three soldiers before the others put him down, but it bought Hesz enough time to whip his arm chains, cracking open the heads of the remaining soldiers like ripe cantaloupes.

Van Rooyen and his sergeant pumped grenades into the tree

line, blowing the forest into kindling. Hesz charged the officer with chains whipping. Van Rooyen ducked just in time to avoid losing his head, but his sergeant was not as lucky.

"Secure the perimeter!" Cal shouted. "I'll handle the giant." He rolled a smoke grenade at Hesz and drew his sword Bòid Géard from its sheath.

Cal rolled as the giant's whipping chains fanned away the gas. For Cal to be safe from the chains, he had to be close enough for Hesz to be able to grab him, but then the giant only needed a second to break him in two.

The chain slammed the earth, blowing up grass and dirt where Cal had just been. Cal shoved his sword through a link and into the ground to the hilt before Hesz could retract, locking down Hesz's left arm. Cal rolled under the arm and hit Hesz in the obliques, a spot as sensitive as a man's gonads for frost giants. Hesz went down on his knees anguished. Cal grabbed the end of the chain slack from Hesz's other wrist and jumped on the giant's back, bringing the arm and chain across the giant's throat. He wrapped the chain around Hesz's neck and pulled as though riding an angry bull.

Hesz struggled, but the angle of his arm did not afford him the right leverage to counter Cal's full weight. Cal pulled with all his strength, knowing full well that if Hesz recovered, he would kill them all. Hesz fainted, but Cal continued the pressure for a few seconds more to be sure. He retrieved his sword, grabbed Balzac off the ground by his scruff, and placed him before him like a shield with his sword at the jester's throat. The firefight slowed. Van Rooyen and his corporal weeded out more attackers.

"Tell all that are left to surrender, or you're going to get a new smile," Cal told the jester.

Balzac pulled a whistle from his pocket and blew it. The remaining men came out of the woods with their guns up.

"Stupidly pointless!" Malcolm shouted. He looked disgusted. Half their men were dead or injured.

Balzac calmly checked his watch. "My men might have succeeded," he said. "I may have been rescued. But most importantly, while we danced here, the necromancer executes his objective miles away unfettered."

Cal grabbed the jester by the throat and lifted him off the grass. "What have you done . . . ?"

Balzac choked under Callum's iron grip. Mal put his hand on Cal's arm, spouting nonsense about needing the jester alive. Cal, however, was certain Balzac needed to die right at that moment.

Then . . .

All of nature screamed.

Their proximity to the lay line amplified the wail. The henge throbbed with power like a wayward engine, its deep thrum vibrating to the core of the world. They grabbed their ears, guardians and enemies alike, trying to shut out the cry of the earth. The jester was the only one laughing; tears of joy streamed down his face. And when Cal thought he could not take another minute of this psychic anguish, the floor of the universe dropped out from under him.

CHAPTER 20

CROSSROADS

1

Trees and sky were the first images to creep into Seth's awareness through the slits of his eyes. Lelani had siphoned his magic like a vampire. He was exhausted, like some hapless weary maiden in the arms of burly Sergeant Urry.

The horses' constant blowing told of their near exhaustion as well. The company stopped at a crossroads. A right turn took them around the base of the Crummock Mountains rising tall in the distance; a left took them toward the Sevren River. The mountain river road was worn and well traveled. The one continuing east straight ahead had grown over, like it'd been abandoned. Seth saw a post on the far corner and behind it, an abandoned grown-over shack. *Ah . . . that road*, Seth recalled.

"Let us rest these animals a moment before they fall apart," Ladue suggested.

Urry placed Seth against a tree with a good view of that road heading east. The touch of the soil and wood rejuvenated like black coffee after a late night—his hangover diminished to a negligible throb.

"The enemy likely thinks we've hidden in Crowe's Porte," Urry told the group.

"Not for long," said Ladue. "Invisible we may have been, but our tracks were not. Our exit was sloppy."

"There was little time for an elegant escape," Lelani said, taking umbrage with Ladue's critique.

"I do not blame you, *ma cherie.*"

Lelani came over to check on Seth. He flinched at her touch, knocked her hand away. If Lelani was hurt by that act, she hid it well.

"I think the reason faerie silver does not affect you is tied to why you grow fatigued after using magic," she said.

That's how Lelani played her game—enticing information dangled on a hook—how she wrangled him back into this Aandor mess five months earlier. Externally Seth remained disinterested. He wished he could whip up a cold egg cream. *Now that would be a practical spell.*

"You store magic," she pressed on.

"He's a Duracell," Daniel joked.

"Quiet, you," Seth warned, not caring about Daniel's title.

"Daniel is correct," Lelani said. "When I cast a spell, I channel magic from the air or some reservoir—I am a conduit, like most sorcerers. I can hold a little of it, but not much, and not for long safely. But you have not learned to channel magic this way because you are the reservoir. It fills you slower than it empties, and so swift depletion of your store unbalances you—leaves you exhausted. I should have realized earlier."

"So, on top of being a crappy wizard, I'm also handicapped. Whoopee! Thanks for nothing."

"Handica . . . ?" Lelani shook a fist in frustration; she glared. "You are a Thaumadyne! An enigma! *One* in any given generation has such a talent. Leave it to the gods to give such a boon to the most feckless and lazy of miscreants. The faerie silver in my blood prevents me from drawing magic from the environment. But you hold a reservoir of magic within you. That's why you were able to cast after the darts struck. Thaumadynes can cast exponential magicks, like the kind Dorn did in New York, without talismans or radioactive components. Their metabolism also removes faerie silver from their blood at an accelerated pace. This is why you're experiencing pai—"

"Not that this isn't fascinating," Cat interrupted, "but where's the next bridge?"

"Wulfhall," Urry said. "We ride around the base of the Crummocks . . ." He pointed at the mountains. Urry mapped out their route in the dirt. "Cross the Grange River at Cuckmere, swap horses, and then ride hard for Wulfhall and then north to the Gate. Four days by most, but we can likely do it in three."

"We don't have *three* days!" Daniel said.

"Attendez," said Ladue. "This Wulfhall . . . she is on the river Sevren, yes? Why must we go around the mountains? The river, she has cut us a beautiful plain to ride through this mountain range. We continue straight, follow the river to this town. It will cut the journey by half."

Lelani and Urry glanced at each other with concern.

"You're telling me that no one's built a bridge between Crowe's Porte and Wulfhall?" Daniel asked, looking at their crude map.

"Meadsweir," Seth chimed in.

"What's a Meadsweir?" Daniel asked.

"Your Grace, you'll not want to be going to that place," Urry warned like a man contemplating amputation without whiskey.

Urry's trepidation brought bittersweet satisfaction to Seth. There was also delight in seeing Lelani balk. "Meadsweir is an abandoned town about twelve miles upriver," Seth answered. "And on the river sits an abandoned castle with an abandoned bridge over the Sevren."

Daniel looked at his crew warily. "What's wrong with it?"

"No one goes to Meadsweir, Your Grace," Urry stressed. "Not for three hundred and fifty years. Every traveler knows to steer clear of that place. I'll not talk more of it." Urry made some motion with his hands as if warding off Satan.

"It's cursed," Seth said with mild amusement. "Haunted."

"Are you kidding me?"

"Some foul presence lurks in Meadsweir," Lelani said. "Even the forest is slow to reclaim the town."

"Whatever's there is related to you," Seth added.

Lelani shot Seth a *don't encourage him* look, which he cheerfully ignored. "About three hundred and eighty years ago, when rulers were still called kings, Aandor's royal family bore a set of twin boys. Custom says that the first twin out inherits the kingdom. Except, back then they hadn't completely bred susceptibility to magic out of the royal bloodline yet. Prince number one had a special sensitivity to magic—and so he was passed over in favor of the spare to the heir."

"Egwyn of Aandor lost his crown," Daniel noted.

"That's it," Seth recalled.

"The boys, Egwyn and Alfred, were called the Fisher Kings in their youth on account of how often they eluded their tutors to steal off in a rowboat," Daniel added. "Historians, however, would remember Egwyn as *the Mad King*. And Alfred was dubbed *the Uncertain* because he had a tendency to change his mind a lot. Jeez, I can't believe all this crap has actually come in handy."

"Well . . . losing a kingdom is enough to make anyone go

batty," Seth noted. "Egwyn withdrew from court, kept to himself, and started experimenting in his private tower . . . no one really cared what he did so long as he kept out of politics—until he blew his tower to smithereens, releasing some entity that took all the wizards and clerics in Aandor City to bottle down."

"Alfred protected Egwyn," Daniel said. "But Alfred couldn't let Egwyn endanger the lives of his family and everyone else in the capital. When Egwyn refused to give up his experiments, Alfred had no choice but to banish him."

"But Egwyn's banishment was one decision that Alfred the Uncertain stuck with until their deaths," Urry noted.

"Meadsweir was hardly a cruel sentence," Lelani countered. "The castle was large, secluded, and, at that time, on Aandor's easternmost border. Under Egwyn's patronage, what started as a frontier fort town grew into a bustling river port with craftsmen, guilds, and artists—a place where merchants from Farrenheil, Moran, and Nurvenheim brought their wares into Aandor and a launching point for our wares to head east. It rivaled the capital in importance and was wealthy enough to afford that bridge to the north bank."

"Aye," Urry said. "But the Mad King went one experiment too far—turned the town into a graveyard. I for one would like to see me wee children again."

Seth doubted any child of Urry's could be *wee*. "We don't know that Egwyn had anything to do with what happened to the town," Seth noted.

"See that post on yonder corner under the weeds?" the sergeant continued. "Children test each other's bravery by etching their mark on that post. It's on the northeast corner of the crossing. This is as far as anyone would dare come. Behind the post, Borin Falk's fishing cabin sits abandoned under all that growth. He was the last man to live this close to Meadsweir. He watched army after army head down this road only to never come back out. And nary a denizen of Meadsweir ever journeyed from the town—not merchant, soldier, or cleric. Only one of King Alfred's men ever came back—half naked, blistered and burned with fever, mad, and babbling gibberish. He didn'a live long. Advisers insisted the king send more soldiers. Alfred refused at first . . . then he sent two companies—two hundred and sixty souls—knights, archers, pikemen, squires . . . they, too, were never heard from again. Borin Falk forsook his cabin shortly after."

"The king just gave up?" Daniel asked.

"The Wizards' Council and banner men whose lands adjoin Meadsweir coaxed Alfred to try yet again. The next group went by river, with powerful wizards this time, members of their council. The town looked abandoned from the docks. Those on the ships claimed they heard the screams of men . . . and something other, but they saw nothing. Neither the men nor the wizards returned to the ships. The river men pushed off and swore never to return. To this day, ships that pass on the river stay close to the north bank as they sail by. They severed one link of the bridge closer to the north bank and used its wood and stone to barricade both ends of the break."

Seth noted Catherine's absence as they argued the pros and cons of Meadsweir. She sat across the road with her back to them. Seth found his legs and walked over gingerly, wincing at the discomfort in his nether regions and hoping to God he wasn't developing an infection. Cat weaved a Winnie the Pooh barrette back and forth through her fingers. Her flushed cheeks were wet. Seth's heart, which had been hard and indifferent for a great portion of his life, broke like a water balloon. Cat had suffered in silence while everyone else plotted.

"You all done?" she asked.

"Cat—"

"Nothing you say will help. I got comfortable with Cal's family—let her out of my sight when I should have kept her at my side. I should have jumped into that carriage; I could have taken Bree with me on the horse. In the end, it's my fault I lost her."

"We'll find—"

"Who's we, Seth? I'm alone here. There are no social services, no FBI. This isn't Disneyland. There are no phones, no buses, and few roads, mostly teeming with rapists and thieves playing soldiers. Right now I'm praying Mina makes it back to her fancy castle, but I don't know. See, that's hardest . . . I don't know if Bree's safe. I want to jump into that river and swim across and run back to find my girl."

"You would not survive the swim," said Lelani, joining them.

Cat looked as though a million thoughts ran through her brain at that moment and her mouth couldn't find a way to merge with any of them.

"I will help you, Catherine—but I must first see the prince safely to the Gate."

"Bree could be dead by then."

"Many could be dead in the next few days. I fear for my kin in the Blue Forest as well. But the only hope of defeating Farrenheil lies with the prince. Did you not see how easily men were willing to follow him?"

Cat's shoulders slumped. The fight had gone out of her. "To hell with you all then," she said weakly.

Lelani reached down and took the barrette. It had strands of Bree's hair stuck in it—she put the barrette in her satchel. Lelani went down on her front knees and crossed her arms over her chest. "I pledge to you, Catherine MacDonnell, when we've seen Daniel to safety, and when my magic returns, I will find Brianna."

"Then I vote for the quickest route there," Cat said. "We should go through Meadsweir."

"There's no voting in Aandor," Seth explained. With a finger toward Daniel he added, "We do what *he* says."

"Putting aside the distance thing, we can't outrun all the soldiers looking for us," Daniel said pragmatically. "Heading south along the mountain just brings us closer to Lord Gillen's duchy, and he's thrown in with the enemy. Meadsweir is the safest option . . ."

Urry harrumphed and coughed.

"And if the enemy's half as superstitious as Sergeant Urry, it'll buy us more than just a shortcut."

"Mount up!" ordered Ladue.

Urry shook his head like an innocent man receiving a bad sentence. The idea of it amused Seth. The biggest and best armed among them was the most chickenshit . . . or maybe he was the wisest of them.

2

Though gnarled and weeded over, the path to Meadsweir was still there even after three hundred years. It led travelers away from civilization (be it as it may)—a ghost road to somewhere ancient, predating man's hubris of taming nature. The forest was dense, thicker than any Seth remembered in Aandor, with a deep greenish-black canopy; roots had upturned road stones and threatened to trip the horses; bad drainage eroded the path's integrity in the thin places at the edges of precipices, which came up with little warning. The company rode quietly, confident that their pursuers would not follow and that the devil they didn't know would prove safer than the one they did.

Seth rode with Daniel, staff in hand, ready to shield them from whatever came up, but the riding aggravated Seth's bladder, stabbing painfully with each step of his horse. The last time he tried to make water, it was like a cluster of needles. Seth didn't know quite what to do about his situation in the middle of the woods. He navigated with a delicate Tabasco-filled balloon shoved in his lower gut.

Ladue led with his *belle fille* fully cocked with safeties off. Urry covered their six. The man looked like he was entering the gates of hell and saw demons lurking behind every tree.

"The bridge is in disrepair," Urry said, trying to convince the others to reconsider. "They cut out a section. We would need planks to cross the gap . . . assuming we reach it."

"Shhhhhh," hushed Lelani.

"It's not just the town," Urry whispered. "Dark creatures are drawn to such places. Witches and gnolls . . . grimlocks, ghouls . . . they have to live somewhere."

"They can dance with *ma belle fille*," Ladue whispered back. Ladue would be lucky to make it through one clip of his M4, Seth thought. Magic was dense in this area, more than usual for Aandor—Seth could almost perceive his body absorbing it.

"Keep your reserve full," Lelani instructed Seth. "Draw from the magic around you when you cast; I may need to tap your store in a crisis."

"I don't know where I pull magic from," Seth admitted. "All my focus is on getting the spell out at all."

The woods were barren of ground life—not a squirrel or

chipmunk—no evidence of deer or fox. A few bats flapped overhead and the only birds they spotted flew west, but never from the town. After some time the forest thinned rapidly and the trees grew smaller and less frequent. Meadsweir's wall rose before them as they approached. It was a tsunami of stone that could repel an army, now covered in a colorful array of climbing vines and flowered plants rooted into the mortar.

The forest was indeed slow to reclaim this land. After three hundred and fifty years, the grass leading to the wall should have been completely grown over instead of waist high, and the saplings should be trees. The horses were skittish. Ladue suggested they walk them—it would provide cover from possible hostiles. Seth didn't want to think of losing his horse in a haunted forest. His bladder pressed painfully as he dismounted. He needed to pee . . . immediately.

Behind a bush it took him a while to get going and a searing fire cut through him like a shard of glass. He stopped and bit his lip hard enough to break skin. The trickle that made it out had blood swirling in it. "Oh God," he whimpered.

Lelani trotted over.

"Really?!" he complained. "You're that interested in my wee human winkie?"

"I've been expecting this," she said.

"You've been waiting for me to piss hot needles?"

"Thaumadynes remove faerie silver from the blood at an accelerated rate. The metal is concentrated in your system."

"Metallic kidney stones?" Ladue said. *"J'ai finalement trouvé quelque chose qui m'effraie."*

"Can you zap the fuckers?" Seth pleaded.

"Magic doesn't affect that metal." She took out a small finely woven cheesecloth sack. "Force it through into this, if you would."

"Uh . . . I CAN'T PISS!"

"Keep your voice down," Urry scolded.

Lelani locked a steely-eyed glare on Seth. "Only a few pounds of pure faerie silver has ever been refined in known history," Lelani explained. "Less than a hundred people know it exists and yet, it's worth one hundred times its weight in gold."

"We've come across a lot of the stuff," Seth argued.

"Only the plating and tips of Dorn's daggers were faerie silver, and those are now lost in another universe. I recovered the wizard squad's darts, the spikes in my collar, and now intend to reclaim the granules from your water." She shoved the sack into his hands.

"H o w d o e s t h i s h e l p m e p e e?!"

"You must or your bladder will rupture. Pee into the sack." She found a thick branch and put it by his mouth. "Bite this."

Seth had a lifetime of sins to answer for, of which he was well aware, and it looked like the universe was calling in a stack of chips. His anguish must have been evident because Cat stepped up and said, "For God's sake, Lelani . . . he stopped being an asshole five months ago . . . do something for him."

Lelani appeared ready to debate Cat's claim. Instead, her face flushed pink. She pursed her lips and reluctantly took the bag from Seth. "I swear by all the gods, if you utter a single jape, your descendants will never come to be." She slipped the sack over Seth's penis with a firm grip. She touched skin with her thumb to tap into his magic and recited something; Seth felt his member grow, but not with arousal—it actually grew in size.

"Go!" she ordered.

The stones passed through his urethra with minimal pain. The bag filled—gold liquid with cloudy crimson swirls filtered out.

Seth couldn't help but sigh in sheer relief. Then she returned him to normal.

"Awww . . . you could have left it," he said.

"Learn the damn spell yourself! Or turn your cock into a blossom for all I care!" Lelani marched away with the sack, red-faced. Ladue, Urry, and Daniel keenly restrained their laughter.

CHAPTER 21

. . . BAD COP

Handcuffed to a table in a windowless room and needing to use a toilet, Allyn Grey contemplated his bleak circumstances. They had strapped a blood pressure cuff on his arm, two more straps across his chest and abdomen, and three fingers were Velcroed to wires that ran into a box he suspected was a lie detector. His metal chair was as hard and cold as the beige walls and fluorescent lights—the mirror was likely two-way. He wondered how many other suspected terrorists had sat here mulling over their future. The chair smelled of piss.

There were no lay lines near this building; no mana to cast his blessings, though he was loathe to force conversions anyway. The rules of his order permitted it solely to save lives. He'd converted the construction workers at Yankee Stadium five months earlier to save New York City, and the soothe he cast was mild and would wear off.

Allyn considered what Cal and Malcolm would want him to do. The other guardians were likely no longer even in this universe. That was scary. Balzac had done a number on them.

"May I use a restroom?" Allyn said aloud.

Three people entered and shut the door. The man at the polygraph epitomized nerd: tall and lanky with black glasses—his ruffled white shirt looked too big on him. The other man could be a linebacker, his white shirtsleeves rolled up over reddish hairs on his thick freckled forearms—his tie was not long enough to reach his belt, making him appear like that fifth-grader who'd dressed himself for class pictures. He set a stack of manila folders on the table. The third was an athletic Hispanic woman—her runner's quads stretching the slacks of her black pantsuit, which matched the sheen of her long dark hair; her white rayon blouse shone in contrast with her light-brown skin. She took the seat across from Allyn.

"I am Special Agent Cifuentes, and this is my partner Special Agent Torrenson," the woman said, neglecting the nerd.

"Quite a coincidence both your parents naming you Special Agent," Allyn said.

The nerd chuckled; neither agent flinched. She opened a folder, laid out photos of Callum, Malcolm, Colby, and Tilcook.

"Can you tell us where these people are?" she asked.

"May I speak with a lawyer?"

"You're not under arrest," Torrenson said, with attitude.

Allyn looked at his chained wrists and back to them.

"You're a person of interest," Cifuentes said. "If you help us, things will go better for you."

"But if I am not under arrest, and therefore not in trouble, what, pray tell, do I need *to go better* for me?"

"Don't be a smartass," Torrenson said. His partner's hand on his arm kept the big man from rounding the table. Allyn sensed a personal grudge in Torrenson.

"There's no record of you in the country prior to fourteen years ago," Cifuentes said. "What country are you originally from?"

"Aandor," Allyn said truthfully. Both agents looked at the nerd and he nodded assent.

"I'm not familiar with that country," she admitted.

Allyn didn't know what to do. Tell the truth and get tossed into a padded room at Bellevue or lie and get thrown in prison ending any hope of reviving the guardians' mission. They might also believe him and he could end up with the same results.

"You're facing a load of potential charges," Torrenson chimed in impatiently. "Espionage, treason . . ."

"Treason?! I have never tried to convince anyone to overthrow this government."

Cifuentes pulled a sheet out of Allyn's folder. "You've organized rallies and protests . . . civil disobedience," she said.

"Those were peaceful rallies at the state capital to ensure fair treatment of African-Americans," Allyn said in genuine shock. "Police seem to develop itchy fingers whenever a black male comes into their sphere of authority. Our events were organized to make our country safer, not overthrow the government."

"Bullshit," Torrenson said.

These two fins were circling Allyn like he was the last fish in the ocean. "I do not know where these people are."

The nerd did something between a nod and shake.

"How do you know them?" Cifuentes asked.

"Malcolm Robbe sponsors scholarships for my church. Mr. MacDonnell is his security adviser. The large fellow looks like that mafia guy on the news . . ."

"Bullshit!" Torrenson said, leaning into the table on large pink fists. "Quit with the games. We nabbed your trucks heading north. We know you've been training mercs on that compound. We know a lot more than you—"

Again, Agent Cifuentes put her hand on his forearm. Torrenson jerked back and teased his hair in the two-way mirror.

"There were nine hundred deaths the day New York was attacked," Cifuentes said. "Three thousand seriously injured. If you're really a loyal American, help us to protect the public."

It was a fair request. Allyn's loyalties were stretched in too many directions . . . but he could not guarantee something like New York would never happen again. But what happened to Aandor's insurgency once the truth was known? It was against the law for U.S. citizens to wage private wars on other nations—and the law would probably hold up for nations in other universes, too—*especially* other universes. The Pentagon would fall into Cold War–level paranoia over invasion. *Aliens.* Allyn decided to keep his secrets until he could consult a lawyer.

"You should know that we've detained your wife and daughter in North Carolina," Cifuentes said calmly.

Allyn's resolve unraveled. Michelle had said all along that Aandor would find its way into their home. He was angry at these agents for proving her right . . . but also, with himself for putting his family in jeopardy.

"That's completely unnecessary," Allyn said. His voice had dropped to a whisper. "They have absolutely—*absolutely* nothing to do with any of this."

"It's different when it's *your* kid in the line of fire," Torrenson said.

"My wife and child were born here." He appealed to Cifuentes. "I must insist you release my family."

"Oh, he's insisting," Torrenson said to his partner. Torrenson turned his full attention on Allyn and came in close, their noses inches apart. "I'm sure my daughter *insisted* one of those monsters that crawled out of the sewers five months ago not bite her in half as she walked home from school."

Lord have mercy, Allyn thought.

Allyn looked to Cifuentes for empathy, but her cold black eyes were compassionless, reptilian. This woman never played the good cop in interrogations . . . there was no "good cop" in this building when it came to him. The authorities were as desperate for their answers as Farrenheil was for Daniel's head. And now Michelle and Rosemarie were at the mercy of these people. Michelle would talk with little prodding.

Allyn looked at his hands—hands that had filled sandbags before the flood, healed the sick, signed petitions, and found missing children. All his good deeds were nothing to them. He could blame Aandor for his family's fall, but the prince had a right to life, too—Allyn swore an oath he wholeheartedly believed in. Was there really any other path for him than to protect the prince?

The agents watched him intently. They'd been hunting for the terrorists for months and they finally had one strapped to their machines. His friend, Sheriff Martin, had said cops had an instinct for knowing when a dam would break.

"The irony regarding he who sent those reports to you," Allyn said methodically, "is that he works for the side that put this city in danger." Allyn let those words sink in for a moment. The agents looked at each other, then again to him.

"Sides?" Cifuentes said.

"Yes. It certainly wasn't you fine folks who stopped that disaster five months ago. New York got caught in the middle of two factions. It's an old story—refugees, insurrections—agents that followed the survivors to stamp out a royal bloodline."

"Like some Hollywood movie," Cifuentes said.

"Balzac Cruz knew where to hit us. He knows how to play governments and private interests. With just some words on paper Cruz accomplished what a very deranged man with all the power in the universe and an inflated sense of entitlement could not do."

"So we're looking for the wrong people?" Cifuentes asked, pointing to the photos. "You're the good guys?"

"The people you want are gone . . . or dead. The guardians were immigrants . . . good citizens, playing our role dutifully until our memories were awakened. The mercenaries are for a war in Aandor."

"Your friend's report was vague on exactly where this Aandor is . . ."

"Balzac Cruz is *not* my friend. Nor is he yours."

"He's the only one who's given us any answers."

"He serves himself with what he gave you. You know how politics work, Agent Cifuentes."

She thought about it. "I'd like to take you seriously, Mr. Grey." She laid out two more photos. "The more you help us connect dots, the better for Michelle and Rosemarie."

"Not for me?"

"Nothing can help *you*," Torrenson cut in.

In the photos, a Hispanic woman lay dead before a church altar, a Middle Eastern man was dead behind the wheel of a cab; both oozed black blood.

"I've never met them," Allyn said truthfully, but cognizant of Dorn's long trail of victims.

"Carla Hernandez was an employee of your associate Mr. Dretch," Cifuentes explained. "Salim Abdullah drove onto the curb outside of a Manhattan police precinct. Care to guess what the coroner found in each case?"

"An empty cavity where their hearts should have been," Allyn responded.

"Now we're cooking," Cifuentes said. "Traffic cams verify that Abdullah was in fact driving the cab to the station. This was no remote-controlled car. So when you, as you colorfully put it, said the other faction had all the power in the universe, what specifically were you referring to?"

"Mr. Cruz's ally, Dorn, kept their hearts in sacks and forced them to do his bidding," Allyn explained. "Then, he destroyed them."

"How?" Cifuentes looked like a cat that had caught a canary.

In for a penny, in for a pound, thought Allyn. "Magic," he said in all earnestness.

Torrenson screamed and punched a wall, sending vibrations through the plaster.

Special Agent Cifuentes sat back in her chair, satisfied . . . all she lacked was a cigarette. "Are you magic?" she asked.

"I am not a wizard," he said cautiously, knowing that those in this reality *would* consider his blessings sorcery. It kept his conscience clear, though—enough that the polygraph did not contradict him.

They promised Allyn his trip to the bathroom contingent on a few more answers. More photos: Symian—burned black and flattened on a city street, Todgarten and Krebe in body bags in what he assumed was Malcolm's private warehouse. Allyn gave them the broad strokes of their conflict. He told them that Symian was a half-troll and the other a frost giant mutt. Talking unburdened him. Allyn was not cut out for espionage.

"And they're from where . . . Scandinavia?" Cifuentes asked.

The FBI was still in denial. "Alternate reality," Allyn said. "A different version of earth in another universe."

The two-way mirror thumped loudly and reverberated. The door opened; a svelte man with a wild mop of brown hair, a visitor's badge, and a cheap polyester jacket stormed into the room chased by an air force colonel and a stout redheaded woman. "Dr. Harrison, you cannot do this!" the redhead scolded.

"You *did* travel across dimensions!" the man exclaimed excitedly, pointing at Allyn.

Torrenson pulled the excited doctor away from Allyn.

"Sorry about this, Leticia," the woman said to Cifuentes. Her badge read "Director Lewis."

"This is fascinating," the doctor exclaimed. "*This one* is actually a traveler from another universe! How did you come here?"

This one? Allyn thought.

"Dr. Harrison, you are compromising this interrogation!" Director Lewis shouted. "Calm down or I will ship you back to MIT in cuffs!"

"I want the wife and daughter, too," Harrison said. "I want to study them all."

"My wife and daughter are not from Aandor!" Allyn insisted.

"Your daughter is a hybrid between an alien and a human."

"We ARE human beings!" Allyn stressed. "Cifuentes, we had a deal. Don't let this idiot near my family."

Dr. Harrison was removed from the room, but the colonel remained, barking orders to transfer Allyn's family to a military detention facility. Cifuentes had that apologetic look; bad decisions were being made that were out of her control.

"My daughter is just twelve . . . ," Allyn pleaded.

"Let's give you that bathroom break," Cifuentes said to get him away from the colonel.

Cifuentes and Torrenson bookended Allyn as they walked him down the hall past other rooms. Despondent, Allyn almost missed it . . . the faintest twinkle of magic—a room near the end of the hall. But the metal doors prevented him from reaching through.

"I hear one of my friends being tortured in this room," Allyn said suddenly, playing a long-shot gambit.

"The rooms are soundproof," Torrenson said.

"Nevertheless, I heard his voice," Allyn lied. "I want to see if he's okay."

"He's fine," Torrenson said. "Only guy with a heart condition that will outlive us all."

"How do I know you haven't dissected him? I've been forth-coming with you."

"No," Cifuentes said.

"Colby!" Allyn shouted at the top of his lungs and kicked the door as they passed.

A confused agent opened it.

"That you, Padre?" Colby asked from inside the room. Allyn could not see the detective, but there it was . . . the faintest ten-dril of magic a few molecules thick connecting Colby Dretch to the nearest lay line. It was the spell that kept him animated. Al-lyn pulled on that tendril, wresting it from its target, and drew the energy into himself. Colby went silent and slumped onto his table—the other agent in the room cried out. Allyn hoped the detective could forgive him. He hoped it would be temporary—just until he finished what he believed he had to do. Michelle and Rosemarie's lives depended on it.

Allyn cried out, clutched at his heart, and went down on a knee. This drew his handlers in to see what was wrong—they put their hands on his back and arm and chest. Allyn grabbed their wrists and cast the strongest soothe he could muster with his meager allotment. Torrenson relented almost immediately; Cifuentes was the more willful of the two—a strong mind fight-ing conversion—but she eventually succumbed.

"How may I serve," she said—her submission transmitting through obsidian eyes.

"Put me in this room with my friend. Introduce me to these agents. Then bring me a damned chamber pot, because I'm surely going to burst. And finally . . . bring me Dr. Harrison, Director Lewis, and that air force colonel."

CHAPTER 22

HOME FRONT

Hard cobblestones pressed into Callum's back. He turned over and retched. Gone was the lush greenery of upstate New York and in its place wattle-and-daub construction, timber, and stone. The incline of the street was familiar . . . he'd walked it many times. Where three streets converged rested a plaque commemorating Egwyn's Square—a small plaza just a few blocks from the wharf. He was back in Aandor.

Catherine! Bree!

Cal's soldiers littered the road, confused about their new surroundings. Beside him, Malcolm retched and groaned. "What happened?"

"We're in the Aavanteen," Cal said.

"Oh Jesus," Mal said. "No."

It was the Aavanteen, and yet it wasn't. The deathly quiet street should have been lively, filled with bustling laborers and immigrants . . . a fair share of hustle by its denizens. The houses were so hot the people virtually lived on its streets. Were they taken away, or were they hiding, convinced this was not their war, and what did it matter who the masters were? No matter who you genuflected to, poor was poor.

"Avan wha . . . ?" asked Tony Two Scoops.

"Aandor City," Malcolm said.

Balzac laughed as though he'd just won the lottery.

Cal slammed the jester against a wall. "Send us back," he growled.

"I am no wizard, MacDonnell. I but set events in motion, and play on the probabilities. Truly, I had hoped to be in Aandor by August. But this . . . this has unfolded beyond my wildest expectations. I am home!"

"Our kids!" cried an agitated Tony Two Scoops. "Our wives! My gumar!"

"The streets are deserted," noted Tilcook. "Martial law?"

"Not everyone," Van Rooyen noted, cocking his ear down the road that led to the wharf. Boots marched toward them.

The streets from the lake were curved to eliminate sight lines, giving a young town an advantage against invading forces.

Malcolm pulled a battle-ax out from under his suit jacket, to Cal's amazement. "Didn't think a dwarv would stand around a frost giant unarmed, did you? Let's teach these motherfu—"

"No," Cal said. "Too many. We retreat for now."

"TO ARMS! TO ARMS!" shouted Balzac. "The enemies of Farrenheil conspire—"

Van Rooyen's right hook ended that, but the damage was done. The patrol doubled its pace, blowing horns to alert other squads. The Farrenheisi formed a line along the width of the street three rows deep with shields up and spears jutting. As the patrol entered the tiny square the mercenaries opened fire, cutting them down like straw before the scythe. More enemy squads rushed in from the other streets, blowing horns as well and drawing yet more of the occupying force to the area.

The mercenaries covered the next wave. One by one, however, their assault weapons began to jam, some even blowing shrapnel back on them. Tilcook and Tony whipped out their pistols and covered the group's rear. The front line, however, was out of firepower.

"More coming up from the lake!" shouted Malcolm.

"Swords!" Callum ordered, whipping out Bòid Géard. The mercs complied.

The adversaries clashed like rogue waves. Malcolm's ax bit through leather and iron scale. Callum took down two men for every one of his friends. Still more soldiers poured into their square.

The ground began to shake, at first Cal thought because of the number of soldiers, but then the structures around them shook and swayed. The shaking grew deeper and even the Farrenheisi looked worried. From behind a house one of Malcolm's Chinook copters boomed into the air, whipping a frenzy of wood, straw, and slate in its wake.

"That's Ligresti," shouted Van Rooyen. "He was in the copter back in New York."

"Our guns are toast!" yelled Tilcook.

The copter hovered thirty feet above the guardians. Ligresti's copilot swiveled the fore pintle-mounted M240 down the street and opened fire on three dozen Farrenheisi rushing the guardians. The enemy succumbed before the weapon, whipped like pureed fruit. The M240 blew the front walls off the house where the street curved before coming to a stop.

"We don't know how long that copter will stay functional here," Mal told Van Rooyen. He waved for the pilot to come down to retrieve the group. Their best chance was to fly out of the city and head for the deep woods. Cal heard a low grunt that sent a line of fear through him—the sound of a frost giant in the midst of great effort.

Hesz emerged from a side street holding his manacles. He whipped the chains round and then threw his whole body into the rotation like a discus champion, releasing them toward the Chinook's rotor mast.

"COVER!" screamed Cal. He grabbed Malcolm and smashed through the door of the closest building.

Shrapnel exploded everywhere; metal bits blew through the walls and shutters of Cal's shelter. Pieces of the blowback took out the helicopter's tail rotor. The flying machine's engines groaned, sparks sputtering from it. Cal rushed back out. The pilot tried to gain altitude and steer the helicopter toward the lake, but it began to spin around, drawing circles of black streamers above them.

"There's munitions on that copter," Mal said.

Ligresti disappeared over the next row of buildings—Cal counted out the three long seconds before the Aavanteen shuddered violently from the explosion. The copter had hit near the wharf, packed tight with shanties, wooden warehouses, and ships. A plume of black smoke rose high enough to be seen for miles.

"Jeezus! The whole waterfront's going to burn," Malcolm said.

"Tell me youse guys got firemen," Two Scoops said.

They didn't.

The last remaining Farrenheisi troops tightened ranks and closed in slowly on the guardians. Cal and the mercs steeled themselves for the rush. The enemy soldiers never got the chance as they were taken down with arrows and spears from behind. Through the dusty haze, hooded men emerged to retrieve their arrows from the dead. Their armor was battered, their clothes soiled and torn, but some bore the markings and insignias of the city watch among them.

"Who are ye?" said the lead man in a tattered Dukesguarde dress uniform. "Name yourselves."

"I am Callum MacDonnell, captain of the Dukesguarde, son of Lord Commander James MacDonnell. Has some blow to your skull caused you to forget your commanding officer already, Renny?"

Corporal Renny Falk was always the one you counted on to defuse a stressful situation with a sarcastic quip or a barb, but today he looked drained of all humor. Renny stepped closer and studied Cal's face and a glint of his former grin emerged. "Good gods, man . . . the invasion's aged ye ten years . . . if you don't mind me saying, Captain. And ye weren't all that pretty to start with," he noted. The man hugged Cal like he was his best friend in the world.

"Where's the prince?" Renny asked.

"Safe," Malcolm said.

"We'd best be going," Renny insisted. "More of these scat eaters are sure to come."

Both Balzac and Hesz were gone. Cal would have given chase if he knew which direction they'd gone. *Shit!*

"We're going to need a place to hole up," Malcolm said.

"Aye, that you will," said Renny. "This way."

CHAPTER 23

THE CRAWL

1

Despite the clear blue sky, the town was thick with a drab mood. Rumblings and a gray line to the west hinted at a soaking soon enough. The consensus was to get across the bridge as fast as possible—not to seek cover in Meadsweir. Only hills and forests awaited them on the other side of the river, settlements having long been abandoned since Meadsweir went dark; bears and wolves were known elements they could take their chances with.

Shops and homes, tightly spaced, lined the street. They were worn with age but otherwise intact—no indication of unnatural disasters. The street ran straight for sixty yards and then curved down to the left toward the river. This was a true street of stone and mortar, not the grubby muddy roads of Yarmouth and Crowe's Porte. Rusting sewer grates denoted advanced drainage. They certainly did have money and people at one time. The usual clop, clop, clop of the horses echoed too loudly for comfort in the desolation. The shadows grew long as the sun fell toward the rumbling line of clouds; they were the only thing that moved in this life-sized diorama and it played tricks on the mind. Not a rat, nor a bird, was evident. Even the insects shunned this place. It gave Daniel the heebie-jeebies.

Most residents had departed long before the final demise, but bodies cropped up sporadically along the street—mostly soldiers. These loyal (or stubborn) denizens were finely preserved for people who had died three centuries ago; except for a pinkish coloration, like severe sunburn, their decomposition was akin to couple of days. Time crawled in Meadsweir.

"Just hole up here," Seth suggested to Daniel. "Farrenheil would never come looking."

"We're getting Danny to the Gate," Cat said tensely. She glimpsed Lelani when she said this. It bothered Daniel to see discord among his friends.

"Please, silence yourselves," Urry whispered.

The curve opened up to a circular plaza with an ornate fountain at its center; four phoenixes back-to-back chiseled from granite—the oxidized tips of water pipes peeked out from their open beaks like green worms. Surrounding the plaza were long-abandoned shops, taverns, inns, and half-timbered trade houses with gabled roofs and spackled white plaster that reminded Daniel of Bavarian architecture. Four streets led into this plaza; to the right, King's Lane led to the castle, which despite its lower elevation by the river, still towered magnificently over all Meadsweir. Where the castle was, so too was the bridge.

"You guys feel that?" Seth asked. Daniel did not feel a thing; Seth was alone in his observation based on everyone's expressions. "The air's like pure oxygen," he continued. "Feels like I just downed a Red Bull."

"Well don't fly away just yet," Daniel said.

The rest of the town was the same—until they came upon a

cluster of fallen soldiers . . . broken and mangled, clawed and bitten . . . but not consumed. Wagons and boxes that had been part of a barrier were sprawled all over the road—a last stand, if Daniel ever saw one.

"Whatever it is, it does not consume flesh," Ladue noted.

"Wicked sunburn, though," said Seth.

The company passed through gingerly, careful not to disturb the dead. Daniel recalled the meadow back in New York and hoped no necromancers lurked here. Past the soldiers, the castle came into view. Daniel expected it to be a dull cold gray thing—perhaps because he thought of exile as a punishment, something one did to bad people—but the stone blocks had a tinge of peach in them, and the exposed wood was burnt umber where dark, and bright burnt sienna where light, giving the exterior a warm, homey veneer in contrast to the black malevolence of its windows. The land surrounding Egwyn's domicile was free of construction, a perfect killing field for archers atop the forty-foot curtain walls and sixty-foot mural towers. A channel of the Sevren flowed around the castle for its moat.

This had been the outer boundary of the Kingdom of Aandor for hundreds of years. Those nonhuman predators of man were halted from coming farther west, and humankind flourished in Aandor. The padre called it the Foothold Period, when thanks to wizards and magic, man ascended to the top of the food chain.

As luck would have it, the outer drawbridge was down and the barbican portcullis open. They moved across the bridge, Ladue and Urry in the lead, until the horses snorted nervously and stopped midway.

"Do you feel that?" Seth asked.

Daniel did not feel anything.

"I do," said Cat. "Something prickly in the air—raised the hairs on my arms."

The stillness of Meadsweir was unsettling. In most abandoned towns, vermin at least vied with the cats and wild dogs for dominance—but not here. Whatever killed those soldiers centuries ago had not left. Aandor simply gave it a wide berth. The sky rumbled; the topmost edges of the darkening clouds were iridescent with the failing light as they shrouded the sun.

"We should get inside," said Ladue, embodying everyone's sentiments. With some coaxing the horses crossed the drawbridge. Daniel looked up nervously at the murder holes, praying no shower of boiling oil brewed. Another drawbridge spanned a second smaller moat behind the barbican. Through the gatehouse they entered into a bailey that consisted of a stable, a barrack, and two small cottages against the curtain wall. Ahead was the castle keep, a majestic, looming structure with six gabled turrets that cleared even the forest's tallest trees.

They stabled their horses and climbed steps to the ornate double bronze doors. To either side of the doors stood a fourteen-foot statue at attention. They looked half finished, with only the most rudimentary hints of facial features and musculature—deep black sockets where the eyes should have been and heavy brows; one statue was cut of bluish stone and the other was molded of fired red clay. They reminded Daniel of the statues on Easter Island.

"Maybe the artist never got around to finishing them," Seth said, reading his mind.

"Are we here to critique sculpture?" Ladue asked. He grabbed one of the door's large metal rings.

"Wait!" Lelani warned.

As Ladue pushed, an orange glow ignited in the statues' eyes. Both turned their heads slowly toward Ladue.

"Step back!" Lelani ordered.

"I got this," Seth said confidently. He cast his purple blossoms spell on the sentries.

"No!" Lelani shouted a second too late. The blowback jettisoned Seth like a cannonball a dozen yards into the barrack wall. The statues now raised their arms and took cautious steps toward Ladue.

"Fall back," said Urry. Ladue took aim at the clay sentry with his M240, but Urry grabbed the stock and yanked up. "What use are bolts against clay . . . except to call every malicious spirit down upon us with your din?"

Lelani and Cat grabbed Seth and the company retreated into the guardhouse. Once Urry crossed the threshold, the sentries reversed themselves and returned to their posts.

"What happened?" Seth asked, rubbing the back of his head.

"You cannot use transmutation on golems," Lelani said. "Their elements are bonded to the divinity that has granted them life."

"*Those* slowpokes killed all of Alfred's soldiers?" asked Daniel.

"*They* did not," Lelani said.

"Can't we go around the castle to the bridge?" asked Cat.

"They built it straight into the castle," Urry said. "This was a border town . . . better for defense as well as collecting tolls and tariffs."

"From the town square, I spied a castle side gate—lower and closer to the river—most likely the road to the bridge," Urry said. "But the portcullis was down and the drawbridge up. The wall is higher in back—we'd have to scale fifty feet with horses and your swollen belly . . ." Then he added, "Um—your ladyship."

"Daniel can touch the door," Lelani said.

"Mon Dieu!" Ladue cried, followed by Cat's "Are you serious?"

"Golems are guardians," said Lelani. "Egwyn never had children . . . Daniel is the rightful master of this castle."

As the others argued about the danger, Daniel walked toward the big doors. The statues remained still as he approached. Urry and Ladue rushed to catch up, competing for nervous looks. Daniel grabbed the ring with little ceremony. Again the orange light flickered in the sentries' eyeholes, and they turned toward him, but instead of reaching for the teen, they contemplated him. The sentries put their hands together prayer style and bowed to Daniel.

"What now?" Daniel asked.

"Order one to show you its shem," Lelani said.

"Can I see your shem?" Daniel asked the clay golem. It remained still.

"Say it as a statement, not a question."

"Show me your shem."

The golem opened its mouth; a small clay tablet poked out like a tongue. The orange glow from its eyes died. Daniel handed the tablet to Lelani.

"Egwyn created these protectors," Lelani said. "Here is written the name of the golem's patron goddess, Dienna—the Gray Hunter. Among its commandments: obedience to the royal family, protection, and also a taboo against taking a human life." Lelani looked over the tablet again and raised an eyebrow. "The taboo against taking life should have been its first commandment, but it is subordinate to obedience. I'm surprised a cleric would agree to this covenant."

"I could use a few thousand of these," Daniel said.

"Golems were forbidden before Egwyn's time. Only the divine may create life." Lelani gazed at the massive castle doors. "What other taboos did Egwyn ignore?"

Lelani placed the tablet back in the golem's mouth. The eyes flickered again.

"Can you open these doors?" Daniel asked them. The sentries remained unmoving.

"Please open these doors," Daniel repeated.

Again nothing.

Lelani said, "Perhaps you contradict their last command."

"Do you have standing orders?" Daniel asked the clay golem. It nodded.

"Whoever gave you that order is long dead," Daniel told the sentinels. "I am Danel, the great-great-great-great-great-grandnephew of Egwyn, and the current prince of Aandor. Disregard your previous orders and follow my commands."

Each golem nodded and extended an arm toward their door. As they pushed, the rusty hinges squealed obnoxiously, clamoring through the castle.

"Stop!" Daniel ordered.

"That made a racket," Seth noted.

"Fucking dinner bell," Cat agreed.

As they waited to confirm nothing was coming up from the depths, the sky rumbled and boomed. They slipped in through the crack one by one, weapons in hand, just as the heavens released their deluge.

Thunder rumbled and reverberated through the musty, stale

keep. Tattered tapestries hung precariously along the foyer's high walls. White and blue squares made up the polished checkered floor. A marble pantheon of Aandor's gods lined the edge—tall columns, intricate moldings, this castle was an artisan's dream. The keep's cathedral-like proportions could house a race of giants. Crepuscular rays filtered through the archer slits and high windows from the sunny eastern side of the castle, illuminating small islands in the darkness. The western side of the castle was black from the storm, and soon they would lose that precious little light as well when the storm rolled over. Daniel and Seth pulled out their flashlights.

"One moment," Ladue told them. He put on a pair of military-grade night-vision goggles and scanned the deep dark recesses of the keep.

Ladue made a sweep of the grand foyer, turning around slowly. When he came to Daniel, the mercenary raised his hand to block the goggles lens. *"Mon Dieu,"* he whispered, stopping cold. "Daniel . . . you glow magnificently."

"Flattery will get you everywhere," Seth quipped.

Ladue passed the goggles around for all to see.

"Dude, you're lit up like a Texas bonfire," said Seth.

"Am I under attack?" Daniel asked.

"It's magic," Lelani said. "The energy does not permeate a royal, and so it congregates around you, creating an aura invisible in the normal spectrum."

"Like an armor of light," said Ladue.

"Huh?" said Daniel.

"The aura's shaped like you, but bigger," Cat explained. "Like you're seven feet tall. Maybe that's why people take to you? They're subconsciously attuned to the heroic proportions of the aura, perceiving Daniel as larger than life."

"Charisma on steroids," Seth said.

"It also explains how the golems recognized him as a royal," said Lelani.

"Can we dial the aura down?" Daniel asked.

"There is nothing to be done," Lelani said. "This is who you are."

Ladue took Seth's flashlight and took point. A double staircase on opposite walls curved to a central balcony above. Underneath the balcony was the entrance to the great hall.

"The bridge is below this level," Urry said. "We must head down, not up."

Their footsteps' echolocation indicated the hall was longer than it was wide. The last of the natural light was bluish and weak, leaving them in near darkness—except for a tiny, pulsing yellow and magenta dot at the far end near the throne.

"Campfire?" Daniel whispered.

Ladue cracked two industrial-grade glow sticks and hurled them several feet ahead. They skittered to a stop on the smooth marble floor. The eerie greenish light ran up the base of a stone support column and radiated about six feet before being swallowed by the greedy darkness. The silhouette of a large figure lay next to the column.

"Zoiks!" whispered Seth.

"Jinkies," added Cat.

"Divine appeals are a poor shield for the evils that lurk here," Urry told the pair.

The "man" lying by the column was actually a fourteen-foot metal construct . . . scorched and melted in place.

Lelani reached into its mouth and pulled out the shattered fragments of a clay tablet. "Iron golem," she whispered.

A few feet from it, black ash and bits of scorched wood formed the murder-scene outline of a large man; bits of a clay tablet lay where the head would have been.

"Wood golem?" Daniel asked.

"Gee—what lives in an abandoned castle and shoots fire so hot, it can instantly melt iron?" Cat waxed sardonically. "Oh wait . . . I've seen this movie . . . we're going to get crisped by a fucking dragon."

Lelani chuckled softly. "Dragons are mythical creatures, Cat."

Seth guffawed loudly and drew everyone's ire. "Sorry," he said. "The *centaur* just set *our* asses straight on mythical creatures."

Daniel shook his head and chuckled, and after a beat, Cat and Ladue joined him.

"Have ye all lost your minds?" Urry whispered tensely.

"Close, *mon ami*," Ladue said. He picked up a glow stick and threw it farther down the hall. Urry did the same, pausing a moment first to examine the stick and the miracles of modern chemistry. More bodies were scattered along the floor.

"Soldiers of the realm," Urry confirmed. "Once."

That pulsing light lay just before the throne dais. The company circled around and tried to come to terms with what they were witnessing—a dead knight of the realm on the ground, grasping a familiar ornate silver dagger, with which he'd barely pinned the corner of a fiery, phantasmal heart to the marble floor. The heart was in the center of a silver painted pentagram, which was itself within a painted circle, with runes written along the edges and at the tips of the star's points. The heart was translucent; it fluoresced like a plasma sculpture, was as large as a football—and it was beating.

"That dagger," Cat said. "Like the ones Dorn used."

"Faerie silver," Daniel said.

"Should we take it?" Seth asked.

"Absolutely not," answered Lelani. "That pinned heart is very likely what has kept the entity trapped here for over three hundred years."

"That thing gives me goose pimplies," Seth said.

"It evokes foreboding in me as well," Lelani admitted. "It should not exist here."

"We can contemplate demon hearts, or we can get the lad to Red King's Gate," Urry reminded them all.

"Here," said Ladue behind the dais.

A stone staircase spiraled down into the bowels of the keep. Urry collected the glow sticks, leaving the great hall behind them completely dark—the sunlight was gone, supplanted by the sporadic intense flicker of lightning and the patter of rain from a rumbling black sky.

2

The light sticks traveled only so far down the spiral stairs. They repeated the action every few feet. Daniel was in the middle behind Lelani and in front of Seth. The space was tight, a true squeeze for the centaur, but she'd proven nimble as she had on so many occasions. The nub of her once-beautiful lush red tail waggled back and forth as she descended. Living among humans in Aandor City—with its fragile tiny furniture, staircases, small doorways, outhouses, water closets, storage cellars, and attics— could not have been easy for her and must have been very lonely. She was an alien being; what human could desire her romantically? Apparently Ladue. The descent came to an abrupt halt— Daniel absentmindedly slammed into Lelani's rear and grabbed her rump.

"Oh jeez—uh—sorry," he said, mortified.

She smiled knowingly and resumed her descent. Daniel put some space between them.

"She's flirting with you," Seth whispered. "She obviously likes men, though the logistics baffle me; think Ladue can make her whinny, Danny boy?" Seth made a vulgar fist pump.

"You are an utter moron," Daniel remarked.

"Is that a neigh?"

At the bottom, they were in a vaulted corridor of stone and mortar that stretched two directions from the staircase.

"Do we pick pitch-black tunnel number one or pitch-black tunnel two?" asked Cat.

"The river is to the right," said Ladue with mercenary confidence.

"Aye," Urry concurred. "Let us make haste for the bridge and be done with this place."

"What about the horses?" Cat said.

"If we can raise the portcullis on the side entrance, I'll go back for them," said Ladue.

"Leave them," Urry urged. "If we make the bridge, we should count our blessings."

"I'm six months pregnant," Cat reminded the sergeant.

He looked at her bump, then at her, and crooked his head toward Lelani. "If the centaur'll na carry you milady, I certainly will."

The corridor was lined with doors. The company ignored them and silently pushed through, leapfrogging their glow sticks, chased by a claustrophobic blackness determined to swallow them. Daniel was grateful for Meadsweir's mystery alpha inhabitant . . . God only knew what things might have taken residence in the castle's bowels if it hadn't scared every living thing away. The corridor was clear and eventually curved to the left before spilling into a rectangular room about sixty feet long.

The room was designed like a mountain lodge—rain patted the gabled shingled roof three stories up, supported by massive beams and braces running the width; rivers of thick white mortar bonded the cobblestone floor, each polished stone the size of a grapefruit in earth tones of gray and brown. An elaborately chiseled oak mantel framed the hearth—plush velvet chairs and a divan squared off over a polished marble end table to form a cozy nook. The room overflowed with expensive-looking statues, jewelry, urns, platters, books, and other knickknacks displayed on tables, shelves, and pedestals. The lack of a door to such a chamber struck Daniel as odd; from the corridor it appeared dark, but once across the threshold, you'd swear it was sunlit, though the source was not evident. Not a torch or lantern was lit, and the stone hearth on the left wall was cold.

At the far end, opposite the corridor entrance, was a heavy door of thick wooden planks banded with strips of black iron and black studs. It had an iron handle, and above that, the keyhole encircled by a severe nest of iron barbs sure to prick even the most expert lock picker. Everything about the door screamed *stay out*. But the room lacked any other egress.

"Touch nothing," warned Lelani.

"But there are all these nifty shiny things laying about," Seth said sardonically. "You'd think a wizard would be smart enough to lock his sanctum."

"This is *not* Egwyn's sanctum," Lelani stressed. "This is the antechamber, and I assure you, this is the most dangerous room in the castle. Nothing is as it seems."

"I've no interest in the doings of wizards," Urry noted. "Let us retreat."

"The river is that way," Ladue said, pointing at the far door. They walked through cautiously, mindful not to brush against or tip over a crystal vase that would be the envy of any Waterford craftsman; a solid gold sextant; a silver dagger with a jade handle encrusted with jewels; a platinum goblet filled with diamonds; gold and silver swords . . . hundreds of such items. The room was stacked with swag. Urry and Lelani had the hardest time slinking through the tight spaces. Ladue reached the door first; Lelani cringed when he tried the handle.

"Locked," the Frenchman said, as though he weren't traveling in a realm of magic, booby traps, and curses.

"Please," Lelani implored all of them. "Touch nothing. Lean on nothing. Sit on nothing. Do not even place an item of yours on a table or pedestal." She turned to Ladue. "Do not open doors."

Daniel studied the room. One of the myriad trophies and doodads was likely the key to the door. Wizards thrived on tests; keys under the mat was too pedestrian . . . if someone could outsmart your trap, you deserved to get robbed. "Should have brought a thief," Daniel mused aloud.

"I can pick this ancient lock easily," Ladue said.

"No," Lelani warned, placing her hand on Ladue's. She took out an ornate brass compact case. Inside, jewels decorated one half and a superbly clear mirror took up the other. Lelani took Seth's hand and borrowed some magic. The jewels glowed, casting laser lights onto the mirror.

"This door is poison to anyone who forces it." She put away the compact and took out a small glass beaker and some vials. "Seth, I will need both hands for this counter enchantment. Please hold me, and do not let go."

"I knew you were pining for me, Red," Seth quipped.

"She's going to kick you into next week," Ladue warned amiably.

"Uh . . . I know you're smart," Daniel said, "and you have many amazing talents as a wizard and a warrior—but are you sure you're up to this? I mean . . . you're trying to outsmart a legend."

"We're in the bowels of a deserted city haunted by an unknown entity that only providence has helped us avoid so far," she said, as though a summation qualified as the explanation. She mixed her ingredients and placed the beaker under the door. Seth put a hand on her back. Lelani made motions smooth and graceful like a hula dancer as she chanted. The beaker fizzed and foamed like yeast in water. Small gray fizzy-foamy caterpillars began crawling out and up the door. The army of squirming foam settled on the door like a blanket; Lelani changed her chant, the language now more guttural, darker, almost ancient. It was painful to everyone's ears but Daniel's.

"Agh! What are you doing?" Seth complained. Unlike the others, he was unable to use his hands.

The foam organisms started to turn black, and then they crumbled into fine carbon cinders.

As the others cleared their heads with a shake, Lelani swept the cinders into a Tupperware container. She swapped the container for a bronze key in her satchel. Lelani exhaled hot breath upon the key and stuck it in the lock. She rubbed the bow with her thumb for several seconds and then waited. Lelani, normally the epitome of confidence, looked hesitant; it was scary to witness.

"What's wrong?" asked Cat.

"I am trying to churn butter with a toothpick."

"If that key's not the right tool for the job, I don't know what is," Seth said.

"If this does not work . . ." They all stared at her. Daniel had forgotten how to breathe. "If something should go awry—run to the corridor and keep going to the great hall."

Lelani turned the bolt.

The door remained locked. It would not budge no matter how much she strained or turned the bolt back and forth. Lelani snapped her hand off the key as though stung. The key glowed red and melted into slag onto the floor. The light in the room dwindled, like dusk descending—the room's contents, a cityscape of silhouettes.

"Run!" Lelani commanded.

The company retraced their steps through the darkened room at twice their original speed. Urry knocked over several pedestals' worth of items. At the far end by the corridor came the reverberation of a huge crack, like a massive ice shelf calving. Six feet of cobblestone floor along the wall, running the entire width of the room, dropped. Cool air carrying the scent of ozone and an ambient bluish light flooded up through the newly formed pit. Daniel and Seth reached the edge first—the corridor lay just beyond it. In the pit, a cool gray mist swirled. Cold winds swooped up and lightning and thunder rumbled below.

"'Tis the gateway to hell!" cried Urry.

Daniel imagined hell a lot hotter and less misty than this trench. A break in the swirl revealed the threatening truth—he spied Meadsweir as one would from an airplane—several thousand feet in the clouds. Spray from the storm and the scent of ozone filled the chamber. Stones along the floor's edge continued to drop, and the gap between them and the corridor widened.

"I can make that jump," said Lelani, pulling a rope out of her satchel and handing one end to Ladue. As she started her charge toward the corridor, stone missiles smashed the roof above the gap with tremendous force, splintering rafter joists and braces, halting the centaur's leap. The stones continued through the opening, hurtling toward the castle again on their second run. The next wave to shatter the roof was closer to the group, forcing the company back farther into the room. The impact of stones on the edge took a large chunk of shelf with it. The gap to the corridor widened to twenty feet.

"You can't make that jump!" Cat shouted against the tumult of the thunderstorm.

"We must find a way through that door!" Ladue shouted.

They returned to the other end of the room. The floor continued to calve a line at a time, except for when a stone hit and took out larger chunks. Artifacts and furniture fell through the sky, only to return with deadly velocity; it made Swiss cheese of the once beautiful gabled roof. Half the room was gone.

"Should we climb onto those rafters?" Cat asked.

"We'll just get brained by falling debris," Seth pointed out.

Assuming the key hadn't been on the other end of the room and was now in eternal free fall, finding it was imperative to survival. "Should we just start picking up objects!" Daniel shouted.

"Absolutely not!" Lelani said.

"What could be worse than this?" Seth asked.

"The whole floor might drop at once!"

Hundreds of items still remained in the room, hundreds of possible keys. Daniel ignored the approaching gap and concentrated on the things nearest him. Something would click . . . call out and say, *It's me—I'm a key.*

The hearth and mantel ripped away. Less than half a room

remained before the hole in the sky, and they were in as much danger of being swept out by the roaring wind as losing the floor. Communication had become impossible. Urry and Ladue used grappling hooks and rope to hoist themselves to a joist. They reached down to pull up Cat. Daniel ignored their pleas . . . avoiding the drop wouldn't protect them from being bludgeoned. Daniel scanned silver spoons and scepters; rubies the size of a baby's fist; goblets, chalices, and platters; shields with banners; gold knitting needles skewering balls of fine yarn; robes of ermine, silk, and linen; curly-toed embroidered slippers. Nothing cried out to him—nothing, except . . .

Sitting on a plain table against the back wall was a large jade bowl filled with valuables: a string of pearls, a silver snuffbox, some copper coins, a gold ring with diamonds and emeralds, and something that appeared out of place with the other items—a brass oarlock. *One of these things is not like the other, one of these things just doesn't belong* . . . Daniel sang to himself. There were other non-shiny, non-bejeweled items like the weather-beaten wood and steel arbalest leaning against that very table. But the arbalest at least represented the apex of technological engineering in this realm. Everything in the room screamed value in some sense . . . except the oarlock—a fisherman's tool. *The Fisher Kings.* Daniel lifted the oarlock without hesitation. He studied it and the door, and slipped the pin into the keyhole. One of the barbs pricked his knuckle. He waited for the chaos behind him to stop while sucking at his wound. Nothing.

Another section of floor fell away—their shelf had at best ten feet. Seth followed the others up the rafters. Ladue and Cat pleaded with Daniel to climb. Even if the hurling missiles were not a factor, Lelani was stuck . . . she could never pull her own weight up there.

This has to be the key, Daniel thought, but lacking empirical evidence, he began to worry. He withdrew the oarlock and studied it. Lelani pressed close against him—the shelf had become little more than a ledge and she would run out of standing space sooner than him. They studied the object together.

The brass inside the ring was scraped, the scratches shining slightly brighter than the tarnished exterior. Daniel ran his finger on the inside and discovered the subtlest dimples in the metal. The metal barbs on the door formed a circle around the keyhole, like a nest of black iron thorns with the hole a black egg in its center. Daniel put the oarlock in front of the keyhole and pushed it over the nest of barbs; it was a snug fit, like a wrench over a nut. Daniel rotated the oarlock, adding new scrapes to the metal, until the bristles found their dimple and the two pieces locked. Again, nothing happened. Lelani reached for the oar ring and turned it—the circle of barbs turned with it. The bolt turned, and the door opened a crack.

The floor ceased its disintegration. Debris closest to them continued to tumble through the room, but at the far end of the room, cobblestones fell back in place along the edge like pieces of a puzzle, building out a new floor. The display items and roof shingles also returned. As more of the room reemerged, the din of the storm subsided.

"I don't understand," said Cat as the men lowered her down. "Was it an illusion?"

Lelani shook water off the way a horse did, spraying them all with drops. "It most certainly was not," she said. "If not for His Grace, we would have fallen . . . and unlike the items in the room, we would not have returned along the magical corridor. We would have perished."

Where they had entered the antechamber, a solid stone wall

had replaced the corridor entrance, with not even a seam of a hidden door to the dark tunnel. They could only go forward.

"Let's move on," said a shaken Ladue. "The sooner we are out of this place, the better."

CHAPTER 24

OLD ACQUAINTANCES

They ran, turning and twisting through back alleys—away from the inferno engulfing the wharf—with deftness only watchmen honed after years of patrol can do. As Cal ran past familiar neighborhoods, his broken heart for the family he'd abandoned in New York smothered any nostalgia for his beloved city.

They exited the Aavanteen, crossing over a canal into the prosperous part of town. The streets here were empty, too. The alley between two houses spilled out onto Atheling's Way, but they stopped short of the avenue. Across was the massive Sacellum of Helene—a white marble beauty of columns, friezes, and domes and cypress trees along the top of the high walls. At the base of the wall enemy soldiers stood guard with no indication that anything was amiss. Cal was grateful his world had no radios; information moved only with the fastest horse. Renny removed a metal drainage grate in the alleyway, and one by one his men dropped into the earth.

"Don't think I'm gonna fit through dat," Tilcook said eyeing the hole.

"Suck it in," Cal ordered. Tilcook squeezed through, and the guardians followed the watch.

"Is this what it's come to?" complained Tilcook, huffing and wheezing as he lowered himself down the ladder. "Rats in the sewer."

"Better live rats than dead men," Malcolm said.

"Easy for you to say . . . Dwarvs love tunnels."

"Why haven't the Farrenheisi come down here?" Cal asked.

"Oh, they come down," Renny said. "But this is a very old city, built on top of older parts, and there are tunnels below tunnels. They'd need most of that army outside the wall to give it a proper scrubbing. Lucky they can't spare the men."

"Not for long," Cal said. "Forty thousand more march north from our southern fort."

The watchmen stopped in their tracks—the weight of this news marked them profoundly.

"They've broken the kingdom's spine," said one solemn old man.

"How?" Renny asked.

"Wizards," Malcolm spat out.

"Then we're lost," said another watchman.

"The prince is alive," Cal said to offer hope.

"Lot of good a babe will do," said Renny. "Is he in the city?" *Was he even in this universe?* "No," Cal said.

Mal added, "He's of age, though." Their saviors looked at Malcolm skeptically. "Long story."

They went through a hidden door, down another level below the sewers to an ancient cistern with pillars and vaulted ceilings. Stone walkways snaked through the cavern toward islands of glazed brick that broke the still black surface. Sconces on the pillars illuminated the great cavern.

"Jee-suss," said Tony Two Scoops, and let out an echoing whistle.

"We're deep below the Domo Helene, where the Sweet Sisters reside on the compound," Renny explained.

"Hiding under the skirts of virgins, huh?" Tilcook huffed.

"There are worse places to cower," said a woman in the shadow of a pillar. Cal caught the glint of a crossbow in her arms.

"Stay your hand, Sister . . .'tis Renny."

"Who are these others?"

"The captain himself, Cal MacDonnell, and his friends."

The woman in a grayish-blue cassock studied him, then stepped forward from the shadows—a white linen guimpe and wimple wrapped her head, cheeks, and neck. Her eyes locked on Callum. She looked familiar. She smiled as he struggled to remember. She pulled back on the wimple to expose the shape of her face and waves of blond hair.

"Loraine?"

"Milord," she responded with a slight bow, though as a Sweet Sister, she was only required to bow for prelates and the archduke's family.

"But . . . but . . ."

"Three years ago," she said. Loraine came closer with the torch and illuminated Cal better. His appearance startled her. "Yeh've aged half a life, milord."

"Old squeeze?" Two Scoops quipped.

Loraine stared Two Scoops down with a glare as deadly as the crossbow she held. "I'll thank yeh not to be spreading rumors, sir."

"Be nice, or she won't let you pass," Renny warned.

Their base was on a flat brick expanse in the corner of the cistern large enough for several campfires. The black water lapping against the edge of the platform lent a serene charm to the camp.

Fifty souls called this home; city watch, castle guards, veterans of past wars, and women and children as well. These were the fortunate ones . . . free of the atrocities above. A few Sweet Sisters ministered to the needful.

Renny led the guardians to his fire—three of his lieutenants joined them. "Are you the only Dukesguarde?" Cal asked.

"Falknyr was with us . . . he was killed yesterday trying to procure weapons. Only half this lot is armed. The city is locked tight. Your fight was the only victory since the invasion."

"That was no victory," Malcolm said. "That was a textbook clusterfuck."

"You killed more enemy than anyone since the bastards arrived—and lived to tell the tale. So tell me of the prince?"

"Proust opened a portal to another realm," Cal said. "One where time passes more rapidly than in Aandor. We've lived years already, as Sister Loraine observed. Danel was fourteen when last I saw him, and—"

Loraine smacked a skewer with something that looked suspiciously like roasted rodent against Cal's chest. "Eat, milord. Yeh'll need yer strength if yeh're to be rescuing yer pretty miss from the castle."

"My wha . . ."

"The lovely Lady Godwynn."

Chryslantha had been a point of contention between Cal and Loraine years ago. "Loraine, this isn't the time . . ."

"I'll have a word with yeh, if it please his lordship." The crossbow was crooked in her arm facing only a little way off to the side. "Yeh fine gents won't object?" She shot them a threatening glare and moved toward a private corner of the platform.

"Rumors, huh?" Two Scoops cracked.

Cal followed her, if only to keep the peace.

In the quiet corner Cal spoke up. "Loraine, I never meant to hurt . . ."

"Are yeh daft, man?" she whispered with a disgusted look. "I'm na carryin' a torch for yeh." Loraine's accent always thickened when she was stressed. "There's a *spy* in this resistance. Yeh needs to quit yer gabblin'."

Cal remained poker-faced. He slowly looked over his shoulder in a conversational manner and studied the people around him. Farrenheil's takeover had been thorough—it made sense they would have anticipated an insurgency.

"Who do you suspect?"

"If I knew who, I'd have put a bolt into the bastard already. We started good at first . . . hit them Heiszers when they strayed too far from their platoons, stole babes out of the city when the white bitch started her cullings. But our group grew quickly. Who were we to deny anyone seeking asylum when the world was on fire? Yesterday our luck turned. Falknyr was the craftiest of this lot, and the Heiszers were waiting for him at the depot. He was set up. We lost six."

"Why doesn't the enemy storm in, take everyone?"

"They're fishing for the prince. The whole city knows yeh stole away with the boy. And here yeh are prating to men yeh've never met about the lad. Yeh should have stayed hid, Cal."

"The prince is safe in another realm. We didn't plan to return like this."

Loraine traced his hairline with a soft finger and touched the few creases around his eyes. "Have yeh really been gone ten and four years?" she asked.

"Aye," Cal said, slipping back into his old vernacular like a favorite pair of boots. "Have you really taken vows, Loraine? What if the prelates discover—"

"There's no rule that yeh need be pure as first snow to be a Sister, Cal. Some of the lasses are virgins; some sent into the order by pigheaded fathers—for the rest of us 'tis a simple vow of chastity. Men are soft in the head about the matters of women."

"Yes," he agreed with a subtle smirk.

"I married Marson Bale, yer father's tenant's son, after yeh left for yer soldiering . . . tall and wiry with eyes like amber in firelight. We moved to Eel's Tooth to help his aunt with her inn on account of his uncle dying. I cooked and he did whatever else needed doing. We had a baby girl, Rose. There weren't nothing Marson would'na do for his wee bairn.

"Eel's Tooth was a wealthy port town; I cooked a delicacy, whisker fish, which the local gentry paid dear for. Ye could not find it in the Spoke . . . ye had to wade into the marshes up north in a flatboat to fish it. Four times Marson came back with a hearty catch, and I could not cook the things as fast as the local lords asked for it. We made enough silver to pay the inn's taxes and extra for a generous Yule.

"But *I* was set on hiring Rose a proper teacher, one that could teach ciphering in addition to letters and how to play the lute. I wanted her to be more than I was, you see—more than the kitchen help—someone who could turn the head of a young lord . . . and *keep* him. Marson went out again to the marshes—but this time he come home sick. Yeh heard of dock fever, Cal? Turns a man the color of butter. We spent all the silver on healers of good repute but scarce skill. The fever took Marson in a week. And then it took his aunt . . . and then it took Rose."

"I'm so sorry, Loraine."

"What have yeh to be sorry for?"

"Your loss . . . what we had . . ."

She laughed. "I'm two years older and knew full well yeh were betrothed when I set me mind to yeh. I was foolish, makin' trouble of ma own doin'. Yeh've always been fair to me, Cal. Always talked true. When I screamed at yeh, I lied about yer father and I having a toss . . . I'm ashamed I said such a thing. Yer da was . . . is a good man. Yeh're a good man . . . and yeh're the only one I trust out of this whole lot."

Malcolm approached cautiously. "Hate to interrupt the reunion, but we are fighting a war."

"Tell the others to zip it about Daniel and our experiences," Cal ordered. "It's not safe."

"That sucks," Mal said. "Wish you'd said something before Tilcook whipped out his phone with pics of him and the prince."

Cal suppressed a groan.

"You sure about this, Cal? We'll need to share info if we want to get it. Renny's already come through with news."

"What news?"

"One of his people spotted Balzac. The clown's at his tavern . . . the Phoenix Nest."

CHAPTER 25

FOOL AGAINST LOVE

1

The White Lady called Chryslantha for a second audience after a day. Magnus said to tell Lara the truth, but why give her any advantage by which to find Callum?

Under normal circumstances Chrys would have confided in Sophia, but her friend slept all day and ate only when Chrys fed her. She did not need new burdens.

Sergeant Kalbfleish had been reassigned, and she was no longer shadowed, to her relief. She was assigned a chamber-maid—a stout Farrenheisi with tightly braided blond buns above each ear who no doubt reported all to her mistress. She was a boon, nevertheless. The maid was sympathetic enough toward Sophia for Chrys to wonder whether the common folk of all kingdoms would live in peace if they but discarded their masters.

A stylish blue dress had been supplied for Chrys . . . low cut and leaving little of the feminine mystique to the imagination. The great hall had been cleared of the dead; vinegar and lye masked the lingering rot. Widow Taker, one of Lara's personal cadre of wizards, paced the hall taking inventory of all the magical items the Farrenheisi pilfered throughout the city and piled into this room; much of it from temples, Magnus's chambers, and his wizards' academy. Widow Taker's true name was lost to the ages. He was ancient; a man of Sunumbreea, with pruned brown skin and cold black eyes, dressed in the pelts of leopards and jaguars whose pacing movements he mimicked. The wizard accessorized his dress and staff with dream weavers of hair and bone and feathers; they dangled on rawhide strips along with hoops of copper and silver. The staff was burned black, the wood twisted like an arthritic finger. On his spindly fingers sat a dozen wedding rings of bone, wood, gold, or silver—all from different cultures. He collected the wives of his vanquished enemies for his harem and was rumored to have fathered a hundred children in his long lifetime. Lara had come to Aandor with four of these formidable acolytes, including her nephew Dorn; was it cause for hope that only one wizard remained?

A table had been set by the window . . . a carafe of wine, candles. *Does the witch mean to woo me?* Chrys wondered; she tugged at her bodice. Their first encounter still preoccupied her, waking Chrys at the cusp of a guilty pleasure in her dreams; leaving her restless and her bedding sodden with sweat.

In Athelstan's seat of power, Lara studiously applied her quill to a scrap of parchment. A scarlet canopy hung over and around the dais. Lara's hair was a rich, luminous chestnut brown likely due to the desiccated servant sprawled on the dais stairs. The witch had started dinner without her. Two squires entered from the room behind the dais and removed the body.

When Lara finished writing and blotting, she rolled up the document and affixed a seal of hot wax, which she stamped with her signet ring. She stood, stretched, and placed the document among others in a basket.

"Affairs of state are tedious," Lara said, rolling wax off her fingers. "Vaulknar has appointed me interim governor."

"Congratulations?" Chrys said, not sure if Lara was vexed or pleased by the appointment.

"Blunt was the more obvious choice, do you agree?"

Chrys nodded.

"The grand duke tries to appease me. I am the most powerful sorceress in the Twelve Kingdoms, and even a man immune to magic would be a fool to rest comfortably around such a thing—family or not. Gardener kings and queens were common in the past. People believe the royals' resistance to magic helped them contain the whims of sorcerers, but in truth, mages realized the folly in trying to run governments. There is a whole world behind the world that no mundane is aware of. We have far more power and responsibilities than any king. Most wizards say 'Why saddle oneself with the day-to-day boredom of bureaucracy?' But then, most wizards are men, and men have different views of power and their entitlement to it. They are weak for it. I've never met a man who could endure what women endure.

"Vaulknar is a confident ruler . . . believes himself to be his own man; but any great ego that panders to its lusts is ripe for exploitation . . . and I am after all a beautiful woman, magic or otherwise." Chrys expected some sly goading expression on the White Lady for her seductive craftiness, but sensed a repressed shudder instead. Chrys, too, would shudder at the idea of some fat old duke atop her. For a second she pitied the lady, but quickly dissuaded herself of that charity.

"I had more wizards when we set off; placed into service by crafty Vaulknar himself. Leashes really . . . assigned to curb my ambitions. Many perished at the archives. If only they'd had a patron to protect them. The spell to transport two armies across hundreds of miles required sacrifices . . . wizards. I donated the grand duke's surviving watchdogs to the cause. And now Vaulknar is concerned. How rich," she said seductively. Her beautiful eyes had a glint of violet to them, that same illumination when they shared the bath . . . heat flushed into Chryslantha's cheeks, her heart raced under Lara's gaze, a betrayal of her most primal urges. Chrys knew full well that Lara fed off these energies—there was no hiding them from her.

"I have good news . . . and some not-so-good news," the White Lady said smoothly, ignoring Chryslantha's unease. "We found your sister. She hid with servants in the stables on the day of our *liberation* from the Tyrant Prince."

Is that what we call it now? Nevertheless, Chrys was elated.

"She will be quartered with you . . . however, you should know that she told her captors she was a tradesman's daughter, thinking it would save her. Can you imagine that?" Lara said amused and perplexed. "Your sister did not comprehend the advantages in being Lord Godwynn's daughter. The brains in your family have fixed squarely in your basket, Rose of Aandor."

Our brother is both smart and deadly, Chrys almost said, picturing the day he might drive his sword through her. Better the witch thought her enemies all fools.

"Anyway, some soldiers captured her for the slave exchange—a side business the more industrious among our ranks engage in. Her owners were not kind to her."

Chrys masked her heartbreak, her anger. "You promised those in the castle would be spared."

"Yes, but she wasn't in the castle—and she did not identify herself. Would you have me punish men for behaving like the animals they are?" Lara said, throwing her hands up in resignation.

Colonel Falkyre brought Niccole out from an adjoining room. Someone had done their best to make her presentable, but bruises bled through the powder. Her hair had been completely shorn, even her eyebrows—the dress was a peasant's shift, drab and plain, the likes of which her sister would never have worn. Niccole did not recognize Chryslantha through her vacant stare.

"She'd contracted lice, so the hair had to go," Falkyre said.

Chryslantha embraced her sister, but Niccole withdrew shaking and shuddering to throw her off and moaned like some soft-in-the-head simpleton.

"Niccole, it's me," Chrys said.

Lara waved Falkyre and Niccole away. Chrys made to follow. "Don't you wish to hear the bad news?" Lara asked.

"Worse than that?" Chrys said accusingly.

Lara looked cross. "Your level of gratitude disappoints to say the least," she said. "Blunt and I had a bet over your reaction. Perhaps my husband's right . . . I lack empathy. It's rare for Blunt to have any thought I have not inserted into his head," Lara said absently. The White Lady looked alone, like every other woman stuck in a political marriage. "I was hoping you and I could enjoy a pleasant dinner, discuss the whereabouts of my nephew, but this thing with your sister has soured the congenial ambiance."

"Congenial? You've threatened to kill my friend, her infant son, and my betrothed. You have Proust chained to a chair, squatting over his own filth like an animal. Your behavior fosters only contempt in me, Lara."

"*My lady,*" Lara corrected sternly. "You grow too bold, Godwynn . . . our familiarity has not elevated your station."

"I have no station! I have no kingdom, no prince, no husband, no title. I have not seen my parents for days, and my sister . . . you've brought me a shell of the girl she once was. By the gods, you've mutilated Magnus; at least release him from that damned chair so that he may feed himself."

"Magnus is an aberration . . . a danger to us all, though Athelstan turned a blind eye because it suited his purpose. The mage would already be dead if he did not have information I need. Or rather, *needed,* because some news has fallen into my lap, darling girl, and I would have you corroborate with whatever Proust divulged to you."

She can sniff out a lie like mongrels in heat . . . and you, Lady Godwynn, are not a skilled liar, Proust had told her. "The prince, Callum, and Lord Dorn are no longer in this realm," Chrys stated.

"I know!" she snapped, slamming the padded armrest of Athelstan's great oak chair. "I've conjured the most powerful finder spells ever conceived, and always they lead to that damnable black mirror in the pantry. It swallows men like a leviathan."

"I speak not of kingdoms, but of the world itself," Chrys explained. "There are other realms . . . other realities . . . beyond the veil of our own. The only way to reach the prince is by the door Proust created. The child is nowhere in the Twelve Kingdoms." It was all the truth Chrys needed to reveal. Let them search for a babe and a man in his prime should they find their way through. If Lara chose to kill her now, so be it—her poor betrothed, white-haired and wrinkled, would not be long for the world after his return—the better, for Chrys would meet Cal in the Elysium Halls sooner rather than later.

Lara stepped off the dais and circled her. Chrys looked straight ahead, trying to keep from her thoughts that hot pulse that came from the White Lady's touch. The sorceress stopped in front of her and closed the space. "But when will they return?" Lara asked. Her eyes became the slits of a predator. "How old will the prince be? And your betrothed . . . will you long to plant sweet kisses on your captain? Or will the mottled, gray wretch reeking of mint oil remind you of your grandfather?"

How could Lara's informant know the truth of it?

"Oh, what a precious look," said a voice that had been absent from the castle these past days. She was not used to seeing him dressed in the finery of a nobleman—but it was indeed Balzac, the court jester, who emerged from behind the canopy. He was older, plumper than when she saw him last. "She lies by omission, my lady."

"I would expect no less from a woman of good breeding, Balzac. She will make an excellent wife for whatever nobleman we bestow her on . . . once she's turned to our cause, of course."

"Do you now juggle and jape for Farrenheil?" Chrys asked the jester.

Lara laughed. "Balzac is the most powerful title-less man in Aandor. And he has been to your guardians' realm beyond the veil and returned."

"As has your beloved," Balzac told Chryslantha. "Older and much changed from the arrogant pup that went through the portal only days ago."

The whole world had turned upside down. Jesters striding great halls like lords, young ladies of good breeding stripped of their virtues, and infant princes hunted like criminals. Chrys stared down the jester defiantly, a glare that conveyed everything she hoped her betrothed would do to this man when he finally caught up with him. Cruz picked up on her judgment as if she spoke her thoughts aloud.

"MacDonnell hides in the sewer like a rat," Cruz continued. He studied her in the gown, but it was a gelded leer lacking the carnal qualities she recognized in other men. A specter of viciousness possessed the jester, and when he smiled again, it was the face of one who set small creatures afire for pleasure. "You are lovely. I am certain that if Cal reunites with you, my dear, he will forget in a heartbeat his commoner hag of a wife—and their brat."

Those words struck her like a slap across the face. "You lie," she said.

"I am many things, my dear, but a liar is not one of them. Callum MacDonnell has shared his bed with another woman, a wife, for the past seven years," he said with a smarmy grin.

Chrys slapped the jester hard.

Balzac rubbed his cheek, appreciating her reaction with the evenness of one not concerned with proving his claim. It contributed to his sincerity. "I was with him when we returned to Aandor." Balzac pantomimed grief. "Saw his wretchedness at having abandoned his true family in that other world."

"Callum would never forsake a vow," Chrys said.

"True . . . MacDonnell is noble to a fault," Balzac agreed. "But our idiot mage miscast a spell and wiped our memories shortly after we arrived in that other realm. Proust's choice of wizard brings into question his renown as a genius. For years we were unaware of our true identities, unaware that Aandor existed. We founded new lives independent of each other. Callum has spent the past fourteen years as a commoner . . . a member of the city watch—so much for the intrinsic superiority of the nobility. MacDonnell and his commoner wife have a young daughter, and Catherine is pregnant again with his son. And every minute that he spends here, she grows more haggard with age, and his children will never know him, and whether he puts his mind to returning to his family or to vanquishing the enemy here, a vow he made will be broken, and it will eat at him like worms in a corpse."

Chryslantha's stomach plunged into a chasm. Her breath

ceased, her skin grew cold and ridged, and her knees began to shake. Balzac continued speaking, but she heard not a word of it—a drumming thumped her ears, her vision darkened, then closed like a tomb.

2

Someone was patting Chryslantha's cheek with a wet cloth, asking her to drink. "You lie," she whispered and opened her eyes.

Lord Blunt ministered to her. Lara's head hovered above Blunt's robust shoulder, mild concern visible on her flawless brow. Chrys tried to stand, but her legs would not support her. Soldiers brought in a daybed and Blunt lifted her onto it. He was solid—as hard as the walls of this castle.

Balzac sat on the stairs of the dais swinging a leg over his knee. He smiled like a fed cat and said, "A hard blow, I know."

"And yet you delivered it so enthusiastically," Lara noted drily.

"Information is my art, my lady. In my exuberance, I perhaps forgot that Chryslantha Godwynn is the best of us all and required a delicate touch."

Liar. Chryslantha wiped her tears. For the first time she felt truly lost. Lara pointed to Balzac's kerchief, which he handed over grudgingly, and she gave it to Chrys. It was overperfumed with lilacs and lavender.

"What of Dorn?" Blunt asked.

Balzac shrugged and waved about. "Still in that other realm. The necromancer's attack on the guardians' most powerful mage worked brilliantly, more than I could have hoped when I left my students behind with messages for our parties. But we could not account for everyone. Those who were miles away may or may not have come back with us. Truly, my lady, other than MacDonnell and his cohorts, I cannot say who has returned to Aandor or whether anyone left behind has the means to try again."

Balzac's tone was one Chryslantha knew well—Niccole used it for half-truths to mask omissions like Chrys tried to do earlier, only Niccole was adept at it . . . and Balzac could probably school her. The jester played a dangerous game with Farrenheil. He was on no one's side but his own.

"Well, the prince need not be here for trouble to sprout," Blunt said. "An insurgency has risen in the woods around Yarmouth, as we feared," he told Lara. "Several companies have been attacked. I've dispatched six hundred men to relieve that giglet, Onyx, before he loses the eastern towns. We need our army at the Gate to arrive quickly and replace our troops around the city before we contend with Athelstan's last remaining army in the west. That one will be an honest, straightforward battle."

"Oh spare me, Kyzur," Lara said. "If not for my magic, you could never have taken this kingdom."

They noted Chryslantha's interest in their conversation and stepped away from her—*and Balzac*. Balzac took the snub in stride and sidled over to Chrys with that ever-present smirk.

"MacDonnell will come for you," Balzac said. "Guilt is a powerful burden. It vexes the soul."

"All you do is lie, Balzac . . . even when you are telling the truth. What has happened to Lara's nephew? Did you kill him?"

"I genuinely do not know where Dorn is. His body, that is— the man is most certainly dead. Killed by MacDonnell's wife, a most unremarkable wench, if you can believe it."

She could not believe it. Callum had a wife . . . not just any woman, but one who killed one of the most powerful wizards of Farrenheil. If not for the turmoil her existence brought to

Chryslantha, she could kiss Catherine MacDonnell for striking Dorn. What would Lara do when she learned Dorn was no more? Right now Cal was assured a quick death. But if Lara were to learn of Dorn's fate at the hands of Catherine MacDonnell, they would make Cal's agony linger . . . he would suffer terribly. "You have grasped an asp by its tail with your games," Chrys told Balzac.

"I've withheld a truth for everyone's benefit, especially yours. In MacDonnell's absence, Lara might take her rage out on you, and the White Lady in a rage would make very poor decisions—or perhaps very good decisions, which also might not work for my agenda. As they say in the other reality . . . that woman is 'bat-shit crazy.'"

Chryslantha rose and exited the hall without taking leave. Lara wouldn't stop her this time. One thing Balzac spoke true. Callum would come for her . . . out of guilt if not love. Could she blame him for his marriage? War destroyed families and destruction came in many forms. One thing was certain, Callum's spirit would be torn. As long as she and this Catherine were both alive, he could never be at peace while a pledge remained broken, whatever the circumstances. But that did not matter right now. She needed to keep him alive. When the war was won—*if the war was won*—there would be time to set right what they could of their future.

CHAPTER 26

FORGE AHEAD

Daniel and the company emerged onto a mezzanine over-looking a fair-sized forge. Lightning flashed through slit-shaped windows high in the room. Even if the company could reach them, only Daniel and Cat might squeeze through.

Lelani found candle lanterns and passed them out. Stairs on either side of the landing led down to the floor. Furnaces, smelters, and hearths sat under racks of hammers, chisels, and tongs. A large dry watermill sat still over a stone slack tub in the far corner.

The floor stones had runes etched into them, as did the sides of the hearths and the walls. Under the mezzanine was an alcove with shelves stacked with bottles, beakers, and books—a small black cauldron and a distillery sat on a wood bench next to a chalkboard with notations. A standing desk was covered in vellum parchment, quills, and bottles of ink dried out long ago.

"Of all the things I considered might be on the other side of that door, a forge was not one," noted Urry.

"Aye," Lelani agreed. "It appears Egwyn was a Magesmyte."

"Let me guess . . . forbidden magic?" asked Cat.

"Not necessarily—like Thaumadynes, Magesmytes are rare—their craft is dangerous. You hear about their works in myth and legend—objects that provide great boons or horrid curses—artifacts that are somewhat alive, have souls. The rewards of such an art, financially and otherwise, are incalculable. Today, they must petition the Wizards' Council to practice."

"Egwyn's experiments . . . after losing his throne, it was all he had left," Daniel said.

Urry was about to pick up a tin cup left on an anvil.

"Do not touch anything!" Lelani stressed.

"I thought we had left the dangerous room behind us," said Ladue. They all looked at the centaur.

"I was mistaken," she said. "Magesmything sometimes results in cursed artifacts."

"My uncle told tales of demons that possess the smith's works through the coke fires," said Urry. "The gateway to the underworld."

"Cursed items are accidents," Lelani explained. "The goal is a perfect fusion of magic and metal—exquisite balance in energy and matter. A Magesmyte serenades his creation. He taps into the harmonics of the universe, crafting a poem for the attributes his work should embody. He hammers the searing metal to the rhythm of this ideal thought. It is complex . . . like conducting an ensemble while playing all the instruments."

"So they make things like your magic key?" Daniel asked.

"No. The creations of a Magesmyte are not so easy to disenchant—they are nearly indestructible and release an intense amount of energy if you succeed. However, when the magic and the object are not in harmony, the artifact is in pain, becomes a cursed thing, angry and vengeful. It can make you miserable."

"And how many cursed items might there be?" asked Ladue.

"All smiths have accidents. There's likely a cursed item for every two good ones."

"I still think it be demons," Urry said.

"Uh . . . there's a dead guy back here," said Cat. She was in the niche under the mezzanine.

The man was slumped against the back wall. He had been tall, his clothes fine and expensive. He wore a satin pillbox-style hat with an exotic red feather pinned to its side large enough to be a plume unto itself. Like all the others in Meadsweir, he barely looked dead. His right index finger was black with dried ink. He had been writing on the wall.

"Egwyn," Urry noted. "A portrait of his brother hangs in Aandor City."

Daniel had seen many dead bodies of late, but something about this one tugged at his emotions. Cat put a hand on his shoulder. She looked at him with motherly concern.

"Your first blood relative?" she said.

"I guess," Daniel admitted. "I was hoping it'd be, you know . . . someone alive."

"You're not going to cry?" teased Seth.

"Only tears of joy after I thump you."

"What has Egwyn written, *ma cherie*," Ladue asked Lelani.

"It's Old Aandoran . . . 'I die as Alfred.'"

The group stood over the wizard king like an honor guard.

"Does he mean his brother was dead and now he follows?" Cat asked, breaking silence.

"Alfred died on the night of the new moon in the month of Meán Fómhair in the year of the gryphon 749 OE," Daniel said. "He was in prime health, fairly young, but mysteriously fell into a coma in his sleep and died later that day. No wounds, no illness, or insect bites . . . he just stopped by all accounts." They stared at him in wonder. "Hey, the padre's been on me like white on rice for this stuff. Who knew it would actually come in handy. Too bad we can't tell when uncle Egwyn bought it, though."

Lelani clopped over to a large stone disk engraved with celestial images: suns, moons, stars, zodiacs, and random lines connecting them. Three stone talismans sat in pegs. "A wizard would have updated his calendar every morning. These pegs were last set into Meán Fómhair in the year of the gryphon. New moon."

"Coinkydink?" Seth mused. He'd had energy since arriving in Meadsweir, but still, he was fidgeting more than usual.

"Take a pill, would you, buddy?" Daniel said. He riffled through some parchments on the standing desk. The notations were gibberish to him, complex equations with illustrations and alien symbols. "Are these important?"

"These are brilliant," Lelani said with reverence.

A guttural roar reverberated outside in the rain; it bounced off the low canopy of clouds and castle walls and froze everyone in their places. The pound of slow heavy footsteps shook the room. Daniel realized the ground level outside was just below the sill of those high windows, putting most of the forge below the surface. In the windows, a magenta glow brightened as the footsteps neared. Everyone blew out their candles, then held a collective breath. The dark gave focus to the cold neon light in the windows. Two massive hooves and a forked tail walked past the forge. The power of the thing transmitted through the walls.

"'Tis a demon," Urry whispered.

"It heads toward the bridge," Ladue noted.

The thing outside roared again, sending spiders down everyone's spine.

CHAPTER 27

WORMHOLES 'R' US

1

The company cooled its heels . . . their options as slim as the forge's high windows; the drain in the slack tub was also too small to squeeze through. Lelani was certain another egress existed, for such was the nature of wizards' lairs—but they could not know if the bridge was clear of danger. The beast had not circled back.

Cat was grateful for the break. The loss of her child had sapped her emotionally; the weight of the baby she carried and the group's near demise in the antechamber had exhausted her physically. Only the drive to reunite with Brianna spurred her on. But with their rations dwindling, they could not stay here for long.

Urry paced unproductively. Ladue continually reminded them that the creature could have returned to its lair through the other side of the castle. Cat was frustrated with Lelani, who read scroll after scroll of Egwyn's work. Her voracious addiction for knowledge had blocked out their present danger.

"Find anything useful?" Cat prodded.

"That creature is not indigenous to this world," she said, still scanning the scroll.

"'Tis from hell, like all demons," Urry said.

"It hails from another reality," Lelani continued. "A being composed of both matter and magical energy."

"Plasma mojo?" Daniel asked. "Is that possible?"

"Egwyn created the spell craft to transition through time, space, and dimensional planes," Lelani said. She waved Egwyn's scrolls, high-quality lambskin vellum that, unlike parchment, would survive a thousand years. "All wizards attempting to break these boundaries have built on the Mad King's work. The design of the antechamber trap is pure genius."

"What of the beast?" Urry asked.

"Egwyn explored universes closer to the center of the multiverse—a center that we theorize is composed of pure energy. He brought this creature here. It stands to reason that the physical composition of life closer to the core would incorporate the energy in its makeup."

"And beastie was none too happy to find itself here," Seth mused.

"You presume much about the creature," Lelani said.

"Huh?"

"You're assuming it's aware," Daniel said. "What if it's its world's version of a silverback gorilla? The beast may not be capable of understanding what happened to it."

"Being trapped here for hundreds of years could have driven it insane," Ladue added.

"I haven't gone more than six hours here without something trying to kill me," Cat said. "How do you all live like this?"

"It's not always like this," Lelani said. "This is war."

"But how do we defeat such a monster?" Ladue asked.

"We do not," Lelani said. "It has slaughtered armies. Weapons are ineffectual, as is magic I suspect. We avoid it by any means—stay beneath its notice. The warriors who came before us gave their lives to trap it here. It's pinned through its proximity to its heart . . ." She paused a second, looking around the desk, and pulled a particular scroll out from under the pile. She scanned it quickly, moving her lips to the words before finishing her last statement absentmindedly. "Which it seems unable to retrieve? Of course!" she said to herself. Lelani retrieved a rock from the bookshelf—black and rough, marbled with silver streaks. "Faerie silver is not natural to this world—that's why it's so rare." She traced a sentence on the scroll with a finger. "Egwyn theorized that meteorites laced with faerie silver originate from across the multiverse—possibly the far edges of creation where magical energy does not reach . . . a place where life is not carbon-based as it is in our universes—and the element came here through tears in space."

"Wormholes," Daniel said. "Some scientists think black holes are gateways to other dimensions."

Lelani pulled out a flyer. "Egwyn sent runners and ravens to the dwarv kings with detailed explanations on how to identify impact sites—he pleaded for them to prospect for the element."

"Hah!" Urry scoffed. "Did he expect dwarvs to mine his rocks out of the goodness of their hearts?"

"He was desperate," Lelani said. "Egwyn never intended to bring the beast here. Think about it . . . asking the dwarv chiefs for help was treasonous. Mastery of magic is the cornerstone of man's supremacy in this world—and he exposed a weapon that could neutralize wizards to a competitor race. But this creature posed a greater and more immediate threat to the entire world. Alfred had sent knights and wizards against it. All perished. Egwyn would have been desperate to correct his blunder—one that never would have occurred if not for the affliction he brought upon his twin brother, the king . . ."

"Okay, now you've utterly lost me," Seth said. "And I'm not the only one from the look of the crew."

She unfurled another scroll and pegged its corners with the meteorite, a book, and a silver artisanal jewel box. She opened the lid to reveal two circular imprints in the crushed velvet interior. Grabbing wooden tongs from a tool rack she pulled from Egwyn's wrist a silver bracelet fashioned as serpents eating their own tails and laid it in one of the velvet imprints. As an afterthought, she studied the feather in the hat and pulled it as well. "This was written in his hand," she said of the scroll.

Our condition becomes more frequent, more burdensome with age. Last week's switch came in the midst of Alfred's lovemaking with the queen—and yet Alfred refuses to tell his wife or anyone of the curse. I cannot blame him. He would be shunned and removed from power. Twice the switch has occurred close to my experimental castings. Should my brother suddenly find himself occupying my form while I were in the midst of harnessing elemental forces, the momentary disconnect could bring ruin to both of us . . . to the kingdom.

My susceptibility to magic was the back door through which Greggor Valkai, the court mage of Moran, inflicted Alfred with this malady, such is the bond between twins—therefore it was only fitting I conceive the solution to our situation. I have studied the clerical arts with a local prelate and by combining their blessings with wizardry, forged bracelets that duplicate the effect of the soul switch, but at a time of our own choosing. As long as my brother and I wear them, we can counter the curse nearly in-

stantaneously. I look forward to presenting them to him at our next name day feast.

"That explains Alfred's 'flakiness,'" Daniel said. "He literally wasn't always himself."

"What does the red feather do, then?" Seth asked.

Lelani handed it to him. "This is a phoenix feather," she said. "To say it is rare is an understatement . . . they usually combust and turn to ash when the bird regenerates. Fix it to your staff . . . it will increase the potency of your spells."

"Sure you wouldn't rather enhance your boyfriend's potency instead?" Seth said looking for Ladue, who had moved to the wall at the far end of the shadowy room.

"I have found a hidden door," Ladue said.

Lelani vaulted across the forge to reach him. "Do not touch it!" she scolded.

"*Ma cherie,* I have promised as much."

Lelani examined the wall and pressed on a stone, which slid back. The door swung creakily on bronze hinges. Behind it was a vestibule and another door. Two stone golems guarded it.

"An exit?" Urry asked.

"Vault," Lelani said. "It's where Egwyn would have stored his artifacts and the materials to craft them. But it will also have an exit that can only be accessed from within."

"Let me guess . . . it's the most dangerous room in the castle," Seth said.

"Aye," Lelani confirmed, missing the mockery.

"I can't go through anything like the antechamber again," Cat spoke up.

"Aye," Lelani agreed.

The centaur went back to the niche and packed as many scrolls and books into her magical satchel as she could cram. She relieved Egwyn's corpse of its rings and amulets as well. She gave one of them to Daniel, a silver ring with his family crest upon it. "Crest rings are never buried, but passed down to descendants," she told him. She placed her hands on Daniel's shoulders. Cat thought Lelani meant to cast a spell on the boy, but she offered only advice. "Of us all, you are the least threatened by whatever traps and protections Egwyn placed over this vault. We are relying on you to see us through the guards."

"No pressure, kid," Seth said.

"Course not," Daniel said. "Why should things change now?"

Cat was frightened for Daniel as he walked into the dark vestibule. The prince looked fragile before the massive golems; the flickering light of his candle lantern cast a sinister glow on their faces. She prayed that Lelani was right, or all their efforts on Daniel's behalf up until now would have been for naught.

"I am Danel, descendant of King Alfred, nephew to Egwyn, and the current prince of Aandor," he said to the two golems. "Open this door."

Two tiny glows slowly emerged in their eyeholes—flickering orange pinheads that floated in the blackness of those deep sockets. Rocks scraped as the golem to Daniel's right tilted his head down to the boy. Its mouth opened.

"At the tourney, four lads competed in the jousts and melee," said the golem. The disembodied voice was very human, though its lips did not move.

"Liam beat Sean in the melee, Edwin came third, and the sixteen-year-old won. Liam came second in the joust, the seventeen-year-old won, Edwin beat the eighteen-year-old, and the nineteen-year-old came third. Tybalt is three years younger than Sean. The person who

came last in the melee, came third in the joust and only one lad got the same position in both contests."

And then silence.

"Well that's just great," Seth said. "It tells pointless stories."

"It's a logic puzzle," Daniel said. "We have to figure out the question first."

"I didn't hear no question."

"Exactly," Lelani said. "That's the control key. Egwyn knew the question. But if we do not solve this riddle, we will die here."

Of course we will, Cat thought. Cat left the group to its scribbling while she took a seat on the edge of the slack tub. She stretched her lower back and massaged her legs. The prince and the centaur deciphered with an omnibus of prerequisite head-scratching, pen-cap biting, and tapping of digits. Cat was impressed . . . not by Lelani, who no one doubted was a genius of the Caltech variety, but by Daniel, who could hold his own in a room of PhDs. But it wasn't his smarts that concerned her—Daniel was still just a kid. Who knew where his breaking point lay.

"Can't we ask the guard on the left if the one on the right is lying or something?" Seth asked.

Daniel's shake of resignation mimicked Cat's internal cringe. Still, Seth had had his good moments lately. He seemed on edge, though, since coming into Meadsweir . . . hyper, overanimated while everyone else was near exhaustion; the man needed to switch to decaf.

"Different puzzle, Jar Jar," said Daniel. "You ask one guard which door the other guard would pick as the safe door, assuming that one guard always lies and the other always tells the truth. Do you see two doors in the hallway?"

Cat would have found the Joey-and-Chandler routine more

amusing if her belly didn't grumble and her throat wasn't parched. "Does anyone have water?" she asked. Ladue had one sip left, which he graciously offered. Cat had no shame in playing the "pregnant mother" card in this instance. The minute she swallowed, her bladder cried for release. "Jeezus, Mary, and Joe, I can't catch a break," she muttered.

"Guys, if we're going to be here more than fifteen minutes, I need to tinkle. Options?"

Everyone except Seth said, "Slack tub" and pointed behind her. There wasn't enough room for her to hide behind the waterwheel; Cat would have to do her business in the open. At this point, she didn't care.

A circular plug lined with dried, cracking rubber of some type covered the drain.

Seth hopped into the tub and lifted the plug for her. Below it a rusty iron grate caught anything larger than a baseball from falling into the pipe. Cat wished she'd worn a dress—a simple squat and tug and the business would be over. As she worked out the logistics of her predicament, Seth examined the waterwheel.

She had just unhooked the waistband and placed fingers on the zipper when it occurred to her—in that time-delayed fashion when you acknowledge words moments after they've been uttered—that she could not possibly have heard Seth say the words *I found the lever for the wheel . . . I can get us water.*

Cat spun around faster than any pregnant woman ever should. "Seth! Don't—" was all she managed to exclaim before he forced the lever into the open position.

The ancient lever, having committed its final task, snapped in Seth's hands, leaving him gawking at the wooden stick he now held. Water rushed in from a flue above the wheel, filling the top bucket. The great wheel groaned as its ancient rods turned. Cat hopped out of the tub just in time to avoid the first wash heading for the drain.

As the wheel reached nominal speed, its loose bolts and rusty rods made a racket on par with its industrial age successors.

"Shut that bloody thing down!" Urry barked. Seth held up the broken lever with the dumbest of expressions. As if it weren't loud enough already, a sound emanated from the drain, louder and more obnoxious than the waterwheel. A pounding came from the other side of the wall next to the slack tub; something buried underground outside the recessed room.

"What the hell is that?" Cat asked.

"This room is at river level," Lelani said. "Egwyn would have had a pump to prevent flooding—but there's not enough water going through." The wheel and the pump screamed to the castle that things were in motion.

Ladue and Urry rushed to the lever station. They tried to grasp the remaining nub and put it back, but could not gain leverage.

Cat pulled a hammer from the forge's rack and grabbed a piece of iron shaped like a rail spike. She nudged Ladue out of the way and drove the spike through the center of the nub with two blows, then pointed to Urry to grab the new lever. Urry cut most of the flow before the spike cracked the nub. The wheel stopped, as did the pump.

"I'mreallysorryguysIdidn'tmeantofuckthingsup . . . ," Seth was babbling like a meth addict.

"Seth, calm down," Daniel said. "Why are you jittery?"

"Feel like I've taken five NoDoz pills."

The runes in the forge lit up hotly, bathing them in the glow of a candlelight vigil. In contrast, cold luminous plasma shone through the window above the waterwheel, but instead of great hooves and a forked tail, the muzzle of a beast pressed against the leaded glass—and three pairs of malicious bovine eyes challenged them.

2

The beast's howl was unnatural, like the high-pitched screech of brakes and stripped gears on an ancient garbage truck. Its very breath rattled the window frame. For Cat, the creature's rage personified evil—furious at the confirmation of life within its realm—an unholy amalgamation of anguish and insanity. It battered the window with hooflike mitts—two thick clawed fingers and a thumb. The glass shattered, it reached in desperate to grab the intruders, but because of its bulk, could not squeeze through the thin window. Its breath was noxious—an alien compound not meant for this world. The group retreated deeper into the forge. Frustrated, the creature looked around, and then climbed up the castle wall.

"It's going to try to come through the ceiling!" Seth exclaimed.

"No, the forge roof is solid stone," Lelani said.

"But the antechamber . . . ," Ladue pointed out.

The click, click, click of the beast's hooves scrambled above them before moving toward the antechamber next door; silence for moments . . . and then the smashing of wooden beams. Lelani jolted for the gallery door. She slipped a four-by-four plank of solid lacquered oak into the staples and keep.

"It'll get sucked into that vortex, right?" Cat said, more hopeful than certain.

"We deactivated the trigger," Lelani said. "This door will not hold."

"That thing had six eyes!" Seth said, shaking.

"Shut up!" Cat cried. "How fucking stupid are you?! Pulling levers?! Really?!"

"We all needed water!" he shot back. "I don't remember you shouting at Lelani for nearly killing us in the last room!"

Cat grabbed his ear and yanked him close to take up her entire field of vision. "I can't die until I know Brianna's safe, jackass! *Stop fucking around!*"

Lelani touched her shoulder. Cat shrugged it off and backed away from them. She passed Daniel, who was scribbling rapidly, a fast-forwarded mimic of his earlier self.

The roof next door relented; the creature crashed into the gallery of priceless artifacts. The next roar preceded a massive thud on that barred door. Cat's blood ran cold—even Ladue lost the casual nonchalance he brought to danger.

"Are you almost done, Daniel?" Ladue asked. The beast hammered relentlessly. The frame shook . . . mortar dust fell from the ceiling.

"I'm ninety-nine percent sure the answer includes the participants' age and rankings in both contests," Daniel said. "Liam came in second in both rankings and he's eighteen." He looked to Lelani who nodded agreement. "Give me a minute to get the others."

The door frame splintered; a crack ran along the length of the oak bar. Everyone gathered their gear and joined Daniel in the vestibule.

"Close the fake wall behind us," Cat ordered.

"It won't stop that thing," Seth complained.

"Damn it, we're buying Danny minutes!"

The beast broke through and leaped from the mezzanine across the expanse of the forge, smashing all manner of items hung in its way. It landed haphazardly before the vestibule just as Lelani and Ladue sealed the wall. The group was entombed. The beast pounded on the wall, which thankfully was sturdier than Seth had thought. Cat prayed the monster would not accidently hit the stone that released the latch.

Daniel turned to the right golem. "Edwin is age seventeen, he came in first in the joust and third in the melee. Tybalt is age sixteen, he came in fourth in the joust and first in the melee. Liam is aged eighteen, he came in second in the joust and second in the melee . . ."

A hoofed fist smashed through the wall. Everyone jumped back instinctively toward the vault door; the left golem perceived them as hostiles. It took one step forward with arms raised, daring them to take another step. The beast would not stop shrieking. The very idea of intruders anguished it. Seth threw his purple blossom spell at the thing's arms, but it shrugged off his efforts. He erected a shield against the wall—the stones and dust bounced against it, but the beast's arms ignored the spell as though nothing was there; the demon was impervious to magic.

"Sean is age nineteen, he came in third in the joust and fourth in melee," Daniel finished. The pinpoints in both golems' eye sockets turned from orange to blue. Both stood at attention before Daniel.

The last of the wall fell—dust billowed beyond Seth's transparent shield, saturating the once great forge. The monster took a step through the shield's threshold.

"We're fucked!" Seth cried.

"Kill that monster!" Daniel commanded the golems. The group flattened against the vestibule's walls as the golems launched themselves at the beast, one hitting it high, the other low, driving it back into the white storm of the forge. From the gallery came the pounding of more heavy footsteps. The two stone sentinels from the entrance burst in from the mezzanine and piled onto the beast with their brothers. "Cool," Daniel remarked, a little too pleased with himself for Cat's comfort. She took his shoulders and spun him toward the vault door.

It opened easily at Daniel's touch. A large, wide staircase descended; Urry barred the vault door behind them, and the group followed Daniel down the stairs.

Thirteen steps took them to a beautifully varnished double oak door dotted with iron studs and trimmed with black iron bands across the width of the wood. Daniel pushed them open. The vault itself was dark and silent—musty and mausoleumlike—with cobwebs across most surfaces. The rush of new air unsettled the dust; motes drifted in great flocks across their meager light.

The rectangular vault was built from stone blocks the size of cars, with high ceilings that echoed the smallest of sounds. They could just make out the wall to their right, leading Cat to think they entered at one end of the room. To their left was a mystery cloaked in blackness.

The beast raged above at the castle's guardians.

"The golems will not be victorious," Lelani said. "Nor will the vault door deter the demon. Our only chance lies in getting out of Meadsweir."

Ladue and Urry braced the lower door with whatever pieces of long wood and iron they could, including spears and javelins from a weapons rack.

Lelani was about to scold them about touching strange objects when Ladue cut her off. "Mademoiselle, if we are yet alive five minutes from now, you may admonish me to your heart's content."

Cat, Seth, and Daniel explored the dark recesses, illuminating with their lanterns. The items stored here were not flashy, nor were they showcased on pedestals and such. If the antechamber was a boutique, then this vault was a warehouse—practical and utilitarian. Only a single dais that they passed hinted at finery. The room smelled wetter, earthier the farther in they walked. They reached the end in a few minutes.

"Aww, shit," Seth muttered, echoing Cat's sentiments.

Her heart sagged at the sight of the cave-in. Hundreds of years of neglect had accumulated on this corner of the castle, piled on earth that was too soft, too close to the river. Repeated flooding and inattention to drainage had softened the ground, and the stone walls and ceiling had fallen in—a chaotic landslide of stone blocks and massive rafters. Whatever exit might once have existed would need a big excavator to dig it out; the guardians were lucky if they had ten minutes left.

"I'm really sorry," Seth said solemnly. "I let you down . . . let Bree down."

"We're not dead yet," Daniel said defiantly.

In a dark corner they heard the hard splash of Lelani making water. It reminded Cat of her own interrupted business. *No one wants to die with a full bladder.* She found a quiet corner herself and finally relieved herself. Her parched throat wished she'd scooped up some of the water from Seth's bungled attempt. In the movies, people seemed to go days without eating or drinking. Cat had gone just a few hours and was already light-headed.

Daniel and Cat backtracked. A sole table sat on the dais; an assortment of weapons was laid neatly on a red velvet cloth: long sword, short sword, dagger, war hammer, hand shield, bow, quiver, and what looked like an overly large but ornate scepter with protrusions that reminded Cat of the tail fins in a pulp fiction rocket ship. All these items had the phoenix—Daniel's family crest—stamped upon them.

"The workmanship is exquisite," explained Urry, who had joined them. "But what good is steel against the beast?"

"Perfect for bashing frost giants," Daniel said of the hammer, a solid block of polished iron with beveled edges. "Must weigh thirty pounds." He grabbed the long handle wrapped in strips of oiled leather. "Maybe we could brace the door . . ." Daniel's lifting of the hammer looked easy . . . almost comical. "Scratch that," he said. "It's as light as a kid's bowling ball." He tossed the hammer to Seth, who fell backward.

"Get . . . it . . . off!" Seth gasped, pretending to be pinned under the weapon.

"Stop fucking around," Cat said. She reached for the handle and pulled. It would not budge. "Let it go," she told Seth.

Seth started to turn purple; his pantomime had reached expert level. Urry joined Cat, and even together they couldn't lift the hammer off Seth's chest. "'Tis no ruse," Urry said, straining. "Weighs thirty stone."

Daniel came over and lifted it again. He swung it back and forth with one hand and hammered the floor, shattering the stone and mortar with a deep indent. There was not a mark on the weapon. Urry tried the fancy scepter and struggled to drag it to the edge of the table. Daniel took it from him with his free hand easily.

"What's the point of a three-hundred-pound scepter?" Cat asked.

"'Tis no scepter," Urry corrected. "Flanged mace."

Lelani and Ladue joined them from the direction of the landslide. The dais was now the only island of light in the blackness. They waited for the centaur's reprimand, but Lelani just sighed in resignation. "At this point, we have little to lose by searching the contents of this room. We need a miracle."

"Why am I not immune to these magical weapons?" Daniel asked.

"Your resistance powers the enchantment," said a disembodied voice in the darkness.

The guardians drew their weapons and formed a circle.

Two points of light floated in the blackness beyond the dais. Ladue rounded the table with his lantern; the outline of a golem sitting against the wall took shape. This one was closer to a man's proportions and sculpted of red clay. Parts of it had melted and dried through the years, its body cracked and flaking. The head was in decent shape.

"Those born of the royal family—those who were not anomalies—would stop the current of energy, which flows through all things in Aandor," it said.

"A circuit breaker," Seth said.

The golem tried to lift its arm; its shoulder joint cracked and crumbled, and the arm fell to the floor and shattered.

"I was once mobile," the golem said. Its voice conveyed exhaustion, a very human quality of sadness. *"I fear motion is beyond me now."*

"What's with that accent?" Cat said, catching only every other word.

"'Tis the old tongue," Urry remarked.

"The beast yet lives?" asked the golem.

"Aye," Urry confirmed.

"What keeps it in Meadsweir?"

"Knights fought it in the grand hall and pinned its heart to the floor with a dagger," Lelani said.

"Faerie silver?" the golem asked. *"The beast is in agony. It cannot approach the dagger to release its heart and yet the dagger stabs it*

from afar. Should it ever escape Meadsweir, it will destroy the king-dom. The world. Such is my bane."

"Are you more than a wizard's construct, monsieur?" asked La-due.

Cat noticed it first . . . the glint of silver about the golem's remaining wrist. She moved her lantern to the armrest, illuminating a familiar bracelet fashioned like a snake eating its tail. "Look."

"I am . . . ," started the golem. *"I was . . . Egwyn of Aandor."*

"Todin's beard!" Urry cried.

"Does anyone else feel like they just got whacked by Danny's hammer?" Seth queried.

"The boy . . . ," Egwyn noted. *"Approach, kinsman, if it please you."*

Daniel stood before the old clay king. *"You have the look of a Bradaanese nobleman,"* it said in an observational manner.

"Mother's side," Daniel said. "My father is Athelstan, arch-duke of Aandor. I'm the prince . . . Do you know what's happened in the world since your day?"

"Glimpses," it said. *"The thoughts of passing wizards on the river when one sails close. I have slept for great periods over the centuries to preserve my . . . sanity. But the spell fails. By my conscious perception I have been alone in this room, immobile, for five years. Buried alive; unable to move. I am perhaps . . . a bit mad at this point. These woes were my own doing. When I realized all was lost, I preserved my es-sence in this golem. But I unwittingly doomed my brother. In my hu-bris, I thought to cheat the curse placed upon us. When I entered this golem, the curse, like nature, abhorred a vacuum. It could not retrieve my soul, but linked to Alfred, it pulled my brother's essence into my former flesh. And there, Alfred was trapped."*

The beast's rage grew louder. It had begun ripping into the upper vault door.

"*I welcome death*," announced the golem king.

"We do not, sir," said Ladue. "We wish to live for our own sakes as much as your kingdom's. Is there another exit from this room?"

"*No longer.*"

"A weapon then?"

"*None,*" said the clay king. "*I would have forged such a thing long ago. The beast is as much magic as flesh. Our spells are useless.*"

"Jesus H. Christ!" Cat shouted in total frustration. "Two geniuses, two world-class warriors, and a legendary wizard king, and nobody has a freaking clue what to do? We made it through necromancers, prison camps, raging armies, mile-high sky vortexes, and my fucking mother-in-law . . . and I'm not ready to quit now! So somebody better start coming up with some crazy-ass outside-the-box answers on how to get us to the other side of that fucking river, or I'm going to plotz before that glowing demon bull ever gets in here!"

"Outside the box?" Lelani said, musing over the expression. She had that crazy look mad scientists get on the cusp of saying "Eureka!"

"It's an expression," Daniel explained.

"It's a solution," Lelani said. "We're going to use a . . . what did you call it? Wormhole? To escape."

"That's major mojo," Seth said. "Lots of power. The White Lady destroyed the entire Wizards' Archive to bend space."

Lelani threw her hands out to indicate the enchanted objects filling the room around them.

"But Lara used multiple wizards, all better than you and me!" Seth continued.

Lelani pointed to Egwyn.

"Aye," Egwyn confirmed. *"I would aid Alfred's scion."*

Lelani chalked out a spell circle on the dais floor. With black grease, she drew a five-pointed star within the circle and placed a candle on each point. "We will not be *creating* a time-space anomaly," she explained. "We will coopt an existing one at only half the cost and effort."

"The antechamber," Cat said, realizing. "The one that almost killed us."

"A mile long, at least," Ladue said. "Enough to traverse the river."

"Deactivated!" Seth countered.

"The trigger was," Daniel said, coming on board. "But the distortion . . . ?"

"Aye," Egwyn agreed. *"'Tis woven into the fabric of the chamber."*

"But moving something like that so that it lays across the river instead of up into the sky . . . ?" Seth pointed out, ever the voice of cowardly gloom.

"'Tis dangerous," said Egwyn. *"If it should shake free of your control, it would roll across the land as the world spins, and unravel reality wherever it touches. To control the distortion properly will require four wizards."*

"Four?! Four?!" Seth exclaimed. "Lelani's neutered, you're made of crumbling clay, and I'm still in the minor leagues!"

Lelani opened her palm and ignited a nascent phosphorescent ball, much to everyone's delight; it sputtered like a Fourth of July sparkler and whipped around to light the candles. "The silver has passed through," she said.

The beast had smashed the outer vault door. It descended the stairs.

"Great . . . we're still short a fourth wizard," Cat pointed out.

"That's not accurate," Lelani said.

"Who?" Daniel asked.

"Cat."

"Yes?" Cat replied.

"No, I meant Cat is the fourth wizard."

A cold wash came over her . . . she forgot about her parched throat, her aching muscles, her exhaustion . . . her daughter. If it had been anyone else who said it, Cat would think it a moment of levity; Cat could count on one hand the number of times Lelani had not been serious—and never when they were in danger.

"You're nuts!" Seth charged.

"For once, I wholeheartedly agree with Seth," Cat said. She hoped this would not become a habit. Lelani just raised an eyebrow and waited for the news to sink in.

There had been talk . . . Cat's father's grandfather was a Sioux shaman, his grandmother, a medicine woman on their Dakota reservation. Suddenly, all of Seth's fears and reservations about wizardry made sense; the power to wave one's hands and speak mumbo jumbo and by so doing alter reality . . . it was too great a burden for anyone.

"I've suspected for some time," Lelani told her. "Your hearing Rosencrantz's death cry as clearly as Seth and I confirmed it."

"There's nothing magical about me," Cat said. Her denial rang false in her own ears. Ever since she was exposed to real magic, something had come alive in her—an undercurrent she'd never known existed before.

"You are not a wizard, Cat," Lelani stated. "Wizardry takes training and education and involves knowledge of the sciences. But your innate sensitivity falls within the spectrum of a sorceress. For our needs this will do. You will handle one of the vectors needed to move the anomaly."

"Huh?"

"You're making sure the couch doesn't smash into the banister while the heavy lifters on the ends carry it up the stairs," Seth explained.

All the time Cat spent studying horticulture and medieval economics might have been better used on books of the arcane. Cat wished she'd at least read past the first Harry Potter.

"You demanded an idea, MacDonnell," Seth reminded her. "Red just pulled a doozy out of her massive horse butt."

"You need to shut up," Cat said mechanically. She was starting to shake. Her only hope of ever seeing Bree and Cal again depended on Cat doing something she'd never done before . . . something fantastical and alien—and getting it right the first time.

CHAPTER 28

A GRAND MAGUS'S LAST TRICK

1

Chryslantha had gone right to bed after her audience. The news of Callum's marriage to a commoner had killed the reserve sustaining her these past few days—depleted the meager cache of hope that insulated her from the harsh reality of their new world . . . a world that could never be set right again. Balzac's haunting revelation stalked her even in her sleep. With no respite in either slumber or wakefulness, Chrys contemplated a life without Callum. Just the very idea of it turned her stomach. If she was to remain sick with grief and longing for the rest of her days, was death any less preferable?

The next day, she forced a respite from her dour malaise to explain to Sophia the truth . . . that Danel was safe in another realm. Sophia had trouble grasping it, believing it a ruse to get her to eat and dress. Chrys would not relent, though. "Why would I fashion a fantasy where you never suckle him again or see his first steps, or hear his first words?" she told her friend. "The infant is gone, but your son lives. Even if he is as old as you when he returns, *he lives*." Chrys oscillated between rage, sorrow, and

320

relief (for she was truly grateful Callum also yet lived) in the space of informing Sophia—but was too numb to pursue a detailed explanation further.

Guards arrived without warning demanding that Chryslantha and the archduchess accompany them. Chrys asked for a moment to prepare, for they both looked a mess, but the soldiers grabbed them by each arm and hauled them out of the chamber. Chrys managed to get her legs under her in time to carry herself, but Sophia stumbled, and the men half dragged her.

They merged with soldiers escorting Athelstan, the high prelate, Commander MacDonnell, Lady Boules, and other nobles. A weight of trepidation settled on Chryslantha. *What has happened?*

A hundred guardsmen lined the periphery of the great hall. Officers ignored the new entrants as they plotted over a long table; piles of parchments and scrolls lay around a great topographical map of Aandor chiseled from a slab of wood with tokens and statuettes upon it. From a side door five elite soldiers dragged in Magnus Proust chained and gagged. Chrys's heart broke for the once proud wizard, who still wore nothing but a soiled diaper. His jailers' uniforms were clean to a shimmer, with the mark of the double lightning bolt on the collars of their doublets. Their commander was a fair knight and beside him walked Widow Taker. They forced Proust to his knees before the dais and continued to hold his thick steel chains.

Lara stormed in and climbed the dais; Balzac shuffled behind her. "The time for games and half-truths is done," she announced. "Let me set the proper tone for our discussion." Guards dragged Earl Francis Gibbons from the crowd and threw him before the stairs. He tried to rise, but they forced him on his knees. Gibbons was well liked at court, fair to a fault and a kind word never far from his lips; it pained everyone to see him treated so. An enormous man in black stepped up with a halberd—he severed Earl Gibbons's head with a single clean swing. The earl's wife shrieked in terror, one daughter was sick and the other fainted, as did some of the other nobles in the group. A guard gagged the earl's wife with a rag to quiet her.

Lara picked up the earl's head by its hair. Gibbons's eyes focused wildly on his wife, his mouth rounded to call to her. Chrys realized, with abject sorrow, that the earl yet held a spark of cognition, but his wife was too distraught to see this. Chrys managed to hold her own stomach down as she stepped between them to block the wife's view. *Better she believes it was quick.* "Take his family from this hall," Chrys begged the guards. They looked to their mistress.

Lara nodded, and the earl's family was dragged out. Chrys looked around at her fellow countrymen: repressed panic, dejected, hopeless. Today marked a turning point. How many of them would live to see the next dawn?

"I trust I've made my level of patience clear," Lara said. "Arnulf, proceed."

The handsome officer stepped forward and read from an officious piece of decorated parchment covered in the stamps, seals, and ribbons of Farrenheil. "Danel of House Athelstan is a heretic, guilty of challenging the rightful authority of Farrenheil, and attempting to usurp the legitimate claim of his lordship Grand Duke Vaulknar Zin of Farrenheil. Danel is hereby declared an insurgent and enemy of the state. The lives of Danel, his men, and all abettors in his revolt are forfeit. *Anyone* caught aiding the rebel will be put to death immediately."

The nobles looked to one another, dumbfounded.

"The prince is an infant," said James MacDonnell, stating calmly what for most would be obvious.

"You can thank Proust for your prince's rapid growth spurt," Lara said. "I promise you, his death now will be slower and far more agonizing than it would have been as a babe."

"That is not possible," said a shaken Mila Boules.

Lady Boules's remark lit a fire in Sophia. "Oh, you would wish it," Sophia scoffed. "Anything to stem losing your tenuous proximity to power. All that scheming and now your hooks are stuck in a gelded duke."

"My, my . . . we've stumbled across a family squabble," Balzac said with amusement.

"Not germane to this discussion," said Lara. "You've all missed the point. Danel is the prince of nothing. He's a vagabond savior in a hopeless cause. A few farmers and centaurs playing soldier in the woods."

"Even lost causes have their patron hallows," the high prelate said. It was uncharacteristically brave of the man.

"If the prince's purpose is so hopeless, why have you lashed out thusly?" Sophia asked. Chryslantha's heart lifted at seeing her friend become vibrant again; but she worried about the White Lady's temper.

"Gibbons was a better man than most, and he knew nothing of the prince's activities," Athelstan added.

"When I anger, someone dies," Lara told her audience. "This is how *you* know I am important. You will not harbor any hope of rescue . . . of recompense. I will not tolerate it . . . nor efforts made within this castle or city to help that brat. The war is done! Your southern and eastern armies vanquished, half your banner men have pledged their fealty to Farrenheil . . . and yet this insurgency will drag out the implementation of the pax I am trying to establish. So here are the rules. I will start killing nobles with each pointless success your bastard manages to pull off. Earl Gibbons was the price for Yarmouth."

"You have a score of hostages," Sophia pointed out. "If you need all our deaths to punish my son's victories you have a bigger problem than you acknowledge."

Lara scowled at the archduchess, looking fit to be tied for having her fears made transparent when she sought to hide them through terror. Chrys was certain Sophia would be executed next. Proust began to laugh under his gag, drawing Lara's attention. The laugh morphed into an uproarious muffled cackle. Chrys knelt by his side. "Magnus, do not provoke her."

Magnus touched his forehead to Chrys's and his thoughts mingled with her own. *"She cannot find him. The prince's possessions in this castle are from his infancy. After many years, items lose their connection . . . doubly so for a royal whose very essence rejects magic. Her spells struggle to find their mark. This is why she lashes out like a petulant child. There is a legitimate challenge to her authority, and she cannot cheat her way out."*

"Do not stir the hornet's nest," Chrys pleaded.

He smiled, his eyes wise and compassionate, like a grandfather consoling a favorite heir. *"I have been brought here for only one reason, child. Allow me to save Sophia and to have my last laugh."*

Chrys rose and turned to face the White Lady, ignoring her own sage advice to the wizard. "You said a death for *each* defiant act. Is this the value of your word?"

"Gibbons was restitution for Yarmouth," Lara explained. "What of brave Lord Onyx, who died defending the honor of Farrenheil?"

"Magnus has value."

"You have no idea who you defend. In all the world, Proust is the wizard all other wizards truly fear. Even his own council's chief was wary of him. Look at how he's aged so rapidly . . . the gods only know what dark arts he's consorted with. We will all sleep easier after today."

The axman had quietly moved behind the wizard. He swung deftly to separate Proust from his neck. The ax, however, stopped at a transparent barrier, elastic in nature, and launched in reverse, sending the halberd's rear spike seven inches into its wielder's forehead. The crowd of nobles (and their guards) hurriedly backed away as the executioner hit the floor. A dozen archers on the balcony shot at Proust. Arrows stuck in the barrier around the grand magus like quills in a jellyfish; they turned flaccid and began to wriggle, pulling their heads from the barrier, then sliding down the shield to become pythons and cobras as they touched the floor. They darted for the guardsmen holding the chains.

"How is he doing this?!" cried Lara.

Widow Taker bowled a fistful of tiny skulls, like marbles, toward the snakes. As they rolled, bones emerged from the skulls, building themselves into the skeletons of some diminutive primate. They attacked the snakes and were quickly swallowed. The bone primates grew within the snakes' gullets, ripping their way out of the flesh. The snake flesh transformed into millions of flesh-eating beetles with pincers cracking the tiny skulls like almond shells. Widow Taker pulled an elephant's tusk from his bag of bones and struck the end hard on the floor. The vibration ran up Chryslantha's legs; all felt the pressure of his spell as the marble floor fractured and the beetles were uniformly crushed.

Aandor's grand magus leaped into the air, nearly pulling his chain handlers with him. They struggled to constrain him like a wayward balloon in a wind, as though the gods themselves summoned him on high. Other guardsmen came to their aid, dragging Magnus back down. Widow Taker chanted frantically in his native Sunumbreean, one hand's fingers jerking in spasms, the other hand clutching his carbon-black cane before him. Runes fired hotly on the stick; his eyes were blank and his head shook back and forth. Magnus's own head convulsed and seized as he fought the spell.

"Now!" Lara cried to her archers. They fired again—this time finding their mark. Magnus's "lift" ceased and he crashed to the marble floor in a clatter of chains. Guards stepped in to cut him down but hesitated when hundreds of bone-white sharp protrusions grew out of Magnus's skin. The guards found their courage, but it was too late. The bony thorns launched out of the wizard, piercing armor, cutting the soldiers in a maelstrom of shrapnel that embedded itself in the stone walls of the hall. None of the Aandoran nobles were touched, though.

Widow Taker doubled his mind attack on Proust, speaking words so dark and ancient they brought pain and despair to Chryslantha's soul. The nobles and even the guardsmen along the periphery clutched at their ears. Magnus cried out as well, also calling upon that ancient tongue—the great room quaked as though two leviathans groaned with rage. Only Lara remained unfazed. The White Lady took position before Proust and called fire around her arms, moving them gracefully like blazing wings. She covered Proust in a thick pillar of boiling red flame. Guardsmen protected their faces with their cloaks as the heat rose to an inferno. The high windows shattered. Chrys could no longer see Proust for the firestorm surrounding him, such was Lara's unrelenting intensity, yet still, the quake from Proust's voice continued and magnified as Aandor's greatest mage battled for his life. And then the voice stopped. The vibrations stopped. Lara ceased her attack, winded and bent, pressing a stitch in her side.

A charred and blackened thing lay where once there was a man. It smoldered, adding to the thick haze, and smelled of meat. Embers of its charred flesh wafted like black snow on currents of smoke. An arm moved. Magnus yet lived! He crawled toward the White Lady, leaving an ashen streak of carbon on the marble. Skin cracked off as he struggled. Chrys prayed there was more to the wizard than this . . . wizards always had another trick. But this burned and blinded thing was no longer a wizard. Arnulf retrieved the halberd and finished the executioner's task; Magnus's neck fractured like spent coal, and the grand magus moved no more.

Chryslantha shivered with rage . . . with sorrow. She felt a sudden longing for her betrothed. Such was her terror that Chrys had all but forgotten Callum MacDonnell was no longer hers to pine for. She had never felt more alone or abandoned. She put her face in her shaking hands; if death took her now, it would be a comfort.

2

A few more nobles and gentry had been brought into the hall, including the return of Earl Gibbons's family; all of them herded into the far corner and barricaded in by a collection of armoires, chests, and hutches. A half circle of guards around the barricade completed the pen. Lara, it seemed, wanted an audience . . . or, they would not be staying long enough to bother with a trip to the dungeons. The nobles breathed in the ashen particles of

Aandor's once powerful wizard. Except for servants clearing out his husk, the beetles, and broken glass the battle seemed like a distant dream. Two hard benches were all the women and elderly had to sit on. The lowest scullery maid had more advantage than Aandor's nobles.

With Farrenheil's strategic consolidation mostly complete, the nobles' importance diminished, as was evident by the reassignment of Arnulf as liaison to free Colonel Falkyre for other duties. Chrys hoped they would not separate her from Sophia, but did not know what arrangements her father had made. For all she knew, Lord Godwynn had bent the knee to Vaulknar Zin, and she would also be obliged to switch allegiances to Farrenheil. The thought of it turned her stomach.

Arnulf came over to inspect his guards and Chryslantha caught his eye.

"Are you being treated well, my lady?"

"As well as can be, sir. Some of the older ladies could use more than a bench . . . something with cushions and a back."

"You'll not be here that long," he said.

"If they could be returned to the archduke's suite . . ."

"That apartment belongs to the governess and general."

"Speak true, Sir Arnulf . . . how many behind me will not survive the week?"

Her forwardness caught him off guard; he appeared awkward for a second, and then motioned to join him beyond the restricted area. "I'd heard you were bold—a lady of uncompromising character."

"You have not answered my question."

Arnulf straightened as if just remembering this was not some carol at a feast. "There's much debate among the high muck-a-mucks about what to do with you lot. It's the dungeon for some . . .

house arrest for others. I'll tell you this . . . Archduke Athelstan was to be next under the halberd. Proust's resistance has unsettled the White Lady, bought him a day."

Chryslantha was shocked. "Why?"

"Athelstan is not important now that his son is of age. He cannot negotiate on Danel's behalf and what's left of his army legally belongs to the boy. Gods help us should Danel actually cobble troops together . . . ," Arnulf said with a sly smile. "Though we will not allow that to happen," he finished.

Arnulf had divulged much, was too familiar with a woman he'd just met—a clear sign that he was smitten. Chrys smiled instinctively, leading Arnulf to believe his wit amused her. If men were too stupid to remain clearheaded, far be it for Chryslantha to surrender the advantage.

"You've met the prince?" Chrys asked.

"Oh yes. And survived. It's his mercy that will be his undoing. He seemed a bright lad, but unsuited for war. My men and I reported what we'd learned to our superiors and the soldiers we encountered en route back. The whole forest is looking for him. And, *we* live to fight another day." He laughed.

"Ha!" Chrys laughed curtly, almost mockingly. It was the first good thing she'd heard in nearly a week.

Arnulf was discomfited. "Pray tell, woman, what do you find so funny?"

"You were outmaneuvered."

"How so?"

"How difficult would it have been for Danel to keep secret his identity when the whole kingdom knew him to be a babe?"

Arnulf did not understand the question.

"Whispers are a funny thing," Chrys continued. "They proliferate like rabbits and grow into legend. Every farmer, merchant, and tradesman from here to Red King's Gate who may have bent the knee to Farrenheil before Danel's return will now hope for the chance to hide him, feed him, volunteer a son to his cause—and the less work for him to convince his subjects that he is legitimate, thanks to you."

Arnulf now looked increasingly uncomfortable. After days and days of defeat, Chrys had grasped upon a minor victory . . . a way to hurt back for the misery she'd endured. "My lady, I doubt . . ."

"Have your soldiers taken vows of silence?" she asked. "He *chose* to reveal himself, and in so doing, used *you* to spread his message that Aandor's savior had returned."

Stillness overtook the young knight; Chrys immediately regretted her words. Too hard, too angry . . . she'd challenged his aptitude and embarrassed him.

"You are quite the astute strategist, my lady. How could one so brilliant, so beautiful have lost the champion of the lists to the lesser wiles of Catherine MacDonnell?"

This time, it was Chryslantha who turned still. "Catherine MacDonnell is in Aandor?"

"She and her daughter were my prisoners." He straightened tall before her and stepped close, forcing her back against the wall. "I'm embarrassed to say I did not at first realize whose wife she was; perhaps I am dim, as you allude."

"Sir Arnulf, I beg your forgiv—"

"Unlike your eyes, however, blue as the waters in a southern atoll, hers are gray as cold ash. Your flaxen hair brings the sun to us mortals, hers is as a moonless night. Your beauty is legend throughout the kingdoms . . ." He took a closer step, pinning her tightly. Chrys turned her head; he whispered in her ear. "And yet Captain MacDonnell chose her. Perhaps he thought you too clever to make a proper wife. I, on the other hand, would have kept you, taught you your place. I may yet do so. I am an adept winner of prizes. Perhaps if I lop off the head of the pretender prince, you will be the instrument of the White Lady's gratitude?"

Arnulf slid away leaving Chrys furious at her own behavior. Here was her handler, a somewhat noble man among savages, and she poked him like an imbecile prodding a hornet's nest in search of honey. Just when Chrys thought the day could not get any worse, she heard Mina MacDonnell cry out, "James!"

Another group had been brought in. James leaped and embraced his wife and daughters. *Three daughters?* Chrys's blood ran cold, for among Mina's brood, a smaller, strangely dressed version of Meghan stood with them. Chryslantha knew every cousin, every ward of the MacDonnells, and this one, who wore her betrothed's likeness as her own face, was not one of them.

She returned slowly to the restricted area. Valeria caught sight of her friend and rushed to embrace her.

"Oh, my dear," said Mina upon seeing Chrys. Tears streamed from her eyes. "I had hoped you'd been spared all this."

"I have been treated well, Lady MacDonnell."

Chrys bent to examine the girl. She took her small face in her hands and wiped dirt from the girl's cheek. She'd been crying recently, her eyes red and puffy.

Mina looked embarrassed, nervous—unable to say what Chrys understood would be difficult for the matriarch to admit.

"I know," Chrys said, releasing the old woman from her duty. "Of Catherine, of Callum's daughter. Is this her?"

James MacDonnell's head swiveled back and forth in search of an explanation.

Mina looked emotionally wrought. She'd likely been drafting her explanation from the moment she'd met her grandchild.

"I don't care for the reasons right now, Mina. This girl is in great danger. They will use her to get to Callum."

"We told our captors Brianna was Mother's youngest," Valeria said.

"There is one here who will know that is not so," said Chrys. As if on cue, Arnulf's voice boomed behind her, ordering guards to bring in more cushioned seats for the older ladies. Terror filled Mina and the girls' eyes. Chryslantha put her back to Arnulf and pulled Brianna tight against her, cradling the girl's head. "She must not be seen with you," Chrys insisted.

Valeria pulled a shawl from Lady Guthrie's shoulders, staring defiantly at her not to object, and draped it over Brianna's head. Chrys guided the girl to the back of the crowd, the corner where the most concentrated group of people stood between Brianna and the rest of the hall. Mina and the girls started to follow.

"What are you doing?" Chrys said. "Stand elsewhere. She must not be linked to you."

"She has no one but us," Valeria said. Val threw her mother a dirty look. "We took Bree from her mother, and the child has been inconsolable ever since. We are strangers to her."

Chrys got down on one knee and looked into Brianna's eyes . . . Callum's eyes. This was the closest she'd been to him in days and she was determined to hold back her own pain. "Brianna, your father is in this city. He is in danger. If Farrenheil discovers who you are, it will go very badly for him. They will use you to get to him and then they will . . . hurt him. Do you understand?"

The girl nodded, tears welling.

Chrys used the scarf to wipe Brianna's tears. "I am a . . . friend . . . of your father's. I will stay with you. Don't be afraid . . . if anyone asks, you are Pearle, my cousin Ian's child. Can you remember that name?" The girl nodded.

Chrys rose and faced the MacDonnells who hovered behind her. James was demanding an explanation. "Go," Chrys whispered, shooing them. "Should Arnulf ask . . . the girl and her mother are in the forest."

A messenger on horseback rushed into the hall. He clopped to the dais and handed Blunt a post. A hush descended on the room; everyone strained to listen.

"The prince has fled Crowe's Porte," Blunt said. "They eluded the winged cavalry and were last seen heading east on the river road—toward Meadsweir."

Friends and foes gasped. The most stalwart guardsmen could not believe what they'd heard.

"We have them then?" cried Lara.

"No, mistress," said the corporal. "Lord Gillen marches north, we close in from the west, and the Skilytes patrol the river. Where else is there for them to go but back?"

"East," said Balzac, ever the pragmatist.

"Madness," said Blunt. "None who've journeyed to Meadsweir have ever returned."

Lara's mood turned dark. "If I had but a token of the prince's."

"But you do, my lady," said Sir Arnulf.

Arnulf plowed into the crowd of prisoners and grabbed Valeria by the arm. Her father tried to intercede, but guardsmen restrained him. Chrys motioned to Bree to stay in back, then grabbed her friend's hand as Arnulf pulled Valeria out of the pen. He brought them both before the White Lady. Arnulf pointed to the small metal pin of a lantern on Valeria's dress.

"The prince bestowed this token upon Valeria MacDonnell, whom he considers his friend and under his protection."

Lara came down from the dais and snatched the pin. "Bring

me a cauldron!" she demanded. She hovered over the great map of Aandor on the table.

Valeria turned her face into Chrys's shoulder and began to cry. Chrys comforted her. *This is not her fault.*

"Can you kill him from here?" asked General Blunt.

"No. He is protected from such sorceries. This spell will destroy the token, but we will at least know his location."

Lara threw the pin into the cauldron waters and recited. It popped, and smoke drifted up. She scooped a ladleful of the bloodred liquid from the cauldron and scattered it onto the map. Beads of red liquid rolled across it, over mountains and through the rivers, pooling into larger beads until the few remaining ones settled into each other directly over Meadsweir. Lara threw another scoopful onto the map; they, too, joined the first over Meadsweir.

"Madness," whispered Blunt. "Does this mean he yet lives?"

"It means his body is there," Lara said. "Alive or dead."

"Then it is done!" proclaimed Balzac.

The Farrenheisi laughed and slapped their cohorts' backs. Lara, however, did not accept this as victory.

"Retrieve his body," she told the messenger. The corporal looked ill. *As he should,* thought Chryslantha. The corporal came off his horse and bent the knee before her.

"Mistress. We chased his party to the crossing—hundreds of men tightened the noose—they could not have doubled back or crossed the river. Their tracks, still fresh, led toward Meadsweir." Sweat trickled down the messenger's face. "The bravest of us trekked half a mile down that cursed road to be sure," he said as if to indicate there was no need to risk the lives of her men.

Lara was not having any of it. "I do not suffer cowards," she said. "Find braver men, Corporal, and retrieve the prince's body—or I shall find you a grizzly bear to wrestle in the pits."

General Blunt approached his wife. He put a hand on her shoulder. "Lara . . ."

"Kyzur, how many troops do we have scrounging through the woods and towns east of here?"

"Ten thousand."

"Send our fastest messengers—every crow, every raven, every pigeon that can carry a note—use the Haderach if you must, to contact the hedge wizards advanced enough to receive messages. Tell all ten thousand to converge on Meadsweir."

"Lara, no," said the general in horror. He'd lowered his voice, but the echo in the silent hall worked against it. "Lord March is delayed coming up from the south, and we have not yet contended with the western army."

"We'll be fine," Lara assured him. "General Koke's troops will replenish us from the Gate. Our plans to breed that cow Sophia hinge on a clean break from this bloodline. There must be no whispers, no stories, no legends. Legends spring from doubt."

Chrys led Valeria back to the pen, away from the mad sorceress. Athelstan had his hand on Sophia's shoulder and she put her arm around her husband and leaned into him for support. The life of their son was worth more than their differences. Lady Boules had the good sense to stay back and keep silent.

"Send the army to Meadsweir," Lara ordered. "And if they find whatever it is there that makes men's knees weak as maidens', kill it as well. It has no place in *my* empire."

CHAPTER 29

HOW TO MOVE A TUNNEL IN FIFTY-FOUR EASY STEPS

Seth's heart broke for Cat as she struggled with Lelani's instructions. Magic was not something to be learned on the fly. Cat fumbled her spells like one who'd never driven a car being told how to operate a fifteen-gear tractor-trailer. Magic had separated Seth from his family, placed impossible expectations upon him; he'd be rid of it if he could. Lelani, still a student herself, never struggled; the motions came easily, even when she winged it, like a master chef who never measured ingredients.

The beast threw itself at the door—its roar amplified in the tight stairwell. Poles in the door staples began to crack. Urry and Ladue replaced them with iron rods, but even those began to bend under the beast's onslaught. Each man braced a door, trying to lessen the strain on the rods. The monster's cold luminescence shone through the widening crack, its radiation making the iron brittle where the light touched it.

Daniel grabbed Egwyn's war hammer and sword.

The door rods snapped, clanging onto the floor just as the prince reached them. The monster pushed Urry and Ladue back as it forced its way into the chamber; Daniel and Seth took full measure of the beast for the first time—sixteen feet of fluorescent muscle, a bull-like head planted on shoulders seven feet wide, its serrated horns twisted like a ram's. The torso tapered down to bovine haunches and hooves; its forked tail whipped frantically.

Ladue was pinned between the door and the wall. Urry drew his sword and attacked. The monster backhanded him, its three-fingered hand searing armor where it touched.

The war hammer had the longer reach, so Daniel took it with both hands and slammed its head into the creature's gut with the force of a runaway pickup truck. The monster bent in half, screaming in pain. Daniel reeled back and swung again, an uppercut to the jaw. The blow drove the creature halfway up the stairwell. Ladue and Urry tried to reseal the door, but the splatter of wood and iron on the ground jammed between the two halves.

"Clear the floor around that door!" Lelani ordered. "Daniel, be ready with the sword." She produced a small beaker from her satchel with rattling bits of faerie silver.

"Didn't you say we could buy a city with that much faerie silver?" Seth reminded her.

"Wealth is no boon to the dead," she replied. As the creature again entered the room, she flung the silver at it. Seth had never heard an anguished sound like when the silver touched the beast. The soft pastel glow of its skin turned an infected crimson. The plasma reeled from the metal bits in concentric rings, like a stone thrust in water. The creature retreated up the stairs backward crying in agony as it expelled the bits of metal lodged in it piece by piece.

Ladue and Urry had cleared the floor and shut the doors.

"Daniel, bar the door with the sword," Lelani said. "Mage-smyte weapons will not crack or melt."

Urry added more iron poles around the sword, and Daniel

wedged the war hammer between the door and ground—temporary measures at best.

"It will lick its wounds and return," Lelani said. "We leave now or die."

Lelani rushed through the final preparations for the spell.

"Good, good," said the old clay king. *"But the centaur cannot anchor this spell."*

"She's the best wizard we have," Cat pointed out.

"You have the other bracelet," Egwyn said. *"Place it upon the male wizard."*

"Whoa! What?" Seth replied.

"I will anchor the spell in his form."

"And where will I be?" Seth asked.

"Your essence will reside in the golem until I complete the task."

A whiff of bullshit just touched Seth's nose. He looked around in case anyone else thought this, too; the weight of everybody's gaze bore down on him. He needed to do this thing regardless of their right to ask. Seth didn't give a plug nickel for any of their wishes—except for Catherine. She was the only true innocent, lost more than anyone else since Aandor came back to their lives. If she did not get out of this dungeon, her daughter and unborn child would suffer for it.

The creature roared in the stairwell.

"Before the beast returns!" Egwyn stressed eagerly. The legend had all the leverage.

Lelani held out the box with the gleaming bracelet for Seth; it beckoned from its crushed-velvet cradle.

"You know this is fishy," he whispered.

She gave him the slightest of nods, a look that confessed they were all out of options.

Seth slipped the bracelet on his wrist. For an instant, his soul, for lack of a better term, was in transit. Egwyn's ghostly finger reached out in passing and touched his mind. It was a pinch, not at all painful, but surprising for its corporeal tactility in their ethereal states. Was that a smile he saw on the ancient wizard's wraithlike face?

Seth was in the golem, but the fit was not exact—like sitting on a small stool, he was on the verge of falling and concentrated on staying put. He realized that he couldn't speak. *But Egwyn had no trouble talking from the golem.*

He saw in shades of gray like supernatural night vision. Egwyn looked at his hands—Seth's hands—relishing flesh again after three centuries. *Don't get used to it,* Seth thought—something in his clay gut told him Egwyn had less noble ideas.

The group convened on the dais. With the sword and hammer on the door, Daniel wielded the flanged mace as backup. Egwyn and Lelani began their spell—Cat and Seth in the golem were positioned for stabilization. Egwyn said a word and the spell began to pull the energy from the room's myriad objects into the circle. Magic was torn out of vases and frames, farm implements, cups and spindles, weapons and shields . . . everything in the room that the Magesmyte had made, cursed or otherwise, was being drawn on and swirled into Lelani's circle like light into a black hole. The objects screamed, as their souls were ripped from them. Only Daniel, Urry, and Ladue did not hear their cries. Seth would have put his only clay hand to his clay ear if he could spare the concentration. They would never have been able to do this spell without Egwyn—he was the only one who knew how to deconstruct his own works. Lelani threw many of her own magical items into the circle as well, including the wizard-hunter Ahbahdaan's amulets, rings, and earrings. Cat chanted and motioned as Lelani had instructed, and Seth mirrored her in his thoughts.

Egwyn caught hold of his anomaly three rooms away and began to draw it toward the vault. The vibrations were enormous, like dragging the *Titanic* through stone and mortar—shaking the ancient castle to its foundations. Seth felt the pressure of the thing as it grew closer—an anomaly that was flat in their reality, but tubular in unperceived extra-dimensional space. The spell sucked the life out of every last item in the room, including Daniel's magic weapons, which were holding the door closed. The monster's last smash bent them.

"We have it!" Egwyn shouted with Seth's voice. They steered the anomaly to the far wall.

"Position it to lay across the river!" Lelani ordered. The four of them moved it with great effort . . . this arduous transdimensional "couch" they carried up a five-story brownstone.

Seth and Cat were exhausted by the time they set the anomaly in place. Egwyn triggered the portal and the wall flicked on like a high-definition screen set to a peaceful meadow.

"Wait!" Egwyn warned, as Urry walked toward it. "Let me alter its purpose, lest we find ourselves trapped in a tunnel leading back here."

The beast smashed at the door.

"Hurry," Ladue warned. "That door has three hits left at most."

"It is done," Egwyn said. "You must close this portal behind you once you are on the other side. I shall now switch places with your friend."

That was the best thing Seth had heard all day. He waited.

And waited . . .

Something was wrong. Egwyn shook his head like a drunk sobering up.

"Are you okay?" Lelani asked. What Seth heard next made his blood run cold.

"I'm fine," Egwyn said, nailing Seth's accent and vernacular perfectly. "The switch back was a little sketchy."

Seth screamed bloody bullshit inside his clay prison. That son of a bitch had stolen his memories, his knowledge, and convinced the guardians he was back in his body. By the time his friends learned the truth . . .

Egwyn picked up a mallet and walked toward Seth-golem. "Egwyn requested I end his suffering," faux Seth said.

In his panic, Seth stopped focusing on his ill-fitted hold of the golem . . . it launched him free of the body. Egwyn was ejected at the same time, and Seth's body slumped to the floor. Seth dashed to reenter his body, but Egwyn's spirit blocked him, and they wrestled.

"I did not anticipate a protection spell about you," Egwyn said as they grappled in the spiritual plane. *"Whoever cast it was adept . . . and wise to protect you so. Your power is trapped deep, preventing your rise to greatness. Too bad I shall reclaim it for you. I will again walk under the stars!"*

Something changed in the balance, and Seth was pulled back into the golem.

The beast put a serious bend into the vault doors—its luminescence growing through the crack.

"Release him, Egwyn," Lelani commanded. "Your time has passed." Seth's face under Egwyn's power turned malevolent. The ancient king grasped her wrist. The short red hairs of her tail grew rapidly and turned into hundreds of red-and-black-banded snakes; they bit her rump and legs. Several grew long enough to attack the back of her neck and shoulders. Lelani could not distance herself from her own tail. Ladue lunged to slice them off with his sword, smashing them with his boot heels; they squirmed away underfoot to find solace in the dark spaces.

Egwyn resumed his murderous march toward Seth. Seth didn't even have two arms to ward off a blow. That's when he remembered . . . the pullback into the golem was like the first time . . . the bracelet was the only thing that made this soul swap possible. Seth strained to lift the golem's remaining arm. Ball and joint that had once moved easily scraped and cracked. A fissure opened from the shoulder to the elbow. With a last push, he raised his arm as high as he could and at the last moment sprang his essence from the ill-fitting clay prison as before. The arm cracked and fell, severing the bracelet's physical connection to the golem's body.

Egwyn was again ejected from Seth's body. Cat quickly snatched the silver bracelet from Seth's limp wrist.

Seth had guessed correctly that once his soul was free, whatever protection spell was on him wanted no part of another driver. Egwyn's ghost grabbed Seth's spirit again, preventing him from reaching his own body, and him from returning to the golem. Seth thrust his ghostly fingers through Egwyn's third eye into his spiritual brain. He could taste the man's memories . . . his first spell, his first kiss . . . the anger and anguish of having been deposed as well as the love of his brother, which was genuine and true. He could taste the madness in the man's mind, a bitter, sour thing—the torture of sitting for an eternity in the dark, cut off from the world by an invincible monster of his own making. Seth was merciless, voracious in his violation, angry with what Egwyn intended for him. Egwyn and Seth snapped back into themselves. He was just getting used to his skin when Lelani hauled him off his feet and threatened to cut him with a knife.

"Wait! It's me! It's me!" Seth pleaded.

"Prove it!" she said. Her knife started to glow hotly.

Egwyn may have had his memories, but there was no way some moldy old wizard king would match Seth's manically depraved personality. "Errr . . . uh, you're so smoking hot, I'd probably hit your ginormous horse vag, if you let me?"

Lelani gave Seth a dirty smile and pushed him toward the portal. Cat let out a relieved bark of laughter.

"Let's move!" Ladue ordered, throwing Seth an evil eye.

Seth called his staff to him and they jumped through just as the beast crashed into the vault. On the other side, they ran across a meadow. Seth looked back—the portal hanging in open space actually looked like a bubble of dark water. Behind it was the river and Meadsweir. The beast appeared at the wormhole.

"Shut that hole!" Cat screamed.

The beast crossed through the threshold in a rage. Seth thought their number was up when it suddenly grabbed its chest and succumbed to pain. A luminous rainbow of plasma energy erupted from its body and arched across the sky, over the river back to Meadsweir Castle. The creature howled and whimpered. It retreated into the portal back to the vault. The streaming energy stopped.

"It can be only so far from its heart," Lelani said.

The beast paced the portal threshold, raging, cursing them in whatever passed for its language.

"Let's get away from here," Seth said.

"Aye," Urry agreed. "There's a stable five miles away . . . from there, the Gate's a day's hard ride northeast."

CHAPTER 30

FROZEN SORROWS

1

The guardians rode hard after Meadsweir, stopping only to change horses and straighten their backs. Their replacement mounts were barely rested; Roland and Daniel's Yarmouth men had come through the same town hours earlier. Folks went out of their way to greet their prince, the oddity that was a babe only a few days ago and was now a young man. Their kindness and good wishes were heartwarming. Daniel was impressed with how rapidly the news of the invasion, and his unorthodox return, had spread—for better or worse, at least the kingdom was finally awake to its new reality.

North of the Sevren the land suffered a dry spell, rain skirting just south of the river for several weeks; the trail of Roland's growing company was clear. Lelani was first to spot the company, just a quarter mile out from the Gate. Daniel was surprised they had caught up, since Roland rode as hard as they did.

"Something's amiss," Lelani said.

The three hundred men and horses in Roland's camp stood frozen as statues. A bird flying east toward the fort town suddenly went stiff over the camp and fell to the ground. The guardians stopped their advance.

"Balzac did say Farrenheil wasn't worried about the Gate," Seth reminded them.

"The enchantment is likely anchored to some object within the fort," Lelani noted.

"Doesn't seem to worry them much," Cat said, pointing to the mountain pass in the distance. The long, red line of Farrenheil's army—fresh from its victory at the Wizards' Archives—snaked its way down the mountain. Only Red King's Gate stood between them and the rest of Aandor.

"Suggestions?" Daniel asked. No one put forth an idea, even Seth, whose inappropriate wit seldom took a holiday. His friends were themselves frozen; someone had pushed out the enchantment to ensnare them.

Daniel dismounted carefully, trying not to tip over his poor horse. Everyone was fine except for Cat, who had been shifting her weight in the saddle and now teetered precariously on the edge. Daniel helped her off and sat her against a boulder. Her joints were stiff, but still bendable. Her pupils dilated ever so slightly when he looked into them. She was in there and cognizant.

Daniel collected his backpack and weapons. "I'm going into the fort," he told everyone, not even certain they could hear. He suspected Cat was burning a hole in the back of his neck with a glare, and refused to face her. He had to find the enchanted item. What else was there to do?

Daniel had been holding the flanged mace in Meadsweir during the escape spell; it must have protected the weapon. The mace was slightly longer than a Major League bat and weighed about four pounds to Daniel, but his warhorse had struggled as though lugging an obese giant with an anvil. Daniel had never practiced with a mace and wished he had the sword instead. He moved through Roland's frozen company of ragged farmers and smiths. They would not have stood a chance against elite Farrenheisi soldiers. Ladue's blowing the bridge in Crowe's Porte had saved these men's lives.

The fort was a self-contained town with its own guilds, merchants, and smithies. Daniel zigzagged through a crowd of revelers, frozen in the act of celebrating his naming day. It occurred to him to come up with a better plan than to walk up to the keep's front door like an idiot. He ducked into an alley and hugged the ground on the other end, crawling under kiosks, carts, and horses, past stray cats and frozen vermin, until he came to the side of the building. The keep was a four-story box-shaped dwelling of stone, brick, and abutments, which made for excellent hand- and footholds. It was fairly easy to climb to the third floor. From up high, he could see that nothing moved except for the army heading down the mountain toward the Gate.

He entered through the nearest window. One of Roland's officers and his young bride were in their bed, their throats cut, their sheets drenched in blood. Their eyes haunted Daniel—open and aware like Cat—trapped in the horror of their pending demise once the enchantment lifted. Daniel left the room, shaken by the couple's unfair fate, only to stumble upon a greater horror— the hallway was full of frozen people who'd also had their throats slashed. Not even the laundress or message runners were spared. This was beyond the rules of standard warfare; Daniel was furious. He weaved through the imminent dead toward the center keep, grateful for his sneakers that made no sound upon the stone.

Each landing had an open view of the box-shaped central

staircase from top to bottom. A large delegation of important-looking people gathered in the foyer at the foot of the stairs, engrossed by a massive ornate copper urn in a crate that two Farrenheisi honor guards had opened for them. The fort's officers' throats were slashed, but the Farrenheisi were untouched. The urn looked to be a naming-day gift from Farrenheil on its way to the capital city. It was also likely a Trojan Horse. *Bingo*, thought Daniel.

On the second landing behind a pillar with a view of the front door and holding a two-bolt arbalest hid the wizard responsible for all this. A young woman, puggish yet athletic; she reminded Daniel of the comedian Amy Schumer. She wore banded leather leggings and a tight burgundy leather doublet, and wisps of her blond hair peeked out the edges of her black felt cap.

Daniel's immunity to magic wasn't absolute protection. If a wizard pulled a rock wall down on him, he would die just like anyone else. He understood that he had a short opportunity before she realized what he was. Retracing his steps, he retrieved an arbalest from the officer's room. Daniel wanted to get in close . . . a sure thing. He programmed the countdown timer on his iPhone, placed it on the floor, and hid in a hall niche just a few feet from the phone.

Megadeth's "Symphony of Destruction" began to echo through the silent keep, calling the wizard to the hall where Daniel waited. She wiggled her fingers at the phone, but Dave Mustaine ignored her and continued to warble his verses of doom. She poked the phone with a cautious foot before picking it up. As she straightened, Daniel stepped out and fired at her chest. The arbalest jittered from the shot—the arrow flew high and pierced her where the shoulder met the chest—no vital organs. She screamed and fired back.

Daniel ducked into the niche in time to avoid bolts whizzing past. He charged her. She made wiggly fingers but nothing happened . . . before she could implement plan B, the prince swung the flanged mace. She ducked; the mace smashed into the stone column beside her and took out the whole pillar.

Another wiggly hand gesture and all Daniel's pockets turned inside out. She seemed to be searching for something on his person. He tried to smash her into the ground, she rolled, and two feet of granite floor crumbled beneath the strike, crashing into the landing below. "This'd be going a lot more mercifully if I had that enchanted sword," he told her in English.

The girl wised up and changed tactics. She touched the floor—the stone morphed and a clean rabbit hole suddenly opened under Daniel . . . and on the landing below, and the landing after that. Daniel would have dropped into the dungeon to his death if he hadn't quickly whipped the mace across the opening to create a pull-up bar. She started to close the hole around his head. He yanked the weapon and dropped, but the stone closed around the mace head. Daniel hung on, swinging back and forth for momentum to land on the edge of that next gap below him. He drew his plain vanilla short sword, and a little can of American magic that Cal had distributed copiously to the group before returning to the upper level.

She must have thought Daniel was a heap of broken bones in the basement, because instead of following up her attack, the wizard was tending to the arrow in her shoulder. Daniel almost felt sorry for her . . . until he saw the frozen grandmotherly maid whose wicker basket full of linens was spotted with crimson from the gash across her throat. Amy Schumer would have killed everyone in the town if Daniel hadn't shown up.

He hit her with a stream of pepper spray. She screamed and, in a fit of panic, waved her arms to blindly hurl the frozen people in the hallway toward the prince. He ducked, unable to stop the poor flying stiffs from crashing in a heap on the stairs below. Daniel leaped at the wizard—her hand rose, and his sword edge skittered across an invisible bubble. The blade just tinked like it hit glass with every hack. It didn't, however, stop his hand.

He punched her hard in the temple. She kicked his legs out from under him and he landed on top of her. Daniel twisted the arrow in her shoulder. Blinded and in agony, her cries were child-like. She slapped his face, flapping her hands wildly, scratching at him, then found his throat—no wizardry, just pure instinct—and squeezed for her life. Daniel abandoned the arrow and tried choking her as well. They rolled on the floor like fatal lovers, her sounds of desperation feral, pleading. Daniel didn't think he could last much longer. He saw the tip of his enchanted mace jutting six inches out of the floor near them—its sharp, curved blades cemented in place. He rolled them toward the mace using Cal's training to end up on top. One of the mace fins cut her cheek . . . her shield wasn't enchanted-weapon-proof! He grabbed the arrow in her shoulder again and yanked up. Her body followed instinctively, and with the last of his strength, he shoved her head down hard on the mace head. The back of her skull cracked like a lobster. He put his weight on her forehead and shoved that mace as far into her brain as it would go.

When Daniel had accidentally killed his stepfather, he thought there could be no worse feeling. When he had intentionally killed another man with his sword, he thought that was rock bottom. He was tired of being wrong. Instead of washing the stains of his sins, he kept adding to them. *What have I become?*

2

Daniel spied the Farrenheisi force with his binoculars—about ten thousand, the same as their strength in the fort. The enemy was about two miles out on the grassy plain between the fort and the mountains. They approached at a leisurely pace. Farrenheil had every reason to believe the fort was out of commission—a virtual cakewalk; every kingdom had a politician who promised easy victories. Daniel had just two hours to prove this one wrong.

The wizard's death had not broken the enchantment. *The urn then?* Backstabbing, conspiring assholes were drawn to irony, and what could be more so than his naming day gift ushering in his kingdom's downfall. The stasis around the urn was so concentrated even Daniel felt a tingle. Even if he could shut it off, it just meant there was going to be a long bloody battle. His army would be worn down. Daniel leaned against a wall and slunk to the floor overwhelmed by trying to keep everyone alive.

"Think, genius," he mocked. He liked it better when his problems came in the size of the Grundy brothers back home.

The wizard had looked him over like a pork chop, trying to find what . . . ? His immunity to the enchantment? Maybe something *she herself* possessed? He checked her body . . . she wore a silver amulet embedded with an amber stone around her neck. Amber was symbolic of stasis. He took it and returned to the urn. The weird tingle was gone. *Turnabout is fair play, right?* Daniel could awaken one person with the amulet. But then what? Two guys dragging the urn would just get showered with artillery.

Artillery!

Red King's Gate had trebuchets—catapults on steroids. The one parked by the rear wall was four stories high and weighed hundreds of pounds. A sergeant stationed near the siege engine was the lucky recipient of the wizard's amulet. After a brief explanation of the situation, Daniel was delighted to learn Samm Biggs was the device's engineer. "Finally, a bit of good luck," Daniel noted.

Biggs instructed the prince to awaken one of the Clydesdales and use it to pull the machine away from the wall and position it so that the mechanisms had room to rotate. Then he used the horse to drag the urn to the machine. Once accomplished, he awoke Samm again. They primed the winch and set the payload for maximum distance, which for something as light as the ninety-pound urn would be a quarter of a mile. That would get Roland's company, his friends, and the front half of the fort out of the enchantment's range. Samm also helped prep the follow-up payloads—the ones that gave the prince pause . . . the recipe for years of nightmares to come.

"You can't stop now, laddie," Biggs said. "Them Heiszers are almost at our door."

Biggs did not yet know of the people in the keep with their throats slashed. Daniel wondered how much of a rush he would be in if it were his son in there, or if his mother were the laundress with the bloody basket. How many people in the history of either earth were faced with the realization that they were going to execute ten thousand people? Hitler? Stalin?

Farrenheil's army camped a quarter mile from the fort's back gate. The grass was high, obscuring the foot soldiers. A squad of four horsemen rode toward the fort. Through binoculars, he verified they wore the same amulets Biggs did. Hard, cold reality hit Daniel like a slap from his stepdad—all of Red King's Gate's residents would have had their throats cut by day's end . . . and the kingdom to follow. He'd made his peace with what he planned for Farrenheil. It was monstrous, but just. They'd broken the accord first.

Samm launched the urn. The arc of the copper projectile against the blue sky was a beautiful thing. It landed in the center of camp, bowling over several people before coming to a stop. The enchantment, however, remained intact—the army from Farrenheil was now frozen in place.

Dozens of heart-wrenching wails ushered from the keep behind them. Samm wanted to check. "We are not done here, yet," Daniel said solemnly.

They loaded the second projectile . . . a ball of packed straw saturated with oil and greasy rags tied with twine. It roared when they touched flame to it. They pitched the fiery ball out to the Farrenheisi camp where it exploded into the tall dry grass. They loaded the second fireball and aimed it at the army's other flank, then a third in the center of the camp. The mounted party turned back, but within minutes the flames had spread beyond anyone's ability to contain. Ten thousand soldiers and their camp followers could do nothing but stare as the flames rose, consuming their tents and banners . . . their oil . . . their clothes. The plain had become an inferno.

The squad of four, unable to save their comrades, charged the fort with raging cries. Daniel took down a horse with an arrow. The sergeant was a much better bowman and took out a rider. The remaining squad tried to ride around the wall to outflank Daniel and ran into Roland's company. The front two-thirds of the fort was free of the enchantment. Samm and four of Roland's men who now wore the riders' amulets started dragging the still-frozen across the demarcation line . . . at least those who had not been cut.

Daniel stood on the wall mesmerized by the inferno. The smell of human barbecue that initiated his arrival to this universe was now by his hand. Aandorans and Farrenheisi smelled much the same when they cooked. *What will the historians call me?* Daniel wondered. *The Vengeful? Danel the Great?* A year ago he'd wanted to draw comics . . . maybe write a screenplay. Today, he put his demented imagination to practice in a world that, far from imprisoning him, extolled such action. His men called him a hero but Daniel didn't feel it. The price for coming home was higher than he'd ever dreamed.

3

From the window of his spacious tower office, Daniel followed Lelani's team, returning from the charred plain with the neutralized urn. Apparently, Seth had just enough faerie silver left in his urine to counteract the enchantment. A detachment of riders passed them on the way out of the fort to put down those Farrenheisi that had survived the fire.

Roland aged a few years after witnessing the massacre in the keep. Lieutenant Bryce fell to his knees and cried for his friends. It was a hard blow to the fort's denizens.

On Daniel's desk were maps, stats, and logistics . . . all the intel any general needed to create a plan. No matter how Daniel looked at the situation, the results kept coming up the same— and they were grim. A knock at the door was too early for the meeting. Catherine didn't wait to be invited in.

"Did you hear?" she asked, flustered.

"Can you be specific?"

"I finally wrangled five minutes with Roland . . ." Daniel

prayed she'd exhibited some tact—Cat could be single-minded and brusque. "That *bitch* took off for Meanmnach Castle against Roland's order to remain with the company. *Why* did he order Mina to stay, you ask? Because the Skilytes had breached the Sevren and put troops north of the river!"

"I'm sorry, Cat. Mina won't let any harm come to Bree."

"What if she doesn't have a say? What if Callum finally makes it home and his daughter is a hostage? He'd surrender in a heartbeat; they'd execute him on the spot! I have to go after Bree, Danny. You have to give me Lelani . . . Ladue at least."

"Cat . . ."

"Please don't make me beg. I'm responsible for her. I let her down," she said on the verge of tears.

Roland entered with Ladue, Urry, and Seth in tow. They took their chairs at the table—Cat invited herself to stay as well.

"The ravens are off to Udiné, Jura, and Bradaan," Roland said. "Miss Stormbringer cloaked them from enemy archers with a spell. We included the tale of your return. Even neutral Jura must accept where its interests lie."

Daniel hated to ask, but felt he must. "Our losses?"

Roland stared at Daniel like a man who'd outgrown war. "All my senior officers, clerks, aides-de-camp—our master wizard. Most of our company and platoon commanders escaped since they bunk in the barracks with the men. I have a short list of new promotions—young men, but competent."

"I'd like Urry promoted and Ladue commissioned," Daniel added.

Roland nodded with no argument. It was all hands on deck. "We're bolstering our fortifications to protect you . . ."

"No," Daniel said. "Prepare the entire army for a march—we're heading west."

This surprised them.

"Is that wise, milord?" asked Urry.

Daniel had thought about this moment their entire journey east. "If our last stand happens here, we'll be overwhelmed," he told the group. "I don't want to watch ten thousand good people die just trying to protect me. It's a waste."

Roland straightened in his chair. "My lord, this fort could withstand—"

"No, it can't." Daniel cut him off. He picked up an intelligence report and waved it. "The enemy left a reserve of forty thousand men in Farrenheil to our east. To our west they will soon have eighty thousand between the capital and us. Once they've secured the south, the east, and the center, they will march here and squeeze us from all sides. This fort will become the last bit of kingdom. Besides . . . in a world with wizards, there's always a way in. It doesn't matter how high or thick the walls are, we can't wait them out indefinitely. I'd rather fight. From a strategic standpoint, doing nothing here only makes them exponentially stronger. We want to put pressure on them, surprise them, take on smaller numbers and expose fractures in their line."

The table was solemn as they considered his words.

"We'll probably lose," Daniel added, stating what they were all thinking. "But I can't hide forever. And I'm tired of running. This way we bloody them up good, give our banner men in the north and the western army a fighting chance to take these wankers down."

A resolve dawned on Roland's face . . . and maybe a little pride for his prince. Urry and Bryce were on board as well. Ladue looked like a proud uncle who would follow Daniel into purgatory. Seth was harder to read . . . worried or happy or both. Cat studied the floor, waiting for the others to leave.

"Cat, we're heading toward Bree," Daniel said. "I'll see if we can spare people for a side mission once we're past Crowe's Porte."

"The hardest, fastest march will have the army at Aandor City in five days," Roland said.

"We need to be faster," Daniel said.

"Not possible," said Bryce with confidence. "We'd kill our army getting there."

Lelani entered, sweaty and soot-stained from work in the field. "The device is secured. The apprentices are scouring all wizards' personal effects for more items."

"We have a plan," Daniel told Bryce. "And Seth, you're pivotal to it."

"Typical," Seth said. "You and Red conspire, and tell me at the last minute. That means I'm going to hate it."

CHAPTER 31

THE PHOENIX NEST

1

They arrived in a steady stream—merchants, teachers, guildsmen, prostitutes, artists, street urchins, smugglers, the titleless rich, even simple country folk who came to honor their prince, now unable to return to their farms and villages. Enemy troops had lodged themselves in people's homes, and some families left rather than risk being abused—to whom could they appeal for justice when their lodgers were the law? No quarter was spared; so many were disenfranchised by the new world order. The brick islands of the insurgents' underground cistern were full.

They'd found the cistern, somehow, but not Farrenheil? Callum was certain that agents lurked among the displaced, and the Farrenheisi remained at bay so long as it suited them. This cistern was a giant roach motel—it would be raided once they found the prince, or the minute they realized it had lost its value to them. The worst was yet to come.

Aandor City was more than just the sum of its dwellings—it was a process, a weight on the world that distorted the land around it for hundreds of miles. Cal had met those who'd never seen it, but spent their whole lives working for it. Cheese, timber, peat, cotton, silk, tobacco, wheat, chickens, sheep, pigs, geese, fish, salt, pelts, antlers, iron ore, coke, copper, heads of steer, and thousands of eggs per day flowed into the city on boats, barges, and wagons to be consumed or converted into something else. The cycle, though sometimes slowed, never stopped—until war came.

The city began to show strain—it'd lasted this long only because of the sheer abundance of food that had been brought in for the prince's celebration. Cupboards grew bare, and what few cellars still remained stocked were pilfered by desperate neighbors. This city of a half million souls would soon starve, and disease would take root. Little made it through the army outside the city's walls—that ravenous mass of thousands and its insatiable hunger—growing fat on the bounty it had pilfered throughout the countryside. Little was left for the city—not that the new rulers cared, secured away in their castle—their tables, it was said, were heaped with delicacies.

Cal assigned Tilcook commander of procurement and intelligence. Tilcook's family had emigrated from Udiné and settled in the Aavanteen slums when he was a child. He had the insights of a street urchin, the culinary talents of a top chef, and the subversive tactical mind of a mafia capo. He understood the cynical mind-set of common folk—no one believed the nobles did anything for the people, only looked after their own interests. To get them to fight, they would have to believe Daniel would help them . . . put his gold and mind to making their lives better in a way Farrenheil never would. Cal believed that the people's interests and the prince's were linked. But Tilcook's genius was his ability to sell it the way politicians back on earth sold lies—he snake-oiled the truth.

Tony Two Scoops was predisposed to acquiring supplies that

"randomly fell off" Farrenheisi wagons. Tilcook and Tony could also spot rubes from a mile away. Three Farrenheisi corporals were already on their payroll—dimwitted grunts, unhappy with their meager spoils. "Looking the other way, doin' nuthin', is the easiest way of raining silver into your pouch," Tilcook had explained. "Someone's always applying for that job."

Renny staked out the Phoenix Nest. Balzac Cruz knew too much to be left to his own devices. The jester hadn't moved, so far. They considered going in, but the gambling den was filled with Farrenheisi officers pitting their wages against lady luck.

Malcolm organized a shadow army through a dwarv network, secretly arming citizens above going along with the invasion program, but eager to answer Captain MacDonnell's call when the signal was given to open the veins of sleeping lodgers and to take the fight into the streets. Cal tried to design such a moment, but it required a distraction for that army outside the walls. Any victory in the city would be short-lived otherwise. He also pondered how to set Magnus Proust free. The wizard must send him back to his family.

A girl slightly older than Bree had trouble tying an infant's clout. "May I help?" Cal asked. The girl was perplexed and even a little starstruck; even the lowest man in Aandor did not do diapers. Cal took over and refolded the cloth into proper triangles slowly so that the girl could follow the steps. "Where are your parents?" he asked.

"I don't know, milord. Some soldiers took our mother yesterday . . . our father was at the duke's castle the day . . . they came . . ." The girl was still in shock—fending for herself and her baby sister.

Cal handed her a stick of deer jerky. "Ask for Sister Loraine," Cal said. "Ask for milk and a pot to heat it in. Tell her I sent you."

He handed her the infant, clean and tucked away. The girl broke into tears and threw her arms around his waist. Cal held her head, thinking of his own family looking for their father.

Cal slogged through bifurcated loyalties. His duties to the archduke were absolute . . . but he could not leave things as they were. Weeks had passed in Cat's reality by now; very soon it could be months. Cat would believe he'd abandoned them. This thought destroyed him; it had been Cat's biggest fear . . . the reason she would not let him tuck her away while he led the rebellion—why she insisted on coming to Aandor. *Another vow broken.* Cal was numb with regret when Loraine appeared suddenly beside him with a young lad.

"Cal, this is Kender. The castle sends him on errands outside the walls for the White Lady's supply master. He returns to the castle and does not have much time before he is missed."

"Milord," Kender said, nervously pressing his hands together. Cal had almost forgotten what it was like to be the kingdom's matinee idol—champion of the jousts—Peyton Manning and Derek Jeter rolled into one badass knight with a crest.

"At ease, Kender." The boy nearly swooned when Cal uttered his name. Malcolm strolled over to listen as well.

"The duke and his family are under guard in their own apartment," the boy started. He was well spoken, clearly not born into servitude. "Master Proust is in the velvet cell. Your betrothed is liaison between the new order and the old. No one speaks ill of her, milord, we know where her heart lies." The boy ran through a list of minor details quickly—who lived, who died, the players in Lara's court. He was anxious to be on his way lest his handlers mark his tardiness.

"Wait," Cal said. "That last thing . . . ?"

"The jester?" Kender asked. "Athelstan's fool is constantly by the witch's side," the boy said. "He dresses as a nobleman and has Lara's ear."

"How'd Cruz get past our surveillance?" Mal said, scratching his head.

"He didn't," Cal replied. "I'm an idiot. How much do you want to bet there's a tunnel leading from the Phoenix Nest to the castle? The Nest was the old burgomaster's home. The duchy owns the building. Rumor is they hold an interest in the Nest."

"Casinos have a good cash flow," Mal said.

"Yeah . . . except that Cruz funneled the archduke's own profits to finance his downfall. Cruz has hands in dozens of trading ventures, all with royal warrants, all under the radar."

"Too bad we already want to kill him. There's not much more dead you can make a man after the initial dead."

"So Farrenheil now knows of Proust's trick," Loraine noted.

"And that the prince is not an infant anymore," said Mal.

"There's rumors of a freedom fighter in the woods claiming to be Danel of Aandor," Loraine noted. "No one thought much of it at first, but then he routed the enemy from several villages. Farrenheil sent several companies east at dawn to contend with them."

"I doubt it's him," Cal said. "Daniel had little interest in being the prince, and less in taking up arms."

"Still . . . someone's rallying the countryside," Mal pointed out. "Might be enough to get the neutral kingdoms off their asses. We should get into the castle and disrupt their command."

Cal thought deeply of the risks in such a plan. "We won't have any help," he said. "Except for lords Dormer and Heady in the west, the rest of the nobility has acquiesced to the enemy . . . secured their future in the new order. They're safer playing along."

"You're joking, right?" Mal asked.

"You heard the boy . . ."

Mal rubbed a hand through his beard, clearly frustrated that he had to explain something so elementary. He pulled up a stool. "Cal, feudal warfare and hostile corporate takeovers are a lot alike. The victors shake out just what they need to still keep things functioning. Then the culling stops for a time and the survivors of the old order think they are part of the new order . . . but they aren't. The new bosses want to be sure first they can run things without them. The cuts never stop, Cal. We tack on severance pay to alleviate guilt. You know how many engineers I'd have guillotined if I could? Instead, my competitors hire them and they take my manufacturing secrets with them. Here, you happily put your sword to those who hate you, and this way you never have to fear them returning to bite you in the ass."

"Do you have a point, Daddy Warbucks?"

"Our nobles won't be staying in their comfy rooms. Farrenheil has to pay its soldiers for the invasion with lands and titles. At some point soon, Farrenheil will determine that retaliation is improbable . . . they won't need Aandor's nobility to negotiate a truce or exchange for their own people's freedom. The rout will be complete, and then more of Aandor's heads are going to roll . . . especially the male bloodlines, while daughters are married off to the Farrenheisi at sword point. There's no lasting peace to be had. The clock is ticking."

Cal cursed silently to himself; too many years upholding law and order in a democracy had made him forget what bastards the aristocracy could be.

The resistance, though necessary, was a distraction. All these desperate, vulnerable countrymen appealed to the protector in him . . . the cop. But who was he fooling? It was easier to play nursemaid in the cistern than to address his own guilt over his fractured loyalties. He was avoiding his old beloved. How could he face Chryslantha . . . endure the joy on her face when she laid eyes on him again, bear up against her embrace . . . her hope for their future reclaimed? How could he ever crush her the way he must? Even in victory.

Tilcook stormed into the camp excited, wheezing from a run.

"Take it easy, big guy," Mal said. "No paramedics here."

Tony followed soon behind. "Didja tell 'em, boss?"

"Tell us what?" Cal said.

"The second Chinook . . . it come over, too," Tony spat out. "It's in a warehouse sitting pretty with a full tank of gas, three mounted machineguns, and sixty thousand rounds of ammunition."

"We had assault rifles and magazines on that one, too," Mal said excitedly. "Grenades, C-4, and a few custom Hellfires I was transporting up for the Apaches."

"How'd you find it?" Cal asked.

"The pilots freaked out after the switch," Tilcook explained. "Left the warehouse trying to figure out what'd happened . . . ran into a patrol. They got cut down, but we got wind of talk about their pistols, strange helmets, and fireless torches. We traced their steps and found the copter."

"Cal, do you know what that thing can do with just few minutes of operation?" Mal asked.

It was the distraction Cal had hoped for. Against an army without surface-to-air response capability, it could conceivably take out an entire division. It was a game changer.

If Cal could decimate the army outside the walls . . . send them running in a superstitious panic over a death machine from hell, then they could spark the resistance within the city, free Aandor's nobles . . . and Proust. He could return to Cat . . . raise the prince's army in a few months and return within an Aandoran day to end Farrenheil for good.

"Mal, you're in charge of that copter," Cal said. "Pick a team from our earth-side crew and guard it with your lives until we're ready to unleash hell. Don't talk to any of Renny's men."

"We're cutting Renny out?"

Tilcook nodded in agreement. "Something about the Phoenix Nest doesn't smell right."

"Let's be cautious," Cal said.

"What about you?" Mal asked.

"It's time I got into that castle."

2

At midnight, Cal and Van Rooyen entered the Phoenix Nest dressed in Farrenheisi surcoats over their armor—just some off-duty grunts looking for spirits and games of chance. Four of their mercenaries had gone in a few minutes before, so as not to tip off they were together. At fourteen years older than his known age, Cal hoped that his receding hairline, crow's-feet, nascent beard, fake gold earring, and black eye patch would throw off any spies in the crowd that might have recognized him otherwise. The front pub was crowded with former city guardsmen looking chummy with the Farrenheisi. It turned Cal's stomach to think they might not be faking their loyalty to the occupiers. People wanted to survive. For the poorest folk, it made little difference who the masters were.

Access to any tunnel would be from either the basement or, also popular, through one of the upstairs rooms or closets. Either way, they would need to go through to the gambling den, and admittance to the back room came at a price. Cal presented the bouncer a gold phoenix standard for the group and they were swiftly let through the velvet curtain.

This room was bigger, brighter, and cheerier than out front—decorated in red velvets, gold, and varnished wood. The lamps and sconces were gilded and radiated warm, inviting light. The serving wenches were beautiful, dressed seductively in lace and satin. In the far corner, a wench led a drunken old man with a fist full of coins up the stairs. To Cal's right, men played faro. A rousing cheer came from his left—the dice had rolled profitably for one happy merchant.

Cal left the upstairs brothel rooms for his soldiers. They were more eager for the assignment than he was comfortable with, but as long as they played the part, they'd raise little suspicion. Cal was eager, too . . . to rescue his father, the archduke's family, and, yes, Chryslantha. He lacked a wizard to take on the White Lady, not that there were many wizards who could, but he would cross that bridge when he came to it. The dice game in the corner was heating up by the sound of things.

Cal and Van Rooyen ordered beers at the bar and studied the room. Cal wished Tilcook was with them; he could have found the hidden entrance with his eyes closed. But Tilcook prepped the city's sleeper agents for their pending assault . . . riling their resentments and establishing triggers that would roll them out to retake Aandor at the proper time. The man was a natural subversive: crafty and brilliant. He had a talent for exploiting people's deepest desires. The Feds in New York called him the Debonair Don—and they all admitted their lives would be less interesting once he was put away. Yet here in Aandor, he was just a castle cook.

A thick white froth dotted Cal's upper lip—the beer was warm yet delicious. He considered the fortunes of the guardians as he sipped. There was a great reversal for some when they fled to a land where aptitudes were properly rewarded free of pedigree. Mal was a billionaire and Tilcook a wealthy crime lord. Balzac had forgotten he was an opportunist . . . yet still ended up a tenured college professor at a top university. How much of what Callum had here in Aandor came because of his name—because of privilege? But that privilege did not transfer to women. Catherine would be one of the brightest and most educated women in Aandor, yet what could she achieve in this world? What of Bree, who took after her mother? Her role in Aandor would be to play up her appearance until Cal negotiated for a husband; and then she would be her husband's property. *It's freaking medieval,* he realized. How much did Cat love him to subject herself to this type of change? She'd spent her life trying to dismantle the last remnants of this kind of world in her own . . . and yet she agreed to join him. He swirled his beer and looked into the mug as though it held the answers. Chief among his revelations was how much he loved and missed his wife.

A drunken Farrenheisi sergeant tilted like an old tree into Cal. Cal pushed him back straight on his stool and the man woke up.

"Sorry, mate," he said in a deep gravelly voice.

"Haven't you had enough spirits, soldier?" Cal said in perfect Farrenheisi.

"Name's Ott," the man said. "My company just got back from the forest. And just in time, too. Let the other mud-gutters chase that pretender prince. Stupid errand—how can a baby suddenly be a man? Might as well tell me the world is round. And too much marching, for what? Damn peasants . . . all they got is tin cups and moth-eaten clothes and not much else."

"You'd prefer that the peasants had toiled harder so that they would have more valuable things for you to steal?" Cal asked.

The thought rolled around in Sergeant Ott's head like a roulette ball. "'S hard work marching everywhere," the sergeant admitted. "Sometimes I don't have drink for three, four days."

"You'd rather sit here drunk than serve your . . . *our* glorious kingdom?"

The sergeant looked at Cal keenly. He let out a toxic burp and said, "'S not *my* kingdom. If Vaulknar Zin wants some serf's tin cup, he can get off his fat ass and get it himself. It's crazy in the woods. This pretender prince defeated two companies—and a squad of winged cavalry. Here at the city is the safest place for an old soldier. The war is nearly over; I want my twenty acres and ox for my efforts."

Whoever this pretender was, he certainly had the enemy riled. With more time, Daniel could have been ready for that role.

Van Rooyen nudged him. Renny and two of his men, former city watchmen named Drayke and Driscoll, came in the door. They spotted Cal and headed over.

"My lord, I wish I'd have known you were planning to scout the premises," Renny said softly. "I would have put more men on."

"Needed a drink," Cal said, raising his mug. He pointed at his eye patch. "Have a disguise. Thought I might try my luck at faro."

Renny didn't know quite what to make of that. Everyone knew Cal as a humorless stick in the mud—all business and no pleasure. The city guard regularly made jokes about the pole stuck up his ass. Cal smiled; letting his hair down, so to speak, threw their perceptions off. One of these men was likely an informant. Young Callum could never relax in the presence of the enemy . . .

in a room rife with debauchery. Van Rooyen also appeared cool as ice sipping his beer as though they hadn't a worry in the world.

"My lord, 'tis not safe to converse here," Drayke said.

"True," Cal agreed. "Less so if you keep calling me that. Why don't you take our seats, while Graeme and I give the dice pit a roll." Graeme patted Cal for his wit and they chuckled.

Renny's face was classic bewilderment. When his men didn't move, Cal said, "Move."

Cal and Van Rooyen put some distance between them. "Just me, or was something odd with that trio?" Graeme asked.

"One of them should have known about the tunnel to the castle. Yet they were happily staking out the Nest for days. Or were they?"

"Any ideas about the tunnel?"

Cal looked around, tapped the floorboards a few times with his boot. He spotted the door to the cellar and concluded it was too far from the staircase. "Upstairs," he answered. "There are probably times when an archduke just wants to quietly get laid. The most famous man in Aandor walking through the casino would raise a ruckus. We should head up."

"The men are up there."

"I don't think they're concentrating on the holes in the wall right now."

Van Rooyen laughed. "You should drink more often," he said with a smirk.

"*Et tu, Brute?*"

Cal grabbed two women from some soldiers they'd been chatting up. When the soldiers were about to protest, he threw enough silver at them for a night's worth of drinks and they backed down. The women led them up the stairs eager to learn how much more coin the men would dispense. Outside their respective rooms, Cal said, "Sleeper holds only," in English. Van Rooyen nodded and let his woman lead him in. Cal did the same. Behind closed doors he expertly executed a lateral vascular neck restraint, as they called it at the academy, and placed the unconscious woman gently on the bed. He tied her, gagged her, and threw a gold coin on the bed for her discomfort.

He checked the room for secret panels and once he cleared it met Van Rooyen in the hallway.

"Should I rouse the others?" he asked Cal.

"They'll check their rooms soon enough. Let them have their night—we might all be dead by morning. We'll scope Balzac's office at the end of the hall."

"Have you been here before?" Van Rooyen asked.

"No. But it had the largest windows from outside, and I caught a hint of bookshelves."

"They could be well-read whores?"

Cal shook his head and picked the lock. The room must have once been the burgomaster's office: floor-to-ceiling inlaid wood paneling with built-in bookshelves, detailed floor and ceiling moldings, polished wood floors . . . everything varnished and ornate. Two leather sofas sat before a grand fireplace with a massive chiseled-wood mantel, but the inner fireplace itself was marble and granite with an iron cradle. The room smelled of brandy, ash, leather, and lilacs. This was the heart of Balzac Cruz's empire, where he likely met with agents of Farrenheil to plot the destruction of Aandor.

They checked the floor and the shelving. Cal checked the fireplace. Then he noticed something odd outside a side window. Just to the left of it, the outer wall took a sharp ninety-degree turn jutting away from the building. But the inner wall was flat, flush with the rest of that side of the room. If the inner wall had followed the outer wall, there should be an alcove in that corner. This jutting outer wall ran all the way down to street level. And it was close to the inner wall separating the office from the rest of the floor.

In the hallway, the first door on his left was much closer to the office than the first door to the right. He tapped the right wall—a deep sound but not part of the room behind the closest door. Cal went back into the office.

"We renovated our building in the Bronx," he said. "I developed an eye for closet space and cabinets. There's too much unaccounted room behind this wall. I think the entrance is here and the stairs turn into the building and head down there."

Cal started pulling on books, looking for the secret lever. On the shelf were also drawings in gilt frames and a two-foot statue of a happy cherub—a floating naked baby with wings and a harp. He tried to twist it, lean it, turn it, but it would not budge. Scratching his head, he tried to think like Balzac Cruz. Van Rooyen was grinning, having already figured it out.

"Well don't keep me in suspense," Cal said.

Van Rooyen flipped the cherub's tiny penis up like a light switch. The entire frame of the bookshelf moved forward on rollers. Cal grabbed one end and slid it to the side.

Two city guardsmen Cal recognized from the cistern were waiting behind that door with crossbows. Renny and his cohorts entered the room behind them. "I told you this was a bad idea, Captain." Drayke, too, held a crossbow. Driscoll shut the office door.

"I can see these others consorting with the likes of Cruz," Callum said. "But you were a Dukesguarde, Renny."

"Yes, well . . . we don't all come into life with family crests and land. Are there others with you?"

"In the cellar," Van Rooyen said. "We were covering all bases."

"Too pure to allow your men the carnal pleasures you deny yourself," Renny said. "That's the captain I remember. You missed your calling as a prelate."

"So judges a man who licks Balzac's boot."

"Ah, Balzac. He has a just grievance against you highborn. Everyone thinks the man a fool, but Balzac was a scholar in Teulada; a young man of letters, married to a beautiful girl of his village. He and Mercedes had a son, and though penniless as a pauper's pauper, they were happy. However, his patron, a count, took a liking to Mercedes. The count had daughters but no male heirs and, thinking his countess the reason, propositioned Cruz to allow his wife to become his consort for a generous commission.

"As you well know, a proposition from a patron is a thinly disguised demand. Cruz would have ended up penniless, his family on the street, with no recommendations and no prospect for employment. So he agreed to the 'request.' Mercedes indeed bore the count a son . . . after which he tired of her and picked some sculptor's wife to continue his debauchery. Mercedes took their son and left Balzac with no clue as to where she'd gone. Some think she threw herself and the boy into the Sea of Sorrows."

"Is your tale meant to invite pity for Balzac?" Cal said. "He failed his woman . . . acted the coward. Or, more likely, Balzac approached the count with the arrangement."

"I owed him ten gold standards for a gambling debt," interjected Drayke. "Balzac wiped my slate and still pays me silver each week. He gives fair commerce."

"Through your own vices, he's made a traitor of you," Cal said. "And how much are you into the fool for, Renny?"

"It is Cruz who owes *me* for services rendered," Renny said.

"Enemies intimidated . . . dispatched. I'm due fifty gold standards—enough to buy several hundred acres along the Sevren. In protecting his interests, I but protect my own."

"Using the archduke's authority for criminal enterprise . . . you're a disgrace, Renny."

"Let's let the victors decide that. I wish you had led me to the prince. His head would have earned me a castle and my own earldom. Since you've worked so hard to find the tunnel, let us utilize it. Balzac anticipates your reunion."

3

The tunnel ran a quarter mile from the Nest to the castle in a straight line under the city. The torches illuminated only a few feet at a time; it had the feel of a tomb. The archduke's castle was on an island close to shore, the lake forming a natural moat around it. Damp air and seepage revealed when they were under the water. Cal decided to stall Renny with conversation.

"I knew all along you were false," Cal said.

"Liar," Renny said. "The way you prattled about the prince. You have that bitch Loraine to thank for your silence. Drayke and Driscoll will pay her a visit later."

"I have a device from my wife's world that knows the truth of what man speaks. It has great value. I will let you have it if you set us free. A bargain."

"That will not happen. But I would know of this device nevertheless. Or I can just as easily find it for myself and deliver your corpse."

Cal stopped. His captors fixed their crossbows on him as Cal turned on his smartphone. The illumination of the screen alone lit a fire in Renny's eyes. Cal tapped the flashlight app.

"Graeme, would you speak the truth," Cal asked.

"My name is Graeme Van Rooyen, I am a soldier."

"You will notice the device does not object. Now speak a lie."

"I am a little girl with pigtails."

Cal tapped the screen subtly with his thumb and the flash pulsated red. Renny's men were suddenly wary—these were men who would keep their secrets. "Now I will lie. I, Cal Mac-Donnell, promise to forgive you for your betrayal of the realm and swear that I will never try to harm you for your actions." Cal switched the app to another setting, allowing him to tap a message in Morse code using the phone's flash, facing it toward the back of the tunnel. To the captors, it looked like another rejection.

"You're lying," said Drayke with a sneer.

"Never thought I'd see a MacDonnell dabbling with sorcery," Renny said. "You are full of surprises. Give it here."

Cal made as if to hand it over then pulled it back. "It may not work for you. It is powered by a pure heart."

"I'll find me a rich prelate and gain gold for it."

"I guess you've figured it all out."

Van Rooyen suddenly cried out and doubled over in pain. He went down on one knee. Cal feigned concern and joined him on the ground. The thunder of semiautomatic weapons boomed from the darkness behind them. Renny and his men were cut down in seconds. Two of the torches hit wet patches and were extinguished. Van Rooyen managed to save the last one.

Emerging from the darkness were Swanepoel and the other three mercenaries wearing night goggles.

"Took you long enough," Van Rooyen said.

"We were . . . uh, distracted," Swanepoel stammered. "Can't believe they let you send that message to aim high. What dummies."

"Samuel Morse never existed here," Van Rooyen reminded them.

Cal had seen the laser from their target scope hit the tunnel support beams. He loved working with professionals. No warrior in Aandor ever executed as tightly. If he'd had time to train a thousand of them, Farrenheil would have been defeated.

"I think most of the men in the cistern are legit," Cal said. "Renny just needed a few bad apples." Turning to Swanepoel he said, "Head back there and tell Tilcook to cut out anyone he thinks isn't kosher and send the rest down this tunnel. We're taking the castle tonight."

But as Swanepoel was about to leave, a pinpoint of torches flickered back in the direction of the Phoenix Nest as did the sound of men coming up the tunnel.

"We may have made a bit of a ruckus at the bar when we couldn't find you," one of the mercs said.

"What are you packing?" Van Rooyen asked.

"One brick of Semtex," Swanepoel said.

"Perfect," Cal said. "Just a crack or fissure will bring the lake down in this spot and flood the whole tunnel." Though it was cut off from the town, the flood would take care of the mob. Four hundred feet ahead, stone stairs headed upward. Swanepoel joined them minutes later huffing and puffing from his sprint. Cal was about to ask what he set the timer for when the explosion went off. Wooden beams groaned and then came the crash of rock and dirt followed by the rush of lake water flooding the tunnel. The guardians hustled up the stairs to get above lake level. Twenty feet up, they came to a landing with a heavy braced wooden door—the stairs kept rising . . . likely there were entrances on many floors, but they had no way of knowing where the doors led out to.

"Do we take our chances here?" Van Rooyen asked.

Cal thought carefully. This low in the castle, the door likely led into the dungeons; locked iron gates and reinforced doors would hinder their access. The rising stairs were more promising. "We go up," he said.

CHAPTER 32

TUNNEL OF LOVE

1

Seth hated the plan.

He looked back at the long column of soldiers. Roland had abandoned the Gate; there was no point to a border fort when the enemy was already in the heart of your nation. Ten thousand lives hinged on Seth's ability to deliver. The hard march had returned them to the wormhole that deposited the guardians north of Meadsweir. Seth had hoped never to see that town or demon ever again. Lelani's plan was certifiably mad, but there were no psychiatrists in Aandor.

Scouts returned quickly citing strange doings in the town. Seth joined the officers on the overlook where the screams carried on the wind. Farrenheisi bodies choked the river. Soldiers had jumped from the broken bridge thinking to swim to the north shore, but the current was fierce. Seth knew exactly what would make a man in full armor jump into deep water. Thousands of dead littered the field beyond the river between the castle and town. They were mesmerized by the slaughter.

"What could have possessed them to go into that town?" Urry asked, dumbfounded . . . the irony lost on him.

A Farrenheisi platoon struggled to haul planks ripped from the castle's rear drawbridge across the bridge. They were just long enough to reach the next pier. Another platoon rounded the castle's curtain wall, firing arrows at their pursuer. The demon trudged onto the scene, tall as a bus and thick as a bull. Their wizard hit it with fire and frost, but the beast was unfazed. It ripped into the platoon, breaking the men like dolls. The beast grabbed the wizard with its tail, smashed him into the dirt, and crushed him under a hoof. Shouts on the bridge drew the monster's attention. It raged as though letting anything escape alive was an affront to its existence.

"Should we start?" Seth asked.

"Soon," said the newly promoted Captain Bryce. "Let it finish disposing of the filth."

A very human part of Seth rooted for the Farrenheisi on the bridge to get their planks in place. The beast was upon them in a blink. Men hurled themselves into the river, choosing to drown instead.

With a running start, that thing could probably clear the gap and be on Daniel's army in minutes—only the proximity to its heart prevented it.

"Jesus Christ," Cat said, looking away from the carnage. "How lucky were we?"

"That's a lot of men," Daniel said.

Roland affirmed that with a grunt. "Good time to engage them at the capital, before that southern army reaches it."

"Are we turning the beastie loose on the Heiszers?" Urry asked with concern.

"No," Lelani said. "It would destroy the city . . . friend and foe alike. But the beast is important to our plan. As is Seth."

Back at camp, Seth continued to frustrate Lelani. Egwyn's

notes on altering time and space were complex, too advanced for even her. She pressed him for any insight into Egwyn's knowledge. "Do you remember anything?!" she pestered him for the third time.

Lelani insisted Seth absorbed the ancient wizard's memories when their spirit forms merged just as Egwyn had stolen Seth's. Seth had had a glimpse of Egwyn's genius for a brief moment, a universe of knowledge, the tabs of creation. But none of it remained with him, much to Lelani's exasperation. The word "useless" had never been uttered so many times in a single day.

Exhausted from Lelani's scolding, Seth joined Cat in a quiet corner of the camp. She passed the time practicing elementary transmutation. A familiar leather-bound book was propped against a rock. She successfully pulled apart sodium and chloride from table salt and then fused them back together. She even had the elements hovering over her palm in perfect spheres.

"Jesus Christ! You only started wizarding two days ago. You're making me look bad—and with my own book."

"Keeps my mind off Bree out there, alone."

"So magic's just a distraction? I've been concentrating my ass off to achieve that level of control. When Rosencrantz helped me, I did it well . . . well enough to know how short of the mark I am when it's just me."

Cat looked up from the book. "We took Bree to the Liberty Science Center last year; there was a magnetic levitation display. We could push this floating puck in the air around a supercooled magnet. I couldn't see it, smell it, or hear it, but I could feel the force at work there. Magic has that same quality. In the fabric of everything there's something to tug on . . . to push. Now that I know what to look for, it comes down to finding the handles. It's instinctual. Does that make sense?"

"Yeah, I call them tabs, but I always forget where they are after I'm done with the spell," Seth confessed. "I've tried Adderall to help me focus. Nothing works. Someone shielded me from magic years ago . . . I thought I took the spell down, but I think I missed a deeper part of it. The only spells I remember easily are the ones I learned at Proust's Academy . . . before the protection spell."

Cat threw the salt into a stack of twigs over dried brush. She made two fists and glanced her minor knuckles against each other the way one would strike steel and flint. The bundle ignited into a small campfire. "Yeah . . . I'm not having *that* problem," she said.

"What's your issue?" Seth asked, taking the bait.

"We got Daniel to the fort safely. Lelani promised to help me find Bree. Now we're going to war. She keeps pushing it off."

"The stakes are crazy high. She did swear an oath."

Cat shook the book at him. "I can't rely on her. I'm not saying she's a bad person, but I have to be realistic. Getting my daughter back is something I may have to do by myself . . . even if it's behind Lelani's back."

2

Everyone was ready . . . except for Seth. He had read Lelani's instructions three times, the scrolls held before him like cue cards by two petrified squires. He'd asked a dozen times if this was a wise idea and a dozen times he was told *no,* but they were doing it anyway.

"Even Egwyn, the greatest wizard of his age, knew better than to fuck with a radioactive plasma demon," Seth pointed out.

"Egwyn was not a Thaumadyne," Lelani said.

She brought out a huge divining rod, a Y-shaped handlebar that looked like it belonged on Paul Bunyan's chopper bike. It pivoted on a wheel clamped to the Y's lower bar. Most of the bar, except for the grips, had been dipped in melted copper from the stasis spell urn. Lelani held the chopper handles, aimed the tip at the wormhole, and opened the portal. The dark vault appeared behind a large floating drop of water. Ladue, Urry, and Bryce stepped through the bubble and began to make a racket, clanging swords against their shields and screaming. Scouts put up flags when the beast was on its way. The three men made it back just ahead of it. The luminous plasma beast stopped at the portal; it would not step through.

"It remembers," Lelani said. "Taunt it across!"

The three who lured it began a ruckus in earnest, then Roland and Daniel joined them, and soon all the army, a cascade of jeers rolling back ten thousand strong, taunting the monster . . . challenging it. The demon, agitated, stepped through. And as before, its essence flared across the sky in a great column of light. It cried out in pain.

"Now!" Lelani said.

Staff in hand, Seth began to read the words . . . this world's equivalent to Latin; ancient words that fought him, squiggling and squirming on the parchment before his eyes.

"Redde mihi potestas universi
Sanguine animae commoda mihi virtutem vitalem
Sanguinem sanguine deorum potentiae
Audire me facies metuenda
Potestas debellandum inimicos
Potentiam transire mundum . . ."

The flare changed course—and the demon's essence began to pour into Seth instead.

The power burned, and Seth believed he'd lived his last second, but he persevered, held his ground preserving every joule he stole. And if the creature's cries were to be believed, its pain had cranked up to eleven.

If Meadsweir felt like a shot of Red Bull then Seth's rush now was a case of Red Bulls with a cocaine chaser. To charge Lelani's diviner, Seth had to eat the demon. *If this beast was the scariest thing in all of Aandor, what does that make me?* Seth wondered.

He grasped the giant chopper handles. Lelani and Cat began their part, and joining them, Saadon Bray, Roland's hedge wizard, completed the quartet. Together, they uncoupled the anomaly from Meadsweir. The wizards felt the anomaly's pressure . . . a tubular distortion in space-time rippling under the curtain of reality.

Lelani aimed it west. This was Seth's cue to push the demon's stolen essence into the distortion as Lelani reengineered it, lengthened it. Seth pushed with all his concentration, chanting the words, screaming them: the pipe lengthened by a mile, then two, five, ten. At forty miles Lelani and Seth hit a limit. The distortion wouldn't budge further.

"We risk rupturing it if we force it," Lelani shouted over the din. "It was never intended to reach this far."

Seth stopped channeling into the anomaly but kept drawing more out of the creature. The beast had turned transparent. It writhed on the ground as Seth sucked at its essence.

Quite suddenly, the flavor of the monster's energy . . . changed. An ancient language became part of Seth's consciousness . . . as with Egwyn, there came a mingling of thoughts and he could understand the beast's mind—the two were one—its yowls, no longer incoherent, were actual words—curses and pleas to a higher deity. A name came with the memories that flowed from the beast's radiation. *Aeshma.*

This was Aeshma. Sorrow replaced rage with new understanding—deep sadness settled over Seth like a shroud. He became the creature for a moment and would have answered to "Aeshma" had someone called to him. The heartache of lost loved ones was prevalent in his thoughts—a weight on his soul, surrender and acceptance—Aeshma sang its death song passionately to reach those across time and space that it would never see again. The physical creature entered a fetal position. Seth absorbed enough sorrow to break a god's heart.

Daemon, not demon. Seth finally understood. *No silverback gorilla, no aimless beast.* It had parents and siblings, cousins and lovers—children. The creature understood hope, for what else sustained it nigh three hundred years through unendurable pain? It would have died long ago if it knew how to. Egwyn had stolen Aeshma from its home on the most normal of days, kidnapped it and brought it to a world where the fabric of existence was continuous agony to beings of its kind. It had begged to be sent home every way it knew how, asked to make the agony stop! The natives read its pleas as the growls of a beast. Slowly, Aeshma went mad.

The soldiers who pinned its heart were brave, but their bravery was misplaced. The faerie silver was greater torture than even the air here. Aeshma had never encountered anything like it; the radiation was anathema to every atom of its being.

Seth began to bawl; despair enough for ten lifetimes. Through their symbiotic connection, he sent Aeshma a pledge, the first intelligent communication the creature had with anyone in this realm. Seth would send the creature home. Not today, but one day soon—or find a way to end its suffering. Seth stopped drawing its life force.

"What are you doing?" Lelani asked.

The creature bounded toward Meadsweir in giant leaps . . . toward the bridge, toward its captured heart. It left all unharmed as it passed, clinging to a glimmer of hope that it might return to its own home and grateful to Seth for this slight nudge away from the brink of madness. *Someone now understood.*

Seth was awash in tears. His sobs were so heavy, he could barely speak. "We have enough for more jumps," Seth said, indicating the divining rod.

"What if Daniel wishes to retrieve the western army?" Lelani scolded.

Seth would have punched her if he weren't so winded—he realized she did not understand.

"Are you okay?" Cat asked him. Daniel came over to inquire as well.

He waved them off, embarrassed to be seen sobbing until the creature's sorrow ebbed. "I'll be fine," he said.

"Did it work?" Roland asked.

"Yes," Lelani said. "It should let us out about halfway . . . near Iibswitch. One jump after that and we will be on Deorwine Plain in the midst of the enemy."

3

It took hours for the ten thousand to march through the portal. Most of the grunts (and officers) had never seen true magic before . . . the few that had, not at this scale. They entered the bubble with suspicion and reservations, many signing the protection of their gods.

Few Farrenheisi were left in the woods at the other end thanks to the Meadsweir debacle. Just like that, a whole Aandoran division was camped within fifty miles of the capital unopposed. Daniel had used the White Lady's own cheat against her. Athelstan's progressive treatment of the other races within Aandor paid its first large dividend when word came from a centaur emissary that they had five thousand warriors ready to join Daniel's army. They'd convinced a few higher-functioning ogres to join as well.

Seth sat on a log cleaning his still-virginal pistol, thinking of his family just four miles down the road. Lelani denied him leave to check on them. This upset Seth because he'd given a lot for the cause and believed he'd earned the boon. He liked Daniel well enough, but everyone's life was bent toward the kid's interests—his royal family's needs. People had their own families to think of. He looked down that road again . . . *Just four miles.*

Cat stepped into view with a dogged expression that gave Seth the chills. Her temper was off its leash.

"I need your help," she said.

"Depends."

"Meanmnach Castle's about sixty miles due north. I'm closer to Bree than at any time since I lost her."

"You don't know that she's there, Cat. And I can't even leave to check on my own family down the road."

"I'm not asking you to come, Seth. I certainly don't need anyone's permission to get my daughter. I'm not a draftee."

"Then what?"

She slammed the grimoire into his chest, opened to a particular spell. He read it and nearly did a double take. "You can't be serious. You want to link the finder spell with the wormhole diviner and have the anomaly lock in on Brianna?"

She continued to stare him down with tight lips and searing eyes. "I lock in on her, grab her, back before you know it. Easy breezy."

"These two spells were never designed to work together. You don't know what will happen."

"Seth, we come from a world where technology is blended all the time—apps running on apps—iPads running Google Maps, Microsoft—"

"Jesus Christ, are you listening to yourself?" He stood, thinking he might need to physically run away; Cat was channeling maternal crazy. "This is magic. What you and I know about it combined could fill half a thimble. And your analogy is awful. You can't run a PC program on a Mac . . . you have to have a version written for the Mac. We don't know if the foundations of these two spells are compatible with each other. The only one who might be able to tell us is Lelani."

"No."

"What? Why . . . ?"

"She'd only stop me."

"Yes! Because you should be stopped! Cat, best-case scenario, you get within fifty feet of Bree. Then as you're looking for her, someone shoots you with an arrow, or a horse tramples you, or you're gang raped by a patrol. Life's cheap during war. Wait 'til we can go with you."

"That's never going to happen. There will always be something and the next thing keeping my friends from looking for her. She needs me. Call it magic or mother's intuition, but she's not safe and if I wait a moment more, I dread it'll be too late. Are you going to help me? Or are we through being friends?"

"That's not fair . . ."

"I've been sticking up for you for months. If you don't help me with this, I'm cutting you off. I'll do this by myself anyway even if I have to ride a horse up there."

Seth put his head in his hands and let out a long moan. He looked at the page with the finder spell. "We need Egwyn's scroll with the anomaly's schematics."

Cat produced it.

"How'd you find this in the nag's bottomless bag?"

"Every woman owns a bottomless bag."

"Don't suppose you have an idea . . ."

"Saadon Bray and I were pondering hypotheticals—just two novices chatting—we can repurpose the diviner to target Bree by spooling her hair around it." She took the book back. "We mix these ingredients with a few drops of mother's blood . . . my blood, and smear it on the diviner. When it homes in on Bree, we activate the anomaly and steer the wormhole toward the target."

"Where are you going to get enough of Bree's hair?"

"I used a spell on page thirteen to lengthen the strands Lelani had saved," she said, producing a robust spool of hair. "See, Seth, *we* know what DNA is."

"Huh?"

"Magic and science are two sides of the same coin. When they use blood or fingernail clippings for a spell, we know why it works . . . none of the wizards here have ever heard of deoxyribonucleic acid. They don't know that the air is seventy-eight percent nitrogen. They don't know that the sun is ninety-three million miles away, or that it takes light eight minutes, twenty seconds to reach the ground, or that sunspots are not ill omens from the gods. A fifth-grader knows more than these people do. You need to be creative with this magic stuff, Seth. Grow a pair."

The insult was disheartening. "Can't believe an amateur actually figured this stuff out."

"Never underestimate a mother with a missing child. I've been cramming."

"Assuming I say yes . . . when?"

"Lelani is mediating with the centaurs in the woods. So now."

The divining rod was under guard, but not off limits to *them*. They spent several hours setting everything up. It was past midnight when they made their first attempt. It yielded nothing. They checked the process again, but the second try was disappointing. On the third, Cat used a lot of blood, looking pale for the effort. The diviner spun and locked on something.

"I think that's it," Seth said. "But which way is it pointing? Is that north?"

"Sync the portal," Cat said.

"But I don't think that's—"

"Seth, I don't care where she is. I'm going to her regardless."

They struggled to turn the anomaly—a forty-mile other-dimensional pipe that at that moment linked them with Meadsweir. Seth thought their leverage would have been better if they weren't at the tip. A few times it almost rolled out of their control.

"We need another wizard," Seth said.

As if on cue, Saadon Bray rushed into the tent. "What are you doing?"

"Grab a vector," Cat ordered.

He did so only to prevent a catastrophe. Soon enough the anomaly was in its new position and stabilized.

"Hopefully Bree's on the other end," Seth said.

Cat was already packed. She kissed Seth on the lips and stepped through.

The distortion bucked . . . something was wrong. They hadn't secured it properly, but the other end was locked on something powerful and in trying to contract, the integrity of the portal was in peril.

"We need to uncouple the distortion from its endpoint!" said Saadon Bray.

Seth cut Bree's hair off the posts with a dagger. The diviner lurched. Seth gripped the handles tightly. The space-time tunnel stretched and contracted like a worm caught between two birds—it threatened to rip itself apart, and two wizards were not enough to stop it.

Lelani stormed in followed by the officers. She wrested the handlebars from Seth, then deftly unhooked it from its snag and retracted the distortion a bit. The magic in the diviner exhausted itself and the distortion finally came to rest.

"It's dead!" Lelani screamed. She flung the diviner against the tent wall. She was furious.

"The wormhole's gone?" Daniel asked.

"It's still there, but we no longer have the ability to move it. It's fixed on . . ." She stuck her head through the portal and pulled out. "The northern tip of Deorwine Plain . . . more than three miles from the city wall."

"Oh, Jesus," Seth realized. "Did we just send Cat outside the capital?"

"*Into* the capital, you feckless hedge-born puttock. The tunnel contracted by at least that distance before it settled."

"She went to find Bree," Seth explained.

"We are in the midst of a war!" Lelani screamed.

"Calm down," Daniel told both of them.

"You promised Cat that once Daniel was safe at Red King's Gate, you'd help her find Bree," Seth said again. "You gave her your oath."

That took the centaur down a notch. She very well knew she had broken her word. For once, Seth was at peace with the anger projected toward him—with his actions. He helped a friend when no one else would. Lelani could bray until the cows came home.

"The plan is still sound," Roland told them. "The terrain's higher, a slight slope and at the forest's edge. We'll have good command of their camp and the field of battle."

Roland ordered Urry and Bryce to prepare the army for transport.

"This is not over," Lelani warned Seth.

"You're threatening me?"

"You have been a curse to this mission since the beginning. Duke's bastard or not, there must come a reckoning someday for your actions."

"Go fuck yourself."

She threw a fireball at him. He knocked it back instinctively with his staff, better than if he'd tried to do it on purpose. Lelani threw a shield up just in time to stop from getting toasted.

"Enough!" Roland commanded. He bravely stepped between the two wizards. "There will be time to rectify grievances *afterward*. We are moving now before the dawn. Ms. Stormbringer, join the vanguard in case we come across a wizard on the plain. Mr. Raincrest, please cover the rear of the line."

It was high school all over again . . . thrown to the back of the class with the other malcontents. Cat was right—they were sneakily drafted into the war to take care of royal needs at the *expense* of their own. Not anymore.

If Lelani resented a fuckup like him being around, she could just get used to not having him around.

4

The last soldier marched through the portal. Seth rested before the entrance a moment before turning his horse and kicking it north toward the river . . . toward his mother's inn and the only family he had left.

CHAPTER 33

YOU CAN'T GO HOME AGAIN

1

Someone famous once said, *You can't go home again*; upon seeing the Grog and Grubb, however, Seth transformed into the child who had played in these woods, the innocent lad full of wonder and love—before his selfish debauchery shamed him. The rising sun on the horizon colored the modest chalet like a Thomas Kinkade painting, heralding more than just a new day—it ushered a turn in Seth's perceptions, a renewed appreciation for life, for family. He would have surrendered all his worldly knowledge, his New York sophistication, for his mother's embrace and a wedge of Belle's apple crumble. The roof needed patching and the diamond-paned windows a good scrubbing, but all was serene—it was all he could do to not run for the door.

A recent scuffle left its mark in the mud—many boots, and the reddish tinge reminded Seth of the mud from Yarmouth. Seth reached for his still-virgin pistol. It was gone.

Cat!

He entered the inn with only his staff.

It was a Quentin Tarantino scene inside—bloodshed enjoying a brief respite in favor of sociopathic depravity. Seven patrons, two workers, his aunt Belle, and his cousin Pipa were darkly alone in collective misery—only the Farrenheisi soldiers holding them captive appeared to be enjoying themselves.

Seth registered the setting in a blink. Clockwise, from his far left, Squire Kale and his wife, Tabitha, in the corner against the wall—forlorn and pale as their young son, Roger, gripped their table sobbing with his trousers around his ankles—the largest of the Farrenheisi soldiers defiled him. Center room left by the stairs, Aunt Belle strained to free herself of the laughing soldier who held her arms, her eyes locked on the other side of the room where cousin Pipa was pinned to a table, and two of Farrenheil's finest were having their fun. Uncomfortably pegged behind that table sat old Hargetty, shoulders scrunched, eyes cast to the floor, mortally ashamed of his impotence before the assault. At the back table on the right near the kitchen, Margery Snit, a functional lush who could lay claim as the pub's mascot, sat on the squad sergeant's lap in her bright red wig, his one hand around her waist and the other on a curdled pale thigh. She looked not so much happy or sad as "surviving." To Seth's immediate right, the Kittle brothers, Henry and Sam, were slumped against each other, the blood from their recently slashed throats drawing flies. In front of Seth, Aylard moaned on the floor; a strong, silent, sweet man who had cooked for his mother since before Seth's birth— his white shirt drenched in crimson, a dagger protruding out his back. Aylard, unlike Squire Kale and old Hargetty, would not have stood idle as Pipa and Roger were assaulted—nor would William the stable boy, having harbored a crush on Pipa since they were ten. William was being beaten at the rear of the pub by the two remaining soldiers.

Seth's quiver of quips and japes was empty, his gut as cold as his empathy for these soldiers. Aeshma also lingered on his soul, a throbbing, stinging reminder of an unfair universe and the cruelty of others. Seth's eyes transmitted all he needed to say to these soldiers—he intended to kill them all.

He wished he knew more than a handful of spells, but they would have to do. He deflected three flying daggers with a shield. For once the barrier was hard, like his vengeance. The soldiers froze at the realization of what Seth was; no one expected a wizard to walk into a provincial like the Grog. The soldiers' clothes and weapons fell around their ankles as heaps of purple blossoms. The naked and defenseless man now holding his aunt gripped her throat, declaring that he needed no weapon to kill. Belle grabbed the man's scrotum, and as he released her neck in a panic to grab her hands, Seth whipped up a hard wind, his anger and focus forcing it into a surgically compact lash to break the neck of the soldier on Roger, and then cast again to propel that soldier like a rag doll into the man menacing his aunt. Breaking bones sounded the alarm to the other assailants. The soldiers scattered out the back through the kitchen. Seth pursued them to the back door, calling up powerful winds to smash the running cowards into the ancient trees.

Inside, Pipa was curled in her mother's arms with William hovering protectively. Roger was unresponsive—his parents called his name, but he stared into space.

"Blessings upon you, milord," said Belle.

She knew Seth as a lad of thirteen, but he and Belle were now almost the same age. "It's me, Aunt Belle . . . Seth."

Recognition came slowly. "But . . . you're still a wee lad?"

"Sorcery," he said. Truth enough without getting into details. "Where is Ma?"

"A soldier took her upstairs."

Seth darted up double time. "Ma!" he shouted.

He burst into her room. The soldier was halfway out the window. Seth cast a wind to blow the man into a nearby oak tree—so hard, his neck wedged between the prongs of two branches—he flailed to catch purchase as he strangled to death. Seth grabbed his mother's long sword that she kept under the bed for emergencies. It had seen too many wars, but was sufficient for Seth to reach out and slice the man's gut open.

A sick cough escaped Jessica. Seth turned to find her steadying a dagger in her chest. "Ma?" Seth said, frozen, helpless as a child.

Belle and Pipa rushed in, horrified at Jessica's situation.

"No!" Belle cried. She made to remove the knife, but Seth grabbed her wrist.

"She'll bleed out, damn it."

"Are ye a doctor, sir?" Jessica asked.

"Jess, it's your boy, Seth," Belle said. "He's come home."

Others from the pub rushed in as well.

"Someone find a prelate!" Seth shouted angrily, scattering the lot. Seth had practiced a healing spell once . . . but like so many of the magicks he'd studied, the damned spell eluded him. He wished he'd stolen a vial of that powder Lelani kept in her satchel. Seth cursed his stupidity, and agreed with every remark Lelani had ever said about him—feckless, cowardly, lazy, useless, imbecilic shit stain of a human being. He hit his head with an angry fist.

"Lot of good that'll do," Belle said.

"My beautiful boy," Jessica whispered. She reached out to touch his face. Even bloody, his mother was the most beautiful woman Seth had ever known. Everyone said Seth looked like her, but he never felt worthy of that praise.

Seth pressed her hand against his cheek. He kissed her

BLOOD OF TEN KINGS

fingers . . . the only person to ever love him unconditionally. If he'd only remembered her in New York, he would not have lived the life he had lived. "Why did you send me away?" he asked. He was crying.

"Danger here. Your father wanted you to learn . . ." She had trouble catching her breath.

"My father has never taught me a damn thing. I've never even met the archduke."

Jessica stared at him strangely. She started to laugh, but fell into a fit of coughs. She shook her head, trying to get something out. Jessica shivered. Squire Kale returned with the next best thing to a prelate: a physician and his spouse, the village midwife. Seth remembered the man—he doubled as the local barber.

The doctor studied the wound. "Yes, this is serious, but not necessarily fatal."

"Seth!" Jessica said, reaching out to him.

"No. Don't move, don't talk," the physician said. "You're agitating her. Everyone out!"

"No leeches," Seth insisted as he let Belle lead him from the room to let the doctor work.

2

In the kitchen, Pipa fixed Seth chicken soup with bread under William's watchful eye. She hesitated to give Seth mead, thinking his appearance some illusion. Seth insisted on the mead.

"How are you?" Seth asked. They'd always been close, the best faux older sister a lad could ask for, though at sixteen, she was still just a girl herself.

"I'm fine."

"You sure? Those men . . ."

"They did not take my maidenhood."

"We're with child," William said solemnly.

"Son of a gun," said Seth in genuine shock.

Belle rolled her eyes that way mothers did when they believed their daughter could have done better. Seth wanted to both congratulate and strangle the boy. "Clean out the guest rooms," Belle told the couple. "Those pigs left everything a mess." Seth missed Belle's accent, which sounded French. She was from southern Jura, which was ethnically more Bradaanese. Pipa had lost her accent, sadly, and now talked like a Cockney librarian.

When they were alone, Belle turned to her nephew. "The archduke is not your father," she said.

"What do you know of it?" Seth asked.

"More than you. Like you, your *maman* is also a bastard. *Our maman* met Jessica's father in Jura—an important councillor at court. A wizard."

"She never told me my grandfather was a wizard."

"She did not want to fill your head with ideas . . . the pear does not fall far from the tree. Your *maman* fell in love with her father's apprentice, a Bradaanese boy with great potential. The lad, like Jessica's father, was ambitious. There was no permission for wives and children where he wanted to climb in his order. Though smitten, he turned Jessica down."

"But the heart wants what it wants?" Seth said.

"Yes. The boy came to Aandor to take a post in the archduke's court—that would be Athelstan's papa. Your mother took a job here as a servant to be closer to the city, yet not so close as to draw suspicion. And of course, the boy from Bradaan rode out to see her, she being a familiar face and a beautiful one. Your *ma-*

man is not easily dissuaded, and can teach the goddess of love the charms of a woman. He wanted her even as he wanted to rise in his order. And you were born. Bedding tavern girls is a common enough thing, but after Jessica had you, it would have drawn suspicion for him to continue to visit, and so he stopped.

"Your father helped your *maman* buy the inn—and I, a recent widow, came north with Pipa to help her. Your bloodline is powerful in wizards, Seth."

"Ha!" Seth guffawed. "I know three spells. Wouldn't my ancestors be proud?"

"With three spells, you sent the wolves who had terrorized our village scattering. Your father feared what you might become with such a heritage. Gardener kings begin somewhere."

"Well I wish he'd told me himself."

"He was a teacher at your school. Did he never reveal himself?"

"Which one?"

"I never met him, Seth."

"You have to know something, Belle. Jeez, there were dozens of teachers."

"Jess would not reveal his identity. Only that he was more powerful than even her own father."

"Wait, this wizard was more powerful than the court mage of Jura? No teacher was in that league—that's why they were teachers. The only wizard in Aandor with . . ."

Seth's brain hit pause.

"What?" asked Belle.

"The only wizard that powerful was . . . Magnus Proust."

"Patrons have mentioned him—but I have never heard your mother say that name."

"Never? Proust was one of the most famous, most powerful

men in the kingdom. Mothers warn bad children to behave or 'Proust will turn them into newts.' Why would Jessica never mention him . . . unless . . ." *Holy shit!*

Much of what Seth assumed about his life had been wrong. He wasn't sent to another universe because he was the archduke's son . . . he was sent because the grand magus of Aandor wanted to protect his own son from a war. Nausea crept into Seth. Resentment from the belief that he was unwanted, unloved led him down a dark path. But his people had been acting on his behalf all his life . . . his existence was a testament to the abundance of love. Seth's hands began to shake. This was more than he could have ever imagined.

Pipa rushed into the kitchen. "Mum, Aunt Jessy!"

The doctor put pressure on a blood-drenched rag on Jessica's chest. "The dagger was not smooth," he said.

"A nick—caught an artery as we extracted it," the midwife explained.

Jess coughed up more blood. She grabbed Seth's hand and squeezed it. She tried to talk but could not catch her breath. Seth moved onto the bed and held her, cradled her. Pipa screamed for someone to do something. William turned her away from the sight of her aunt and held her tightly. Jessica's face turned purple as she struggled. Then she stopped and slumped in Seth's arms.

His head hung low, the doctor said, "I'm so sorry."

Seth buried his face in Jessica's hair like he had as a child and screamed himself raw. Her hair still smelled like the local flowers. Belle and William drew Pipa and the others out of the room and shut the door. Seth had returned from across the multiverse for what . . . *to see her die?* The grief threatened his sanity. He wanted so much to prove himself. He *needed* to prove himself. He would have been a better son than the person he'd become. Seth's heart had never felt this empty. Everyone he ever loved left him.

Suddenly he remembered a healing spell. It was so fucking simple. How could he not have remembered that stupidly simple spell? Just ten minutes . . . he wanted to die.

He remembered another spell . . . Lelani's phosphorous balls. *Was that all it took?* He could do that in his sleep. Another spell came to mind. Spells flooded his brain by the second—an orgasm of synapses firing like a rumbling thunderhead; the magic Lelani taught him, and Rosencrantz—any spell he'd ever cast with help or without was there. In the face of this exploding knowledge, Seth struggled to retain his grief. Jessica deserved to be mourned.

He knew what Magnus Proust had done . . . placed an enchantment on him to protect others *from* him. Love had been the key to dismantling it. First Darcy and Caitlin, and through them love of himself, for only when he forgave himself did magic flow through him once again; and now his mother—pure, unconditional affection—the primordial turmoil of her loss so deep, it broke the shackles upon his mind to free his spell book.

"Greetings, my son."

Magnus Proust appeared before Seth. He looked as solid as flesh, but Seth knew he was not actually there. He could see the mechanics behind the illusion.

"You have achieved a level of maturity that satisfies my concerns. This spell was designed to alert me upon your achievement . . . but if you are seeing this illusion . . . it means that I am dead.

"I did this thing to instill in you the virtues that would make your power a boon to humanity instead of a bane. Do not be angry with me. Many with our gifts succumb to the power. I had a good father, a

better one than you, and I worried, for we have no shortage of gar-dener kings in our ancestry. Humility, responsibility, the frustration of powerlessness, and the value of power will make you wiser and more compassionate. These are the traits that serve a wizard in society. We are blessed with this burden, my son. I bequeath to you the years of knowledge you yourself have acquired, unencumbered, unburdened. My estate is also bequeathed to you in its entirety. In my chambers are my spell books and other writings . . . use them well. Wield these spells to protect the realm from those who would subvert it. I'm proud of you. I wish only that I could have held you in my arms again. May the light of Pelitos shine on you and your heirs."

Seth remained shaking on the bed as the image faded. The same power that had coursed through him before was sharper now . . . more focused. And yet, even if he got his hands on his father's spells somehow, would that be enough? Magnus was as powerful as they came; yet he died at Lara's hands. Power was fickle. There would always be someone more powerful. No wonder wizards pushed the boundaries of knowledge. Rever-end Grey's warnings made more sense now. One day, eventu-ally, a sorcerer was going to blow up the world.

As wonderful a boon as it was to have access to all the magic he'd studied, Jessica's loss was much, much too high a price. Wiz-ards were no better than lords or kings when it came to the lives of innocents. He stroked his mother's cheek and cried like the twelve-year-old she'd exiled to Aandor. Her glassy eyes haunted him. He closed them and kissed each eyelid. He kissed her one last time before rising.

Orphaned again.

This time, someone would pay . . . or he'd die trying.

CHAPTER 34

KISSY FACE

Chryslantha, like many in the pen, could not sleep. The great hall was dark and quiet; she shifted restlessly on the cold floor, trying to ignore the lingering rot of the dead that had lain there days earlier. Chrys had sacrificed a thicker blanket to Brianna for softer bedding. But sleep was no solution to their dilemma . . . she had to get Callum's daughter out of the castle. He was out there in the city somewhere . . . Did he know that his family had followed him to Aandor?

The nobles who remained were loyal to Athelstan, the ones Farrenheil didn't trust or want. Most would soon be dead—some, forced into such pacts that life would forevermore have no semblance of what once made it worth living. Chryslantha feared her fate. Her parents had cultivated her to be a great prize—tutors equal to any male, art masters, and the latest fashions. The ruling families of eleven kingdoms had had designs on her, and men of low rank lusted for her dowry, among other things. It was a testament to her father's love that he had allowed her to choose Callum over more advantageous matches.

Until now, she'd honored her pledge not to abuse her freedom around the castle—a position she leveraged to advocate for the captives. One subversive act would end all her privileges—and if they were to discover later that Callum MacDonnell's daughter was in their grasp, they would punish Chrys brutally. But playing it safe was not the memory she wished to relive in the ennui of her last days, regretting what she could have done to save this child—to protect Callum. Chryslantha shook the girl gently. "Brianna . . . ," she whispered.

"Friends call me Bree," the girl whispered back.

"Are you a brave girl, Bree?"

The girl pouted like she intended to cry but challenged herself not to. The MacDonnells likely told her to "be brave" in the carriage as Bree pined for her mother. To her *brave* was associated with loss.

"Your father is in this city," Chrys said. "We are going to escape from this castle to find him." Chrys sounded surer than she felt, but it improved Bree's mood.

Chrys had heard of the resistance in the city from the castle servants. She knew some folk in the Hog's Gate district, dwarv merchants with no love of Farrenheil and connections around the realm. Perhaps they would hide her until they found Callum.

Two familiar guards were on duty—Sergeant Kalbfleish at the front entrance and at the rear exit behind the dais a corporal that had been in Sophia's suite the day Lara coaxed Chrys to interrogate Proust. The Farrenheisi had seen her throughout the castle acting as liaison between the old order and new; was it possible that with all that happened, no formal order rescinding her privilege had taken place?

Chrys rolled Bree's blanket and put it in her strange pack that was neither leather nor loomed cloth and had an ingenious tie that the girl called a "zip-her." The prisoners had been allowed to spread out for the night; together Bree and Chrys trod softly through the sleeping nobles. As they passed Sophia, Chrys felt a tinge of guilt for leaving. Who would look after her and the Mac-Donnells? But this was Callum's daughter. Devastated . . . humiliated as she was at her broken betrothal, she would let no harm befall his child.

"Pretend that you need to make water," Chrys told Bree as they approached the guards.

"Where are you are going, milady?" whispered the pikeman, pronouncing his Ws as Vs. Chrys took it as a good sign that the guard had whispered. It showed respect to the sleeping prisoners. This man's parents had raised him well. She was not so sure about his shifty companion—a short, acne-scarred youngling playing with the wisps on his face as though they validated his manhood. The type of man who thought Chryslantha's eyes resided in her bosom.

"Corporal Esser, is it?" she said to the one she knew.

The pikeman was pleased that the Rose of Aandor knew his name. "Ya, milady," he said softly.

"My cousin Pearle is in need of a privy."

Bree hopped from foot to foot in a syrupy display.

"I'm not to let anyone out tonight, milady."

Chrys thought of Arnulf's words about Athelstan's fate. She had to sell this, for tomorrow would likely be a bloody day. "Surely you know that I have free rein in the castle?" she bluffed. "I stayed in the hall only to calm my anxious kinsmen."

Esser considered her explanation before saying, "You were not provided buckets for your needs?"

"Pearle is shy," Chrys countered. "I will take full responsibility with Lara—or does a lass of six present a threat to mighty Farrenheil?"

The corporal looked to the other end of the hall at Kalb-fleish. Chrys did not want more opinions brought into this discussion, especially *that* sergeant's. It was his crew that had enslaved Niccole . . . sold her. She tapped Bree's foot.

"Pleeeeeeze," the girl whined, ratcheting up an act that would make any mummer proud.

"Corporal, Lara and I share an intimate bond. Surely you recall that we bathed together."

The young man turned red. "I did *not* see anything, milady," he said nervously. "I faced the wall as commanded."

"You're a good man, Esser. I want to spare you any consequences."

"Consequences?"

"When I inform Lara of your resistance in this minor request . . . next time we bathe . . ."

Esser looked uncomfortable. "There is a garderobe down the back hall behind this room and at the bottom of the servants' steps."

"I know it," Chrys said.

"We're letting her go alone?" complained his companion in Farrenspiel.

"I have walked these halls unfettered for days," Chrys protested in perfect Farrenspiel, impressing both guards as though a fair-haired goddess of the homeland itself had come down among them.

"Nevertheless . . . Hans will escort you," Esser said. "In this way, the child makes her water and we are covered."

With the guard in tow, they left the hall and arrived at the garderobe. Chrys was at a loss . . . the kitchens were down the hall, the perfect nexus to several exits from the castle.

"Well?" the guard asked.

Bree pulled Chrys into the water closet and closed the door. It was a large closet, but the walls were all stone, no windows, and it had only the one door. Chrys checked the hole in the platform to see if the drop was big enough for them to squeeze through. Bree might have made it to the lake below, but Chrys would not. And Bree could very well get stuck or drown in the lake. The girl pulled down her drawers and sat on the hole.

"Now I really need to go," she said. Her manner reminded Chrys of Callum—a more serious man the gods never made, but he still contained a bit of the child that remained in every man.

Chrys put the candle in the sconce and stared at the door, nibbling on a thumbnail. They needed an excuse not to return to the hall.

"Is he a bad man?" Bree asked of their escort.

The girl had her father's instincts. "I'm sure his mother does not think so," Chrys responded. "For us, however, he is not good. He will not let us alone."

"My friend Kayla wanted a Twinkie, and she pretended to like a boy who had one at lunch, and he gave it to her."

"A Twinkie?"

"You never had a Twinkie cake?!"

"This is more serious than a pastry, Bree."

"The soldier man will like you if you pretend to like him. You look like Barbie, and everybody loves Barbie. Even her boyfriend Ken . . ." And with an impish whisper she added, "And he's gay!"

"So he's . . . happy?"

"Kayla's sister said it means he likes nice shoes more than girls. Anyway, the soldier wants to make kissy face with you, and once he's your boyfriend, he has to do everything you tell him to, and you can ask him to go get you something, like a pie, and he has to do what you say."

"What a strange culture you hail from, child. Do all women exert their will upon the men? Is that how it is with your parents?"

"Daddy has really big muscles, but he does what Mommy tells him to," Bree said innocently.

Catherine MacDonnell was developing into a most horrid person in Chrys's mind. *Did she bewitch my betrothed?* Chrys wondered. Bree had said her mother was a scholar, but what poor taste to order a man about under his own roof. *How undignified.* And yet, how like Archduchess Sophia did this Catherine begin to take form—Sophia, who was truly a queen in all but title and the strongest woman Chryslantha had ever met. Bree had said that her mother also worked in trade before rearing a child. *A woman of strong will and many talents.* Chryslantha suddenly felt woefully inadequate. Catherine was obviously a powerful, confident leader worthy of a great knight such as Callum. Did Callum find a queen in that other realm? A human personification of Helene, the goddess of wisdom and battle . . . was that why he could not remember his own betrothed?

Chrys's insecurities did not serve her at that moment. They needed a ruse. Some elements of Bree's plan had merit. There was nothing in the privy with which to subdue the guard. Chrys literally had only a candle and her wiles; she gave Bree explicit instructions on what to do next and opened the door.

"All done then?" asked the guard.

"Not quite," Chrys said. "I need your help, if you wouldn't mind."

"You want me in there? With you?"

"If it's not too much trouble?"

The guard entered cautiously, suspecting a trap.

"Your name?" Chrys asked.

"Spitznoggle, milady."

Chrys touched his face with her hand and gently stroked the wisps of his beard. The lad tensed up. The rank and file had been warned to leave the castle dwellers alone, no doubt Chryslantha especially so. He tried to say something, but she put a long finger over his lips and said, "Shhhh . . .

"The archduchess is a poor lady's maid," Chrys told the boy. "She tied the laces of my dress too tightly today. It pains my chest. The girl is not strong enough . . . I need your help, Spitznoggle. Would you untie my laces and bring me relief?"

"Is that all?" He looked more relieved than disappointed.

He undid her from behind, but before he could retie the laces Chrys turned around and pressed him against the wall. She kissed him gently on the mouth, ignoring the taste of liver and cheap beer lest she gag. She pressed her untethered breasts against him as they kissed. The lad barely moved, eyes wide, frozen and confounded as though wondering if he would wake up soon. "I might be executed tomorrow," she whispered, taking his hand and placing it on her rump.

"Oooh weee, they're in luuuv," Brianna said rather loudly behind the soldier.

Chrys kissed the soldier again, while Bree continued to remark obnoxiously on their romantic affection.

"Mu-must the child keep talking?" Spitznoggle complained. "Should she even be witnessing our . . . uh . . . what are we— uh, you, intending?"

"You are so very wise, my lord," Chryslantha said. "Pearle, guard the door from the hall outside. Do not let anyone disturb us. Will twenty minutes suffice, my lord?"

"Twen . . . ? Uh, yes. That's good."

Bree shut the door. Chrys suffered the man's bumbling,

groping hands, slowing his passions expertly and blocking his attempts to completely disrobe her even as she managed to get his britches down around his ankles. She'd put a lot of faith in Bree. If the girl failed to remember the layout of the castle, this would end badly for Chryslantha. Five minutes in, the knock she'd prayed for came.

"Damned brat!" Spitznoggle cursed. "Go away," he shouted.

"Open in Vaulknar's name, or I shall tear this door apart," came a very angry *male* reply.

Spitznoggle released Chrys to pull up his britches. She slipped away, fussed to produce a scandalous amount of cleavage, ruffled her hair, and unbarred the door.

"What is the going on here?" said a stout Farrenheisi knight. The knight then recognized Chrys and turned back to Spitznoggle. "You know full well Lord Blunt gave his word no one in the castle was to be touched. Especially her."

"I do!" Spitznoggle pleaded. "It was she who desired me . . . She who started— The girl! She'll tell you. Where's the girl?" he said in a panic, looking around.

"A young lass came by our station and told of a soldier that had dragged a crying noble lady into the garderobe."

"Not true!" Spitznoggle screamed. "Tell them!" he pleaded with Chrys.

"I asked if we could relieve ourselves in private. I am Colonel Falkyre's liaison, and thought it a simple enough request. This guard threatened me not to tell a word of his desires to anyone. I did not know what he would do to me if I fought . . ." Chrys put her face into her hands and sniffed loudly.

The officer dragged Spitznoggle out of the privy by the scruff.

"Where is my young cousin?" Chryslantha asked. "She was terrified."

"We were stationed near the kitchen, milady. I'm sure she is somewhere about."

"I shall retrieve her while you contend with this scalawag."

The officer dragged Spitznoggle off. Chrys hadn't a moment to spare before the Farrenheisi grew suspicious. She found Bree in a hallway nook just outside the kitchen entrance, exactly where she instructed her to hide.

"Well?" the girl asked.

"They have carted the scoundrel off for attempted 'kissy face' with a lady."

Bree presented Chryslantha with a fist in midair.

"Is your hand injured . . . ?"

"Make a fist," the girl said, and she bumped Chrys's with her own. "Daddy does this whenever the Jets score—but Mommy and I do it more because she's a Giants fan."

A truly strange world, Chrys thought.

It was the early hours, still dark out. The kitchen was hot with the firing of the ovens. Tomas the baker had begun boiling water and rolling dough for the day's meals. Guards were stationed in the pantry next to the main kitchen; there lay the portal to Bree's realm—the world that both protected her betrothed and stole him from her.

"Tomas, might I ask a boon of you?" Chrys said quietly.

"Anything, milady," he whispered back.

"Capes and hoods for me and the lass—a discreet door by which to leave."

Tomas rummaged through a chest in the corner and produced burlap cloaks with hoods dusted with flour.

"The lads use these to bring in sacks from the dock in cold weather," he whispered. "To the right of the pantry the corridor will take you to a service door . . . unused since they built the south bridge, so it may stick. The water is at low tide, and you can cross on the old north bridge's piers just at the waterline. The path will put you below a dock in the Aavanteen. There was a fire a few days ago, you'll blend in with the scavengers picking through the debris."

Tomas reached into a basket and pulled out two loaves of bread. As he handed them to Chrys, a crossbow bolt pierced his throat. Bree screamed as Tomas fell choking into Chryslantha's arms—she could not support his weight and together they crashed into the worktable and went down. He struggled with the arrow, his hands bloody and slippery.

"Abetting an escaping prisoner is a capital offense," said Sergeant Kalbfleish in a slow and smarmy manner. He was fat and oily . . . a great unshaven weight upon the earth that three men could not budge. Behind him were three more soldiers, including Corporal Esser. Two guards from the pantry rushed into the main kitchen to investigate the commotion.

"Esser gave us permission to use the privy. I simply came to talk to a friend."

"Esser, is this true?" asked Kalbfleish. "Did you give Lady Godwynn permission to leave the hall?"

Esser looked about as unhappy as a man could be. "I did not, Sergeant," he lied solemnly.

"Ah," Kalbfleish said. "Your word against one of my most trusted men," he told Chrys. "Did it stick in your craw to await slaughter in the great hall like a dumb herd beast, milady?"

"We needed to use the privy," Chrys repeated. "I came to the kitchen to find Pearle."

"Your cousin? The girl looks more MacDonnell than Godwynn. Spitting image of the old commander's youngest wean. Perhaps she knows the truth of it," the sergeant said. He cupped

Bree's face tenderly with his large gloves. "I shall take her into the pantry and speak with her alone."

Chrys stepped between him and the girl, severing their contact. "You would not enjoy conversing with *this* one . . . she is not of your tastes," Chrys spat back at him, nose to nose.

"My pleasure surges from the fearful whites of the eyes and the cry of misery," Kalbfleish said, pressing his face closer. "I care not for gender or race."

Chrys retreated, pushing Bree back with her until they reached the worktable. She lifted a cleaver from the table. "You shall bloody well have to kill me before that will happen," Chryslantha said, threatening to cut the first man to come near them. Chrys gambled that she still retained some value to Kalbfleish's masters.

"Whatever shall we do?" mocked the sergeant. The soldiers chuckled.

A soldier rushed her from behind. She slashed him. Chrys picked up Bree and backed up against the ovens and open pit. The heat was sweltering. The soldiers closed in with daggers out. There was no avenue of escape. She waved her weapon back and forth, straining to hold the girl with one arm.

"Don't look," Chrys whispered. Bree put her face where Chrys's neck met her shoulder, her blood pumping wildly through the artery against the girl's ear. The men rushed, disarming her, pulling at Bree. Chrys screamed violently, kicking and biting, and clutched the girl with all her strength. The men began to punch back. Chrys put the girl under her, shielding Bree from their savagery. The soldiers dragged them from the ovens. One got his hands around Bree. Just when Chrys thought she could hold no more, thunder rang out in the kitchen.

Everybody froze. One soldier fell—a dark stain sullied the

crimson of his overcoat, which was spattered with chunks of his lungs and heart. Thunder rang out again and again. Chips exploded from the bricks behind Chrys with each hammer. The soldiers before Chryslantha fell, bringing into view a strangely dressed woman, pregnant, with raven-black hair and eyes gray as wise Helene's. She held a smoking piece of iron in her hands. The remaining soldiers charged her and she dispatched them with ridiculous ease. Only Kalbfleish, who was in the rear of the charge, remained standing . . . wounded in the thigh. He hobbled wildly for the exit. The woman aimed, but her iron choked, and he limped away. She cursed in the most unladylike manner.

Bree wriggled out of Chrys's grip and ran to the woman, crying with terror and joy. "Mommy! Mommy!"

Here in the flesh was Catherine MacDonnell—the usurper who'd crushed Chryslantha's dreams and stolen the one who'd been her only true love since they had played as children. Did Catherine know how she'd cast Chryslantha into a pit of dark despair? Did Catherine know that she had killed Chryslantha's future and left it for the vultures?

Chryslantha asked the gods to protect Callum no matter the cost; they had answered and taken her joy for payment. More than safe . . . her beloved thrived away from their war-torn land with *this* woman—*lay with this woman*—and now, her sudden appearance, a slap to bring Chrys forth from deep slumber to the new reality. Her loss at this moment was more concrete than she had been willing to accept when the other woman was still some phantom menace from a fantastic tale.

Lady MacDonnell approached with studious gray eyes, mouth open, ready to introduce herself—for Catherine, too, must know whom she beheld before her and took Chryslantha's measure. Something in that gaze infuriated the young lady.

Chryslantha Godwynn did not remember raising her hand to strike Catherine. She did not acknowledge the pain in her palm, the rain of tears from her face. These things occurred to some other woman standing in her spot, in her dress, in her skin.

Catherine MacDonnell, stunned, touched the pink imprint of the hand on her face. Whether it was Chrys's throbbing wrist or Catherine's wounded expression that slowly reasserted reason upon Lord Godwynn's eldest child, it was clear Catherine Mac-Donnell did not deserve such a greeting. She had never conspired to steal another woman's man. She had in fact saved their lives just now.

Chrys dropped her arms to her side, ready to receive whatever punishment Catherine deemed just. Catherine might kill her, the only challenger to her husband's devotion, but Chrys prayed for a sound beating instead—physical pain to match the emotional turmoil. She held herself together by only the slimmest of grips.

Chrys was greatly disappointed, and astonished, when Catherine reached out and embraced her. Only compassion emanated from this stranger, no less so than if Chrys had been her own daughter. What Chrys misunderstood as Catherine's measure of her was in fact sympathy from a wise and caring soul. Cal's wife knew exactly what burden Chrys bore—a cruel hardship that she would never have wished on Chryslantha for all the wealth in the world. Chrys melted into Catherine's embrace with acceptance as though Catherine, too, were her long-lost love.

CHAPTER 35

MY HUSBAND'S BEAUTIFUL GIRLFRIEND

1

Catherine emerged from the anomaly in a badly lit brick room under a cavernous fifteen-foot groin ceiling. A long worktable was stacked with half-eaten dishes and pewter mugs. Shelves around the room were filled with preserves and pickled foodstuffs, baskets of potatoes, yams, onions, burlap sacks of flour, and pots and pans. Behind her was a large mirror frame. Instead of reflecting her image, it was black as outer space.

"Shit," she whispered. This was not the secluded country road she'd hoped for.

The powerful cross-dimensional portal in the castle pantry had captured their smaller anomaly. She checked to see if the return way was still open, and her hand touched dark, cold glass. Not only was she no closer to Bree, she was now in the heart of the enemy's stronghold. Cat clamped down the urge to panic—made more difficult by the angry voices rising just outside the room.

"You shall bloody well have to kill me first," said a woman that, even with just a glimpse over a guard's shoulder, looked too much like a certain Hollywood actress to be anyone other than Chryslantha Godwynn. She wielded a cleaver.

Great . . . my husband's fiancée is picking a fight with murderers.

As Cat drew Seth's pistol, two streams of thought ran through her mind concurrently: acting here would give away Cat's presence, her advantage, and especially the limited shelf life of the only remaining virgin gun; but, doing nothing would solve a dilemma for her husband . . . for Cat's marriage. Cat closed her eyes, trying to convince herself she could shoulder the guilt of this decision for both her and Cal. She tried very hard, but could not fool herself. If Chryslantha Godwynn was a threat to Cat's marriage, it was through no fault of her own. Cat could no more allow them to hurt Chryslantha than she could her own sister, and she could never look Cal in the eye again if she did . . . could not lie about it the rest of her life. Chryslantha was pressed desperately near to the ovens with a child in her arms . . .

She is protecting Bree.

Cat opened fire and took out the lot. Only one fat soldier limped out alive after her pistol jammed.

Chryslantha and Bree stared, both with the same unbelieving expression. Bree jumped out of Chryslantha's arms, bolted into Cat's. Her tiny, warm, fragile body was the finest sensation Cat ever had.

Cat approached Chryslantha to ask about an escape. The young woman was in a stupor, crying and shivering without realizing it. When Cat drew close, Chryslantha slapped her hard. Cat's head rung, and her cheek throbbed like hell.

I guess she knows, Cat realized.

Chryslantha came out of her trance, horrified. The young lady was immobile before her, as if waiting for Cat to return the strike . . . *even daring her.* All of Cat's resentments, her fears, her petty jealousies about the fantastical Lady Godwynn, drained from her. This was just a girl . . . flesh and blood, an heir to the hardships and injustices all women suffered since Eve took breath. Godwynn had risked herself to save Bree, even though the girl was the personification of the greatest betrayal in her life. No wonder everyone placed her on a pedestal—Chryslantha loved unconditionally. If Cat's orientation had run toward the feminine, she would have married Chryslantha herself. Cat hugged the woman for a debt she could never repay. Lady Godwynn, after her shock waned, returned the embrace.

2

The women made for the side exit near the old southern bridge. Troops could be heard tramping and shouting beyond the door.

"This way is cut off," said Chryslantha.

A call to arms rang above in the castle. "All exits will be cut off in a minute," Cat said. "We need a secret tunnel."

"I am not privy to such secrets, Lady . . . uh—MacDonnell."

"Okay, first rule—that honorific should never pass through your lips again regarding me. I don't care how formal the occasion; call me Cat."

Chrys nodded gratefully. "The second rule?"

"Pending as we figure out our lives."

"I want Daddy," Bree said.

"Oh, honey," Cat responded. "Daddy's not here. He's back home."

"Callum is in the city," Chrys said.

"What?"

"He's leading the resistance. Even the Farrenheisi cannot contain the whispers. Their soldiers are found dead, their supplies pilfered. I was attempting to find him with Bree. But now we cannot leave."

"They're expecting us to try to get out," Cat said. "What if we go up instead?"

"To where?" asked Chryslantha. "And to what end?"

"It's a huge building. Wherever's the last place they'd expect us to go. We just need to sit tight for a few hours . . . soon they'll have bigger problems than us. The prince is about to drive a whole army up their ass. In the panic, we'll look for an opportunity."

"The service well," Chrys said. "The high-ranking Farrenheisi are not familiar with it . . . and no one will expect us to be going up." Cat unbolted the side door and cracked it open to confuse their pursuers—then she followed Chryslantha back, down a narrow corridor behind the pantry. At the end was an obscure service well. They climbed three floors, listening to soldiers running in the main hallways.

"And no one's going to check this service well?" Cat asked.

"Eventually," Chrys said. "People of rank rarely acknowledge the service passages. We like our breakfast to mysteriously appear in the bedroom when we awake."

"What's on this level?" Cat asked.

"The duke's and duchess's bedchambers; the library, which serves as council chamber; the station of the Dukesguarde commander. Let us survey the hallway."

The service well was obscured by an optical illusion of overlapping stonework, giving them some cover. Guard presence on this floor was concentrated by the main staircase. They were looking for escapees below. A young chambermaid walked toward them carrying folded bedsheets.

"Justine," Chrys whispered. The maid almost dropped the

sheets in fright, but once she realized who it was she joined them in the well.

"Milady, the castle is mad looking for you."

"We need a place to hide before the soldiers check the service well."

"The bedchambers are filled with valets and footmen," Justine confessed. "The library! The entrance is right across, and the great marriage chest is all but empty and will fit the three of you," she said excitedly.

"But would the council chamber not be guarded?"

"Aye, by a single, handsome night guard who has flirted with me since he arrived. Count to four hundred and come across. The door will be ajar and the top of the chest open as though I'd meant to put something in it. Be quick and be silent."

"What are you going to do?" Cat asked, concerned about putting Bree's life in the hands of an ingénue.

Justine simply smiled.

At the count, the women followed Justine into the library. Cat's stomach was in knots at the thought of getting caught; Cal would surrender, and they would kill him for sure.

The library council chamber was a large, high-ceilinged room with massive diamond-paned windows overlooking the north terrace. Its polished marble floors were checkered in the blue, white, and gold of Aandor. The walls were amply decorated with rows of variously shaped and painted shields from the old houses that swore allegiance to Athelstan's rule. Behind a curtain came a duet of grunts, high and low. Justine had capitalized on the guard's desires for her . . . and Cat thought Justine was likely equally smitten toward the boy. Cat put her hands over Bree's ears and guided her head toward the marriage chest.

The chest, like all the things in the room, was a thing of

exquisite beauty; massive with detailed varnished woodwork and polished black iron trims. Inside, Justine had laid down the bedding for comfort as well as a vase full of water and a chamber pot. It was a tight fit for the three of them, but not impossible for the few hours before the war started. The women shut the lid. Light filtered through the vent slits, over which carefully chiseled replications of grape vines hung. They could see out, but no one could see them in the box. Cat and Chrys took opposite ends, legs toward each other with Bree in the middle lying back against her mother. Chrys shifted their legs around into an intimate, yet comfortable formation, as though expert in sharing confined space.

The real war—*not some cheating, sucker-punch ambush*—would begin on the plains outside the city in a few hours. Farrenheil was due a punch in the nose for its ambition. And if Daniel lost, or if, God forbid, Cal was killed, at least Cat was near the portal back to her universe. She was a sorceress; she would figure out how to get home come hell or high water.

3

Chryslantha's snoring grew until Cat gave her a soft kick. *Not so perfect,* Cat thought, with a smidgeon of guilt for pettiness.

A rush of voices burst into the room. Arnulf stood out over the rest. "Check behind the curtains . . . the side chambers."

Two soldiers opened the marriage chest.

"Here!" they shouted. One grabbed Bree by the hair and hoisted her out screaming; Cat lunged like a panther with a right hook to his cheek. Another soldier—the fat one from the kitchen, now wearing a tourniquet on his leg—restrained her.

"Did you think you could elude the greatest wizards left in this world?" Arnulf said. He pulled a twig wrapped with long blond strands from a bowl of water. "Unlike the prince, you have left so much of yourself in the White Lady's quarters, Lady Godwynn."

A woman in white robes with silver-streaked chestnut hair who had to be Lara joined them. A thrum of power surrounded her, unlike anything Cat had experienced. More than Dorn or even Rosencrantz. She was followed by a large, bald, important-looking officer, likely her husband Blunt; a svelte, more severe-looking old knight; and Balzac Cruz. Lara surveyed the scene. "Who was on duty here?"

The soldier who Justine seduced sheepishly stepped forward.

Lara kissed the boy like a lover until only a withered husk clattered at her feet. Cat's gut lurched at the sight; even the witch's own entourage was discomfited. The White Lady, her hair now chestnut to the roots, bore the radiant look of exquisite ecstasy. "It's been long since I've eaten hometown fare," she quipped.

"Mistress . . . Lady Catherine MacDonnell," Arnulf said, introducing them as though they were at a formal party.

"So you are the infamous wench who stole the champion of Aandor from its Rose. You must be quite the tempest in the sheets." Lara looked over at Chrys with a disappointed leer. "Such is the risk of surrendering the milk before the purchase."

Chrys took the insult with a stiff upper lip.

"Well . . . at least no husband of *ours* has to worry about his prick drying up when we screw," Cat said, glancing at the dead guard.

Blunt was not amused—the soldiers were shocked. Cruz, however, laughed hard. "I told you she was a wit."

A soldier ran in and reported quietly to Blunt.

"That's not possible," the general said, staring down the messenger as if he meant to beat the man. He hurried to the library's terrace. Looking east, he pounded the balustrade. "There are ten thousand soldiers at the edge of Deorwine Plain," he told his wife.

"Bradaan?"

"No. Roland's army from the Gate. I should have led that attack personally."

"The prince would have killed you, too," Cat said. "Looks like we're both having an Excedrin type of day," Cat said to Lara.

Lara didn't understand the reference, but guessed the spirit of it. "Send a raven . . . have the southern army double their pace," she ordered.

"But they are not here *now*," Blunt argued, seeing all the battlefield strategies and tactics that Lara was ignorant of. "We must assume the army we sent to the Gate has been neutralized."

"Deal with it!" she commanded her husband.

"I need Widow Taker."

"Take him. I will use the Haderach to inform Vaulknar of the situation . . . he must prepare his forces at home."

Blunt froze, shocked by her words. "That is our last army," he said. "It would leave our homeland defenseless."

"*Everything* hinges on winning Aandor!" she countered. "Ending that threat . . . ending that bloodline!"

"The grand duke will not release his army from the capital."

"Vaulknar will finish what we started, I promise you that!" Lara argued. "Do *your* job!"

Blunt exited the library in a sour mood with his officer in tow. Lara turned to Cruz. "This insurgency you've been fomenting . . ."

"Hiding in the cistern," Cruz said. "All the city's malcontents in one place, us gathering information."

"They've outlived their purpose. Finish them . . . before the fighting begins."

He bowed graciously. "I'd already given the word, my lady."

Lara turned to her captives, seemingly vexed by the disruption of her carefully laid plans. "I shall leave you ladies to the whims of these loyal soldiers."

"How empty your sympathies over Niccole seem now," Chrys told Lara. "You don't care what happens to the weak or defenseless . . . to anyone, other than yourself."

"I cared when you were my friend. You are clearly my friend no longer." She looked at Arnulf. "Just see to it they remain recognizable. We'll barter them for the captain's surrender in the end." She left the room.

Cat turned to Arnulf. "Who knew crazy witches and their warmongering husbands bickered just like every other married couple."

"You are a very strange woman," Arnulf noted. "You jape when you should fear for your life."

Cruz came off the desk he'd been sitting on and passed them on the way to the room's eastern wall. "Much as I would love to see what you have coming, Catherine, I must attend to the end of the insurgency," he said. He pressed a panel on a bookcase and it swung open, revealing a passage.

"Poor Cat," Arnulf said. "If only you'd known that exit was there all along."

"You always seem to be where I show up," Cat told Arnulf. "Admit it . . . you're sweet on me."

"That may well be true. Perhaps you'll be my mistress after I've taken Lady Godwynn in matrimony. The captain may have walked away from her lands and dowries, but I will not."

"I would end my life before joining with such as you," Chrys said.

Cat was angry with herself for ever thinking well of Sir Arnulf. She'd been taken in by his princely good looks when the evidence of his character had been there all along. He was just another arrogant, privileged jock. "Have you ever bedded a woman that Cal hasn't had first?" Cat said impulsively. "Or are sloppy seconds your thing?"

Arnulf backhanded Cat with his gauntlet. She spun into Chryslantha, who caught her but ended up going down with her. The guards laughed. Cat's temple was bleeding.

"What a brazen mouth you have," Arnulf said. He looked at them with derision. "Does MacDonnell attract only cows with serpents' tongues?"

"You had so much promise when we first met," Cat said. "Bragging about your grandfather's chivalry. Sad that you're just a well-dressed thug."

Arnulf turned crimson. "I wonder how brazen you will be strapped naked to a barn hitch, when we mate you with a horse."

"One of us will be dead before that happens," Cat said, wiping blood from her eyes. She pulled out a dagger and went for his face. Arnulf easily evaded the attack, disarmed her, and grasped her wrists. He shoved her backward toward the marriage chest in a spastic tango. The knight jammed her against it, and the top slammed closed. He forced her back against the rounded top.

The other guards jumped on Chryslantha and brought her to the ground, licking her face, manhandling her.

Bree slipped her captor's grip and began punching Arnulf's legs. He kicked her with a temper and sent Bree reeling head-first into a table.

"Bree!" Catherine cried. Cat tried to bite through his leather gloves, but Arnulf ignored the pain.

He gripped both of her hands in one massive fist and placed the other hand on her breast. He licked her from the nape of her neck to her cheek. "Shall we have a bit of fun before the horse has his turn?" Arnulf asked.

A grown man's scream cut through the air, warning all of a threat. Balzac Cruz flew into the men on Chryslantha and scattered them like bowling pins.

An impossible voice, the most welcome sound in any universe for Catherine, said, "Your days of *fun* are ended, knight." The honorific dripped with contempt.

Standing before the bookcase passage was Callum gripping Bòid Géard tightly before him. Van Rooyen and three of their mercs followed close behind. Cal's brows were deeply knitted, teeth gritted, cheeks and forehead glowing hot against the blue steel of his eyes—Cat had never seen an angrier man in her life.

CHAPTER 36

PARLEY

"For real? We're actually going to talk to them?" Daniel asked astride his destrier. The enemy had signaled a parley, and much to Daniel's astonishment, Roland was honoring the request. But Roland made the representatives from the other ten kingdoms conditional.

They had a commanding view of the plain and the city beyond. Aandor dwarfed the other towns Daniel had seen here by far. The white stone of its walls gleamed in the morning sun, increasing the vibrancy of its other hues by contrast—patchwork neighborhoods of terra-cotta, burnt-sienna, and cobalt-blue roof tiles. Behind the city, the terminus of the Sevren River fed a vast freshwater lake from a beautiful cascade of waterfalls. His parents' castle sat on the shore of this lake, on an island to hear Roland tell, as it used a sliver of the lake for a moat. It was a castle, expanded in recent regimes to become more palacelike as the kingdom prospered. Somewhere in that building—just two miles away—were his actual mother and father. This would have been his home if not for Farrenheil.

You couldn't ask for a nicer day. Daniel, Roland, Ladue, Urry, Lelani, and four soldiers rode with measured pace to the agreed-upon spot. The Nurvenheim delegation set up a tent.

"They won't just try and kill us?" Daniel asked.

"Blunt doesn't care for magic or dirty tricks. Probably asked Vaulknar for an old-fashioned fight instead of his wife's schemes. He's as honorable as enemies come."

At the meeting site, representatives from Udiné, Bradaan, Teulada, Karakos, Moran, Jura, Hodonin, Inakura, and their host, Nurvenheim, greeted them.

Daniel started to dismount when Roland grabbed his leg. "We'll speak our piece from our horses," he said. Roland had mastered that area between subordinate and teacher, which Daniel appreciated. Most kowtowed in his presence, something he was far more attuned to since discovering his aura.

"I hoped we might speak like civilized men over a table, out of the sun," said the ambassador from Moran, a kingdom that pretended neutrality but supported Farrenheil.

"When you lick General Blunt's boots, Stefan . . . ask him to throw his cape over your head to protect it from the sun," Roland responded in an even tone. A few of the other representatives turned their own heads to hide their amusement.

"There's no cause for discourtesy," Stefan said.

"My kingdom is in tatters partly because Moran would never dare to send its army into Farrenheil . . . would never press them to honor the accords," Roland replied. "You may not have actively engaged in this invasion as Verakhoon has, but your capitulation made this war possible."

"Well said," said a Eurasian-looking man in white silk shirt and green silk pantaloons.

"That's Prann Chua from Hodonin," Lelani whispered. Hodonin was the easternmost kingdom of the continent. They weren't especially friendly with Aandor, but shared a mutual interest in keeping their neighbor, Farrenheil, in check.

Blunt arrived with the ambassador from Verakhoon. They, too, remained on their horses. The one standout of the party was a black man in animal pelts and bones with a gnarled black cane, a wizard if Daniel ever saw one. Everyone expected a battle, so Daniel didn't understand the point of this exchange. Farrenheil broke the continental accords that had kept the peace for several generations. Half the signers did nothing to uphold accords. What remained of the Wizards' Council was afraid of Lara and even the clergy was powerless.

Blunt studied Daniel in his hybrid modern-medieval armor, his crudely painted sigil on the shield, which Daniel superstitiously insisted on for luck. Blunt turned to Roland. "You are outnumbered four to one and completely surrounded." The man was aptly named.

"Three to one," Roland corrected. "The division you sent to Meadsweir is gone."

"As is the army you sent to Red King's Gate," Urry added. "And they all died badly."

Blunt considered this grimly; he'd already suspected.

"We're not surrendering or retreating," Daniel added. He hadn't been sure if he was going to speak during the parley, but he was getting the idea behind it. It *could* be a negotiation, a way to avoid a fight, but it was also a battle in and of itself, each side mining for insight on the other for strategy's sake, and maybe dealing a psychological blow. The fact that Blunt had no soldiers to the east to block Aandor's retreat was a win for the home team. Oddly, Daniel wanted to thank Balzac Cruz for his ability to read Blunt—the jester had elevated Daniel's game against lesser players.

A portly representative in bright blue with thick woolly dark hair and matching mustache stepped up. "We have permitted

Lord Dormer's forces in Gull Harbor to cross Udiné," he said. "They will join our own army to reclaim Aandor's southern fort."

"Lord Heady cobbled together enough ships in White Hag to transport half the western army south of your approaching force," the representative of Teulada added. "He's hampered their rear quite successfully, which is why they're late. Imagine what he'll do when the rest of his army catches up."

"Bradaan has sent six thousand men north to contend with Lord Gillen's betrayal," said an older, white-haired gentleman in red robes. His eyes were the same color as Daniel's. "I am Valerian, your mother's cousin, Your Grace," said the man. "Your grandfather will clear Aandor's eastern region of Farrenheil's lackeys."

"Hodonin stands ready with eight thousand spears to reclaim its ancestral lands on Farrenheil's eastern border," said the man in green silk.

"Your perfect victory frays at its edges," Roland said. "Go home, Blunt."

"We hold the archduke and duchess."

Daniel's heart skipped. Roland turned to him and with a most somber tone said, "They are dead anyway if we surrender. As are you."

"I think we are done here, Roland," Blunt said, turning his courser around. "Lara will not retreat. You should consider that carefully. She is by far the most powerful sorceress I have ever encountered . . . in truth, even I am not certain I know my own mind around her." The dark wizard beside the general glared at Blunt for admitting this. Blunt could not care less and added, "Please consider your surrender quick—"

"You're going to lose," Daniel interrupted. He didn't know why he was compelled to say it, but it wasn't bluster. The parley had given them no advantage—Farrenheil still held the advantage. Offering to let the enemy go home without demanding restitution was pitiful. All those innocent lives destroyed . . . a kingdom on the brink of famine and ruin . . . *And we offered them a chance to leave without consequence? No wonder he's not taking us seriously.* Blunt's worst-case scenario was to end up putting his feet up on his own damned ottoman in his own castle tonight. To say Daniel was incensed was an understatement; the stakes had not been raised enough for Farrenheil. This was not how Alexander or Julius Caesar would have let things stand.

"Farrenheil has no grace in this conflict, nothing righteous to fight for," Daniel said. "You're a bunch of thieves. Oath breakers, opportunists . . . just perpetuate your false superiority, your hatred and fear. Every other sentient race on the continent despises you and half the men do as well. Aandorans toiled on this land for generations . . . you're doling it out to your accomplices like bread for pigeons. But land is just part of what makes a nation. It's what we happen to stand on whether we farm or fight. Aandor's more than just land. It's also the ideals that Farrenheil rejects, a place where men and dwarvs and centaurs and the quarterlings of Fhlee cohabitate peacefully. This challenges Farrenheil's worldview. But, not to advocate for an open and pluralistic society dooms our descendants to more conflict. Using magic as a crutch to hammer others into subservience is not a long-term solution. How many times do we need to rebuild a society before we're too exhausted . . . before the final time from which there's no return? It's happened in the universe I grew up in. Aandor fights for its ideals as much as its land. The opposite of war is not always peace . . . not always preferable. There is grace to war when fought for noble ideals—when it is necessary. We'll win because we must, because we hold the grace here."

Blunt was transfixed. Daniel had tapped into the man's own reservations, his fears about their dishonorable attack, breaking the accords. Blunt, loyal and patriotic lackey that he was, struggled not to believe these things.

"When we do win," Daniel continued, pointing the next remark at the ambassadors, "I will slice Farrenheil and Verakhoon into parcels and distribute it among those who stood with us."

"You have no right!" shouted the Verakhoon ambassador, his blood hot as if Aandor's victory were a possible thing. Blunt could have kicked the man into a coma.

The representative from Hodonin laughed. "Such is the character of the Farrenheisi and their allies—having determined to steal your lunch, if their plan should go awry, they become incensed when you eat your own lunch before them . . . as if they were the party that has been robbed."

"Right?" Daniel pressed on. "You've eradicated the law and replaced it with anarchy. The accords are dead. Forget them. No law limits me to the title of prince regent any longer. I have an army behind me, and the blood of ten kings in my veins. When this battle's ended, I will either be the *king* of Aandor or dead."

"Athelstan will not agree to that," said the ambassador from Moran.

"I doubt my father will advocate for you losers. *You* have broken the peace and written your own laws in the air with a finger. *I* will do the same. I will take this war to your land . . . to your family's homes and I will do so with an army of dwarvs and centaurs who want their homes back. So go back to your people—make peace with your gods. Tell them that you spoke to a king today and he found your honor wanting."

The wizard hissed. A black smoke emanated from his lips and

twisted toward Daniel like an ethereal snake on the hunt. Lelani raised a shield around Daniel to keep the gas at bay.

"Widow Taker, you will cease!" cried Blunt. The wizard clearly acted on different orders. Daniel's guards fired bolts at Widow Taker, but they skittered off the wizard. He deflected Lelani's spell attack just as easily.

Daniel rode at Widow Taker with his enchanted mace and brought it down on his shoulder, crushing the joint; the wizard cried out, trying to hold his useless dangling arm. Blunt rode up and took the reins of the wizard's horse.

"This was not my doing," Blunt said.

"We know whose doing this was," Roland said. And with that, the time for talk had ended. The tent was struck, the two groups returned to their armies.

A hundred knights on winged warhorses took to the skies over the enemy's air. That was the company Roland had been most afraid of. Death on wings, these knights were each worth twenty men on the ground.

From the city, a noise echoed through its streets; a familiar, mechanical slap, slap, slap that vibrated off building walls, from a machine Daniel had thought impossible here. The others gawked in fear, thinking it a new weapon of the enemy . . . but as the craft flew toward the winged cavalry, Daniel thought it was the sound of hope.

CHAPTER 37

OTT AND MATZ

Ott awoke with a pounding headache made worse by the commotion around him. He couldn't remember how he got back to his tent from the Nest. Men ran around the camp frantically, arming themselves for battle. A group craned their necks north where the plain stretched a bit before touching the Blue Forest.

"When did we send a division to the forest's edge?" Ott asked a fellow sergeant running past.

"You're as blind as you are stupid, Ott. That's not any army of ours. It's the damned pretender prince. And he's brought ten thousand angry warriors with him, not to mention centaurs."

Ott scratched his stubble trying to sort that one out. The war was over. *Didn't they win?* "We still outnumber them, right?"

"Aye, but no one's heard from them the white bitch sent to Meadsweir. Write them off I say . . . we'll never see their like again. A cakewalk, the grand duke promised . . . plots of land for every soldier to enlarge the glory of the fatherland. Pigshit! Get Matz, grab your furs, and fall in!"

Furs? It was warm as summer.

"The generals have parted!" someone shouted. A decision had been made. There were only two options. Fight or retreat. Blunt never retreated. To Ott's south, all three hundred of the dreaded winged cavalry took to flight. *Perhaps they could defeat the enemy without any help from the rank and file?* The more Ott thought about it, the less likely that seemed. A day like this, when things seemed to be turning wrong, he would be lucky to avoid horseshit as it dropped from the sky.

Ott kicked his snoring tent mate. "Get up."

"What's all the clamor?" asked Matz.

"Some high muck-a-muck screwed up. A prince that's supposed to be dead snuck an army that's also supposed to be dead up our front door. Damned if I'm going to fight the dead. We're heading for the flank."

Matz started to roll his blanket, then caught a sound in the distance. "Do you hear something?" he asked.

Ott thought Matz was still in his drink, until the low rumbling reached his ears . . . and his feet. The sound emanated from the city walls. Something rose above the city . . . an iron beast with wings that blurred to the eye. It flew toward them. With weapons forged by the gods of war themselves, the beast began to fire bolts rapidly from several ports, laying waste to the winged knights. Men and horses fell around them. From its ass the beast belched rockets, lines of smoke tracing their flights to the ground. Essen Company to their left disappeared under an inferno of black and orange smoke leaving a thousand burning bits of meat and metal in a charred crater. Men cried for their lovers, their mothers . . . for every god that ever existed.

Ott and Matz turned the other way and ran along with the rest of their troop, only to witness the Scorpion cohort of Verakhoon disintegrate much the same way as Essen.

Their battalion was in full panic, men running screaming,

bleeding with broken or missing limbs. The beast unleashed another round of its vengeance, taking out company after company.

"Where do we run?" Matz shouted in a panic.

Ott was never the brightest of soldiers, but this much he figured out as the flying death machine belched forth yet another missile—this one flying directly toward him.

He should have skipped this war.

CHAPTER 38

THE GOD OF WAR

1

The copter took to the air smoothly. *But for how long?* Malcolm wondered. News of Roland's army was a welcome surprise; the very distraction Cal had been hoping for. Van Rooyen's men had hurriedly prepped the copter for battle, while Tilcook prepped the insurgency for its citywide assault. A merc with binoculars on the wall fed them real-time intelligence. Mal just wanted to know when the parley ended—the fight was inevitable.

Malcolm took the copter up two thousand feet. He relished this bird's-eye view of Aandor—*a beautiful city for any era.* The froth on the waterfalls shone from the glint of the morning sun, the cascades poured in short runs through the city's streams and canals. Only the enemy's presence sullied Aandor's splendor. The van of Farrenheil's southern force was just a few miles away, their black and crimson uniforms a festering wound on Aandor's terrain. Assuming Roland pulled off a victory here, his army would be too exhausted to fight the newcomers.

Fluttering black dots below caught his eye—the dreaded winged cavalry launched like a swarm of locusts. Mal would leave the logistics of the next battle for later—the copter's limited shelf life in this universe made *this* battle his only priority. That airborne cavalry needed to be grounded. Mal aimed for the heart of their camp. "Light 'em up," he told his crew.

The airborne knights did not know what to make of Mal's iron dragonfly. His port, fore, and starboard machineguns cut through armor and horseflesh with vengeful fury. The copter released hell on a scale that no Farrenheisi had ever witnessed. They tried to attack it, but Mal angled the blades to puree knights like a blender. Before the winged knights could even call to retreat, Mal's guns had eradicated half the company. But that was not the worst of his attack.

Mal had been contracted to develop thermobaric weaponry for the Pentagon . . . by playing with the oxygen mixture in a missile's unspent fuel portion, generating a cloud of vapor, and igniting it, Mal had tripled their explosive force. The Chinook did not have mounted rocket launchers, but Mal MacGyvered a work-around using the payload bay as a launchpad. While his gunners were busy with the airborne knights, the crew fired thermobaric Hellfire missiles at the ground forces. By the time they were done, several dozen Farrenheisi and Verakhoonese companies were charred ruins.

Mal brought the copter around in a wide arc just in time to witness the two armies clashing on the ground. Roland had jumped on Malcolm's advantage. The Farrenheisi were in shock. Aandor's cavalry plowed into Farrenheil like a blue, white, and gold tsunami, quickly followed by nine thousand very motivated footmen, centaurs, and ugly fifteen-foot ogres.

One Aandoran warrior in particular appeared to be the scourge of the battlefield. He had his own personal guard, but scarcely needed them. With sweeping arcs of his flanged mace, he blew men apart before him like a killer hurricane. Mal brought the copter in lower. The warrior was dressed in Aandoran colors, but one of his personal guards, a familiar white-haired man in commando black, was not. And that's when Mal saw the sneakers.

"They're here!" Mal said into his helmet mike. "Son of a bitch! And Danny's leading the fight!"

Mal maneuvered the Chinook to give Daniel cover. He ordered his gunners to clear out a five-hundred-foot perimeter around the prince. One enemy combatant however was not buying it. An ancient-looking black man in animal pelts walked through the carnage and mayhem like a phantom—he was headed for Daniel.

"Animal Skins!" Mal shouted, pointing out the dark warrior to his fore gunner. The bullets rained around that man, but he continued to move on unaffected.

"Fucking wizard!" Mal shouted. "Where the hell is Lelani?" Mal looked around for the centaur and spotted her north of the prince fending off two Verakhoon hedge wizards. Mal was not sure she would get to Danny in time.

The wizard began making motions at the copter, limber fingers dancing wildly. Mal gained altitude, hoping to get beyond the wizard's range, when the engine began to sputter. Determined not to crash on his own troops, Mal punched the copter forward with the last of its juice toward the Farrenheisi. The engine quit soon after.

Contrary to popular opinion, copters did not come down like bricks once their engines quit. Using auto rotation, Mal changed the pitch of his blade, converting it from a fan, which blew down to create thrust, to a pinwheel that created drag as air rushed up into it. He guided the craft through a gauntlet of thrown spears and arrows, landing hard, and skidding into a Farrenheisi platoon too slow to get the fuck out of the way.

"Grab what you can, boys," he told his crew. "It's a slog from here." Mal's axes would drink much blood today.

They peppered the area with smoke grenades to add to the copter's plume. It helped that they weren't dressed in Aandor's colors—in the smoke and confusion, Mal and crew managed to get into a ditch a few hundred yards away. Farrenheisi swarmed the machine, jumping on it, kicking it, spitting, dancing on its corpse, and chanting victory songs. Mal pulled a detonator from his pocket. Thermobaric science wasn't just for missiles . . . and Mal knew long ago he would never waste an ounce of his jet fuel when he returned to Aandor. In the air for just fifteen minutes, the copter still had an hour's worth of gas in the tank. He waited for another hundred men to show up, and then detonated the copter. The mushroom cloud rose higher than the tallest tower in Aandor.

2

Daniel watched Mal's copter go down behind enemy lines. A glimpse of the diminutive billionaire in the cockpit told Daniel the man was as happy to see him. Cal was probably here, too. If only Cat hadn't gone AWOL. Daniel didn't want to face his captain if something had happened to her.

He was grateful for his personal guards. He had the fighting part in hand, but what no novice understood about hand-to-hand was the exhaustion—hours of exertion that only stopped when you were dead. It was also mentally taxing. Daniel's flanged mace would have been the talk of the war if not for Malcolm's barnstorming debut. Roland had wanted him in the rear, some-place safe, but Daniel understood it heartened the men and tied them to his cause to see him beside them. The enemy had become wary of approaching him despite the promise of great wealth for bringing him down.

The dust and smoke suddenly switched direction; Widow Taker headed toward them holding his staff with his good arm. Daniel's guardsmen tried to take the witch doctor down with crossbows and arrows, but the dark wizard deflected them all. Widow Taker's mouth opened into a grotesque exaggerated maw and a tornado of angry wasps emerged to attack them. The insects could not hurt Daniel, but his men swatted and rolled for cover as welts appeared on their faces and hands. Widow Taker marched directly toward the prince.

Wizards at this level were masters at indirect combat. Daniel's immunity would not help against this ancient mage. With a tap of his stick, Widow Taker called up huge nodes of quartz behind Daniel to cut off his retreat, then with a swish of the staff, raised the plethora of fallen swords, dirks, and arrows around him and launched the sharp swarm of death at the prince. Daniel rolled to grab a second shield, crouching tightly behind both. The weapons hit him with the force of a subway train, slamming him into the quartz nodes, the sharpest blades piercing through to cut Daniel.

Lelani vaulted over him, coming to a stand between Daniel and Widow Taker. She threw several of her white-hot phosphorous balls in quick succession. Widow Taker deflected them with his cane easily. He was about to counter when a golden arrow pierced Widow Taker's broken shoulder. The old wizard cried out, but not one to waste the moment, he spewed another swarm, this time hornets, from his distended maw to attack the new shift. Klaugh vaulted into the battle with his golden bow. His squad's arrows, however, could not touch the wizard, leading Daniel to realize Klaugh's bow was enchanted. The bone wizard knocked away Klaugh's next several arrows with his cane fast as Klaugh could get them off, then took a knee and grabbed ground. Rumbling like an earth digger moved beneath; tree roots sprang up to ensnare the centaurs. Daniel swiped at the base of the roots with his mace, smashing them apart. His guards hacked with their swords.

Lelani dropped the wasps and hornets with smoke. With his cane, Widow Taker called for the dream weaver Lelani wore around her neck; the leather cord snapped and it flew to that ebony stick. Widow Taker struggled to raise his injured arm, his fingers dancing frantically against his chest. Lelani choked and stiffened. She turned around at his bidding, fighting each step. "Run!" she implored hoarsely to her team.

Lelani threw a phosphorous sphere at Daniel. He deflected it with his lucky shield. The heat was incredible . . . singeing his painted sigil off the metal. One of Roland's men was not so lucky and combusted. He threw himself to the earth screaming as he rolled the fire out. Klaugh got off another round of arrows, which Widow Taker again knocked away with martial-art precision that belied his age. With Klaugh's next shot, Daniel decided to double down and hurled his flanged mace at the wizard. Five hundred dense pounds of death spun through the air at Widow Taker, who was too distracted to see the mace until too late. It hit him like a speeding truck. Daniel advanced, ready to attack the witch doctor with his shield. The wizard was on his back gasping for breath, the mace sunk deep in his collapsed chest. An iridescent yellow cloud came out of the wizard's mouth and eyes. It flew toward the castle in a pattern reminiscent of a flock of migrating birds. Daniel retrieved his mace and brought it down on Widow Taker's unprotected head.

Lelani was herself again.

"What was that cloud?" Daniel asked her.

Lelani shrugged. This was her first war, too, and no one was sure of anything anymore.

Daniel stood on Klaugh's back to survey the theater. They were surrounded by their own men . . . the front line had moved forward a hundred yards, reaching the smoking ruins of Malcolm's copter. Behind that line of scrimmage, the enemy still outnumbered them by a lot—and Blunt appeared to be pulling them together from their chaotic state for a cohesive counter assault.

"We could use another miracle," Daniel said to no god in particular. He was ready to worship whichever one showed up to help.

CHAPTER 39

NOBLE WOMEN

Callum MacDonnell moves with lyrical grace in the art of death, thought Chryslantha. He had lost nothing with age. The beats and rhythms of his movement—the arc of his sword, the drive of his thrusts—wrote the poetry of your demise before his steel ever touched skin. It blazed her passion to watch him dance.

Sergeant Kalbfleish, lost in a delirium of an easy payday, stupidly attacked Cal alone. One swipe of Bòid Géard cleaved the sergeant's blade in half. Kalbfleish wasted a precious half a second registering shock, which Callum used to put his sword through Kalbfleish's throat.

Arnulf turned to join the gang-up on Callum. Cat tripped him, lost her own footing, and fell to the ground against the marriage chest. Chryslantha grabbed a heavy ceramic vase and bashed Arnulf on the skull. She collected Bree and brought her to her mother. The girl had an ugly purple bump where her head had met the table.

"Oh my baby," Cat cried.

Guards rushed in from the hallway, and the room became a crowded free-for-all, except that Callum dispatched his assailants at twice the rate of any other combatant. Balzac Cruz crawled to the front door and escaped the room. Chrys barred the door to the library to cut off reinforcements.

The men fought savagely. This was her betrothed returned. *And yet . . . this is not my man,* she realized. The lines of his face were etched by a different life, another world. He had lived fourteen summers without the memory of her, sharing his bed with Catherine, whom under different circumstances might have been as a sister to Chryslantha.

Chryslantha had always been haunted by a premonition that she would lose Cal. Since they were children, the fates had conspired against them. It had been her mother who defended her choice, threatening to bear no more offspring if her father went through with his plan to betroth her to a richer, more powerful family. She almost died of the pox when she was twelve, then he of the fever a year later. She suffered through Cal's dalliance with Loraine. He confessed it seeking absolution, swearing upon the gods his lips would never again touch another woman's. Chrys sobbed to her mother that whole night. *These are the things young men do,* her father had said to console her, all but confessing his own indiscretions by not looking her in the eye. *They made better husbands for it,* her grandmother had said. They did not know Cal—if Loraine had been with child, Chrys would have lost Cal to a matter of honor. Then came the Mourish queen's rebellion, an ugly brutal conflict that took two of every three warriors to their grave. Their love was cursed from the moment they realized it. This was why she surrendered her maidenhood early . . . she might never have known him if she'd waited for the prelate's vows.

Cat watched the battle wide-eyed and in abject terror. Chrys was sympathetic to the emotions of witnessing a loved one fight for their life. She helped Catherine off the floor. She took Bree from her mother and cradled her.

"Catherine . . . ," Chrys said.

Cat did not hear. She was transfixed by the pikemen who jabbed at her husband with halberds.

"Catherine!"

"Aren't you scared?" Cat asked. "For him?"

"He is not mine to worry for any longer." A harsh statement; it was both truth and lie. Cat faced her, mouth agape. Chrys regretted her cavalier comment, blurted out to hide her pain.

"Don't you love him?" Cat asked accusingly.

More than you will ever know. "These are the things men do," Chrys said, borrowing her father's words. Cal dispatched his assailants with three moves before Chrys even finished that sentence. "You must listen to me, Catherine. Callum cannot believe he has a choice as to which of our pledges he will honor."

Cat looked at her with a stupid expression, as if to say, *We're talking about this now?* All Chryslantha had gleaned of the world Catherine hailed from told her they did not value honor and pledges the way knights of Aandor did. It was not a matter of life or death to them. And yet, she had been married to Callum seven years. She must have some idea of what was at stake.

"We must choose for him," Chrys insisted.

"Say again?"

"He is a man of high honor, Catherine. Tightly wound, as even his closest friends will attest, but filled with an abundance of love. I have never known Cal to break an oath, even the most minor of promises. We both understand that he will not abandon you. Marriage and family are the ultimate commitment. But allowing him to make such a choice would kill his soul, regardless. He cannot win with either choice. Cal is not like other warriors . . . he is a paladin. His strength comes from the confidence that what he does is morally right. Choosing which pledge to honor would erode him, he would consider himself a lesser person. Without belief in his virtue, it would distract him . . . cloud his mind. It could see him fall in battle. Your children deserve the best of him, Cat—as do you. And by releasing him from his betrothal, it will also go better with my father and for his family."

"So it was *our* choice?" Cat asked. "Yours really. We hashed it out?"

"We did."

"Not to sound ungrateful, but why are you giving up? Your claim is not . . . unjust."

Chrys let out a laugh born of sadness. "How many reasons need I list? I cannot destroy a true family; I owe you a debt for saving my life; he is literally no longer the man I once knew; one cannot fight fate . . ." Then, after a beat she added, "You are worthy of him."

Cat's eyes welled with tears. She said, "I've never met anyone else deserving of Cal until today, either."

Chrys touched Catherine's cheek and joined with sympathetic tears. "Worthy praise, Lady MacDonnell."

Arnulf had recovered and made short work of one of Cal's mercs. There were four left apiece on either side, plus those banging on the library door. Cal, Van Rooyen, and their two remaining men blocked the way to the door and moved the women behind them.

Arnulf squared off with Cal to make sure they would fight. "The irony," he said. "Those doors were built to withstand a revolution, but the insurgents are already inside."

"You speak of yourself," Cal said. "This is Aandor, and you're wearing red and black."

"Cal, be careful," Cat warned. "Arnulf is special forces; also, ambitious and a social-climbing sociopath."

"I am Sir Arnulf of Eindhaven. I am a champion of the lists in Farrenheil." He tapped Cal's sword with his in a playful manner. "I have never been bested in swordplay."

Arnulf lunged at Cal. The other guards attacked, too. Five times Cal parried plainly. On the sixth, Cal counter riposted with a circular parry that brought his sword hacking up ignobly between Arnulf's legs. Arnulf froze with the shock of his castration. Cal brought his sword back, slicing the large artery in Arnulf's inner thigh, and drove a dagger into the man's sternum with his other hand. Arnulf's leg buckled. In a poor display, he feigned weakness, a chance to convey his last will, to draw Cal in for a jab, but Cal blocked the thrust and severed the tendons in Arnulf's sword arm.

Cal helped finish off the other guards; they were finally alone in the room.

Cat rushed into his arms, kissed him passionately. He returned her love with fervor. Witnessing this was the final curtain for Chrys's betrothal. Callum was gone from her life.

Chrys approached them awkwardly, trying to discern her role in his presence. "Cal, the resistance in the cistern is in danger," she said. She still longed for him to hold her. The shock of a world where Cal was not hers would take forever to overcome.

"They are not," Cal said, in a neutral tone. He tried to downplay his emotion for Chrys before his wife. Cat spurred her husband toward Chrys.

He approached her cautiously. Chrys always knew it when he fell into her eyes—his pupils large and dancing with desire, a gaze so fixed that all the rest of the world ceased to be. She still held Bree in her arms, and Cal saw before him a life that might have been. He stood there, hesitant to touch, like Chrys was a vision.

Cal took his daughter. He kissed her bump. "You okay, pumpkin?"

"My head hurts," Bree said. "I want Mommy." Cat took her and glared at her husband. Cal misinterpreted and remained standoffish.

"Oh for Christ's sake . . . ," Cat said to him. "It's been fourteen years and this is how you greet her? *Kiss* your damn girlfriend!"

Chrys had never seen a smile so warm on Cal when he was a younger man. Catherine had done much good with him. He opened his long arms to her. She embraced this facsimile of the man who was once her best friend. His body had changed, the embrace recast for a different mold. Nor did he smell the same. Callum squeezed with all his regret for ever having left her years ago—*a week ago*. He kissed her on the head as though she also were wounded there, and they wept in each other's arms for a good while.

CHAPTER 40

QUEEN BEEYATCH

In the great hall, Lara laid out five candles symbolizing the points of a pentagram along two concentric containment circles drawn in white chalk. Two circles was an improvement over the spell she had used in the invasion. She had wasted much magic then—it was clear that she herself had provided Proust with the power to send the prince to another realm. The second circle would channel the excess magic from the artifacts back into the portal to Höllentor. With Vaulknar's personal army, she could quell the rebellion and finish off the prince's tattered remnants . . . the final blow to Aandor.

Blunt and Vaulknar Zin were anxious old men too used to inheriting their privileges. With Aandor defeated, Farrenheil had no obstacles. Those kingdoms aligned with Aandor on this side of the continent would keep their soldiers at home to fend against the Farrenheisi force poised upon them, while at home, thousands of retired Farrenheisi warriors would don their armor once again to defend the homeland from paltry eastern threats. Farrenheil would at last rule the continent—and Lara would rule Vaulknar as queen of a new age. Thus would end the indignity of her illegitimate birth . . . of the snide remarks and whispers at court for being born bold and clever in the form of the *fairer sex*.

The nobles shifted nervously within their pen, their women and children behind the men as Lara put the finishing touches on her spell. *That's right, fear what you don't understand,* she thought. *Fear me.* This magic came to her in drips and drabs, a scroll here, a clay tablet there, over the years. The final components were created three hundred years ago in Meadsweir, hidden in a vault at the Wizards' Archives. This portal would be smaller than the last one—she lacked wizard sacrifices to fuel it at the same intensity as the first one, but had cataloged a few of her own troops with sensitivity to magic, unbeknownst to them, that she'd quietly had stationed in the great hall. Someone's pending sacrifice would be blamed on the enemy, of course.

Ever cautious, Blunt requested they move the nobles into the dungeons, but Lara wanted the audience for her masterstroke . . . and a ready source of life energy to siphon if needed. No one, not even Blunt, knew the full extent of her powers . . . she could suck out everyone in the room in one fell swoop. Blunt would never have married her if he truly understood the depths of her power and her ambition.

Balzac Cruz rushed into the great hall breathing like a racehorse. His face was cut and one eye blackened. "They're here," he said in a panic. "*He's* here."

Lara studied him placidly. "The insurgency in the sewers—have they been dealt with?" she asked.

"I already told you . . . I sent the agents. But did you not hear me? Callum MacDonnell is in the castle."

"We have two hundred armed men in this keep. Are you sure you have the stomach for this line of work, Balzac?"

"Cruz has the right of it," said James MacDonnell from the pen. "You should leave. On my best day, I could never defeat my son in a duel."

The questioning of her tactics, her authority, scraped at Lara's patience. She'd eliminated one council wizard in his sleep with a dream spell, the second she outdueled at the archives. Proust was greatest of them, and he, too, was gone. If the remaining council wizards were too fearful to stand against her, what had she to fear from a blade-wielder like MacDonnell?

Colonel Falkyre rushed into the room looking very much a man who'd stepped out of a battle—none of the blood on his armor was his, though. With him was Balzac's manservant.

"Has Blunt won the day?" asked Lara.

"The enemy's thrust was successful," Falkyre reported. He was haggard and showing his age. "Our camp is in tatters, most of our winged cavalry dead, and a quarter of our force down. Blunt regroups to counter."

"He'll soon have plenty of reinforcements," she said.

"The general requests your help directly, my lady."

"I've already given you Widow Taker." Her friend and mentor had once sat on the Wizards' Council. Aandor no longer had such talent among their ranks.

"They had a flying steel demon, the likes of which I have never seen—and Widow Taker struggles. He was wounded in the parley . . . the centaur's companions fight with enchanted weapons."

Balzac's man did not have the bearing of someone bringing good news, either. "Well, spit it out," she urged him.

"The insurrectionists are gone from the cistern, milord," the servant told Balzac.

"Gone?" repeated Balzac, dumbfounded. "You mean dead."

"Our assassins discovered the camp abandoned except for the bodies of our agents. Renny cannot be found."

"Where are they?" asked Falkyre. "I wanted to bring two thousand soldiers out with me to the plain, but if we have open rebellion in the city . . . ?"

"This is what becomes of not executing the prince," Lara said. "Without a leader the people are sheep. But give them hope, and every merchant, farmer, and whore that can hold a blade thinks they can . . ."

Lara's eyes rolled back. She whirled suddenly, her fists gripped in tight spasms. "No!" she cried. An iridescent gas moving like a flock of birds swept in from the high windows and settled into her. Her nature consumed this essence like a worshipper devouring the host of their god. "Widow Taker!" She cried like a daughter who'd lost a father. His life energy nourished her . . . a parting inheritance from her mentor. "He's gone!"

The White Lady spread her arms out and raged in a high anguished shriek. A second shriek, and her dress tore away, revealing her naked beauty. Balzac and the messengers had to duck for cover as pieces of armor flew out of the magical swag pile to replace her dress: chest plate, besagues, rerebraces, lobstered gauntlets, skirt of leather-studded lappets, greaves and poleyns with fan plates . . . a galea helmet with a black brush plume. She transformed the hodgepodge suit into a uniformed gleaming thing of beauty. A sword flew into her hand, which she sheathed, and then a redwood staff. A glistening black winged horse flew into the room and landed before her. It knelt to give Lara access.

"I *will* join my husband," she said in a grave tone. "Kill the nobles."

"Wait!" Balzac pleaded. "What about Callum MacDonnell?"

She looked at the effete fool with a modicum of disgust. "When he arrives, perhaps you can tell him a joke."

Reality puckered before her like an invisible giant thumb pressing on a canvas, darkening the indent to rival the horse's coat. A portal opened in its midst and Lara kicked the horse into the blackness.

CHAPTER 41

THERE MUST BE SOME KIND OF
WAY OUT OF HERE . . .

1

Three bangs on the great hall's front door; death itself requested entry, for that was what MacDonnell had become: a harbinger of vengeance.

Cruz had ordered all the entries barred and doubled the guard. Falkyre had their soldiers positioned around the pen to execute Lara's orders . . . it took all of Cruz's cunning to distract and delay the good colonel from executing the command. Good hostages were invaluable, and Balzac was alone in thinking they hadn't enough men to quell Callum MacDonnell.

The colonel was not aware that Farrenheil no longer held the reins in this grand scheme. The evidence of its fraying was subtle, but even Balzac's chief protector, Hesz, understood enough to have all but vanished into the wild; too many unquantifiable factors. Cruz did not care who won the war . . . he'd see both kingdoms destroy themselves. The problem, as he listened to that infernal banging on the doors, was being caught in the middle, having miscalculated his exit strategy. Whoever imagined young Daniel Hauer of Glen Burnie, Maryland, could come marching on the city with an army . . . an army Lara had assured everyone was eradicated? Damned amateurs.

Meghan MacDonnell fidgeted under Balzac's viselike grip. He would not be letting this one go. She was his shield—his ticket out. Farrenheil had no one like Callum MacDonnell. Even Balzac fantasized about the good knight. Men were drawn to Callum, and he drew out bravery as honey draws the bear.

Crossbows took out their guards on the half balcony above the great hall. Castle servants with empty quivers replaced them, but as there was no path from the balcony to the hall floor, they simply sat above the scene awaiting the real soldiers. At the balcony entrance, he spied Catherine MacDonnell staring at him. He pulled Meghan closer, gripping tighter until the girl cried out.

"Calm yourself," Falkyre whispered. It took Cruz a second to realize the colonel was speaking to him and not the girl.

"Calm from a man who cowers behind children?" said a furious James MacDonnell at the head of the pen. The tips of long, sharp halberds destined to end him hovered before his face. The weaponless nobles stood bravely before their families. The men intended to fight barehanded if it came to it. Even feckless Athelstan made a show of it.

Too little, too late, thought Cruz.

"That one will be the death of you," the old commander told Falkyre, communicating along an exclusive bond all old soldiers shared. Cruz was not sure what irked him more—James MacDonnell's assessment of him, or that Falkyre likely agreed.

The walls were not thick enough to quell sounds outside the grand hall. Callum MacDonnell was having his way with the castle guard. And more clashes heard through the windows said that the city rose against its masters as well. Callum's family was the only leverage Balzac had to barter with.

The next hit on the door came from something much heavier. Falkyre drew his sword, as did the soldiers not holding the hostages at bay. The hinges rattled with the next hit, and the door fell on the fourth to reveal a wolf's-head battering ram.

Callum MacDonnell—six foot five in white chain mail coif under a Dukesguarde surcoat of blue, gold, and white—gripped his sword and red phoenix shield as he calmly walked across the threshold. The Farrenheisi, though greatly outnumbering him, parted before him, backing away at a pace just short of cowardly. Cal's soldiers for hire followed him close behind, and behind them castle servants holding "borrowed" weapons.

"This castle is ours," Callum said to the enemy. "Choose not to die today and mercy will be given."

Mercy to the rank and file who bear no fault for planning the invasion, but none for me, thought Cruz. "Surrender and the White Lady shall make a meal of every one of you!" Balzac shouted at his defenders from atop the dais. "Does anyone doubt Lara will return from battle victorious?!" The men hesitated, but Balzac knew how to drive desire when fear alone failed to deliver. "Five thousand gold standards to the man who brings me Captain MacDonnell's head!"

The room erupted at the promise of such a fortune. Callum cut down soldiers like a scythe at harvest. James MacDonnell, too, led a charge from the right flank, quickly relieving his young tormentor of his halberd and making short work of the men who faced him after that. Falkyre cut his way across the hall to challenge Callum, though he did not do it for the money. Career military types ran on honor—*the muse of more stupid deaths than alcohol and autos combined,* Balzac believed. It worked to his advantage as he dragged Meghan to the door behind the dais.

"Where are you taking me?" Meghan asked, struggling.

"Across the Blue Sea," he said. "I will free you when I am safe. If you fight me, though, I will sell you to slavers in the desert, and you will never see your family again."

She struggled, regardless, all the way down the hall to the kitchens. She bit his hand three times. He slapped her hard but Meghan MacDonnell would not relent. Every member of that cursed family was a bane to Cruz's existence.

Blocking his way into the kitchen were Cat and Chryslantha.

"You guessed correctly," Chryslantha said to Cat. She held a sword and heater shield with the Godwynn family crest, like a shield maiden of old.

"I got *his* number long ago," Cat responded. "We have men blocking every exit, Cruz. There's no way out."

Balzac put a dagger to Meghan's throat. "I beg to differ." He had hoped to elicit a more emotional reaction from Catherine MacDonnell—after all, Meghan was the spitting image of her own daughter. But Catherine was stoic in the face of Meghan's jeopardy. *Ice in her veins? Or . . . what does she know that I do not?*

"I swore *never again* after Dorn," Catherine told him. "Never would I take another life. It was the only way I could cope with the burden of such a horrible act. But then I found myself here, completely off guard and in the middle of all these murderers and sociopaths that you brought to Aandor through your schemes and machinations. And to survive . . . to protect my family, you made a liar out of me."

"Here is your chance to save another family member," Balzac said, pressing the dagger point against Meghan's throat. She squealed. A trickle of blood ran down her neck. "Let me go. I promise she'll be safely returned once I am out of your reach. You have my word."

"No one in my family will ever be safe so long as you're free. And that's why, hypnoatremia," she said.

The woman had cracked; she made no sense. "Hypno . . . ? Out of my way!"

"I've been studying this one spell over and over. It's supposed to be practice, the easiest spell for any novice to show they have talent. Funny thing about archaic medicine . . . they didn't know how crucial salt was to the body."

"What are you babbling about? Move!"

Catherine strode toward him casually. "Didn't anybody tell you? I'm a sorceress. Keep up, Balzac, or your rep as the smartest asshat in the room will go to the next jester."

"Sorcer . . . ?"

"Not a good one, but I did master one easy-breezy basic piece of magic that even Seth realized back in New York had potential outside of an exercise; except he's not the best wizard. The way I envision it is complete desalinization; massive . . . instantaneous . . . and utter hypnoatremia. Like so . . ."

She turned an invisible air dial and suddenly held a clump of white powder that streamed between her fingers to the floor. Balzac Cruz was in instantaneous hell—agony all over, weakness, nausea, cramping muscles—he could barely hold the dagger much less press it. The girl wriggled herself free of his flaccid grip and ran to Chryslantha. *When? When did Catherine MacDonnell become a sorceress?* he thought. A factor not entered into his methodology; a contingency he had not accounted for.

Balzac slumped to the floor, weak and fatigued beyond reason. Catherine hovered over him.

"You can live this way for a little while," she said. "But I don't have patience for you anymore. You were the one who orchestrated the reveal of my husband's other relationship in the cruelest and most callous way. You tried to kill me in New York. How much crap can a girl take from one asshole? Now this I promise you, Balzac, I'm going to again vow to never kill. But . . . and here is where this is very important as it pertains to you . . . I'm starting *tomorrow*. Let me show you a second spell I've practiced ad nauseam in case we met again. Wizards and clerics call it different things, but I like to call my version, 'Going Darth Vader on Balzac's Sorry White Ass.'"

She reached out as though holding an invisible broom handle between them. Balzac could not catch a breath. He could not fight and he could not run. Of all the people he'd known and ever met, all the enemies he'd made in his life, he could not believe Catherine MacDonnell would be the one—still could not believe it, expecting some last-minute reprieve, as she crushed the life from him. Catherine MacDonnell was his last vision before he blacked out. His final coherent thoughts were a running loop: *I should have killed her in New York. I should have killed her in New . . .*

2

Colonel Falkyre bent the knee and yielded his sword to Callum. The air in the hall had become cold as winter, yet the old warrior was sweating profusely and breathing much too hard. Cal had issued the man his first defeat in battle after several minutes. All the others surrendered soon after. Cal made a conscious decision not to kill the old soldier. They would need officers like Falkyre to keep any surrender from falling into anarchy.

Swanepoel escorted the prisoners to the dungeons where they were to be treated well, and let out the Dukesguarde who'd been imprisoned. The nobles finally left that horrid chamber and its overflowing chamber pots and hard benches. Cal vowed to root out any occupiers in the nobles' town homes.

Mina and Valeria shot across the hall into his loving arms. He cried with them, not having seen them in fourteen years. His old man approached limping, holding a stitch in his side.

"Are you injured?" Cal asked.

"A scratch," his father said, waving a hand. "You're looking a bit long in the tooth, laddie."

"Aye, Da," Cal laughed.

"Mind yourself, you old bawheid," Mina told her husband. "You taught the gods to read when *they* were bairns."

"Meghan!" Valeria cried. "That dreadful fool's taken our sister."

"She's here," Cat said, walking in with Chryslantha and Bree. Meghan rushed to her brother. For the first time in what seemed like forever, Cal was happy. He had saved his family . . . both parts. And by some miracle, Chryslantha did not despise him. It would be hard to watch her marry another man one day, as she surely would—few were deserving of her—but these were selfish thoughts, and surrounded by his family Cal was grateful for the bounty life had granted him.

Tilcook marched in with Tony Two Scoops and a large, ugly war party. Blood dripped from their armor and weapons. The mobster had promised not to light his last Cohiba until the city was scrubbed clean, and it gladdened Cal's heart to see him puffing away happily.

"All thems Farrenwhatsis mooks was dyin' to meet us," Two Scoops said, resting an arbalest on his shoulder. "Literally."

"We got the women and children into the temple before Ball Sack sent his stooges," Tilcook said. Cal was in awe of the big man. He'd predicted the betrayal, routed out the moles, and was a street-level tactical genius. "Once we sent the signal, every resister puttin' up a Heiszer slit the bastard's throat while he slept. That took out 'bout five hunnerd men in three minutes. Then we all headed out into the streets and started taking back blocks. Went pretty quick. Lotsa Heiszers surrendered when they saw our numbers. We got 'em locked in a warehouse. Bunch of them holed up in the Phoenix Nest, so we got dat surrounded." He took a puff and looked Cal squarely in the eye. "By the way . . . that's my reward . . . the Nest. I want it. You make it right with the higher-ups."

"Everyone's gonna freak when they taste his chicken parmesan and linguine carbonara," Two Scoops added.

Tilcook would probably become the new kingpin of Aandor's underworld with the Nest as his base. Years ago, rigid and righteous Cal would never have stood for it; but with age he understood that market would develop regardless of who ran it. Better the devil he knew than the one he didn't. Tilcook was never a bloodthirsty mobster. He was just smarter than the Feds, which pissed them off to no end, and they let a lot more murderous bastards thrive as they put resources into getting him. Tilcook would give the archduke his proper cut, and they needed money to rebuild the kingdom.

A young male staffer ran into the hall in a panic, reporting to Cal and James that a demon had entered the castle from below and was now making its way up.

Cal and his father went to investigate. With the White Lady still free, anything was possible. It rose up the stairs slowly and hovered in its gleaming whiteness before them emitting whirs and beeps. Cal put his face up to the lens and laughed at the sight of it.

"You know this sigil?" his father asked.

There were still thirteen stripes of white and red, but one more star on the field of blue than when they left.

"What does it mean?" James asked.

"And justice for all."

CHAPTER 42

THE LADY IS THE TIGER

1

With Widow Taker eliminated, Daniel hoped Roland would push through the rest of Farrenheil's line and scatter their center. But Blunt thwarted every attempt. The Farrenheisi general was equal to his reputation, keeping pressure on the flanks with his superior numbers and forcing Roland to pull and replenish men from the center. General Blunt's prescience was uncanny, ordering troop repositions before Roland executed his own force changes. The man could smell Roland's thoughts in the wind. Blunt would eventually overcome one of their flanks, forcing Daniel's army to defend from being encircled.

The remaining winged knights were swift, swooping into the fray from above with spiked flails and razor-sharp chains between them—a single pass lopped off ten heads, and they were gone before Aandor could respond. If Malcolm hadn't cut down that force, the battle would already have been lost. Several Farrenheisi hedge wizards kept Lelani and Saadon Bray too busy to help with the flying knights.

Daniel sensed a physical change in the atmosphere— something that transcended mere vibration or atmospheric displacement. A dimensional rift opened in the midst of the battle bringing physical discomfort to both armies—reality was violated, as though the perpetrator dug through the flesh and bone of the universe. Thick woolly black smoke, pungent as sulfur and old rust, poured from the gash ahead of an armored woman on a black winged destrier. *Shit, not another one,* Daniel thought.

She swooped the length of the battlefield in a long arc to the cheers of her soldiers. The air had grown considerably colder—winter poured into the plain as though an arctic door had opened. Daniel slowly realized this was no typical knight . . . this was a game changer. The White Lady of Farrenheil had arrived.

Heavy gray clouds blotted the sun. The plain grew darker, and it began to hail and snow. "This storm will plague us," Roland said.

"Them, too, right?" Daniel asked of the enemy.

"The Farrenheisi fought at the wizards' citadel in the mountains. We did not bring winter gear."

True to Roland's prediction, the enemy covered themselves in furs. Blunt had planned this. "Do we retreat?" Daniel asked.

"*She* will not let us withdraw," Roland said gravely.

Lara flew over them, toward the flank closest to the city wall. She called down lightning and cut a swath through hundreds of soldiers to scatter Aandor's line. The wind carried the smell of ozone and charred meat with it. Lara looked fatigued from the effort, but when she spotted Daniel, she turned her horse toward him and charged.

Lelani vaulted into Daniel's retinue and just managed to put up a shield. Captain Bryce and Klaugh, however, were caught outside the protected zone. They screamed as they desiccated into mummified versions of themselves, their life energies stolen by a ravenous evil.

"Klaugh!" Lelani cried. Daniel had never seen her so emotionally distraught.

Lara appeared recharged and continued to fly over Aandor's army, feasting on hundreds more men.

"Jesus Christ!" cried Daniel. The White Lady was a bigger terror than the demon of Meadsweir. "We're pinned."

Lara passed over again. Lelani's attacks were countered easily. In minutes, Daniel and his officers were isolated in the center of a crop of withered human husks. The White Lady was luminous as a bright moon; the points of her armor flared like starshine. Lara set her horse down ahead of them. Aandor's center weakened—Blunt advanced with his main force toward his wife.

Lelani's spell hurled all the dirks, daggers, and spears of the dead at the White Lady. Lara rerouted the weapons' course, traveling along the battle line to find targets in Aandoran warriors along the flanks. Lelani charged, hurling phosphorous balls and fireballs. Lara swatted them away, again blasting Aandor's troops. Lara's schooling of Lelani was clear—anything the young wizard did would end up killing her own.

Lara motioned at the centaur. Lelani suddenly cried out. The centaur tried to cast a counter spell, but she was out of her league. Lelani began to smoke and her cry turned into a wail of anguish.

"La chienne la fait cuire vivante!" Ladue screamed. He grabbed a fallen bow and shot the sorceress twice in succession. Lara waved two small portals into existence, one before her, the other behind Ladue—his arrows went in one and emerged behind him. One lodged into his Kevlar vest, but the second pierced Ladue at the base of his head. The mercenary went down hard.

Lelani struggled to recover from her roasting. Lara gave no quarter. She whipped her staff around, lifting Lelani off her hooves, raising her high . . . five stories—and then let go. Four hundred pounds of centaur impacted the cold hard ground with a sickening crunch. The bones in her legs, her ribs, and her back cracked.

Lelani just lay there whimpering incoherently. Daniel was heartbroken and horrified for his friend. But Lara was not finished—she taunted them with Lelani's enchanted dream protectors, swinging them around on their lanyards. The White Lady possessed the centaur's mind just as Widow Taker had earlier. She forced Lelani's broken body to rise. Shards of bone splintered further and pierced the young wizard's flesh. Lara forced the centaur into a palsied walk toward Daniel. Lelani cried to the gods to end her agony.

Ladue forced himself to his feet, ignoring the arrow in his skull, and trudged toward the White Lady with a blade. Lara blocked Ladue's pitiful swing. She dropped her hold on Lelani and grabbed Ladue's face. The Frenchman kicked and jabbed as she drew his essence from him; in seconds, Francois was dead. Lelani lacked the strength to scream . . . only a low guttural moan denoted her loss.

"Prince?" Lara gloated. "All the world is *my* kingdom now. I assure you, *Prince*—I will defend it more vigorously than your father did his parcel—than all the men of this world."

Daniel's fears at Red King's Gate were validated—the guardians would never had withstood Lara hiding out in a fort. He was out of ideas. How did one fight a force of nature? Memories of his sister Penny flooded his thoughts, of happier days with Adrian and Katie; memories of Luanne. He'd lived twice as much as most boys his age and regretted nothing. At least he was going out on his feet, like a prince, instead of hiding like a coward. He had taken down two armies, giving Aandor's allies a better chance of defeating Farrenheil.

Horses behind the White Lady began to neigh in panic; a chorus of screams erupted. Lara turned to them. Large swaths of her army . . . hundreds—man, beast, wagons, and anything else not nailed down—began to float in the air behind her, like Lelani a few minutes prior, except these did not stop. They rose faster and faster into the sky until they vanished.

The rest of the enemy army backed away from the event. Then a second group, including Lord Blunt, began to rise. Lara quickly counter spelled to retrieve her husband's retinue.

Daniel stepped backward slowly, trying to steal away in the confusion. Malcolm appeared with mercs, grabbed him, and double-timed their retreat with a bum's rush. They coopted a few stray riderless mounts and retreated away from the field of battle along with the remnant of their army.

"Your doing?" Daniel asked of the levitation.

"I'm a weapons master, not a wizard," Mal said in that *don't look at me* way.

One of the mercs tapped Malcolm and pointed to a rider charging in from the east. "Uh, sir . . . I think it was him."

2

Seth charged from the wormhole at the edge of the Blue Forest to find Daniel's army already engaged. The sky was black; the air full of ice and hail—but his rage kept him warm. Jessica's death turned in his mind, stoking the fires of hatred. Seth drew upon the predator inside him, but instead of exploiting the innocent and desperate, he would aim his ire at Farrenheil. He knew he would die; even his father could not defeat Lara. But he would bloody Farrenheil's nose before he fell and give Aandor's survivors a better chance. Seth whipped his poor beast into a lather to close the league between himself and his enemy.

The spells continued to build in his mind, including those he'd forgotten he'd learned. Oddly, Seth's vision was sharper than ever. The world looked different, though for the life of him, he didn't know why coming into possession of some two-dozen low- and midlevel spells would affect him so.

As the hail battered him, Seth could see the magic causing the bad weather. Ahead, the White Lady glowed with an ethereal luminescence as she fought Lelani. Like a prelate or druid, Seth could see the concentration of magic around Lara. *My God, she's powerful.* Her castings were solid, precise . . . the most efficient magic he'd ever witnessed. He was about to get his ass handed to him. Lara lifted Lelani into the sky like a rag doll.

Seth's heart stuck in his throat. "No!" He regretted his last words to the centaur . . . his anger.

Lara's magic was visible to Seth; black gold-tinged runes around her hands. "What the fuck?" Seth whispered. The beauty of the magic was breathtaking—formulas made up of runes encircling the White Lady. He could see the invisible mechanics of the spell, the latches and tabs, for lack of a better word, of the magic. This was not anything he'd ever studied. More strangely, he understood the spell even though he'd never cast it before. Lara was diminishing the planet's mass around her target. The spell wasn't lifting Lelani up so much as the centrifugal force of the spinning world had become more powerful than the planet's mass that held her to the ground. *Does Lara even understand these concepts?* Seth wondered. *Or are wizards just children playing with loaded pistols?*

Lara dropped Lelani and turned to Daniel, preparing her deathblow.

Seth wasn't quite there yet . . . he needed a distraction, and the first spell that came to mind was the one he had just witnessed. Seth had little trouble replicating it. Circles of luminous equations branded the air like hot irons around him; they were a deep lavender instead of black with fiery energy halos around the symbols. Rather than ponder what this was, he cast the spell on Lara's army, stronger and with a wider field. Behind the White Lady, hundreds rose—armored knights and horses, too. Winged knights who flew into the field lost their thrust. Seth dialed it up to eleven—he wasn't diminishing the mass . . . he was negating it. The soldiers rose faster. Lara saved only a handful of them; the others literally flew off the world. Seth had succeeded—Danny was no longer her biggest problem.

While the Farrenheisi army retreated from the field, the winged cavalry flew at Seth with spiked flails whipping. Seth whipped his own staff one-handed to swat them from the skies with wind as hard as concrete. He broke the horses' necks, and as they smashed into the cold ground, crushed their riders. The remaining knights left the wizard to their mistress.

Lara hurled a column of flaming magma at Seth so intense it could have spewed from Krakatoa. Prewoke, Seth would have been fried because his old rickety shield had no way to channel the heat. Seth pulled on the tabs of his shield and curved its shape into a convex bowl, closing it around the column of fire until he caught the last of the magma in an arcane containment field. Seth now possessed a miniature raging sun; Lara would just swat it away, so he shot it toward the Farrenheisi's left flank. Lara moved to block it, but Seth hit her with a righteous hard wind that slammed her across the plain into Aandor City's wall. The magma lit up the Farrenheisi companies like the last days of Pompeii. The remaining army retreated from the theater of conflict.

Roland gathered his troops and pushed the advantage, coming at Farrenheil around the flaming flank to pin them against the city walls. Daniel gave Seth a salute, and pointed at the wall where Lara had impacted.

Lara had survived. She pushed herself off that wall, into the airborne saddle of a black flying horse. She banked left to circle around the city, buying herself time to recover. Seth was okay with this. He was having difficulty sorting the spells that continued to pour into his mind. They were no longer the magicks of a student and far beyond the number Seth ever remembered having studied.

Seth found one of the downed flying horses still alive, a chestnut courser mare with broken wings and legs. As he cast a healing spell, Seth thought of his mother and the price for being able to mend the horse. He also cast a soothe on the horse to calm it. *Wait a minute . . . How am I casting a soothe? I never studied clerical blessings.*

"Egwyn," he mumbled to himself. The mad king knew clerical magicks. "When our spirits merged, he took stuff from my mind . . . and I got spells from him," Seth finished out loud. Coopting the spell book of the greatest wizard that ever lived was a score beyond imagining. And Rosencrantz? *How many times did I commune with the tree? I'm remembering spells he never taught me—heavy environmental magic.* Proust could never have predicted that his son would merge minds with so many powerful wizards when he designed that mental chastity belt.

"But why can I see the magic?" he asked his horse, who, after the soothe, was now in love with Seth and licking his face. Every tree, every rock and person, every molecule had a change-undo lever with unlimited options, and Seth could see them all. "I'm pretty sure Egwyn and Rosencrantz couldn't . . ."

Aeshma!

Sharing minds with the Meadsweir daemon had altered Seth's brain. He saw the world the way a creature of magic saw it. Seth suddenly knew that the energy from the core of the multiverse *was* sentient. Lelani said that magic was the art of asking the universal energies to alter the physical world—but Seth could now utilize that language with something more akin to a demand . . . he could direct it, tell the energy how to transform a thing. He remembered every spell he'd ever read, every spell Egwyn and Rosencrantz knew plus Aeshma's unique type of science and view of the universe. Seth owed it to the daemon to survive Lara— to free it from Meadsweir and send it home.

A spider crawled along the courser's belly. Seth took him gently in his palm.

"She'll be no one's meal today, little guy," Seth told the arachnid.

Lara picked up a squadron of flying cavalry as she came at him over the lake from the right. Others of the winged cavalry re-grouped to Seth's left—they were going to pin him, divide his concentration. Some of those winged knights were hedge wiz-ards based on the runes circling them. He cast a soothe on the spider. "I need your help, little guy."

With spider in hand, he launched his courser into the air. What Seth saw from above scared him more than the approach-ing winged knights. Farrenheil's southern army, forty thousand fresh troops, was an hour away from the city. That army's winged cavalry launched ahead of its ground troops. They would wipe out the rest of Daniel's force in minutes. Seth pulled the columns of quartz that had been called up from the ground higher, as tall as Aandor's greatest towers. He manufactured a few more col-umns around the plain. Borrowing from the spider, Seth cast massive webs of sticky proteinaceous silk, anchoring them to the jutting quartz towers, Aandor's wall and tallest towers, and across the skies of the war theater to make access to the ground difficult. The closest knights and their horses were ensnared as they flew into the webbing. He cast several more webs across any anchor points that he could find to turn the sky above the battle into a nightmare for airborne combatants. He enlarged the spider to the size of a car and let it loose in the webbing to feast on the entrapped Farrenheisi.

Seth borrowed from Lara's weather spell to create hot and cold fronts between them and the Farrenheisi reinforcements— massive tornadoes touched down at the head of the approaching army to keep them at bay.

Holy crap, he realized. *I didn't know any spell to create tornadoes. I used my earth-taught knowledge of weather science and wrote a spell on the spot to bring about tornadoes.*

As amused at his ingenuity as he was, Seth had ignored Lara for too long . . . She pressed into his head with her magic, trying to wrest control. The struggle toppled him from his horse. Seth fell into a stretch of webbing that saved him from a hard landing.

How dare a novice challenge me, said Lara's voice in his mind.

She was right: he was a novice. Knowing a thing and having experience at it were two different matters. Cat had the right idea of it, though. Seth needed to utilize his knowledge of science to gain more advantage over Lara . . . and, he needed to play dirty. Seth cast the most unique spell he'd ever attempted; it wasn't physical magic like what he'd done so far, it was arcane . . . sublime . . . utilizing elements of Rosencrantz's and Aeshma's spell books he didn't fully understand, but it would protect him from *her.*

When Lara reached out with her power to choke Seth, she

discovered she, too, could not breathe. The harder she crushed his throat, the less breath for herself. When she tried to enter his mind again, she felt her own mind violating herself. She was forced to stop. One of her knights started a run on Seth.

"Stop!" she commanded, blowing knight and horse off their course with a hard wind. "He's bound us, you fool. Any harm you inflict on him happens to me." Seth pinched his arm to prove the point and she slapped the same spot as though a wasp had stung her.

Not bad for a novice, Seth thought. Her face changed into an evil sneer that sent a cold shiver through him. Lara was the scariest chick Seth had ever met. A great wizard was more than just knowing spells . . . it was about knowing which to use in any given circumstance. It kept the magic from creating worse situations and helped you get out of jams brilliant powerful people put you in. In Lara's expression, Seth saw that her problem was picking from a multitude of options. Every fiber of his being wanted to run right now.

Lara deconstructed Seth's tornadoes to unblock the southern forces. The Farrenheisi hedge wizards, however, were a big problem—Seth had to contend with Lara, and with Lelani down, it would be a short fight for the army. Seth tapped into his innate ability as a Thaumadyne. He absorbed magic out of the air for miles around him, draining the swamp, so to speak. It would be many minutes before magic seeped back into the void.

Lara was impressed. Her consideration of him changed . . . almost the way a woman looked at a potential lover. She'd held on to her own power. Seth didn't think he could handle what she had stored anyway; Lara was not entirely human.

"I feel as though I know you," she said to Seth. "Please tell me you're not one of my own whelps, angry at Mummy for giving them away?"

"I know who my mother was."

"Was? Take heart, you'll see her again soon enough. I've already crafted my final play."

"Can't hurt me without hurting yourself."

"I'm fascinated to have encountered you," she continued. "I thought I had gotten rid of all the great wizards."

Explosions came from inside Aandor City. The thunderous clap of helicopter rotors reverberated again. A squad of Apache attack copters took to the air over Aandor, headed straight for the southern army. A dozen Chinooks followed and landed around Daniel's army. Platoons of black-clad mercs rushed out of the cargo bays, the pop, pop, pop of uniquely quiet automatic weapons fire pushing Blunt's army back farther.

Son of a bitch . . . they pulled it off, Seth realized.

Lara looked dumbstruck at the reinforcements.

"Give up," Seth said, praying she'd quit—or run.

Lara's scary dialed up so high, Seth had to concentrate on not pissing his pants. "I'll be home soon enough, wizard, but not to hide. Today, either Aandor ends or we do."

She turned green and grew scales . . . her arms transformed into dark green bat's wings and her rear legs into ostrich-sized drumsticks of a scaly bird. Seth was mesmerized by the mechanics of the magic—the beauty of its engineering. Her tail was thick and serpentine, her head transformed into a scaly rooster-like visage. Seth had never seen a cockatrice before, but Egwyn had. Lara-lizard sprang at him. Seth leaped to avoid her, but she scraped him on the ankle with a claw.

He turned around for the counterattack, but the she-beast

paced around him chortling, like something funny had happened. Lara had a similar cut on her leg where she scratched him. His cut's bleeding turned gray like wet concrete and then hardened. Seth's leg grew heavy. The skin around the wound hardened as well, turning to stone. His leg below the knee had stiffened and the effect was spreading.

Fuck!

Cockatrices were part of the basilisk family—poison lizards that turned you to stone with a touch or stare. Except . . . they were immune to their own bites and scratches. As soon as Seth was dead, his binding spell would be canceled, and Lara could safely change back. Lara-lizard flew off for the castle leaving Seth to die.

Seth had one minute to effect a plan. He looked at his staff, a surviving piece of his old mentor whom he loved and missed. No help there. Even the phoenix feather, which increased its spell power, was no help as the stone effect reached his pelvis. He could no longer walk.

The feather?

Seth grabbed the phoenix feather and toggled it magically, opening its secrets, peering into the feather's foundations down to its DNA. He recalled everything about Lara's transformation spell, every rune. Seth started to cast a transformation of his own. The language of his magic burned brightly around him in flaming letters, and he felt himself transform, becoming something other. Becoming a phoenix. After he'd finished, Lara's poison completed its course quickly. Seth felt his beak turn to stone, then his eyes and he went blind. His ears, and then all sound stopped. Finally his thinking slowed until all perception went dark.

The first new perception was the acrid smell of ash and cinders. He cracked open an eye. Daniel's giant head was gawking at him. The boy looked twelve feet tall. Seth shook his head and ashes scattered about him. He tried to sit up and found wings of red and yellow feathers where his hands ought to have been.

Holy shit, I'm a bird, he thought.

He got up on his clawed feet. Daniel and his guards backed away. Seth could still see the tabs of creation. He remembered the spell, but had no hands to cast it with. *Some wizards didn't need staves or wands or the motions of their hands,* Lelani had told him. *They cast spells with their mind alone.* Seth thought about the transformation, cast it again in his newly refined mind, then reversed it and played it over like a song on repeat. It hurt like a motherfucker, but the feathers molted off, and soon he had opposable thumbs again and a voice box with which to complete the transformation. Another problem remained: he was a baby.

Seth searched for a good spell to remedy this. The one with the event horizon Lelani used to initiate contact when they first met Rosencrantz. They had sped up time around the tree.

He put his hand up and asked Danny to back off, but his new vocal cords were not broken in, and he had no teeth, so it came out, "Eh wun bah wfff."

Imagining a circle around him, Seth established an event horizon and cast that sorcery. He aged a day for every second at first, but then he accelerated the effect. He stopped at eighteen, realizing no law forced him to return to twenty-seven. This was his do-over—to make the years he'd squandered on earth count again. The sinner burned into a pile of ash. He had literally been born again.

"Holy shit, you were a bird!" Daniel said in awe, draping a blanket around Seth's naked body.

"I'd be dead if it wasn't for that phoenix feather Lelani gave me."

"She needs you right now," Daniel said.

"I have to get after that white bitch. She's up to something evil."

Daniel grabbed his shoulder. "Ladue and Urry are dead. Lelani won't make it if you don't come right now."

Seth had avoided these moments his whole life—adult choices, hard decisions. Lara was the greater threat—the master of end-games. She could be torturing Cat or Callum right now. For all his newfound power, there still wasn't enough of Seth to do everything needed. But Lelani was his friend. She could have kept the feather for herself, so valuable it could buy a country, but she had given it to him because he needed it. He looked appre-hensively at Aandor's old gray sentinel and prayed he would not be too late as Daniel led him to their friend.

CHAPTER 43

ENDGAME

1

Lara circled the castle and found that someone had moved the mirror portal from the pantry to the library's terrace. It had grown to ten times its original size. She shrank it back to its original size, seized it in her claws, and slithered through the high windows of the great hall, throwing the mirror atop the magical swag pile. Its glass shattered into a million pieces. *There will be no more reinforcements from other realms.*

The nobles were gone from the room, her soldiers replaced by men of Aandor. She slithered through, evading the guards' attacks, and landed on the very spot Magnus Proust met his end. A remnant of his power remained. She sucked the soldiers' life forces to replenish herself, and they clattered to the ground shriveled. Lara magically sealed the doors.

The binding spell faded the very moment that young mage on the battlefield died, and she safely transformed back into a woman. She regretted his death; he would have made a fine acolyte. Lara was exhausted, but victory was slipping from their grasp.

Like a queen bee in a broken hive, Lara rebuilt her spell

circles. Aandor refused to die—but with forty thousand fresh troops in the heart of their city . . . she could break this leviathan's back for good. She would make Farrenheil great again. Widow Taker's essence, his parting gift, would be the requisite wizard's death imbued into the spell. The world shook as she bent time and space inward, drawing from all the magical artifacts in the room. She had drained the world of its magical legacies for this invasion. This portal across the world would be her greatest.

2

Seth's horse flew through the castle's main door, past MacDonnell and his family, swooping Cat off her feet, past Chryslantha Godwynn (*Wonder how that's going*), the archduke and duchess (*Hope Danny lives to meet them*), and landed at the great hall's entrance.

"What the hell are you doing?!" Cat shouted, flushed from the scare.

"We need to kill Lara. Lelani's down and I need your help." Seth didn't have time to decipher Lara's lock on the door. He made Cat and himself intangible with one of Rosencrantz's spells, and phased them through the stone wall. The dead were scattered about. A dark anomaly resided in the center of the hall inside two circles. He looked at the portal with newfound understanding. *Smart—no excess magic waste there.*

"Why is there a portal?" he asked.

"She's bringing their last army from their capital," Cat said.

"So this stretches two thousand miles to Höllentor?"

Shutting down the portal wouldn't end their war. She'd come back some other way. Seth had to science the shit out of this. It was the only advantage he had . . . he could not go toe-to-toe with her anymore with the element of surprise gone. A radical idea formed—something else Cat had said earlier. The idea scared him. It was probably immoral. But they had killed his mother and father. *So fuck them.*

"Vector control," he told her.

"We need two more."

"No, I got this."

Seth sat lotus style within the circles of power. He reached out to his anomaly in the Blue Forest, the one that had brought them to Aandor, and cannibalized it for parts. Sub spell for motion, for integrity, spell for length, etc., and he applied these component magicks to the portal in the room, hijacking it from Lara. He unhitched it from this end and raised it toward the ceiling of the world. Seth had alternatives, like putting this end at the bottom of the ocean so that the pressure would instantly crush emerging soldiers. But that would not stop Farrenheil. *No one else will lose a loved one because of these bastards.*

The walls of the anomaly were thick. Like a ceramics artist he spun it upward, lengthening it. Unlike in Meadsweir, he could extend this one much farther. He closed his end tight and stretched it up and up, beyond the atmosphere thousands, then millions, of miles. *Ninety million miles.*

Rosencrantz protected the earth from rogue solar flares by manipulating the earth's magnetic field. The tree had learned to identify flares from his pristine meadow, and Seth now had that piece of magic. Seth pulled in power around him from farther and farther reaches, ten miles out, then twenty—no mage within sight of Aandor City would be able to light so much as a cigarette with their power. He pushed that anomaly toward a dark spot on the sun . . . a million-mile-long solar flare with the explosive force of a thousand hundred-megaton bombs bursting in a fiery arch. He would only open the portal for the briefest time . . . enough to destroy the castle with Lara and Archduke Vaulknar. *Let them try to wage war without a leader and sorceress.* He placed the head of the portal before the flare, and opened the way to Höllentor.

3

Everyone in Aandor City, wherever they stood, gazed to the east, shielding their eyes from a light that was momentarily brighter than the sun. A mushroom cloud two thousand miles away rose to the roof of the world and curved along it, turning the eastern sky ashen. Minutes later, a violent westward gale hot as an August wind passed Aandor City, blowing away the clouds of winter and thawing the land.

Seth held the portal open for only a few seconds, lest he evacuate the atmosphere into open space. From the force of the blast, he realized it was a second too long. The spell obliterated more than just the castle. Much more.

"What the hell did you do?" Cat asked, her mouth quivering.

What the hell did I do? "I stopped it," Seth said, trying to convince himself. He was shivering. He'd gone too far. His rebirth—his new innocence—already ended.

Callum and his father burst into the hall—Lara's spell was down. They looked at the dead around the room.

"Did you do that?" Cal asked, pointing at the sky outside the high windows.

"She killed a lot of people," Seth said, defensively. *Don't the bodies around the room prove my point?* "I just—just wanted to make it stop."

Seth saw the runes of a nascent portal appear in the hall . . . another wormhole was about to open. He readied himself in case the user planned to repeat his trick with the solar flare. Toxic brimstone rolled onto the floor—the heat was choking. Instead of hellfire, a pitiful naked creature stepped through, wretched, charred beyond recognition—its deep crimson, black-crusted husk covered with cinders and blisters, all its hair burned away. It had but one working eye with which to convey that it was certifiably mad. They all knew who it was.

"Yooouuuuu . . . ," Lara said accusingly, her voice a scraping asphalt of sound.

Guardsmen rushed her. She drained their life forces; a patch of skin healed on her shoulder and she regained her other eye.

"Yooooouuuuuu . . . ," she cried again, her bloody soot-stained steps slow and erratic.

Seth shot her with a lightning bolt. Her reaction was clumsy, amateurish. Seth did not wait for her to regain her wits. He hit her mind with a brain hex. Her "you" turned into "gaaaaghhh . . ." Then he entombed Lara in a layer of ice. He negated the planet's mass around the block and launched her through the roof, through the ceiling of the world. Seth shot her straight toward the sun.

"And this time . . . stay dead, you bitch," he said.

"Seth . . ."

Captain Aandor himself, Callum MacDonnell, approached Seth cautiously. His hands were open, his sword sheathed.

"The—they killed my mother," Seth said, divorcing himself from all accountability. "They killed my mother *and my father.*"

Callum braced Seth's shoulders gently. He pulled the young man toward him—hugged him, the way Seth always imagined his father might if he'd met the man. Seth cried, letting all the anguish of his loss out. "All this power—I couldn't save her."

Callum stayed, protecting Seth from the world and himself.

Men rode in from the battlefield, breaking the moment, shouting to all that Farrenheil's southern army had surrendered. Lord Heady had cut off their retreat. Prince Danel had won. The cheers rising from all the corners of the city and the castle met the empty silence in Seth's soul.

The war was finally over.

CHAPTER 44

FLOURISH

Daniel entered the great city astride his warhorse. Adoring subjects cheered, and those close enough touched his legs as he passed. Banners and streamers filled his view; musicians played scores of victory. Rose petals littered the avenue before him. Sharing these accolades were Roland, Malcolm, and Lelani riding alongside—Blunt rode behind them in manacles, flanked by Aandor's four biggest guards. Daniel was grateful for his companions, but also saddened by the ones missing. Lelani, still healing, bore her losses like a stoic warrior. In addition to friends Klaugh and Ladue, half of the centaur force had died in battle.

Their grand duke and White Lady dead, their capital obliterated, Farrenheil's army was demoralized and despondent. Daniel had offered to allow the rank and file to return home; the officers, however, had to stand trial. Blunt accepted the terms with no contest. Their crimes against Aandor were as obvious as they were abhorrent.

They crossed the drawbridge onto the old gray sentinel's main grounds. In the courtyard, everyone of rank awaited Daniel in a large semicircle—to his right the surviving nobility. Half of them had begun striking bargains with the Farrenheisi. Their cheers were more subdued, like managers meeting the new CEO and wondering what he intended for them. Unlike Reverend Grey, whose view of monarchy was a bit Pollyanna-ish, Colby and Tilcook had schooled him well on the realities of power and what it meant to be at the top of any organization, legal or otherwise. Daniel could read through his nobles' smiles; they all wanted something. Favors. Forgiveness. Advantage. Freedom didn't seem to be enough.

To the left, Callum's entire family . . . you could not mistake the MacDonnells for anyone else. Their joy and admiration were genuine. Tilcook and Tony's wives and kids had come over with the mercenary army, and they stood with their husbands, as did Reverend Grey and Colby Dretch. Colby was beaming like a proud godfather. The ambassadors of the friendly kingdoms were also present. In the center, the castle servants had turned out, headed by the archduke and duchess of Aandor.

Daniel imagined meeting his true parents under different scenarios for years, none of them remotely close to this. All his daydreams were of a private intimate moment. He expected them to be a lot older than him. He hopped off the horse and froze. What should he say? Were they convinced that he was the same child sleeping in their crib only a week ago?

His mother didn't need convincing . . . Daniel's eyes told her all she needed to know. Slowly, Sophia broke protocol and moved toward Daniel as though he were a dream that might evaporate. No one had ever looked at him with such unconditional love; she radiated only joy upon seeing him, none of the regret of not getting to see his first steps, hear his first word, the things that endeared child to parent. Daniel's blood raced as she wrapped her arms around him, their hearts beating in unison against their collective chests. She was slightly taller than him—she kissed him over and over on his head and face.

"I love you," she said.

He cried with her, despite promising himself not to. This beautiful woman would *never ever* abandon him. Not a dry eye remained in that courtyard. Daniel's heart threatened to break from happiness . . . from closure.

His father joined them. He placed his hand reassuringly on his son's back and joined their embrace. Athelstan stepped back and pulled Sophia as well. He took a knee. All in the courtyard followed suit, including his mother.

"Hail, the king of Aandor," his father said.

"Long live the king!" the crowd shouted.

Daniel let them stay that way a moment before allowing them to rise. Malcolm gave a thumbs-up; Cal a subtle nod.

EPILOGUE

Daniel had slept for an entire day in the most comfortable bed he'd ever known. When he awoke, he was informed a celebration would be held on the terrace gardens that afternoon. A hot bath had been prepared for him, and his clothes, a brilliant blue-and-gold high-collared doublet, black tights, and calfskin boots, were laid out.

The castle had kept as much of Lara's food as it needed and distributed the rest of the cache to the city. The lords of the north and west, whose farms had been spared, pledged to distribute as much food as they could to the war-torn regions in the coming weeks. Udiné and Bradaan also pledged aid. Aandor would not starve this year.

His entrance was announced. All turned to him silently, until he told them to carry on. Daniel mingled among the colorful crowd, introducing himself to his new subjects. They were polite even while feeling him out, trying to figure out his views on the world and how to raise their own standing in it. He was grateful Colby and the reverend joined his court; Cal and Malcolm were amazing advisers for war and commerce, but Allyn would keep him morally grounded and no politician could outmaneuver Colby Dretch's Brooklyn street smarts. He inched his way to them through the indulgent gathering.

"I see they got you, too," Daniel said, noting Colby's local dress. The detective looked pretty sharp in a white linen tunic, leather jerkin, and wool breeches. Grey, whose salt-and-pepper head had turned entirely white, wore the traditional robes of a prelate.

"So do I finally get to hear how you pulled it off?" Daniel said to Allyn.

Grey looked reluctantly at Colby, as though embarrassed, and then to Daniel. "Without intending to, I became the president's spiritual adviser," he said peevishly.

"President of what?" Daniel asked.

"Of America," Colby said. "The Fibbies nabbed us. It was looking pretty grim until the padre whammied them."

"It was a soothe. Nothing violent," Grey added.

"But the president?"

Grey kept mum. Colby continued. "When the higher-ups questioned their subordinates' release of us, Allyn had to *soothe* them, too. Then, to cover them, he was soothing the top directors of the FBI, senators, congressmen—you name it, just to stay ahead of everyone who wanted to lock us up. Eventually we got to the top. We *convinced* the whole government we weren't the droids they were looking for. Being the prez's spiritual adviser was a good inside position. We gave Scott Wilcock elbow room to build our invasion plan. Scott had people developing pneumatic rifles 'cause you can't curse a gun that don't explode bullets. The Apache copters were all electric, which was better than combustion. They lasted about twenty minutes before conking out. We sent a drone through to see what the status was, and Cal scribbled us a note, so we knew the action plan. We came through with five thousand mercenaries, plus the Ginas, and two trunks of Malcolm's gold bullion. Son of a bitch is as rich here as he was there."

"But they killed Rosencrantz," Daniel pointed out.

"He entrusted a seed to me," Grey said. "I planted it in the Uwharrie Forest. Junior was a great wizard in his own right."

"You didn't bring *your* family," Daniel said to the reverend.

"Rosemarie's out of college and married to a good man. None of this stuff ever sat well with Michelle. It was too much on our marriage. In truth, I had to leave. I started getting ideas. What if I visited North Korea, Iran, and soothed some common sense into their leadership? I was starting to rationalize my abilities for the benefit of the world. Having influence over all the world leaders scared me. I know I am a moral man, but that kind of power corrupts. The road to hell is paved with good intentions. On that world, I was no better than a wizard. I should not exist there. It was time to come home." He reached into his robe and pulled out the silver dagger Lelani had last used against Chasaubaan in the meadow. He handed it to Daniel as a gift. "Just in case anyone should ever get such notions here again, hold on to this."

Daniel was touched by Allyn's gesture of faith in him. "What of Scott?" Daniel asked.

"He would not leave his daughters," Colby said. "He didn't want to be the 'other person' over here, playing second to Malcolm's wife and kids . . . said that he spent too many years in the closet already. But he did all right by us. We told all the respective loved ones their people were alive. Cat's mom took it hardest. She died of cancer a few years back . . . haven't told Cat yet. We've been looking out for Cat's sister and her kids. Scott will continue that as well as taking care of Tristan's family and watching out for your stepsister, Penny."

Seth walked by with a plate full of food and a large goblet of wine. A beautiful young lady was on his arm. He stopped as though remembering something at the last minute and turned to them. "Hey, you still got that heart thing?" he asked Colby.

"Yes, I'm still dead. Thanks for asking."

"No, definitely not *dead*," he said, looking Colby over acutely. "You're not alive . . . but not dead."

"You smokin' funny tobacco, kiddo?" Colby asked.

Seth handed his plate and goblet to his lady friend. "May I see?" he asked of Colby. The detective pulled out the thumping velvet sack. Seth took the heart out of the bag.

"You wanna make these fine folks hurl their lunch?" the detective asked.

Seth looked at the heart and Colby. He spoke to the organ in a strange language and appeared to be reading the air around it and the detective. He plunged the heart into Colby's chest wrist-deep and chanted. Seth removed his hand, wiped it on his tunic, and retrieved his plate and his goblet. Without ceremony, he moved on with his date.

Colby made a choking sound, which morphed into a cough and then subsided. A ruddy pinkness came into his cheeks. The detective drew breath . . . real breath for the first time in years. Colby laughed with unadulterated joy and Daniel and Grey joined him. They all stared at Seth, who was telling the girl a bad joke.

"Yeah, he's like that now," Daniel said. "Colby, take tomorrow off. Enjoy being alive again. You can help me figure out what the hell's going on around this place after that."

"You got it, boss."

Tilcook and Tony Two Scoops saluted him with their wives Gina and Gina, who were doing their damnedest to introduce Jersey high hair and fingernails to the masses here. Their teenage kids resented every minute they weren't on a smartphone. "We got the Nest running again, Your Grace," the big man said. "Gonna take it upscale for big rollers and we'll open another joint in the Aavanteen for the low-rent crowd. Your cut's thirty percent. Ladies on the house, of course."

"Why so generous?"

"Don't need to bribe no judges, no police, no business taxes, don't need accountants or lawyers. I just pay you and everything's dandy. I fuckin' love monarchies." Tony and the wives laughed at Tilcook's wit, leaving Daniel to ponder if maybe a constitutional monarchy might not be better sometime down the road. Future kings might not be so honest. Balzac's morals and methods were pure shit, but his complaints were not entirely without merit.

Daniel continued his rounds, sure to stop by his mother and father's table. They had spent hours with him before he went to bed, asking about his life and sharing stories of Aandor and their families . . . things Prelate Grey was not privy to. Daniel looked forward to meeting his grandfather, the duke of Bradaan. Sophia was currently in mother-hen mode, straightening his collar, patting his hair, making up for lost years of fussing. Her youth was awkward for him. She was only a few years older than he was. His father was kind, but had less to say. Athelstan was naturally awkward. It was bizarre supplanting your own father as head of a nation. Daniel definitely got the sense of mixed feelings. But any father was an improvement over Clyde. His marriage to Sophia was arranged, and though not passionate, he was kind to her . . . courteous. At least Daniel had escaped that fate. With the accords broken, Danel, king of Aandor, could marry whomever he wished.

Valeria MacDonnell approached with a friend and they genuflected. "Your Grace, may I introduce Chryslantha Godwynn."

"I've heard a lot about you," Daniel said, feeling odd that he could not shake her hand, according to the rules.

"We are eternally grateful for your bravery in battle, Your Grace," Chryslantha said. "I look forward to hearing tales of your life in the other realm. Valeria's recounting is fascinating, and she'd been there but a few days." The woman's demeanor set Daniel at ease in a way no other Aandoran had managed to do . . . the only new face so far that didn't seem to want anything from him. She was confident, comfortable in her own skin.

"And you both can fill me in on Aandor's secrets," Daniel responded. "On the earth I grew up in, women always had the best gossip on what was going on in town." They agreed on a picnic two days hence before moving off to join Sophia. The three of them glanced at him over their shoulders as they talked.

"Well that wouldn't make anyone self-conscious," Daniel mumbled to himself.

"They're plotting," said Cat, coming up behind him. She was noshing on pickles, radishes, and roast chicken with a half goblet of white wine to wash it down. Her flowing dress followed the shape of her big belly and she was most radiantly beautiful for it. "Deciding who's a good match for you . . . for the sake of the kingdom, of course. I got roped into the discussion earlier, hence the wine. This place is going to take some getting used to, but at least the cheese is amazing."

"I think I should get my bearings before I start dating."

"Your role right now is to produce an heir—and a spare. Your mom wants grandkids," Cat said mischievously. It was good to see her so relaxed that she was stirring up trouble for the fun of it.

"My mom's only five years older than me. She's not even done having her own kids."

Cat chuckled. "Hey, are you sweet on Valeria?" she teased. "You can be my brother-in-law. Then I can hammer you when you do something boneheaded, and not get thrown in the dungeon."

"You're as bad as they are."

Cal joined them. He looked heroic in the blue, white, and gold of the Dukesguarde commander. Daniel had promoted Cal after elevating his father, James, as the proxy governor and lord of Farrenheil.

"Danny's right not to rush," Cal said. He turned to the prince. "You'll need to go on a tour of the kingdom soon. You can meet every subject, and when you're ready, find the right one for you."

"I don't want him to be alone," Cat argued.

"He's not alone; he has us."

"It's not the same," she told Cal. "It's the not the same," she repeated to Daniel. "You're in a high-pressure role. Having *someone* makes a difference. This is why there are no single presidents of the United States. Even Malcolm had Scott. What about Chrys?"

"Cut it out," Cal said.

"I fucking love her, you know," Cat argued. "She's awesome. A king makes a great consolation prize."

Cat was stirring up an awkward tension in her attempt at humor.

"I think I'm going to concentrate on restoring the old empire," Daniel said. "It'll bring peace to the continent. I should keep my options open in case I need to marry into the two remaining bloodlines needed to make those kingdoms feel like they have a stake."

"Very wise," Cal said, gratefully. "I'll arrange a council meeting to start planning strategy."

Cat and Cal left to check on Bree, who was enjoying her pony with her grandmother.

Daniel moved off to a remote spot at the edge of the terrace whose sole occupant was a convalescing centaur. Seth had done an admirable job saving Lelani's life on the battlefield, but she still had a few weeks before she was fully recovered. Physically, at least . . . She had not been the same since the battle.

"Why are you alone in the corner?" Daniel asked.

"Not all humans are comfortable around other species," she said, nodding to the nobles in the crowd.

"Where are your tribal leaders? This is as much their victory."

"Not all centaurs are comfortable around humans."

Like everyone else, Lelani had wanted something from Daniel. But she was always honest about it.

"You're my friend," he said. "I'll always be grateful for what you've done for me. I hope you know, we'll not only maintain the Blue Forest Accords, I think we can improve on them. Different species remaining a mystery to each other just breeds mistrust. We have to do better."

They passed a moment in silence taking in the vista. "I'm returning to my village," she said. "With so many dead, the centaurs need leaders. Klaugh had a family . . . I will hunt for them." She faced him. "Hesz has reached out to factions in the nonhuman communities, including the centaurs—factions that do not want peace with man and do not want to abide by our agreements and the lines drawn on your maps."

"How worried should we be?"

"I'm not sure. This war killed most of the proficient wizards in the kingdoms as well as those with latent talents. Lara sacrificed hundreds to open her portals."

"We have Seth."

"Seth is not himself," she warned. "He sees the world differently now. He plans to settle in Meadsweir . . . to take up Egwyn's studies and return the daemon to its realm. You would be most fortunate if that is his only ambition."

"Talk about a downer."

"Enjoy your parents, Daniel. Relish the love that has been denied you most of your life. You haven't experienced it yet because of the war, but Aandor is a wondrous and beautiful place. All leaders have burdens, but make the best of your life as you deal with them."

"Can I count on you?" he asked.

"I hope so," she said solemnly. She kissed his cheek and left the party.

Daniel observed the festivities from his private corner. All these people—more family and friends than he'd ever had before. He still felt isolated. *Heavy is the brow that wears the crown.*

From across the terrace he watched his mother hold court. He caught Chryslantha Godwynn's eye. She nodded and smiled in a sympathetic way—a quality in her gaze suggested she knew his troubles. To Daniel's surprise, relief settled in during that fleeting connection; like someone shared his burden and made it lighter. Warmed by that brief moment in which he was not alone, he started across the terrace, returning to the company of friends and strangers, putting aside the work of nation-building, and looking very much forward to a picnic.

ACKNOWLEDGMENTS

Thanks to the folks whose time and efforts have helped me succeed: Chris Cooper, Evan Gunter, Seth Kramer, Amy Stapp, Zohra Ashpari, Tom Doherty, Ron Gwiazda, Amy Wagner, Irene Gallo, Christian McGrath, Peter Lutjen, Seth Lerner, Rayna Bourke, Thomas and Dolores Bourke, Paul Stevens, and Alice K. Turner.